QUIET TREACHERY

Marcus found a path and picked up speed as he entered it. He felt the muscles in his neck and across his back tighten, as if he expected an arrow. He had every reason to expect an arrow; he was a soldier, sworn to suppress the Apache by matching wits and nerves, hot lead and cold steel against these great Indian warriors. But this was too easy, too quiet; he was suspicious. Suddenly, after he had covered only twenty paces, an arrow flew by his right ear, so close a feather in the fletching brushed it. Marcus froze. The arrow had lodged deep in the tree trunk ahead, just where the path curved to the left. It vibrated with a soft, twanging sound. Someone was laughing behind him. With his heart pushing up to his throat, Marcus slowly turned.

It was Juh, the invincible Geronimo's war brother.

"Son of a bitch," muttered Marcus. But he was ready. . . .

TUSCON

The first saga in a blazing new trail of adventure—

FORTUNE'S WEST

S0-BSM-041

FORTUNES WEST

TUCSON

FORT LOWELL

A. R. RIEFE

A SIGNET BOOK

NEW AMERICAN LIBRARY

PUBLISHER'S NOTE

This book is a work of fiction. Names, characters, places, and incidents either are the product of the author's imagination or are used fictitiously, and any resemblance to actual persons, living or dead, events, or locales is entirely coincidental.

Copyright © 1988 by Alan Riefe

SIGNET TRADEMARK REG. U.S. PAT. OFF. AND FOREIGN COUNTRIES REGISTERED TRADEMARK—MARCA REGISTRADA HECHO EN CHICAGO, U.S.A.

SIGNET, SIGNET CLASSIC, MENTOR, ONYX, PLUME, MERIDIAN and NAL BOOKS are published by NAL PENGUIN INC., 1633 Broadway, New York, New York 10019

First Printing, September, 1988

1 2 3 4 5 6 7 8 9

PRINTED IN THE UNITED STATES OF AMERICA

— 1 —

August 1865

olonel Thompson Bragg Betteridge's orders
were delivered clearly and calmly, but this
did not make them acceptable to Major Marcus Venable.
The only senior officer with experience in fighting Apaches,
the major had been shackled with a dangerous mission.
He examined the strategy and it looked the same from
every angle: a suicide mission.

A two thousand-man search force had been assembled
in an all-out effort to find and capture the legendary
Geronimo. The bluecoats had combed the mountains of
Sonora in northern Mexico, where the Apache chieftain
and his followers had fled. Their quest had brought them
to the brink of a horseshoe *cañón*.

Venable was to lead his hundred men down a narrow
trail to the bottom of the *cañón* yawning below the army's
main camp and up the opposite side to the rim. The major
was certain that Geronimo and his people were concealed
up above the camp on the *cañón* rim. The men filling
the trail leading down and up the other side would draw
the savages' fire, thereby exposing their own positions.
Betteridge's main force would then attack the attackers.

"Protect your men and wipe out the red mongrels."

Colonel Thompson Betteridge was enthusiastic over
his idea, conveniently ignoring the hazards involved for

5

those assigned to carry it out. The colonel was a muscular, powerfully built man—one who, as might be expected, used his size and deep voice to awe and intimidate. He needed to do neither, however, to Major Venable. An order was an order, regardless of how ill-conceived or downright stupid it might be.

At thirty, Venable was ten years younger than the colonel, and a veteran of three years in the Indian wars—a man whom women would describe as dashing. In uniform he looked classically heroic, with his blues meticulously tailored and gleaming with brass. His lithe body did not contain an ounce of excess fat, and his stomach was as flat as a pan. His hair was blond from birth, but the Arizona sun had bleached it almost white. Thick, pale eyebrows crowned light-blue eyes that displayed frankness, sincerity, and a boyish joie de vivre. That joy of living had been quashed by the colonel's command, however, and over the ensuing hours until darkness fell, the perils of the impending assignment threatened to eradicate it permanently.

Darkness had arrived and clouds effectively concealed the full moon when Major Andrew Colclough, Venable's newfound friend on the expedition, stopped by. He discovered Marcus toying with an engagement ring, which he hurriedly stuffed in his pocket.

"Finish your letter to her?" Colclough asked.

"I changed my mind."

"Won't she be disappointed?"

"She's not expecting it; it's better we leave things as they are."

"And how are they?" Colclough caught himself. "Don't answer, I'm prying, I'm sorry."

Marcus told him the whole story. Pouring it out brought him something akin to relief. He imagined it similar to what a devout Catholic must feel in the confessional.

"And you don't think she expects to hear from you? She might like to," Colclough said.

"I don't know what's in her mind."

Sergeant Brennan, a burly butcher proud of his fondness for blood, suddenly stepped into the tent. Colclough left. Brennan looked gray with worry, his beady eyes questioning.

"The men are ready, sir, ready as they'll ever be.

Weapons checked, gear. It's gettin' near time." Brennan's voice lowered as he took a step closer. "Can I ask you somethin' off the record? I know this ain't your idea, but what's with Betteridge? He's orderin' us to our deaths is what he's doin'. I been ten years in this man's army, I never seen the beat o' this. He must be loony to give such a' order."

"It's given, Sergeant, we obey it. That's what it's all about, right?"

"We're ready when you are, Major." His voice was even, but Brennan's expression clearly condemned Venable for his refusal to take a stand against an insane order.

"I'll be there in a minute," said Marcus.

"Mmmm."

"What was that?"

"Yes, sir."

Moments before the signal to start out, the malicious moon slid into view, staring down like the daunting eye of an executioner, lighting the trail all the way to the bottom, across the *cañón* floor and up the opposite side. The men groaned; some crossed themselves. Colonel Betteridge was nowhere to be seen. The men continued to grumble.

"All right, quiet down. I'll be leading the way. Sergeant, you stand to one side and send the men down one at a time, three paces between," Marcus said.

"Yes, sir."

"You'll bring up the rear. And remember, all of you, this is tactical. Not a whisper. And watch your footing."

Marcus shook his fist in a sign of encouragement and started down the trail. Mixing with the Apaches over the years had imbued him with some special instincts. He could *feel* eyes watching him and pinpoint their location. Instinct also warned him when trouble lay hiding ahead. Both powers, if they were in working order, would be helpful tonight. He glanced upward. The moon looked fixed and formidable, threatening, determined to hold its position and shower its light.

Venable looked back over his shoulder. The men were coming down one by one. If they kept the distance between them, the line would stretch nearly to the bottom before Brennan, the last, fell in.

Marcus moved along in a crouch, gun out and cocked.

His mind returned to the tragic night of the ambush in the Tortolitas. It had been the last battle he had led his men into, and he hoped this would not end in the same bloody, terrifying way. But thus far, the settings were nearly identical. He looked back again. The men were dodging from one cover to the next, avoiding the trail as much as possible. Venable wanted to get to the bottom as fast as he could and find the easiest way up the opposite side, one that might escape the keen eyes of the Apache. It was a faint hope.

Marcus stopped once to listen, straining his ears. He could hear only the breeze punctuating the dull thudding of boots behind him and the swish of foliage. There'd be no owl call signals—no need. Every blue coat was clearly visible when each man popped from behind a tree, bush, or boulder to rush to the next.

He was within twenty yards of the *cañón* floor, a dried-up streambed lined with small stones, the banks nearly hidden by weeds. He clattered across and started up the trail on the opposite side. Above, about thirty yards ahead, an outcropping jutted forth. When he got to it he would be safe from firing coming from the slope at his back, but he would have to swing around one side or the other and gain the top before going on.

He rested a moment in the outcropping's shadow. The man behind him came scrambling up out of breath, pale with fear. Neither spoke. Marcus jerked his thumb upward, the other nodded. Another man joined them. Marcus grasped the edge of the outcropping, swung, kicked himself over to the top, then started up the trail. He had not taken ten steps when the mountain erupted with rifle fire. Bullets slammed the ground from every angle. A volley of arrows followed. He could hear screaming and scrambling behind. The man behind him was hit and dropped from the ledge with a sickening thump. Panic seized the troopers up and down the line. High along the rim, the others had opened fire, shooting at unseen targets.

One cold consolation came to mind as Marcus reflected on the situation. This was not like that time in the Tortolita Mountains the summer before. At least this time he would get to die with his men. He thought back to that sweltering summer night, and the metallic taste of fear coated his mouth.

June, 1864

"Eyes all over your heads, men," barked Captain Venable, casting a wary glance to the top of the mountain. He had taken a mounted squad of eight men into the Tortolita Mountains after a band of renegade Mogollón Apaches who had reportedly raided a ranch, killed four beefs, and made off with two horses. It was not a crime that screamed from the front page of a newspaper, except in the eyes of the ranch owner. He demanded the army catch and hang the offenders.

The Apaches had better than a two-hour lead, and up in the mountains their tracks vanished in the stony and rutted ground. Among the eight men accompanying Venable were his two most reliable veterans: Corporal Tumble—John Francis Tumbelsky—veteran of Chickamauga and native to Springfield, Illinois; and Private Orph—Orpheus Constantine Tchakarides—survivor of more battles than he cared to recall, born and raised in Lorain, Ohio, which happened to be the captain's hometown.

Venable had enlisted in 1860. He had fought with distinction in seven major battles in the East, risen to sergeant, and was commissioned an officer. After the grueling bloodletting that was Chancellorsville, in which he incurred minor wounds, he was reassigned to Fort Lowell, bringing with him twin silver captain's bars.

Riding single-file, the squad came to a grassy knoll set like an oval platter of sunburnt hay among the boulders. The horses were hobbled, the men assembled around Venable's upraised hand. He ordered them to the cover of a nearby overhang. The peaks rose fifteen hundred feet higher above, the slopes festooned with scrub, the number of trails to the top dwindling. Having cooked the territory to a turn, the sun had lowered to within the width of a man's hand of the horizon over the distant Tucson Range.

The captain and his men were familiar with the area. To the left near the summit a series of caves penetrated the slopes, although none could be seen at the moment, boulders and outcroppings effectively obstructing their view. The caves provided an excellent place to defend, however. The savages knew they were being followed, and had only to lead their pursuers up and get them within range before annihilating them.

"Sir," said Corporal Tumble, "something's going on up the way. I heard scramblin' plain as day."

The source of the sound was immediately apparent. A wild-maned, worn old sorrel, which had been cut in one flank with a lance and had badly infected leg sores, loped into view.

"One of theirs," said Orph, "sure as blood's red."

"Abandoned," said Venable. "Climb is too steep, it couldn't make it." He ran a gloved hand down its tangled mane. Blood and sweat had dried on the horse, confirming that it had been left and had dawdled in the area for at least an hour.

"They're already holed up in the caves, Captain," said Orph.

Venable did not answer. All eyes fastened on him. He buffeted ideas about in his head and churned out his decision.

"That horse is a decoy. They want us to think they're up there. They're below. Thanks to this overhang, they can't see us from above or below at the moment. We'll leave the horses where they are, all night if need be. We'll separate: three men to the left of the trail with you, Corporal. Orph and you three will stick with me on this side. When you get into position, make sure you can see the knoll."

Orph corrugated his brow. "You figger they'll come up to steal the horses?"

"Let's hope," said Venable.

The sun was turning into a drop of blood, purpling the bellies of the clouds above it. The shadows lengthened, flinging black carpets down the slopes. It was getting colder. When darkness came, the temperature would drop noticeably. The men broke out cold beans and hardtack of the consistency of firebrick and began to eat. They washed the meal down with the tepid water from their canteens. Across the narrow winding trail to the left, the horses stood patiently, the Apache mount in their midst, content to stand without hobbling as they nibbled the dry grama that carpeted the knoll.

Far below, Tucson huddled: tiny, sunbaked, a clutter of adobe and wooden buildings surrounding the old military

plaza, at too great a distance to betray movement in the
streets.

Venable thought of beer and drank from his canteen,
imagining the flavor of hops and barley mingling in the
cool, refreshing amber liquid, his upper lip lacing with
foam. He waited. Someone laughed. He jerked at the
sound.

"Keep it down."

The sun, darkened to a menacing crimson, embedded
itself in the distant peaks. The wind swirled down from
the summit, whining about among the boulders. Venable
refastened the top button of his tunic and fought back a
shiver.

Given no choice of posts, he had accepted reassign-
ment to Fort Lowell. At the time he had never heard of
Lowell or Tucson. His CO had handed him a single sheet
of paper after congratulating him effusively on a job well
done. He then described his new assignment: its "strate-
gic importance," the need for officers of his scope and
experience "out there," and cited the nation's gratitude
for his willingness to serve "where most needed."

After a month's leave he had journeyed west, arriving
in Tucson, walking into Colonel Schreiber's office, saluting and laying the envelope containing his orders on the
desk.

Now Schreiber was laid low by pneumonia and Marcus
was in charge: of Fort Lowell, of this mission, responsible for the lives of eight men. He had to guess where the
enemy was, where they'd move, what they'd do. It came
down to a guessing game, all because four steers had
been slain and two horses stolen. The Apaches didn't
want either; what they wanted was bluecoats chasing
their ponies' tails and the chance to wipe out the soldiers.

Fort Lowell was short personnel, down twenty men
from the one hundred ten originally assigned to duty
there. Not a single replacement had arrived in nearly a
year and a half. There was a war on. He put himself in
the enemy's moccasins. The Apaches had to know there
were only nine of them pursuing.

Nine from ninety leaves eighty-one.

Private Henry Colclough, two years in blues and still
green as spring grass, spoke.

"Captain, Apache!"

He was standing at the trail end of the edge of the overhang.

"Down!" barked Venable.

Colclough flushed and obeyed. He came duck waddling toward them, pointing up through the overhang.

"I saw one come out of a cave up top, turn around, and go right back inside."

"You're seeing things, boy," growled Tumble.

"I saw him!" Colclough's jaw was thrust out belligerently.

"No doubt he did, Corporal," said Venable.

"Then they're up there after all," ventured another man.

Everyone but the corporal and Orph nodded.

"I doubt it," said the captain quietly. "More than likely he's the one who brought the horse, let him loose, and went up to the caves."

"And showed himself on purpose," continued Tumble. "To make us think they're up there. Think like a Apache, boys. When the hell you gonna learn?"

Darkness fell rapidly. The sky was strewn with clouds. The moon would show, brighten the slopes, enabling one to see a hundred yards in every direction, then vanish, plunging the area into blackness. All eyes were on Venable, the men awaiting the expected order to move out. He hesitated to give it. Lingering doubt nagged. The wind whined above them and died.

"One last word," he said. "When you locate cover, take it, use it. When you shoot, shoot with the moon, when you can see what you're shooting at."

Tumble was staring at him; he stared back defensively. The corporal grinned.

"Pay attention, boys, your lives'll depend on your cover."

"Pay no attention to the man up top," added Venable. "Keep your eyes on the knoll; when they come for the horses, follow them down. Keep out of sight. They should lead us straight to the main body."

Should, he thought. Why did he feel the need to qualify the assertion? No doubt because he was guessing, hoping. He fell silent, waiting, eyes on the moon. It slid slowly behind a cloud.

"Move out," he snapped.

Off they glided like shadows, picking their ways through the rocks without a sound. Captain and corporal held their places and continued to wait. Then Tumble started away to the left toward the trail and down.

"Wait," whispered Venable. "Let's stay here. It's as good a spot as any we'll find. Listen . . ."

They froze, their attention riveted on the knoll and the horses. There was no sound.

"What is it, Captain? Somethin's buggin' you . . ."

"Four steers, two horses. That's the extent of their marauding. Doesn't make sense. Radlund, the owner of the spread, has at least three hundred head. Two weeks ago he sold off a hundred over at San Carlos. And he must keep at least twenty horses."

"They killed the steers. They didn't *try* to steal 'em."

"Stealing the horses smacks of an afterthought. The whole thing has a fishy smell to me. What do you think?"

"Real fishy. Raid sure didn' net 'em beans, but they got one thing. Got us up here."

Venable looked grim. "The main idea. The whole idea."

Up the slope an owl hooted. A second echoed it below, then one to their left, the fourth to the right.

"Oh my God," murmured Venable.

Owl hoots surrounded them, softly chanting in a weird chorus, repeating louder, louder still; fifty voices, a hundred. Fear seeped into the corporal's eyes.

"Surrounded . . ."

"Lemme go for help, sir," murmured Tumble. "Sneak my mare out of the bunch, ride like hell down through the bastards. They gotta be spread out. May not even have men close to the trail either side. I'll ride low right through 'em." He pointed skyward. "Just have to wait for that long, fat cloud; it'll be good for five minutes of pitch dark, maybe more. That's all I'll need."

"No."

"Sir?"

The hooting resumed around them. A chill chased up Venable's spine.

Tumble held his breath and eyed him. "Sir . . ."

"Listen. We'll wait for the cloud, then I'll start down afoot. You head for the knoll. Free every horse, then swat them away. Head them downtrail. Yell, shoot, raise the loudest ruckus you can, anything to spook them, send them charging off. Then duck for cover. They'll be coming at you from all sides."

"Captain—"

"Let me finish. By then I should be a hundred yards down, maybe farther, maybe through their line. I'll catch a mount coming by me."

"They'll be at full gallop; you'll be trampled before you can get a hand on a rein. By then the bastards'll attack, start closing in—"

"You'll just have to burrow deep and give back as good as you get. Hang on. Give me half an hour." Marcus added an edge to his tone, making it an order.

Venable handed him his carbine, checked his issue Colt, his right hand finding the grip, and got out his Green River knife. It was not government issue, but reliable in a hand-to-hand fight.

"Best keep that thing in its sheath, sir; moonlight'll bounce off the blade like the sun off a mirror."

Venable winked and slid the knife up his sleeve. The cloud crawled over the moon, blotting it out. Off he ran, moving in a crouch, straining his eyes to pick a path through the rocks, reluctant to go anywhere near the trail until he got well down the slope, below the lower line of attackers. But the rugged terrain slowed his progress, forcing him to follow a pattern that zigzagged even more severely than did the trail. He slipped behind an outcropping and set his back against it panting, sweating furiously, than suddenly turning freezing cold. Nerves and the night air, he mused. The slope spread below him. It was another two hundred yards at least; double that and more by way of the tortuous route he was obliged to follow.

He held his breath and listened. Tumble was cutting the hobbles; any second now the horses would be free and starting down. He waited, panting less now, catching his wind.

"Start them, Tumble, get 'em going. What's the matter?" he whispered fiercely.

He resumed running. Rounding a ledge, his right boot found a hole; he plunged down halfway to his knee. Had the ledge not slowed him, he would have snapped his leg stepping in the hole. He lifted himself and took a single step as a dark shape sprang in front of him. He smelled the Apache before he glimpsed his face or his knife glinting in the moonlight. Before the Indian's blade could descend, Marcus had shaken his own knife into his palm, swiveled it in his hand, and started driving it upward.

Each dodged, avoiding the other's thrust. The way was narrow, the rocks close on both sides. The brave fell left, hammering his rib cage, grunting, leering viciously. Venable had pulled back when the attacking blade sliced downward, barely missing his chest. He fell back, jolting his spine, sending darts of pain from tail to nape.

The brave had righted himself. He sprang. Venable's feet caught him full in the gut and launched him into the air. He landed on his head, his neck crunching with a sickening sound. Venable scrambled to his feet and spun about. The brave lay motionless, his head at an awkward angle on his broken neck. His knife still lay in his grasp.

Venable began running again. Above him the rumble of hooves filled the night. He pulled up short and moved swiftly off to his right to the trail. No sooner did he gain it than the mountainside exploded with howls and arrows came whirring at him. He ducked behind a rock and threw a glance up the trail. Its narrowness forced the horses into single file. The leader's eyes whitened with fear. Shooting erupted above left and right. All hell exploded. The horses crashed down the trail, spurred to even greater speed by the din. The first one, then the second rumbled by; snatching for one, then the other's reins, Marcus didn't come close.

He drew his Colt and fired in the air. The third horse, now in the lead, braked so abruptly that the one behind it bowled squarely into it, knocking it headlong; quickly the others, unable to stop, piled into one another. In a frenzy one after another rose, pawing the air, shifting to one side, then the other. Only one, a big chestnut mare, remained calm, vaulting gracefully over the pack, landing just beyond where Venable crouched watching. The surface it came down on was uneven, jagged; it landed and staggered briefly. In that instant Venable's hand shot out, grasping the reins. He swung up into the saddle and thundered away.

The moon failed to cooperate. It emerged, painting man and mount a bright blue-gray as the horse moved surefootedly down the trail. Venable flattened himself along the saddle; arrows whizzed at him from both sides. He prayed that none would strike the horse. He pictured one lodging deep in her flank, her hind leg caving in. She would fall, rolling over onto the shaft, pinning him under her.

He spurred her and prayed, speaking soothingly and encouragingly to her. She fairly flew down the mountainside, picking her way adroitly. Level ground came inching toward them; she had almost made it when the black shroud fell again.

She reached the base. Through the steady rattling of her hooves Marcus could hear firing. He threw a quick glance back over his shoulder, but all he could see in the darkness was the occasional flash of a rifle, like a pulsing lightning bug. Guns cracked like fingers snapping, cleanly, sharply.

He spurred on, tearing across level ground toward the fort. Officers and men would have finished their evening meal by now; the officers would be sitting on their tiny porches with their families or visiting their friends, a lazy end to a lazy, uneventful day. The men would be relaxing: playing cards, craps, or just talking.

On and on he rode, the sound of gunfire fading. The mare was big, strong, showing astonishing endurance, but the pace he was demanding of her would wear out the strongest horse in ten short miles. He cursed himself and his blind stupidity in leading his men into the lion's mouth. Had he taken the time to think it through he would have realized from the outset what the Apaches were planning. But at the outset there hadn't been the luxury of time for thinking, only for action. Radlund had come storming into the fort demanding action. Marcus had been sitting at Schreiber's desk when he heard the commotion and ran outside. After listening to the rancher, he rounded up the nearest eight men and stormed away from the fort.

How much time had elapsed? Fifteen minutes? Twenty? How long could they hold out? The Apaches obviously had no rifles, or they would have been using them from the start.

How many were there? Too many. They would pin the soldiers down; they'd use the moon. When it was concealed, they would tighten the circle. When it appeared they'd isolate their targets and rain arrows at them.

Had Tumble been able to find decent cover after shooing away the horses? Knowing the corporal, he had probably picked his spot before he cut the first set of hobbles, then worked his way through the horses to the one closest to his rock. Once he had freed it, he would send them all running down the trail and jump for his life.

"Hang on, hang on . . ."

The fort rose, a huge rectangular shadow a mile directly ahead. He jammed his rowels again and again. Hang on, Tumble, Orph, Colclough. We'll be back in force! Every man; we'll cut them down like ripe cane!

The shadow before him broke into separate, smaller boxes. No stockade fence surrounded the post; no gate forced him to pull up and order it opened, wasting precious seconds. He barreled through the entrance, pulling up in the center of the parade ground, his horse wheeling about in a small circle. He emptied his gun in the air. Men came running.

"Mount up! Every man! Carbines! No saddles! No time! Move!"

Schreiber's striker appeared at the office door buttoning his tunic, his sallow face etched with puzzlement.

"Don't just stand there, get me a fresh horse. Your own! Move, goddamnit!"

It was only a few minutes in the incalculable total of all time, but it seemed like eons before the men were mounted and off. Lieutenant Robert Sutherland, a veteran of the war in Virginia, rode on Venable's right; on the opposite side rode Lieutenant Russell Gaines. Sutherland was a good officer, Venable knew—a bit standoffish, perhaps even a snob, which was not surprising, considering he had been a proper Bostonian in civilian life. But he was able and courageous under fire, a man his men looked up to. Gaines, on the other hand, was something less than Venable's ideal junior officer. Why such a man ever even joined the Army was more than Marcus could understand. He had been a schoolteacher, had never fired any kind of gun in his life prior to enlisting. He couldn't hit the sky with a twenty-second aim, according to Corporal Tumble. He rode poorly, uncertainly, and became ad-

dled and confused under pressure, commanding more
derision behind his back than even grudging respect.

He did try, but he was so hapless that on more than
one occasion Venable found himself wishing Gaines had
stayed at school with his chalk and his books, and left the
fighting to those blessed with heart for the fray. Sutherland, sadly enough, was not twins.

Marcus turned to Gaines. "Russell."

"Sir?"

"When we get there you and your men stick with me."

Venable glanced toward Sutherland. The lieutenant
accorded him a thin smile of understanding. He understood if Gaines did not that the captain did not trust the
schoolteacher on his own under fire. His own men needed
protection from him.

The mountains rose before them stark and forbidding.
They were still not close enough to hear gunfire, but the
closer they drew the more concerned Venable became.
Within a half mile of the foothills they still had not heard
a sound. He guessed that roughly forty minutes had
elapsed since the onset of the shooting; forty minutes
under siege. In an open area on level ground it would
have taken the Apaches all of thirty seconds to wipe
them out. Among the boulders and outcroppings stud-
ding the slopes it would take considerably longer.

How long?

And if any were still alive, why weren't they shooting?
Even blindly?

The troops pulled up at the base, 65 strong, spoiling
for battle, supremely aware that their friends and com-
rades were halfway up the mountain fighting for their
lives. Sutherland, Gaines, and the other officers assembled around Venable. He sat motionless staring at the
backs of his gloves.

Not a sound, not so much as a whisper of breeze came
floating down. The moon brightened the slopes. There
was no sign of a living soul. His heart sank, his chest
tightened. He felt like jelly. He had lost the race, lost
them.

All.

Thrown them away!

"Too late," mumbled Sutherland.

"Dismount. Spread out left and right ten yards between. We'll go up on foot."

"Too late," repeated Sutherland. The others nodded. "It's all over, Marcus."

"I heard you the first time, Lieutenant! Stop gabbing and do as you're ordered."

They went through the motions, positioning themselves in a line, starting up the mountain. The moon came out and stayed out. They climbed and searched. In two hours they found the bodies of nineteen Apaches and eight soldiers. All eight bodies were stripped naked. All scalped.

2

Gabriel Cowan wore his broadcloth frock coat unbuttoned; the sleeves were long, reaching to well below his wrists. His collar stood straight and stiff with the points turned backward. His tie was a small black satin bow, his trousers a dark-striped cashmere. His elegant clothing was stiff and glazed with blood, the blood of many patients blending in a proudly displayed badge of his profession.

The patient had been laid on a bare wooden table. He wore his street clothes but for his trousers, removed so the surgeon could work on his leg. The wheel of a wagon loaded with barrels of syrup had passed over the limb just under the knee, and the break was grievously jagged.

The operating room was gloomy and windowless, tucked away in the hospital basement. The only light came from a lamp suspended above the patient. Its glow barely reached the small square table on which the surgical instruments had been laid out and covered with a cloth.

"Carbolic acid solution," said Dr. Cowan, snapping his fingers.

His assistant, Dr. Marion Sturges, uncorked a small unlabeled bottle of carbolic acid to which a quantity of linseed oil had been added. After moistening a cloth with the solution, she began gently laving the afflicted area. Dr. Sturges was suddenly more woman than physician in her solicitude. A curly blond hair fell across her brow, and she wiped it back with her wrist, only to have it fall back again. Under the single oil lamp her pale complexion seemed to glow. Her eyes, hazel flecked with gold, smoldered with dedication as the patient flinched and groaned softly.

"Easy, Doctor," said Cowan. "Even unconscious, he can feel it."

Marion sighed sympathetically. "He looks drained."

"He's lost a lot of blood. The break's so jagged it was like a fistful of knives stabbing the veins and arteries."

She paused to readjust a clamp fixed to the femoral artery. "It's seeping," she said.

Cowan shrugged. The anesthetist had removed the chloroform cone. Cowan moved around the table, stepping in front of him to examine the wound from a different perspective. Two rats scratched in combat in the wall opposite the foot of the table. Water stains browned the ceiling; cracks laced the walls, dust was everywhere. The mawkish, ever present stench of pus permeated the stale air.

Cowan squinted astigmatically at the wound, clucked, and moved around to Marion's side.

"Give me the full strength."

She handed him a second bottle of carbolic acid. He poured it undiluted into the wound. The exposed nerves twitched in reaction, the liquid seeping through the interlacing of muscles, nerves, and tendons into every passage. He clucked resignedly.

"No simple green stick break, this one."

"It's completely overriding."

Using a fork retractor, she held back the flesh while he carefully reset the bone.

"We've got to get all the fragments," she cautioned.

"You dig for the one down below there," he said. "It's jammed so deep just the tip is showing. See it? Try to ease it out. Mind the clamps."

Using an artery forceps, she slowly extracted the sliver of bone and restored it to its place.

"Good girl, good hand. How's he breathing?"

"Not strong, but steady."

"We're going to save this leg, Doctor," he said. "It beats hacking it off, tossing it in the ash bin, right?"

"Mr. Hamilton will think so."

Marion eyed Dr. Gabriel Cowan admiringly. Nine out of ten surgeons would have taken one look at the break and reached for their amputation saw. He straightened and eyed her.

"That takes care of all the fragments. Work on that popliteal vein. Try and open it back up so he can get full circulation."

It was delicate and tricky work, like massaging a flattened hose back to roundness, but she succeeded.

"Good girl, what a touch . . ."

She smiled appreciatively. "That about does it."

He had realigned the two pieces of bone and restored the remaining fragments, the last one no bigger than the locking bar on a cuff link.

"Take over, Doctor," he said.

Marion began dressing the wound, using a mixture of putty and carbolic acid, the putty holding the disinfectant so that it would not be washed away by discharges of blood and lymph. She applied the mixture outward to a distance of about three inches around the wound to forestall infection, then covered the leg with tinfoil to reduce evaporation of the carbolic acid. The leg was then splinted and the splints bandaged to hold them in place. The unconscious patient was lifted onto a stretcher to be returned to his bed in the ward.

Doctors Cowan and Sturges walked down the echoing corridor and up one flight to Cowan's office near the landing. Dr. Gabriel Cowan, chief surgeon and associate director of Wills Hospital, Philadelphia's largest and most prestigious hospital, was seventy and his hands shook slightly from palsy, except when he operated. Under the stress of performing surgery they seemed to draw on some hidden reservoir of strength that steadied them. He was in poor health, suffering with a frail and overworked heart and a variety of lesser ailments. His health and age, however, in no way hampered his work. His dedication recognized neither as drawbacks.

He was ungainly, slope-shouldered, thin-chested, his face bony and gaunt, and at first glance he appeared cold, humorless, a man overly concerned with propriety and detached from and indifferent to those who came under his scalpel. But if one took careful notice, Cowan's twinkling blue eyes, ready smile, and warm voice attested to his humaneness. He was kind and caring; he respected his patients as fellow humans and was sympathetic toward their suffering. He made it his business to allay their natural fear, to comfort and indulge them.

Away from the hospital and his duties he was a different man. He was captious and outspoken. His acid tongue made enemies easily, but his reputation as Philadelphia's foremost medical man saved him from becoming a pariah. Quite the contrary, he was something of a social lion—roar, fangs, claws, and all.

His associate, Dr. Marion Sturges, was one of only two woman doctors on the staffs of the city's four hospitals. Had it not been for the wartime shortage of doctors, it was doubtful—even with her enviable qualifications—that she would have been accepted by Wills. Were it not for Cowan's faith in her and his campaigning on her behalf, she would have been struggling to overcome the prejudices against her sex in the field and eking out a living in private practice.

It was nearing six-fifteen. He had performed and she had assisted in eleven operations that day. The one prior to setting the fractured leg had been an attempt to remove a cancerous lung from a sixty-year-old woman. It had been strenuous, difficult work which had turned out to be in vain: the patient had died shortly after being returned to the ward.

The two of them were exhausted. He hung up his coat, undid his tie, settled himself in his swivel chair, and lit a foul-smelling stogie. It was getting dark out; the evening star had appeared and the rumble of the traffic in the street below seemed to diminish with every round of the second hand on the watch which he had laid on the desk, coiling its chain neatly beside it.

She stretched, leaned back, and fussed aimlessly with her tight blond curls. A victorious smile masked her fatigue, but it quickly faded to a frown.

"Too bad about Mrs. Grady. All that work for nothing, poor soul."

"Her lung was too far gone by the time we got inside," he murmured. "A miracle couldn't have saved her. I don't believe in miracles. I believe in vacations. You need one desperately, Dr. Sturges. You look like the wrath of Jehovah."

"Thank you, Doctor."

"You're welcome." Concern furrowed his slender face. "Still no word?"

She shook her head. "Last I heard they were going into battle at Petersburg, Virginia."

"Didn't they fight that one last year?"

"You're thinking of Bull Run."

"Right. They had such a good time they reprised it. Sweet Jerusalem, they can't even settle accounts on one piddling patch, they have to fight over it a second time. What a war." He laid a slightly shaking, comforting hand on hers in her lap. "He'll come through this one all right. He always has."

"So far. Just please don't say no news is good news. It looks like the Confederates are digging in for one last stand. They'll be fighting like tigers."

Cowan studied her over his glasses: her emerald eyes, flawless complexion, the perfect balance and symmetry of her features.

"How've you been sleeping?" he asked.

"Oh, splendidly." She rolled her eyes, belying her words.

"Don't overdo the luminol."

"I don't use it. I don't take anything, only warm milk and pleasant thoughts. I crochet them out of air and phony optimism."

"He *does* write you regularly. That's more than most husbands I know."

"I get three letters in one day, then not a whisper for a month. I wish to God he'd never joined. We could have been settled, raising a family. This disgusting war could drag on for another ten years."

"It can't. The South can't sustain itself much longer. Cheer up, you'll find a letter waiting when you get home tonight." He puffed. "Nasty fracture, that Hamilton fellow."

"It must have been terrifically painful," she agreed.

"We'll give it four days. If we remove the dressing and there's no rancid smell or any other signs of putrefaction, he'll be okay. If anything does go wrong, it'll show before the four days are up. Thank God for carbolic acid. What a blessing. Did I ever tell you that from 1860 through to the end of '62 I performed thirty-five amputations? Couldn't save a single leg; didn't dare try; seven-

teen patients died. Beginning in '63 up to now—what's
that, eighteen months? I've performed six, saved thirty-
four legs and not so much as a speck of pyemia. Three
cheers for modern medicine, Doctor."

"For carbolic acid and your skill." She stood up,
stretched, and smothered a yawn with her fist. "I have to
make last rounds."

"Look in on friend Hamilton. He must be awake by
now. Come back and let me know before you leave.
Then go straight home to bed."

"Is it all right if I have supper?" she asked with a small
smile.

"Only if you eat fast."

"Bless you, Master."

He turned from her in his swivel chair and picked up a
month-old and somewhat bedraggled copy of the British
medical journal *Lancet*. He pretended to be immediately
engrossed. She threw her arms around him from the
back, hugged, and fled.

He leafed through the magazine, pausing at an article
which attacked Dr. Joseph Lister's germ theory. He was
convinced to the point of castigating anyone who dis-
agreed with him that Lister, whom he greatly admired,
had long been right in urging acceptance of the antiseptic
system for preventing the spread of germs. Carbolic acid
was the key to the system; why most of Lister's col-
leagues refused to recognize its worth Cowan could not
understand. Articles ridiculing it infuriated him. He was
tempted to send off a blistering letter attacking Lister's
critics, but decided that any support that came from this
side of the Atlantic would do the cause more harm than
good.

Marion went upstairs to make her rounds, nodding to
orderlies and nurses, but thinking only of First Lieutenant Tyson Sturges. How she missed his warmth beside
her in bed, his embrace, his manly scent, his kiss that left
her limp.

But she missed him in a hundred ways outside of the
delirium of their love. She missed their conversations
that often stretched into the darkest hours of night. Apart
from Gabriel Cowan, there had never been anyone she
had enjoyed talking to like Tyson. They had fallen in
love and married nearly three years ago. It had been as

romantic as a fairy tale, all rainbows and rosy clouds, sunshine and joy. He had been away two of the three years, coming home only once about a year ago for a weekend. The hours were devoted to his arms, his love, to insatiable lust for each other, hours that had sped like seconds then back to the war and now into his fifth battle. Five times his life in jeopardy and not a scratch; how long would his luck last?

Depending from the silver chain around her neck was a carved pewter locket that had been her grandmother's. She opened it to his smiling face: the heavy brows and shining dark eyes, the smile, the faultless carving of his handsome features. Picture and memories were all she had of him. Petersburg had him: the snapping guns, the cannon, the blood and destruction. For what did they fight and suffer and die? Southern pride, and Northern. To erase the secession, force the Confederacy to disband and the states it embraced back into the Union.

She walked into Ward B. The beds set four feet apart flanked a wide aisle that ended with four large and grimy windows. All but two of the beds were occupied; the patients lay on flock-sodden mattresses fitted with the same filthy sheets used by the previous occupant. The prevalent odor of illness defied flowers, perfumes—everything introduced to mask or minimize it. Like the smell of death over a battlefield it hung in the air around each contributor, a mix of sour-smelling linens, suppuration, and ammonia fumes.

A nurse was standing by Hamilton's bed. He was awake and obviously in pain. Marion hurried her step. She took his pulse, felt his forehead.

"Nurse, prepare two cc's of quinine and morphine. The quinine first. And repeat both in two hours. How are we doing, Mr. Hamilton?"

"I got some terrible soreness, ma'am. Can I see the doctor?"

"I'm the doctor," Marion stated matter-of-factly.

"Oh." A flicker of suspicion overrode his expression of pain.

The nurse, a freckle-faced girl whose engaging grin had been replaced by a furrowed brow of concern for her newest patient, speedily prepared the injection of morphine. The quinine was to be given orally.

"Dr. Cowan saved your leg, Mr. Hamilton, just as he promised you," said Marion.

"The man's a saint. I was afraid I'd be hobbling about on a crutch the rest of my life or worse."

"You're going to be just fine," she continued. "By tomorrow morning you'll be over the worst of the pain. Anything I can get you?"

"No thanks, I'm fine. Good as can be expected, as they say."

Her eyes had been drawn to the empty bed opposite him. Mrs. Grady, minus her cancer-savaged lung, now lay in the morgue. Who decides who lives, she reflected. Not the doctor. How valiant the fight, how determined, how noble. How futile.

Dr. Cowan's stogie had gone out. He was relighting it when a young man in his shirt-sleeves stuck his head in.

"Doc . . ."

"Doctor, Hubert. A dock is for boats."

"You seen Doc Sturges?"

"She's on rounds."

"Telegram for her."

"I'll give it to her."

Hubert went off whistling. The boy walked like he was on a bicycle, thought Cowan. He closed the door and sat holding the telegram against the feeble light of the setting sun, wishing he could make out what it said through the yellow envelope. He turned it over as worry spilled into his heart and began to fill it. Why take it for granted it was bad news? Why was it the first reaction to the unique yellow envelope?

"Damn."

There was no way of telling who the sender was from the outside. Cowan's stogie went out again. He jerked it from his mouth and stumped it forcefully in the ashtray, but continued to hold the envelope in a manner that suggested it contained some kind of explosive that was threatening to detonate. Fear displaced concern and fast became dread.

He shut the door. He sucked his lungs full of the smelly, warm air, bit his lower lip and opened the telegram.

THE WAR DEPARTMENT REGRETS TO INFORM YOU THAT
YOUR HUSBAND FIRST LIEUTENANT TYSON MATTHEW
CHARLES STURGES HAS BEEN KILLED IN ACTION AT PE-
TERSBURG VIRGINIA STOP THE PRESIDENT EXTENDS TO
YOU HIS DEEPEST AND MOST HEARTFELT CONDOLENCES
FOR YOUR LOSS STOP MAY YOUR BEREAVEMENT BE AS-
SUAGED BY THE KNOWLEDGE THAT YOUR HUSBAND MET
HIS DEATH WITH FORTITUDE AND HONOR.

RESPECTFULLY

E M BROWDER
WAR DEPARTMENT
WASHINGTON D C

Light steps approached the door. Cowan crumpled the
paper and flung it in the wastebasket just as Marion
walked in.

"Mr. Hamilton's doing nobly. I gave wards B and A a
quick once-over. Mrs. Childress needs her dressing changed
every two hours, not four; I instructed the floor nurse.
And Mr. Hampton, the ancient mariner—you remember,
the appendectomy—is infected. I washed his incision.
You may want to take a look. Lord, it stinks in here. He
could stand another suture or two."

She threw the window wide.

"I'll take care of it. You go on home." The flatness of
his voice only alerted Marion to his troubled state.

"What's the matter?" she asked immediately.

"Nothing. Why should there be?"

"Something is. What?"

"Don't badger me, woman."

"Gabriel . . ." She clenched and unclenched her fists,
as if battling to keep from throttling him.

"Sit."

"What is wrong?" She pleaded for explanation with
her gaze.

"Sit down, Doctor! First, shut the door."

She did so, but the question remained in her eyes. She
sank her teeth into her lip and began to move her hands
nervously.

"Gabriel?"

"Christ . . ." He shielded his eyes with his palm and rubbed his forehead wearily.

"What is it!" she cried, an edge of panic creeping into her voice.

"Don't shout!" he shouted.

"It's Tyson. You've heard something. He's dead. Oh my God!"

"Marion, Marion . . ." Already Cowan's gentle approach had been shattered.

"He's not?"

"Will you calm down?"

She immolated him with her eyes. He could feel himself shrink under their assault. He retrieved the balled paper from the basket and began to smooth it on the desk. She snatched it away and scanned the page. Gabriel sighed and studied the tips of his shoes. Marion finished, stared at the paper, and sank slowly into the chair.

"Tyson, darling . . ."

Her voice was weak, her words barely audible. Cowan stood by her, hands on her shoulders. She twisted her head and pressed her face against his chest. He held her; stroked her hair, fumbling for words of comfort. The hollow platitudes were well intended but meaningless, so he shut up and let her cry softly. She straightened, sniffled, swiped at her eyes, and stared at him. Initial shock and heartache began to yield to resentment.

"I'm not surprised, I'm really not. You think I am? You're wrong. I knew it was coming. A woman knows."

"Marion—"

"It would have been a miracle if it hadn't. There's your miracle neither of us believes in. You can't be in the thick of it day in day out and not have it catch up to you. Gabriel, he's dead."

Somehow her words sounded like a challenge to him, and made him feel to blame.

"My dear—"

"Dead!"

"Sssssh. Come, let me take you home."

Her rage increased. "I don't want to go home. For what? What do I need with empty rooms and silence. He's . . . dead. They've . . . killed my husband, my . . . Tyson. Dead!"

The door opened. Two orderlies and a nurse gaped blankly. Cowan slammed the door in their faces, bolted it, and went back to her. He held her, patting her back gently. His heart sank in his chest. The telegram lay where she'd dropped it—words from a stranger on a piece of cheap paper, words to wrench the heart and mutilate the spirit.

Tears continued to pour down Dr. Marion Sturges's contorted face.

3

General William Tecumseh "War is Hell" Sherman called General George "Old Gray Fox" Crook the "greatest Indian fighter the United States ever produced." Crook did not disagree. He ran his silver-backed brush through each fork of his magnificent beard, mounted his favorite mule, and rode off to war, greatness, and fulfillment of Sherman's estimate of him. He warred against the rebels and against the Indians. No gold-braided Napoleonic chapeau or Custer-style sailor-suit collar with stars for him, he wore a corked helmet and the white canvas suit of a cavalryman on stable detail. His puritanical streak was as wide as his fame; he did not smoke, drink, or swear. He was, however, outrageously eccentric beyond his attire; he was also the most decent, humane top officer in the West.

He had arrived in Tucson on the Santa Cruz River in southeastern Arizona Territory, where earlier General James Carleton had established a military plaza near the center of a tiny settlement. Its focal point was the Tucson Depot, erected to store military supplies. At first it was a small encampment occupied by a single fifty-eight man company of the 32nd Infantry, and the men had all they could do to escort the supply trains and maintain a couple of outposts on the Mesilla road.

Camp Lowell, as it was then called, was a hellhole

when Crook rode in. He took one look and promptly deemed it "unfit for the occupation of animals, much less troops of a civilized nation." Construction of a new post was ordered northeast of town. It was built in a square with storehouses, stables, and other buildings girdling the interior officers' and men's quarters. To the north stood the sutler's store flanked by the laundresses' quarters and ordnance depot. To the south, ranged in a line in proximity to the officers' houses, were the guardhouse, the water tanks, and quartermaster's residence. East and west storehouses backed up to the enlisted men's barracks. And surrounding the whole was barren, mesquite-littered and sunbaked land fit only to walk and ride on, typical of most of the land in the immediate area.

In command of the post General Crook placed Lieutenant Colonel Justin Schreiber, a man who did not share his humane view of the Apaches. The Old Gray Fox was a minority of nearly one in his belief that Indians were humans who should be dealt with fairly rather than savages to be exterminated. He posed for one final photograph in Napoleonic style, one hand tucked in his blouse, face aglower, and departed to assume command of the Department of Arizona. One year later to the day, Lieutenant Colonel Schreiber fell ill and took to his bed. Captain Marcus Venable, his aide, sent the colonel's striker into town to bring back Dr. Artemus Shaw, Tucson's only physician. Colonel and captain awaited the doctor's arrival with mixed feelings. For eight years Shaw had been the only doctor not only in Tucson, but the area. He was in his late fifties, hard-bitten, ornery, overworked, and militantly intolerant of human stupidity and weakness. If humans were the creatures they most closely resembled in appearance and character, Artemus Shaw, M.D., would have been a horned toad. His steely glare, practiced scowl, and rumbling voice commanded attention and obedience. He had a habit of treating his patients like small children, patronizing them mercilessly, dismissing disagreement and any questioning of his judgment. He gave the impression that he wanted to be considered as God with a satchel, or, at the very least, St. Luke.

While the captain and the colonel waited for the doctor in Schreiber's bedroom adjacent to his office, the conversation turned to the grisly events of the night before.

"It's very simple," said Schreiber, "you shouldn't have gone. It's not your place to go out after marauding savages. You have junior officers for that. You, Marcus, are acting CO."

"I went because I—"

"Felt obligated to. It was your chance to prove I made the right choice. Great Scott, who else would I choose? You're the last man around here who has to prove himself."

This came from the colonel's heart, Venable knew, but it passed through one ear and out the other, flying cleanly by the captain's ego. He had lain awake the entire night brooding over the slaughter, blaming himself. The sight of Corporal Tumbelsky lying dead with four arrows in his chest, his scalp ripped off, a bloody cap in its place, had sickened Marcus. The eight bodies had been brought back and placed in a shed to be buried that afternoon with full military honors. These eight soldiers in blue had been doomed from the moment they set out after the raiders.

There were eight needless deaths sitting in a row on his conscience, shaking their mutilated heads.

"My God, man, look at you, your face! One would imagine you'd killed them yourself." Schreiber made a disapproving sound. He looked annoyed.

"*I* think I did."

"You're a fool, Marcus."

"Stupid, I know."

"Overeager. The Apache's the wiliest savage in the land, and the Mogollóns, the wiliest of the breed. You fight a clever enemy in his backyard and the odds are against you every time. Accept it, man, chew it, spit it out, and go on. You let it prey on you like you are and it'll destroy you. This post needs a leader with a firm hand on the reins, not a moping, brooding, conscience-striken martyr." His eyes softened and his tone. "Shake it off, Marcus, put it behind you."

"I wish to God I could," Marcus said levelly.

"You'd better." Schreiber coughed and wiped his mouth with his handkerchief. "Damn lungs. They're like tissue paper."

"You don't feel any better?"

"The same. I had trouble with my lungs when I was a boy. Not consumption, but something like it. Doctor never did pin it down. I was out fishing with my dad, I was only about thirteen, I fell overboard. Nearly drowned. Caught a devil of a cold that lasted six months; to this day whenever I catch cold I get pain in both lungs." Schreiber stopped and looked at Venable's weary and dejected form. "When will you bury them?"

"In about an hour." He could feel his eyes misting. He turned his head. Tumble, Orph, Colclough, all the others; so young, most so green. He'd be thankful when this day was over. What a beginning to his tenure as CO.

The inner door opened. It was the man who'd replaced Schreiber's striker while he fetched the doctor. He snuffled noisily.

"Man here wants to see you, Captain."

"Who?" Marcus asked.

"Didn't say. Civilian."

Venable turned back to the colonel. "Get some sleep, Shaw'll be here—"

"When he gets here, I know." The colonel smiled thinly.

Venable went out, closing the door. His visitor was a barrel-chested individual in riding breeches and a deerskin shirt. He was in his fifties, square-jawed, ruggedlooking, a no-nonsense expression draping his large head. An ivory toothpick was jammed between his teeth in one corner of his mouth. He was Luther Radlund, whose ranch the Mogollón Apaches had raided.

"Remember me? Luther Radlund. It was my spread them filthy ragheads stole the horses from, killed four head of cattle. Do I understand rightly it was you led the party that chased 'em? What the hell happened? Couldn't you get my horses back? Catch them miserable ragheads, blow their heads off? Jesus Christ, you boys are supposed to protect us, our property. They come waltzing by, raise hell, kill and steal, ride off and get away clean."

He dug a paper out of his chest pocket, unfolded it, and proffered it.

"What's this?" asked Venable.

"Just what it looks like. My bill to the U.S. Government. That's who you're working for, ain't it? Some job you're doing."

Steam had been slowly building pressure in Venable's maw from the rancher's first outburst. It blew.

"Listen to me, mister, we broke our backs chasing them. Caught up with them in the mountains only to run into a goddamned buzzsaw. Ten or twenty hit your place; by the time we caught up they were five times that number. It was a setup." He leaned over the desk and eyed him hard. "They killed eight of my men."

"So?" Radlund stared blankly.

"What do you mean, 'so'?"

"They're soldiers, aren't they? They're paid to take chances; it's their job."

"Paid sixteen dollars a month! Nickels and dimes to risk their lives protecting you civilians."

Radlund sniffed and lifted one corner of his mouth in a sneer. "Don't seem to be doing a very good job of it."

"Are you deaf? They died trying to do 'your' job. Surrounded, trapped, outnumbered."

"I lost four goddamn steers, two—"

"I don't give a damn! You're talking animals, I'm talking human beings!"

"Like I say, risk goes with the uniform. Anyways, this here's my bill. Forty bucks for each of the steers; one hundred sixty; sixty for each of the horses. Total of two hundred eighty. I'll thank you to submit it to the proper official for payment."

Venable was shaking in anger. Radlund's face remained scornful until Venable snatched the bill from him, crumpled it, and threw it at him. Radlund's face darkened; he bristled.

"You bluecoat sonovabitch!"

"Get out of here." Marcus could barely control his boiling fury.

"Who the hell you think you're talking to, tin soldier!"

"Out!" roared Venable.

He went for his gun, drawing it slowly. Radlund's eyes widened. His hands came up defensively and he began to back off.

"You're loco! I'll get you for this, I promise. I know Governor Jack Goodwin personally. You're finished!" Radlund sputtered.

"Get out of here before I blow your head off."

He was gone. Marcus heard the squeak of a buggy and the pounding hooves of Radlund's horse as he sped away.

The striker's replacement returned silently, obviously having heard every word.

"Private, pick up that crumpled paper there, flatten it out, make a copy and mail it off," Marcus snapped.

"To where, sir?" came the meek reply.

"I have no idea. On second thought, to hell with it."

Marcus picked up the wastebasket and held it at an angle. The man tossed the ball into it.

Olan, the colonel's striker, arrived with the doctor. Venable stood by as Shaw perched on a three-legged stool, his bag open, the clamps of his stethoscope meeting at the nape of his scrawny neck, his eyes slit, his expression intimidating.

"Headache, shivering, backache. Temperature one hundred and three. Blood-flecked sputum." He paused and set the flat of his hand against the left side of Schreiber's chest. The colonel grunted and grimaced. "Severe pain, shallow breathing, shortness of breath. Color high, tinged with blue. Lobar pneumonia."

"Bad cold," murmured Schreiber.

"Rubbish, you telling me I don't recognize pneumonia? You, Captain, fetch another pillow. Two. Prop him up. Listen to me, Colonel. Are you listening?" Shaw barked.

Schreiber grunted, but the pain in his chest tautened his jaw and the cords in his neck.

"You're to see and talk to no one. No disturbances, no work, no giving orders. Rest. Are you listening? Captain, are you going to get those pillows today?"

"Right away, Doctor." Venable strode out the door.

"Colonel, stay awake. You're to stay in bed, understood?"

"How long?" Schreiber stiffened so Shaw had to fight back a smirk.

"Follow orders, do as you're told, grin and suffer, and you could be on your feet in two weeks. Or eight."

"Jesus, Mary and Joseph—"

"Relax, be thankful you're not being measured for a pine box. Not yet."

Shaw folded his stethoscope and placed it in his bag, then pulled out a hot water bottle and slapped it across Schreiber's knee.

"Food. Soup only today and tomorrow. Hot as you can

stand it. Water if you want it. No coffee, no tea, no solid food. Understood?"

Just then Captain Venable came back with the pillows.

"What kept you?" Shaw grumbled. "Prop him up. Gently. Then take this and fill it with hot water. Are you his orderly?"

"I'm second in command," responded Captain Venable, bristling slightly.

"Where's his orderly?"

"Gone back to barracks. Inspection."

"Second in command, are you? Well, now you're number one. Hot water. Hot as you can get."

Venable left a second time after setting the pillows under the colonel, raising him to a sitting position.

"He'll take over," Schreiber murmured when Marcus had left.

"Somebody better, you're not fit to stroke a cat, much less run this pesthole."

Artemus Shaw paused and eyed his patient with softened features, uncharacteristically lapsing into warmth and human concern. "What are you doing here, anyway? Can't you get a decent post? Heat and bugs, scorpions, sand, dust, Apaches. Why in blazes I ever left LaCrosse, Wisconsin, I'll never know. Why'd you come here? Don't answer, you're not supposed to talk. Besides, I'll bet they ordered you. Is the captain a good man?"

Schreiber nodded.

"Then the fort's in good hands, so you needn't worry. What's taking him so long? Does he have to go to Phoenix for hot water? And what is he looking so gloomy about?"

Schreiber beckoned him close and told him in brief about the massacre. Just as he finished, the outside door opened and Venable reappeared. Shaw took the bottle from him, tested it with the back of his hand, wrapped a towel around it, and set it against the colonel's chest. Then he looked up at Venable.

"I'll be back in the morning. Late. I've got a baby coming and a tricky case of blood poisoning to see to. Keep an eye on him. If you spot anything that looks like it's going wrong, come running. But please, no false alarms in the middle of the night, okay?"

"Right," said Venable. "You could use two more hands."

"On another doctor, you bet."

Shaw lingered outside. He set down his bag, filled and lit his pipe, drew enjoyably, and surveyed his surroundings. Lowell was typical of Western posts. It had no outer wall; its only stockade was an interior one, built to protect the post trader's goods from light-fingered soldiers. Officers occupied the row of small private houses across the parade ground, where each man had two to four rooms, depending upon the size of his family. The enlisted men were crammed into barracks to the left and right, where rows of bunks stood head-in to the walls. The barracks were small, poorly built, poorly ventilated, freezing in winter, and blistering hot today. In damp weather the dirt floors sprouted mushrooms and toadstools. Candles provided flickering light and a round iron stove offered a small circle of warmth on winter nights. Senior enlisted men had the best places, near windows in summer, near the stove in the winter.

Privies were outside; there were two bathhouses, both built at Shaw's insistence. Although War Department orders stipulated that each man bathe at least once a week, no provision for bathhouses had been made when the fort was built. The two later acquisitions represented Dr. Shaw's personal triumph over the federal bureaucracy and its benign neglect of the poorly clad, poorly fed, poorly trained, poorly armed, poorly paid, poorly treated men.

Army posts in the Southwest were particularly uncomfortable in summer. The men got some relief from the heat by hanging large clay ollas inside and outside to keep their water cool. The water in the jars evaporated quickly in the heat, cooling their surroundings. To protect themselves from the sun the soldiers erected remudas fashioned of saplings covered with leafy branches in front of the barracks.

Even more troublesome than the Apaches were the centipedes, scorpions, tarantulas, and snakes. As Schreiber had once groused to Shaw, "At Lowell everything that grows, pricks; everything that breathes, bites."

The sun glared viciously off the four square metal plates embedded in the ground at the east end of the parade ground, the four holes where prisoners were incarcerated for punishment, to cook and reflect on their crimes and nearly suffocate. In the center of the parade ground stood a flagpole, Old Glory hanging limply, ingloriously, unmoving; fittingly marking, reflected Shaw, the U.S. Army's less than effectual presence in Apache land. He shook his head, thought fleetingly of LaCrosse, Wisconsin, then puffed and boarded his buggy to return to town.

One week and two days had passed since the telegram arrived. At the end of the first week, when Tyson's remains failed to be returned to her, Marion wired the War Department, inquiring as to the reason for the delay. The day after she sent the telegram she stopped by the Army recruiting center on Chestnut Street and talked to the sergeant in charge. He told her what she did not want to hear, but had half-expected. Some bodies of men killed in action were irrecoverable; not enough pieces of them could be found to put together. "Just the head with the face, you know . . ."

A second telegram to the War Department confirmed that such was the case. She began hoping she could at least get back his wedding band. She got nothing.

At Gabriel Cowan's stern insistence she stayed home for the first four days to mourn, but from the first hour the walls of her apartment began to close in, Tyson's eyes in his photograph on the mantel followed her about the place, and her loneliness set her heart aching from morning till night. She took to wandering about the city, visiting the Art Gallery, the Academy of Music, the Academy of Fine Arts, museums and parks, sitting by herself on a bench watching the pigeons and suffering.

She came back to work on a Thursday. She was sitting in Cowan's office when he entered in his bloodied coat, puffing from the stairs, his gray-white hair disheveled, his humor not the best.

"What are you doing here?" he rasped.

"Back to work." Her tone implied that any objection would be a waste of his breath.

"It's only been a week."

"And two days. So what? You need me, I need to *do*

something. I'm fed up with wandering about the City of Brotherly Love. It's a bore."

"You can't come back so soon. Look at you, you look as if you got five minutes' sleep the last two nights together."

"Ten at least." She smiled thinly. "Must we argue? I want to work today, tomorrow, Saturday."

"And then?" he pressed.

"I've made a decision, Gabriel."

She sat at his chair at his desk. She had on a tight-fitting, dark green, full-length skirt and frilly white blouse under a long-sleeved jacket which matched the skirt. She refused to wear black, insisting that every mirror only reminded her of the tragedy, that it was no one else's business, and she would prefer not to advertise her widowhood. In her eyes was a plea for understanding of what she was preparing to say. He'd seen the look before; he knew her penchant for prefacing her words with her eyes.

"I'm . . . leaving."

"Sweet Jerusalem, what now? You going home to Baltimore and hang out your shingle? Don't be a ninny, girl," Artemus scoffed.

"I'm going out west. Arizona."

Artemus did not miss a beat. "Why not Zanzibar? Ultima Thule?"

He was already into verbal flailing in retaliation for the shock she'd given him. But then abruptly and unexpectedly his face softened, his jaw sagged, he pushed his glasses back up to the bridge of his nose, and frowned worriedly.

"You're serious." He bolted the door and took the visitors' chair.

"I want to start over as far from here as I can get," she said. "My cousin Lillian and her husband have been out there nearly six years. I got in touch and she insisted I come out."

"Sweet Jerusalem, is that any reason to go?"

"I've been reading up on Arizona at the Free Library. On Tucson. It was occupied by the U.S. in 1856."

"Skip the history lesson, I'm not interested."

"Will you at least let me tell you my reasons?"

"Whatever they are, they're not good enough. Has

your brain suddenly jumped the tracks?" He studied her seriously. "Marion, I know what you're going through. At the moment your grief is more than you can bear, but what makes you think running off to Arizona will relieve it? It's stuck in your heart, child. It'll be the last thing you pack and the first you unpack when you get there."

"I need a change. In everything."

"So move. Get a place on the other side of town. Those new apartments near the Old Swedes' Church in Southwark are supposed to be excellent. Lovely view of the river. New surroundings, new neighbors. Let me tell you something—"

"*Let* you? Can I stop you?"

"Don't be impertinent, Marion, this is serious. You're not a housewife or a schoolgirl. You're a doctor—a very good one." He held out his hand. It trembled. "Paralysis agitans. My operating days are numbered."

"You're right-handed."

"I'm seventy-five going on ninety," he said.

"Seventy," she countered.

He took her hands in his and peered deep into her eyes. "I need you. Wills needs you. You, lady, are my best man. You'll be taking over for me in a few years, perhaps even year after next. I intend to see that you do, and I still carry some weight around this mausoleum. Chief of Staff Marion Sturges. How does that sound?"

She shook her head. "I'm sorry, Gabriel."

"Of course you are!" he burst petulantly, coupling it with an appropriate hurt look.

"I am. I know it looks like I'm ungrateful—"

"What in hell has gratitude got to do with it? How in God's name do you expect to carry on a practice in such a dismal backwater? Under such conditions? Danger and deprivation, surrounded by murdering scum, rampaging redskins, drunken soldiers. You won't last two weeks."

"We'll see."

"So your mind's made up. Why tell me?" His eyes narrowed maliciously. "Are you looking for my approval?"

"I don't need anybody's approval. I'm telling you I'm going, not asking your permission."

"You know what you're going to have to do? Refight all the battles you've already won to establish yourself. I shouldn't have to remind you that medicine and surgery are a man's domain. You've no business being here, but you are. You worked and sweat and took the slings and arrows from every quarter and made it. Now you want to junk it all and start over."

"Don't you think I haven't considered all that?"

"Not long and hard enough, evidently."

She fished his watch from his pocket. "A quarter to eight. Isn't it time we got started?"

"I started an hour ago."

"I'm sorry I'm late. When I got up I couldn't decide whether to come in or give it one more day. It wasn't till after breakfast—"

"You're a fool, Dr. Sturges."

"Could be. Buck up, I may be back here in two months, less. You'll be able to say I told you so."

She patted his shoulder, he shook off her hand.

"Okay, have it your way, leave. But please go somewhere other than Tucson. There's nothing romantic or adventurous about the wild frontier, no matter what drivel you read in the dime novels. What you're really doing is running away. Fleeing the pressures, responsibilities, the daily battles: Mrs. Grady, Mr. Hamilton. Running from civilization into the bushes."

"I'm a coward." She smiled indulgently.

"I didn't say that."

"But you did. I'm going to prove you wrong, Gabriel. I'm going and nothing can stop me. And when I don't show up on your doorstep two months from now, you'll have to admit to yourself you were wrong. Let's go to work."

That night at dinner Marion's resolve began to weaken. Though Cowan did not persist in belittling her decision, her own second thoughts tested her determination. They shared a table at Locker's Restaurant on eighth and Vine, lingering over coffee.

"I'll miss you, Marion," he said gravely.

"I'll miss you."

"Have you set a date to leave?" he asked casually.

"This coming Monday. I wrote and told Lillian."

Cowan's eyes gleamed. "Are you going so soon because you're afraid you might change your mind?"

"No," she replied quickly.

"I wish you'd given us a little more notice. Sweet Jerusalem, who'll I get to replace you?"

"Dr. Hawkins is dying to replace me."

"A lightweight." Hawkins was dismissed with a flip of Cowan's hand.

"He's very good," Marion persisted.

"He hasn't got your eye or your hand." He leaned closer and assumed a solemn expression. "Or your heart or your stomach."

"You know he deserves a chance." Marion stared directly into Cowan's eyes, and for a moment she envisioned him standing on the platform, waving as her train pulled away. His shoulders sagged in surrender, a solitary figure fading with every click of the wheels, disappearing from her life forever.

Heavy silence blanketed the table. Gabriel stared into space. Marion added sugar to her coffee to keep her hands busy.

"That's the sixth spoonful," he said.

"Is it? I'm not paying attention." She stared into her cup. "I don't want it anyway."

He had the look of a defeated champion; shock mingled with disbelief. "Want to go?" he asked.

"Do you?"

"In a bit. The waiter's not staring; it's too late for somebody else to want the table. It must be almost eleven."

Another awkward lull replaced conversation, but this one did not hang like an anvil. This was unpressured, as comfortable as could be expected under the circumstances. He seemed to be signaling his acceptance of her decision.

"You must do what you think is best, of course," he murmured. "I shouldn't be second-guessing you. It's times like these a friend should be understanding. Still, it will take some getting used to."

She covered his hand with hers and squeezed it. "And I'll have to start getting used to being alone."

"Not having me around to blister you, eh? Who'll take care of you out there?"

"Me."

"You'll be a babe in dangerous woods," he warned.

"But this babe can climb trees."

Gabriel sighed resignedly. "In some wildly deranged

way, I suppose it makes sense. I don't know anybody else who'd make such a leap, but you—you can handle it. I've probably known since the first time we met."

"My interview?" she asked, a smile pulling at the corner of her mouth.

Gabriel rolled his eyes. "You showed up at the worst possible time."

"You set the time," she countered.

"I'd come straight from losing a young man to peritonitis. His appendix burst before I could even open him up. In his prime and good-bye. I was in a rotten mood when I sat down opposite you."

"I remember your expression," she said and shuddered. "I thought you were going to pick up a chair and hit me. Then you opened Pandora's box."

"Had to see how strong your stomach was, didn't I? What better test than a human leg sodden with carbolic acid, shrunken and yellow. You turned pale as a sheet." He laughed and pointed. "You nearly passed out."

"I did not," she scoffed. "I'd seen dozens like it."

"Nothing as lovely as that one. I handed you a scalpel and held my breath, because I was afraid you'd cut yourself." He snickered.

"Why did you do it?"

"The leg?"

"No," she laughed, "hire a woman."

"Why not? What's unusual about a woman doctor? Do you have horns under that absurd hat?"

"You're in a tiny minority, Gabriel," she said, shaking her head. "You were perhaps the third man between Geneva Medical College and Bellevue who didn't snicker when I said I was determined to be a doctor. Do you know the snide remarks, the sarcasm, the infantile practical jokes I put up with all through school? The skeleton dressed in a wedding gown paraded through Geneva by my fellow students. The nasty little notes in my books or on the blackboard before class. I was made to feel like a black man insinuating himself into an all-white environment. I was barred from attending lectures on reproduction, asked to leave the room when a female breast was dissected, denied access to information on diseases affecting sexual organs—"

He dismissed her with a wave. "Ancient history. All that matters is that you made the grade."

"When you walked into the interview with your devilish box under your arm and that look on your face, I was just waiting for you to call me Doctress. Tell me the truth, why did you accept me?"

"I have a good eye for talent," he replied. "I only hope Tucson has the sense to appreciate what it's getting. I doubt it will."

Having abandoned his initial frontal assault in favor of compliments liberally interspersed with regrets, he cleverly maneuvered the discussion back to poking holes in the fabric of her resolve—which badly needed stiffening at the moment.

He was smiling. Did he think he was making headway?

4

The train tracks stopped at Garden City in western Kansas, about sixty-five miles from the Colorado border and roughly seven hundred fifty miles from Tucson. Civilization stopped with the tracks, Marion reflected. Welcome to wilderness America. She could complete her journey by stage coach in a series of runs that, according to the conductor, "shouldn't take more than a week."

"I hope you're packing a gun, little girl," he said.

"I'm not."

He mumbled something about fools rushing in as he swayed down the aisle.

The ride across the nation's belt had been scenic until Kansas, but the seats were granite, the food was stale, and her berth in the sleeping car was only slightly wider than an ironing board—and less comfortable.

But compared to a stage coach, travel by train was like floating on a cloud. She was given insight of what to expect by a drygoods drummer, who was to be a fellow passenger as far as Trinidad, Colorado. His name was Hoopes and he looked like Humpty-Dumpty. He was a permanently pleasant gentleman, almost fawningly solicitous of her well-being. He was also an indefatigable bore.

They sat with the other waiting passengers in the little

46

building housing the Garden City offices of the Ben Holladay Overland Mail Express Company.

"Best seat inside is the one next to the driver. You ride with your back to the horses, which might make you squeamish, a little like being seasick, you follow me? But you'll be riding so far you'll get used to that. And in that seat you'll get more rest with fewer bumps and jars than any other. If some slyboots offers to swap seats, pretends his seat is more comfortable, pay him no mind.

"Now, if the road turns really rough or if there's a quagmire or a bridge is out and the driver orders the passengers to get out and walk a bit, it'll only be 'cause it's necessary, you follow me? It doesn't happen that often. If the team panics and runs away, it's best to sit still and take your chances; if you jump out, nine times out of ten you'll bust a leg or maybe your neck. Follow me?

"Now, I have to warn you, the food at the home stations isn't near as good as at train stations—"

"*Good*, did you say?" She finally found an appropriate spot to cut into his endless monologue.

"Oh, I know, it does take getting used to. Stage companies do provide the best they can get. Here's some other things to keep in mind," he continued without a breath. "You must never keep the stage waiting. Musn't smoke a strong pipe inside, especially with the shades drawn, especially early in the morning when some folks' stomachs aren't fully awake yet. Don't ever spit to the leeward. If you drink, don't be afraid to pass it around. I always pack my own; ranch whiskey can kill a bull."

She fled into her thoughts, forcing his voice to fade, closing and locking the door to her mind against it and stopping time, reversing it, chopping away the weeks and months. Tyson, my beloved, my own. Never again would she feel his arms; it was like losing her own. What did she need with arms without him to cling to?

Her mind reeled as a rush of memories washed over her. She remembered their first kiss, his lips pressed gently and hesitantly against hers. The slight touch sparked her desire, and she closed her eyes, her brain whirling with the world, making her giddy, setting her heart thundering.

She surrendered herself so eagerly that she would have been ashamed had her mind not been blinded by passion. Their hands shook as they awkwardly shed their clothes.

The room was so dark they could barely see one another, though they stood close enough to feel the heat of anticipation between them. He reached across the velvety blackness and caressed her, his fingers gliding slowly down her shoulder. She shivered and arched her back as a cry of joy caught in her throat.

Flesh to flesh they met, and through it all his mouth was pressed to hers. His kiss was no longer tentative; his tongue glided over hers, and she pressed her hands against his head, wishing he would never stop. The desire gathered and rose like an ocean wave, cresting, curling, breaking with a deafening roar. It ebbed and slipped back, recaptured by the sea of emotions from which it sprang.

In her heart he would never die.

"Try not to lop over on your neighbor if you doze off. Don't ask how far to the next station till you get there. Don't discuss politics or religion or point out places along the way where horrible murders have taken place. Don't lollygag too long at the pewter wash basin at the station. Don't grease your hair before starting out; it'll catch dust and it'll stick. If you've got a silk handkerchief, tie it around your neck to keep out the dust. A little glycerine is good in case of chapped hands; I always carry some. You'll enjoy the scenery. Cross your fingers we don't get held up or stopped by Indians. All the way to Tucson, did you say?"

"Tucson," she barely mumbled.

"My, my, by the time you get there you'll be a seasoned traveler like me."

She gathered that stage coach travel—like a diet—took willpower, endurance, and, above all, getting used to. Seven hundred fifty miles . . .

The westbound stage departed at seven-thirty in the morning. It pulled up in front promptly at seven. The team of six glossy brown Kentucky trotters looked fresh from the stableboy's brush. A stock tender kept a watchful eye on them as they stomped impatiently and swished their tails, and he helped the conductor with the loading. Leather pouches crammed fat with mail went into the front boot, below the driver's seat. On top of the mail in the boot went an iron strongbox, containing valuables. Lumpy canvas bags of newspapers, magazines and other printed matter, and express packages were stowed in a second, larger boot behind the carriage, with the overflow placed inside. Passenger baggage, limited to twenty-five pounds per traveler, with an additional dollar charge for every pound over, also went into the rear boot as well as into the rack on top of the carriage.

Fortified by a hefty breakfast, the nine passengers emerged from the office into the cool morning air for a look at the rig. Marion's ticket through to Tucson had cost $292. She got a glimpse of the interior of the coach, not quite eight feet long and about five feet wide. The upholstery was leather, with polished wood paneling and brass fittings. Leather curtains at the windows served in lieu of glass.

"Leather," explained Mr. Hoopes, loudly enough for everyone to hear, "doesn't shatter and it absorbs the dust, stops the wind, rain, even snow."

Standing close to Marion, he lowered his voice.

"I'll hold the door for you. Get in first, grab the seat right behind the driver there in the corner, you follow me? You'll bless me by sundown."

"You're very kind, Mr. Hoopes."

The last of the mail and baggage was stowed. The driver, a tall, swarthy man sucking on a crooked cheroot, came out of the office and climbed onto his box. The express messenger joined him, his double-barreled shotgun in its boot alongside his right leg.

"All aboard!" shouted the driver.

The passengers climbed into the tiny coach. The stock tender tugged on the cinches, drawing the harness snug, the driver cracked his whip, and off bowled the coach. Hoopes had settled in beside Marion, doffing his curly brim derby and setting it on his lap, the inner brim sneaking under his capacious belly.

"We'll be averaging about eight miles an hour. And stopping every hour and a half or so at a swing station. We change teams at the swing stations. Home stations, where you can eat and walk out kinks, are forty or fifty miles apart, you follow me?"

"Will there be beds at the home stations?"

The only other female passenger, a frail-looking spinster, leaned forward, cocking an ear for Hoopes's answer.

"Bunks, only not for passengers. For the drivers, conductors, shotgun messengers changing shifts. Drivers change at every home station. Don't worry, by day after tomorrow you'll be used to sleeping sitting bolt upright. It's a knack. Everybody learns it, you follow me?"

With every seat occupied and the overflow baggage placed between parapets of knees, the coach was ridiculously cramped. Each passenger was limited to about fifteen inches of seat space. The unlucky three on the center bench had to clutch leather loops suspended from the ceiling. Marion sighed from deep in her soul. Nearly one mile down, a hundred thousand to go.

Gabriel Cowan had asked, "Why Tucson?" She had not had much of an answer for him then, she certainly did not have a better one for herself now. She hardly knew her cousin Lillian, hadn't even seen her since they were children. But it had struck her that the farther away she relocated, the greater need for her services, and the greater the challenge. The inevitable shortages and deprivations, didn't worry her, nor did the dangers that went with the territory. The only flaw in her logic was that countless rural areas east of the Mississippi, right in Pennsylvania, as a matter of fact, desperately needed doctors.

Why indeed Tucson? Why not some place within the circle of civilization that curved outward from the eastern seaboard? Arizona threatened to be a spiny and superheated corner of paradise, though it was attractive in some ways, such as its perpetual sunshine. She was leaving behind the bitterly cold winters. She despised and dreaded sleety weather, slippery pavements, the biting wind.

There was another good reason to test a new environment. Outside of Gabriel, she had no real friends in Philadelphia. It wasn't that she was incapable of making friends, but that she could not—or never tried to—make the time.

It would have been different if Tyson had come home from the war and they had settled and started a family. They would have met other couples and had a whole circle of friends. Had there been even one or two while he was away, losing him and the dismal days and nights of mourning that followed might have been easier to bear. Only Gabriel had truly been there for her, even when he displayed his kindness by trying to convince her she was too spoiled to survive in an uncivilized town.

She didn't consider herself pampered, and rarely indulged herself, apart from an occasional expensive dinner or an overpriced but desirable article of clothing. Still, except for her college years in upstate New York, she had never lived outside a city. Baltimore, New York City, and Philadelphia offered so many luxuries, so many little things one came to take for granted.

She'd never drawn water from a well, never worked a pump. Of course, water wouldn't be any problem out there; Gabriel insisted there was none. She smiled to herself. And sobered, wondering if when she became settled she would still miss him as much as now. Curiously, she did not miss the hospital. The patients' faces were continually changing; she had never become close to anyone except Gabriel. She would not miss her apartment, but she worried that she would long for the clamor and pace of the city. She tried to keep a positive attitude, but the conflicting emotions boiled inside her. Getting away from the East for the first time in her life was healthy; she would be getting out of a rut. And she'd have to make all sorts of adjustments. Gabriel was right about one thing: she'd have to gain the acceptance of the community. If Tucson needed her skills as much as most frontier towns she had heard about, it might be easier than in the East.

They rumbled across the Arkansas River; dust rose in a cloud from the bridge and poured through the window beside her. She rolled down the leather curtain to block the dust's intrusion; others seated near windows also lowered their curtains. Within two minutes the interior became stifling. The curtains could not be partially raised. They hung from two leather straps that buttoned on the inside; unbutton them and down they rolled. She lifted hers an inch. In rolled the dust. The others eyed her critically. She dropped the curtain, got out a hanky, and patted her neck and face.

Dr. Artemus Shaw waited impatiently in front of the Buckley House for the Butterfield Overland stage from Silver City, New Mexico. The stage was already nearly an hour late. Hands joined behind his back, he paced up and down muttering to himself, every now and then casting an eye north, looking for a telltale pillar of dust. It was mercilessly hot. He was sweating; patients waited.

It was not yet nine and already he had dug two bullets out of two antagonists in a bar fight, set a broken leg, and delivered a daughter for schoolmaster and saloon-keeper Augustus Brichta's wife, Bertha, the couple's ninth child.

The Buckley House, as the station was called, was on the corner of Calle del Correo—Post Office Street—and Pennington Street, a hundred yards west of Main Street near the gate of the old presidio. Calle del Correo was the business center of Tucson, and the biweekly arrival of the westbound and eastbound stages added a bit of life to the sleepy town.

Tucson was a "timetable" station, meaning that drivers made every effort to arrive on schedule. The westbound mail generally came in at 8:00 A.M. sharp on Tuesdays and Fridays. The drivers were conscientious about the schedule. The stage today, reasoned Shaw, must have run into something serious to cause such a delay. Indians? A holdup? He lit his pipe and began worrying in earnest.

He recalled his own arrival in Tucson eight years earlier—or was it eight hundred? He'd gotten in exhausted, thrown himself on the floor of the first place he could get into, a saloon, and slept for twelve hours. Awakened by a pistol shot, he'd gone in search of something to eat.

Welcome to Tucson.

Postmaster Mark Aldrich's office stood opposite the Buckley House and the station in front of it. Aldrich came out in vest, gartered shirt-sleeves, and cap; he waved to Shaw and came over.

"Late today," he said affably.

"Fifty-eight minutes so far."

"Expecting somebody?"

"New doctor."

"Do tell. Where from?"

"Philadelphia."

"Some jaunt. Know him?"

"Friend of a friend of a friend. Wouldn't know him from Hippocrates himself, but I plan to greet him with open arms. Anybody shows up here with one good arm and a stethoscope who can cut my workload by half is welcome as the flowers in May."

Aldrich looked northward, shading his eyes from the sun. A window flew open on the second floor of the building next door to the Buckley House. A booze-ravaged, toothless, and pasty-cheeked old man stuck his head out.

"Hey, Doc, you gonna dawdle there all day? I got a busted wrist needs setting. Little tad waiting's got the stomach miseries, lady with a baby—"

"Keep your shirt on, Mordecai, be up in a jiffy."

"Here she comes," announced Aldrich.

"Stage coming!" bawled Shaw to his impatient patient. "Sit back down and keep that wrist still like I told you."

The man vanished. Doctor and postmaster watched the stage come dusting in. It looked as if it had been driven through a sea of mud which had caked, dried, and cracked over every inch of the carriage.

"No arrows," observed Shaw. "No fresh bullet holes."

"Tucson, Tucson!" barked the driver. "All passengers for Tucson get off here and get your luggage down. Mr. Albright'll help you ladies. Take care you collect all your goods; Butterfield ain't responsible for stuff left behind. Take all that's yours and only yours, and thank you for riding Butterfield."

Three passengers disembarked: two women and a man. Shaw recognized the man and one of the women as Charley Meyer, the local druggist and his wife Elvira, who had gone off to Denver to visit Charley's ailing brother and his family.

"Where the devil is my new boy?" Shaw grumbled.

"Missed the stage, so it looks," said Aldrich, smirking at his disappointment.

The other woman passenger was young and pretty with tight blond curls peering out from under her pert bonnet. She quickly collected her luggage and stood on the wooden sidewalk surveying the town. From her expression she appeared a trifle shocked by what she saw: a line of one- and two-story adobe buildings. A few wooden structures. Three saloons, one drug store, and various other business establishments. Not a single church, at least in view. The wide streets looked deserted. It was not only empty, but the driest town she had ever seen. She got the impression that it hadn't rained in fifty years and that the yellow dust was the residue of adobe houses that had crumbled and vanished, only to be replaced by new ones which would be prey to the same fate in time. But there were flowers everywhere: in huge clay pots, window boxes, hanging upside down in bunches from cross timbers and logs to dry. Dominating the scene, tyrannizing it, was the fiercest sun she had ever seen.

In the otherwise empty military plaza stood a whipping post; behind it an American flag drooped from its pole. Something stirred at the base of the post. She recoiled and gasped as a rattlesnake slithered out of the shadow into the bright sunlight. Aldrich went back across the street.

Shaw had approached Marion. His hand went to his hat, he left it on.

"Morning, miss."

"Good morning." She continued to look about. "My cousin was expecting me. Would you happen to know Mrs. Gibson, Lillian Gibson?"

"Sure." He spat and looked past her down the street. "Carved a ganglion out of her husband Joe's backside just last week. Expecting you, did you say? That's funny. Gibsons left town day before yesterday. Heading for California. Joe got bit by the gold bug." He laughed. "Infected." He sobered at the effect his words had on her. "She didn't tell you they were going?"

"She probably did, only I left before the letter came. Wonderful."

"Hey, you're not the only one disappointed, I've been standing here baking for an hour, waiting for a Dr. Sturges. Name familiar? Would you by chance know if he missed the stage in Silver City or before there? Oh, I'm Dr. Shaw, Artemus Shaw."

"I'm Dr. Sturges."

"He's coming all the way from Philadelphia, according to an old friend of mine there. This Sturges's first name is Marion."

"Dr. Marion Sturges, that's me."

He flinched like he'd been pinched. His jaw sagged. His face proceeded to run a gamut of reactions: shock, amusement, skepticism, shock again, distress. He ended up looking appalled.

"You must mean nurse. Or are you a midwife?"

He looked more than crestfallen; devastated was closer to it, she decided. She screwed up her gumption.

"Doctor."

"Rubbish."

"Rub-bish?" She laced the two syllables with a thick slab of disdain which sailed over his head.

"Rot. Women aren't doctors, no such critter. It's against nature. Women clean, sew, bear children. Women, young lady, do not doctor."

The last came out with the finality of a judge pronouncing a sentence of death.

"Is that so? Well, this woman 'cooks' surgical instruments, 'stitches' wounds, and *delivers* babies."

"The devil, you say . . ." He gasped. "What's the world coming to? What's happening back East, has everybody gone loony?"

"Sorry to disappoint you, Doctor."

"If this isn't a hatful. I took it for granted, I mean . . . Marion *is* a man's name, you know."

"It's a woman's, too."

He grunted, narrowed his eyes, and brought his face up too close to hers.

"You really a doctor?"

"I can show you my diplomas."

"Don't bother, anybody can buy a fake diploma. You better get out of the sun. Come up to the office, you look a mess. What was the holdup, Indians?"

"No, a wheel fell off the other side of Wilcox. It wasn't damaged, but the end of the axle got bent. It took them awhile to straighten it."

"I guess Marion can be a woman's name, too. Artemus can't, thank God. Don't look at the office, I don't have time to clean up."

"You must work day and night, Doctor."

"And Sundays . . . Doctor. I expect I should get used to calling you that, while you're around."

"Call me Marion."

He said nothing, telling her with no uncertainty that he'd prefer not to. Three steps up the stairs her knees gave way. He dropped her bags and grabbed her from behind.

"Mordecai. Mordecai!"

The man with the fractured wrist appeared at the top of the stairs.

"Give me your good arm, help me get her upstairs.

She's exhausted. Come all the way from the railhead in Garden City, Kansas, by stage. We'll get her up and into my bed. She'll sleep a week."

"Then turn around and go right back, right?" Mordecai leered.

"Bet on it. You should have seen her face when she looked around the town. But what do you expect? She's a woman. Grab hold."

◄5►

I'm gonna get drunker than six hoot owls!"

"Swimming in a barrel of hooch, right, Zack?"

"Drink till it splits me in two, then get myself twice as drunk. Hee, hee, hee."

Shortly after the sun vanished, taking with it its spectacular hues, eleven soldiers came into town, their pay folded in their pockets, their spirits down following the burial of their buddies massacred on the mountain. Thirsts up, they proceeded to make the rounds of the saloons. By nine-thirty the lot had become outrageously intoxicated. With inebriation came arrogance and hostility. They picked fights with each other and with locals. They smashed furniture and store windows. They accosted women and behaved rudely. One broke a bartender's jaw, another shot holes in seven ollas hanging at the front of Solomon Warner's store. Two others carried off the gate to the garden of a residence on Old Ott Street. Yet another shot and killed a dog, whose capital crime was his yapping insistence on joining the carousers. Word drifted back to the fort. Captain Venable dispatched a dozen men to round up the rowdies.

Marion slept through it all. She did not awaken until

57

eight the following morning. When she checked her watch she could not believe the position of the hands. She had slept twenty-three hours. It was impossible; the body's waste disposal system could not be restrained for such a length of time. She held her watch to her ear. It ticked. Sunlight streamed through the window. The tiny room barely had space for the narrow bed and twelve-inch square night stand alongside it. A rickety chest of drawers that looked as if it had been deliberately distressed by a dozen knife wielders stood against the wall at the foot of the bed. The room was definitely a man's: no frilly, feminine touches, not even curtains framing the single window. And it smelled like a man's room: stale tobacco, a hint of stale liquor, the easily identifiable pungent scent of Genuine Yankee Shaving soap, Gabriel Cowan's favorite.

She sat on the edge of the bed fully clothed, and stretched and yelped. Every bone was broken, every joint on fire. Hoopes had not exaggerated in describing the ordeal a long stage coach ride put the human body through. It was, she decided, a mode of transportation devised by the devil, a torture rack on wheels. Never again would she set foot in such a vehicle.

She could hear movement on the other side of the door: muffled voices. A child began to cry. She got to her feet with pain and difficulty and washed up at the basin stand. In the slightly clouded mirror her face looked wretchedly pale and drawn. She yawned, fussed with her clothing and with her hair, getting her comb and brush out of one of her bags.

A knock sounded.

"Yes?" she answered, clearing her throat before speaking for the first time in nearly a day.

"Are you decent in there . . . Doctor?"

"Yes, come in."

Shaw entered with the same tight scowl of disapproval he had worn when she passed out on the stairs.

"I'm sorry I monopolized your room for so long. I must have been dead tired," said Marion.

"That's all right. Oh, I'm forgetting the most important thing. You're in luck, there's a stage coming through heading east in three hours. Give you time to get something to eat."

"I'm not leaving."

"What about Lillian and Joe?" he asked.

"I'm not going to follow them," she said. "I've had my fill of traveling for now." He seemed more than disappointed. He looked slightly aghast. "Why the rush to get rid of me? You said you were overworked."

"I was expecting a doctor."

"I *am* a doctor, remember?" The syllables fell from her lips like stones. "You need a hand, I can help."

He eyed her for a long moment. She could almost see the wheels grinding in his brain: rusty, they were, well used, overworked. He oozed disapproval. It hung in the air between them.

"Well," he muttered at last, "if you have to stay there's a rooming house up the street. Inez Alou's. It's no palace. This isn't Philadelphia."

"Is it clean?"

"Cleaner than this, but the street's noisy. All the streets are at night. And it's not cheap. She gets five bucks a week. Hungry?"

"Starved," Marion answered immediately.

"You slept almost twice around the clock."

"I didn't sleep, I died," she joked, but Artemus took no notice.

"Best eats, if you value your digestive tract, are across the street down two doors. Mama Elena's. Best coffee in town. When you finish breakfast, come back. I can probably find something for you to do."

"That'd be nice."

"I hope you can handle a mop and the sight of blood." He cocked his head and narrowed his eyes. "You any good?"

"We'll find out, won't we?" It was as much a dare as a question.

"Good, bad, or lousy, there's plenty to do. Lazy won't cut it around here." He turned to go.

"Just one thing."

Shaw stiffened expectantly as if afraid she was bringing up money. She suppressed a laugh.

"What?" he asked guardedly.

"You say rubbish, I say rubbish. One of us will have to come up with something else."

"It's yours, I've worn it out. Oh, don't order the sausages at Mama's. In this heat they tend to rot at the speed of light. I really don't need another patient . . . Doctor."

In the full glare of the morning sun Captain Venable dressed down the eleven offenders in a line before him. Their heads were down, expressions sheepish, brains ringing with hangovers, uniforms disheveled, stomachs churning, regrets over their actions piling up in their fuzzy minds. They stood with wrists manacled behind their backs. Lieutenant Sutherland and two other junior officers standing behind the captain glared at the hapless group. Venable could barely bridle his temper. He had passed the second night in a row wrestling with his nagging conscience, sleeping fitfully. His head and eyes ached separately, his tongue was furry, and all he wanted in the world at the moment was his bed and four hours of decent, unbroken sleep. But the matter at hand commanded his immediate attention.

"Colonel Schreiber, I myself, and the other officers drum it into you daily, but it obviously goes straight through and out. Maybe you don't have brains enough to even slow it down. Attention, goddamn you! We are here for the express purpose of protecting the residents of Tucson and their property and that of the ranchers in the surrounding area. Not destroy it, pick fights with them, insult their wives and daughters, and carry on like lunatics running riot in the asylum.

"This has happened before, I'm sure it'll happen again. Your drunkenness is no excuse. I'm going to discipline you and harshly. Because, unfortunately for you, you've caught me at the worst possible time in the worst possible frame of mind. I see no need to enlighten you further on that point."

He began pacing up and down the line, bending, looking up into each face as he passed it.

"You should be very proud: you're a disgrace to your uniform. A disgrace to your country. My only regret is that I can't collar you with dishonorable discharges and kick you back to where you've come from. McAllister."

The third man in line stepped forward, saluted, and set his sickened eyes on the captain. "Sir?"

"You, I'm reliably informed, are the prize of the lot. You shot and killed a dog."

"Was a accident, sir. It tried to bite me—" the soldier started.

"Shut your mouth. You also attacked the bartender at Brichta's when he cut you off after you demanded he sell you a second bottle. Knocked him cold. Broke his jaw. Stand up straight, you son of a bitch!"

"Yes, sir."

Venable stepped forward and bowed his neck, bringing his nose to within a half inch of the offender's. "Thirty hours in the hole."

"Thir—"

"Shut your mouth, soldier. Don't tempt me to double it. Soldier, some soldier. Thirty hours to begin immediately."

"I'll cook to death!" The man trembled under Venable's glare.

"Lieutenant Sutherland, hole number one."

"Yes, sir."

McAllister was marched off. The first iron plate was lifted and he descended into the hole, complaining loudly. The ringing of the plate dropped back into place caused the other carousers to wince. Sutherland returned and reassumed his stance behind the captain. Three others were incarcerated in the remaining three holes: sentenced to twenty hours in four-hour shifts. Venable cleared his throat.

"Four more of you will go down when their first four hours are up. The rest will go down in their turns. No food, no water, no contact. Grit your teeth and take it like men. And use the time to think about your drunken, disgusting ways.

"And this is just for starters. Additional punishment is richly deserved. As of today you are restricted to the post for six months."

A chorus of sighs swept the line.

"Take over, Lieutenant Sutherland. Lock them in the stockade until their turns."

Doctors Shaw and Sturges were busy with office patients until mid-afternoon. Marion assisted him in removing the nail from the thumb of a patient whose hand had been partially crushed by a stone. It promised a painful procedure.

"Wash me a knife and that forceps in the basin there. Nice and clean now," he ordered.

"But—"

"What's the matter? They've got to be washed, got to get rid of the germs . . . Doctor."

Why must he always emphasize the first syllable, degrading the word, ridiculing it applied to her? And the instruments should be boiled, not merely washed. Washing even in antiseptic soap was worthless. But instead of pointing this out in the presence of the patient, she did as he told her.

She handed him the knife. "What about chloroform?"

"No need. We'll have this bugger out so fast he won't feel a thing. Caleb, relax, you're tight as a floor pin."

Using the knife, he began debriding the afflicted area. The patient yelped when the knife point found live tissue.

"Whoops," said Shaw.

"I'll do that," offered Marion.

"I can manage nicely, thank you," he all but snapped back. "Just have the forceps ready."

When he'd finished removing the dead flesh, having set the area bleeding instead of staunching it, he tightened his fist around it and reached for the forceps.

"Just about done now, Caleb. Relax, it'll be all over before you know it. Grit your teeth. Good boy. Here we go."

To Marion's horror he took hold of the mashed nail with the forceps and jerked it free as he would a sliver. The patient let out a scream that rattled the windows in their frames.

"Goddamn, Doc!"

"All done. Bandage it for him, missy."

"Doctor," Marion corrected.

"You'll find gauze in the cabinet."

"Do you have any antiseptic salve? Montfort's, Barfield's?"

"Never use it. Wrap it clean, and don't get the bandage wet, Caleb. Keep it dry day and night. If the pain doesn't go away in two or three days, come back, we'll have another look. That'll be one dollar. Who's next?"

Welcome to medical science as practiced in Tucson,

reflected Marion wearily as the white-faced Caleb headed for the door. She took a break. Having paid the first week's rent on her accommodations, she took the time to inspect them more closely. She found them more than satisfactory. Before unpacking, she took a bath. She lolled in the tub for nearly an hour. Shaw showed up just as she was done dressing.

"I figured you'd take a bath, but I was beginning to think you'd drowned."

"What's up, more patients?"

"Only two. I took care of them."

I'll bet you did, she thought.

"I'm on my way out to the fort," he went on. "The CO's down with pneumonia. Come along and keep me company."

"What type pneumonia?"

"Lobar." He ticked the signs and symptoms off on his fingers.

"Could be bronchio, they're very similar."

He was eyeing her strangely. Up to now she had not really second-guessed him on a single patient, much as she'd been tempted to, but it was bound to arise sooner or later. At that, she wasn't exactly second-guessing him now; how could she without having seen the patient yet?

But their newly formed alliance was giving every indication of becoming increasingly uneasy. How could she expect it to be otherwise? She had come from a modern, big-city hospital, as good or better than any in the East. He had come from a small town in Wisconsin. Whether he'd ever even interned in a hospital he hadn't said, only that he'd left there eight years before.

Eight years practicing in Tucson by himself. Not another doctor for a hundred miles in any direction, so he'd told her. His isolation had understandably caused him to fall into some curious bad habits. Apart from being behind the times, he was negligent, careless and sloppy—dirty bordering on filthy. He was also staunchly loyal to outmoded and discredited techniques and practices, many of which were brutal and dangerous. Most of the time he sterilized nothing, not even bothering to wash his instruments. He was always in a hurry; he preferred to wipe off on the seat of his pants any instrument used on one patient before using it on the next. He did not bother to wash his hands between patients; he seemed wholly ignorant of the efficacy of carbolic acid or any other disinfectant. He talked about the threat of germs, but didn't seem to worry about them enough to take even basic precautions. He did use chloroform, but on only two of more than a dozen patients whose injuries warranted it. He admitted he'd never used ether. He had set a badly broken forearm around two-thirty, giving the unfortunate patient a slug of whiskey against the pain.

And with a bottle of chloroform standing within easy reach!

She had looked on, saying nothing, wishing for a stick for herself to bite down on to hold her tongue.

His office was a shambles. The wastebasket overflowed with bloodied gauze, used cotton swabs and balls, filthy bandages; the basket looked as if it was never emptied. He proudly referred to it as his "slop pail." Had it been her office she would have closed for the day and cleaned: scrubbed the floor with ammonia, washed the windows and walls, boiled every instrument and instituted dozens of other improvements, every one an ally in the never ending battle against infection.

He was not a bad doctor, certainly not one of that disgraceful legion that should never have attended medical school, much less hang out their shingles and subject helpless patients to their botchery and butchery.

Not bad, but his methods, techniques, lack of technique, and slovenliness would have given Gabriel Cowan absolute fits. Watching him she got a curious feeling: when he was done with one patient and had moved on to the next, his mind was still on the previous one. He was always one behind.

But he did have one outstanding character trait that warmed her to him: he clearly liked being a doctor. He got satisfaction out of easing discomfort, helping people, curing what ailed them. He liked people. It was evident from the way he talked to them. He was particularly gentle with women and children, and, like Gabriel Cowan, did his best to allay their fears.

He was no charlatan, which he could have gotten away with being this far from the centers of population. He knew his stuff. He could look at a patient, listen to their woes, listen to their chest with his ausculator, as he humorously called his stethoscope after the name given the technique for listening to sounds inside the chest by the inventor, Rene Laennec, and diagnose the ailment correctly most of the time. He did not, however, seem interested in taking the time to pursue each individual diagnosis fully, which would have enabled him to ascertain the condition precisely before treating it.

He did not take the time because he did not have it to take. Colonel Schreiber's pneumonia was to prove a case in point. Artemus as good as admitted that he'd read the symptoms in seconds and prescribed treatment accordingly. He filled her in on the colonel's condition as they rode his buggy out to the fort.

"He's holding his own," he added. "Responding to treatment. In a way."

"In a way?" Marion was immediately curious.

"I can't figure it. Ordinarily, he's healthy as Hercules; he just doesn't seem to improve from day to day. Not a smidgen. Doesn't get any worse, but doesn't get any better. I'm anxious to see what you think."

You may sincerely be, she thought discouragedly, but if she diagnosed the colonel's condition as something else, something he'd never even considered . . .

"Does he smoke?"

"Like a locomotive. Cigars. Not while he's been ill, of course. Oh, I put my foot down on that right off the bat."

It could be consumption, could be lung cancer. She would examine him as thoroughly as was possible, given the fact that he wasn't hospitalized—and out here had no hope of it. She could then offer her diagnosis. The fun would begin. Artemus would question it; his ego would thrust itself in the way of his common sense. They would argue until their throats cracked and come to no acceptable resolution. It could end up alienating them. She sighed and vowed to tread the path of the next hour with great care.

They had come to within a few hundred yards of the fort.

"You're very quiet," he said. "What are you thinking about, Philadelphia?"

"What makes you say that?"

"I don't know, first thing that popped into my head."

"You think I'm homesick already?" She tried not to sound defensive, but there was an edge to her voice.

"I don't think anything, I haven't the faintest idea. Are you usually prey to homesickness?"

"No."

"Can I ask you something much too personal?" She smiled and nodded. "Whatever possessed you . . . No, no, let me start again. Why Tucson? And please don't say, 'why not?' "

"A number of reasons. Put them all together and they make up one good one. Don't they always?"

"If you think so," he said with a nod.

She told him about her marriage, Tyson's death, the sudden urge to drop everything and find an environment as different from Philadelphia as "Zululand is from the North Pole." Close the book on the past, lock it in perpetuity, start over.

"Every place out here is more or less beginning, can only grow," she said.

"Or be abandoned," he countered. "Plenty are."

"You don't think Tucson will be; you wouldn't have stayed this long if you did."

"Maybe I'm too lazy to pick up and git."

"Lazy you're not. You've got the vigor of a twenty-year-old."

"Thank you, kind lady. But you're right, I do like this pesthole.

"Tucson is Tucson today and will be forever because of one thing: the Santa Cruz. They call it a river, I call it an overgrown creek. It comes flowing up out of Mexico through a wide valley lined with trees and brush, spreading out into swampy areas, reaching here, and a little ways out of town it goes underground. So when anybody tells you there's no water here, they're ignorant. It's here, you just have to dig for it. The Indians did a thousand years back. They irrigated their corn and other crops. The Santa Cruz was their lifeline before it even got the name. In its own small way it's done for Tucson what the Nile and the Danube do for Egypt and Central Europe.

"The soil, water, and climate are all good, although I grant you, the summers do get hot."

"Broiling."

"This is cool compared to what it can get. This can't be more than ninety or so. Stand in the center of the military plaza on a real scorcher at high noon. Stand sixty seconds without a hat on and don't pass out and I'll give you two bucks cash." He glanced to either side. "This valley is a gem: there's game, wood, pasture and people, the originals, what the Spanish called Papagos. Bean people. They were here long before the Apaches. Here we are," he said as Fort Lowell came into view. "Not exactly Fort McHenry, is it? I'll pick up on my indoctrination lecture on the way back. Unless it bores you to screaming."

"You're not boring me."

"Listen, my sense of smell isn't what it used to be. When we walk into the sick room, take a whiff. See if you smell cigar smoke."

They rolled dustily up to the colonel's office. Shaw got down and came around to offer a hand to help her down. Olan, the colonel's striker, stood at the open door. Marion started around the rear of the buggy in front of Shaw. She stopped abruptly, squealed, and danced awkwardly clear. A fat, gleaming scorpion marched across her path, tail raised, stinger menacing.

"Somebody's house pet," said Shaw airily. "Don't worry, they'll get used to you. We've got all the best-loved species: scorpions, tarantulas, centipedes. The rattlers outnumber the people fifty to one. Just don't panic when you see little green lizards on the walls of your bedroom; it's not the d.t.'s. They're real but harmless."

Marion hurried up the steps. She looked to her right and blinked; the sun bounced off the four iron plates under which the hell-raisers cowered in darkness, sweating furiously and gasping for air. Olan snapped his heels together and saluted smartly. He looked to Marion sufficiently unlike the sergeant and the other soldiers at the Chestnut Street recruiting office in Philadelphia to be from a wholly different army. He wore no cap, his tousled, tangled hair flew in all directions. No web belt; his tunic was unbuttoned and badly rumpled and two sizes too large for him; the sleeve seams hung well below his narrow shoulders; one button was absent, another hung by a thread as he hastily buttoned up. His trousers were as disheveled as his tunic, his shoes wretchedly scuffed. A portrait of slovenliness, she thought.

This was not the Army, she told herself, but a ragtag collection of tatterdemalions drummed out of the military, assembled and whisked off to here to thirst, guard cacti, and play at soldier while the real fighters waged the War of Secession, and bled and died with honor.

"Orderly!" barked a voice from inside.

He stiffened and turned slowly.

"Go back to your barracks and clean up. Wash yourself, change into full dress if you've nothing else presentable. You look like a tramp. And polish those shoes. And next time I catch you without head cover I'll put you on report. Move!"

Olan mumbled a "yes sir, Captain" and sprinted off past the two arrivals. Captain Venable, standing in the doorway, introduced himself cordially, his mild voice at odds with the anger in his face. He couldn't possibly be *that* angry at his poor orderly, reflected Marion as they shook hands. Venable looked deeply troubled, as if he'd just been told he'd lost his best friend. He ushered them into the office and to the colonel who, at first sight of Marion, pulled the sheet up to his chin modestly. Shaw introduced them. The captain, meanwhile, grinned away his irritation. He was strikingly handsome when he smiled, she thought, his light blue eyes beautiful pools that sent a tiny flutter through her heart; his hair surmounting his handsomeness was so light as to be almost white. He appeared to feel the need to say something.

"Welcome to Tucson, Doctor," he said, studying her lovely features and faultless complexion with equal intensity. It had not been long exposed to the brutal Arizona sun by the look of it, for it was unlined, as fresh as a flower in the morning.

"Thank you," she responded.

A beauty, he thought. He tried, but could not take his eyes off her. A doctor? A woman doctor? What was the matter with him? Was he become so jaded, so deeply rutted in life that the unusual surprised him? Why not a woman doctor?

Shaw excused them both and brought her in to the colonel. Like the captain, Schreiber seemed neither surprised nor disappointed when Shaw introduced her as

"Doctor." Shaw was a trifle disappointed that neither of them was. She got out her stethoscope and listened to Schreiber's chest, then to his back, sitting him upright and tapping it in a number of areas. She examined the dried, blood-flecked sputum in his handkerchief. It smelled foul.

"How exactly do you feel?"

"Sick to my stomach, exhausted, no appetite, chest aches constantly."

She ran a hand down the undersheet. It was dry.

"Any sweating?"

"Only at night."

She took his temperature orally, continuing to question him; he moved his head to answer. She read the thermometer.

"Slight fever," she said to Shaw. "There's blood in your sputum, Colonel; do you just spit up or cough it up?"

"Cough."

She had taken the chair beside the bed. Shaw stood behind her. In spite of himself, he seemed to be warming toward her. That was her plan: win him over with sweetness, patience, and professionalism. Stubborn he might be, but not stupid.

She straightened and looked about the room. Both windows were open two inches from the top and bottom to admit fresh air. Outside, the sun was glaring, but it was dark in the room. The air had a sickly smell to it, but no odor of tobacco.

"First we have to get you out of here. No fresh air, no sunlight. You need both. Let me ask you, have you at any time during your life suffered a severe and or prolonged illness affecting your lungs?"

He told her about his near-drowning and the chronic trouble with his lungs that followed. Shaw looked unpleasantly surprised.

"You might have told me about that," he muttered.

"I haven't had any real trouble for years." Schreiber looked apologetic.

"Your doctor's the best judge of what real trouble is." Shaw was obviously miffed.

"You say you were thirteen," Marion went on. "Do you recall what the doctor who treated you said? Did he identify your condition specifically?"

"Bad cold, pneumonia. To this day whenever I catch a cold my lungs hurt."

"How long were you laid up?" she asked.

"Off and on about a year. I'd get to feeling real good, get out of bed, go to school. In a few days I'd catch the sniffles and end up back in bed. Didn't matter what time of year, what sort of weather."

"He called it pneumonia," said Marion.

"Called it pee-neumonia." Schreiber tried to chuckle. And quit it; it hurt.

"No specific type?"

"What type is there?"

"I don't think you have pneumonia this time, Colonel."

"See here—" began Shaw curtly.

She had spoken too soon, kicking the props from under his diagnosis. Schreiber was staring at him questioningly.

"On the other hand, all your symptoms do point to it," she added hastily. "So it does make sense to treat it as such."

"Lobar pneumonia," said Shaw flatly as if to remind her.

"Right. Now, as I said, the two things you need most are sunshine and fresh air. I'd like you to sit in a chair outside in the sun at least two hours every morning and two more every afternoon. Even if it clouds over, you'll still be getting fresh air. And your being outside will give the orderly a chance to air this room out. I also think your bed linens should be changed every day, including your pillowcase. I want you to do something else: when you've used up a handkerchief, regardless of how it may look to you, I want you to keep it just as it is so Dr. Shaw and I can examine it under the microscope."

"I don't have any microscope," said Shaw.

"I do. A Zeiss, excellent instrument." She turned her attention back to Schreiber. "Every night before you go to sleep see that the last handkerchief you use is put in an envelope and marked with the time and date. What we see under the lens day by day will give us a good insight into the progress of the infection. I'll be back tomorrow."

"Thank you, Doctor, and again, welcome to Tucson. Believe me, you really are most welcome."

She had gotten up; her glance drifted to Shaw to see his reaction to the comment. He showed none.

Once outside, Shaw filled his pipe and lit it.

"Why did you tell him you don't think it's pneumonia?" he asked, his tone inviting argument.

"Because I don't."

"Rubbish!"

"My word, remember? I say it's consumption."

"I say rubbish." Arteemus was being as difficult as Marion had imagined.

"Very well, we'll wait and see what shows up on the slide."

She looked off at the four iron plates. Three men were standing around the one farthest from her. It was opened. Two of the men reached down and lifted a man out of the hole. She gasped. "What on earth!"

They had laid the man flat. A fourth man came up with a bucket. Water was tossed on the prostrate man. He lifted one shoulder slightly, then let it sink back down.

"Good God!"

She started toward them. Shaw grabbed her arm and held her.

"Don't. He's a prisoner."

"What did he do? Rape? Murder? What is this place, Devil's Island? I've never seen anything so barbaric in my life!"

The two who had removed the man from the hole began to put him back.

"Look!" she burst.

"It's none of our business, Doctor, just ignore it. He'll survive."

"In this heat? Under that metal plate? It's a wonder his blood isn't boiling in his veins!"

Still clutching her arm, Shaw helped her up onto the buggy seat. He took his place and they started toward town. She looked back and saw the plate being dropped. The three men then moved on the next hole, lifting its plate, peering down into it.

"There's another one! There's probably one in each hole."

"Probably."

"How can you be so blasé?" she demanded.

"It's none of my business. I don't pretend to know why

the Army does anything, including how and why they punish their own.

"It's barbarous! I can't believe Colonel Schreiber sanctions such cruelty. Savages, that's what they are!"

"Look ahead there if it's savages you want."

She turned toward the entrance. A dusty troop was coming in. The last rider in line was leading three prisoners afoot: Indians joined by a single rope around their necks, their hands tied behind their backs. They shuffled along heads down. Shaw reined up as they passed. Apaches. One looked ancient. All looked utterly defeated. The two younger ones were bleeding about the face and neck. One's hand appeared broken; it was badly swollen.

"Good Lord," murmured Marion.

"What is it now? You don't like the way they handle prisoners? What would you have them do, bring them in on a flower float preceded by a marching band? They're lucky they're still breathing. If their situations were reversed, the soldiers wouldn't be. Apaches don't take prisoners."

He slapped the horse's rump with the reins and they rolled off again.

Lieutenant Sutherland halted the troop and dismounted. Captain Venable had come out of the office. They exchanged salutes. Sutherland turned for a look at Shaw's buggy's dust.

"Who's the lady?"

"Shaw's new assistant," Marcus replied.

"Pretty. When did she get here?"

"I don't know."

"Where's she from?"

"What happened? Run it down," Marcus said, snapping Sutherland back to attention.

"We roamed around all morning between here and the Tortolitas. Nothing but jackrabbits and snakes. We stopped around noon. Somebody spotted dust. We chased, caught up with about fifteen of them. Armed and all worked up for it. We went at it like wolves and coyotes for about an hour."

"Any casualties?"

"Not us, not a one. Beat the bejesus out of them. Must

have killed at least half. Collared these three. The older one's Shosagat, overage in grade would-be warrior. Sharp as cactus, though, we questioned him. Would you believe he admitted the three of them were with the bunch that surrounded you on the mountainside the other night?"

"You think he's telling the truth?"

"It was a confession, Marcus; why would he lie about something like that? Why incriminate himself?"

"Whether he was or not, he's automatically incriminated. He's an Apache, isn't he?"

"He knows what happened, described it to a tee. He claims a subchief by the name of Namasa has taken over in place of Gold Eyes. Says Gold Eyes has bad bones: arms and legs. Can't ride, can hardly walk."

"Arthritis."

Sutherland shrugged.

"Anyway, Namasa's now in charge."

"Mmmmm. Take the two bloodied ones over to Barracks B and see that they get washed off and patched up. Take the old man to the stockade. Untie him, lock him up. Tell the corporal of the guard to keep a sharp eye on him. I want him to stew and wonder for a while before I talk to him. Namasa's bad medicine, vicious. Hates the color blue."

"Show me one who doesn't," said Sutherland. "You got a plan, Marcus?"

"A sketchy one. I have to talk it over with the colonel. If the old man can tell us where Namasa's holed up and it turns out right, if he's willing to play square with us, we can do him a favor in return."

"Not hang him. What about the other two?"

"Clean 'em up. We'll hang 'em at sundown. In front of him."

"The taller one's his son." Sutherland turned toward the three.

"Good," muttered Venable. "Seeing his son hang should make a vivid impression on him."

He saluted Sutherland away and looked across the parade ground. The second group of prisoners was being brought over to the holes. He glanced at his watch. Four hours on the dot. He watched them approach and reflected on his words to Sutherland. *Hang 'em at sundown.* No one could accuse him of wasting time. He told himself there was nothing personal in his decision, but of course there was: an act of pure vengeance. The Apaches took no prisoners except women and children, leaving the army little choice but to duplicate their example. In every respect it was as much of a war as the fighting more than two thousand miles away.

He watched the plates being lifted one by one. The prisoner in the second hole looked dead. Venable wiped the sweat from his brow and went back inside.

Picking on Indians seems to be a popular pastime. Military and civilian," said Marion.

"You don't see me picking on them, do you?" Shaw muttered.

They were bumping and jiggling toward town. Marion saw two white men and an Indian. The white men were drunk; both wore guns. The Indian stood between them. He wore no headband, making him most likely a Papago. He was ancient, bent, slender as a rake handle, and ragged-looking. The two white men were taunting him. One drew his gun and fired at his feet. He jumped. The other man laughed raucously and also fired. The air rang with gunfire and smoke rose as they emptied their weapons and their victim jumped and kicked to avoid being hit. When they'd emptied their guns he broke away, hobbling painfully around the corner and out of sight.

She glanced at Shaw's profile. He was trying hard to make her think nothing had happened.

"Even the peaceful ones are treated like stray dogs," she went on. "They settled here, lived peaceably. The white man comes, pushes them off their land, cheats them, abuses them."

"I must be psychic. I was just thinking it was about time we got around to Tucson's Indian problem."

"Does Tucson have an 'Indian problem'?"

Shaw smiled sardonically. "Not unless you plan to create one."

"Not me. I'm not here to stir up racial trouble. All I'm saying is—"

"I hear what you're saying. Can I offer you a gem of advice?"

"Mind my own business."

She glanced back. The two men stood in their gunsmoke reloading and laughing uproariously.

"Close," said Shaw. "I was thinking 'keep your mouth shut.' You're from the East, those three Apaches back at the fort are probably the first Indians you've seen."

She cut in, "You're saying I should pack up my liberal views, take them to the post office, and ship them back to Philadelphia."

"Exactly."

They had begun to warm up to each other at the fort; she consciously felt she was getting to like him. He *was* a character: colorful, unique, conceited, and such a raging chauvinist, he was more entertaining than annoying. His blindness or indifference to the Indians' plight, on the other hand, wasn't amusing. How dare he presume to lecture her!

"Forget it, Doctor," she said between clenched teeth.

He flicked the reins to speed up the horse and modulated his tone. Here it comes, she thought, if he can't browbeat me into agreeing with his way of thinking, he'll sweet-talk me.

"Believe me," he said, "I'm telling you for your own good."

"I'm sure you think you are. I'm sure the Army has good reason to march prisoners back like pack mules with ropes around their necks."

"Nooses. If those three are not hanged by now, they will be shortly."

She gasped. "For what? Fighting for their rights? Their lives? Bows and arrows against guns? They looked like they got the worst of it to me."

"This time. Not the other night up in the mountains. It may surprise you, but there's a war going on here. The government wants to put the Apaches on reservations, where they'll be decently fed, decently treated, taken care of. But the Apaches don't like the idea."

"Do you blame them?"

"It's better than being hunted down, shot, and hanged."

She could hardly argue that, but he did seem to want to paint the picture in black and white only.

"What about the Papagos?"

"They're peaceful as cows. Their reservation is down near Tubac on the Santa Cruz. They don't make trouble, don't get any. And they like the Apaches about as much as the Army does. Trouble is the only thing the Apaches know how to make, not blankets, not baskets. I'm not judging them, even though it sounds like it. It's just the way it is. A lot of settlers have suffered at the hands of the Apaches. Women raped, men scalped, horses and cattle stolen, barns and houses burned. They didn't bring their prejudice with them from back East. It was a gift of the Apaches when they got here. You start mouthing off about the plight of the poor Indian, the innocent victim of the white man's depredations; you start reciting *Hiawatha* and you'll put yourself on the wrong side of a lot of people."

He had pulled up. He sat turned toward her. He kept his tone free of passion, refusing to raise his voice. "Believe it or not," he went on, "most people around here are tolerant. Oh, there are a few bigots, there are anywhere, and bullies like those back there, but the Anglos and the Mexicans get along and both hate the Apaches. Not the Papagos. *They* hate the Apaches, too. They do their best to earn people's hatred. The longer you're here, the clearer you'll see it."

He started the horse. The dust rising from under its hooves drifted back onto them.

"Perhaps, but I doubt if it'll change my thinking. And relax, I didn't bring any soapbox with me."

"Good. That'll be a load off everybody's mind."

She ignored the sarcasm. So much of it came from him, she could wear herself out lashing back.

"But I'm entitled to my views and I'll keep them, thank you. I don't care if people snub me because of them. That's their problem. There isn't a town in the South that doesn't have a handful of individuals who've spent their lifetimes protesting the injustice of slavery, people with the courage to tell the majority where they stand."

"Sorry I brought it up," he said dryly.

"No you're not." She paused. "On second thought, I'm sorry. I know you're only thinking of me, but all my life I've spoken my mind."

"And the devil take the hindmost."

"If my opinion's asked for in polite conversation, I'll give it."

"I guarantee it won't be asked for. Anybody who knows you're from the City of Brotherly Love will be able to guess what you think and won't be interested. I guarantee you something else: six months from now you'll feel different."

"Not a chance."

"We'll see."

"Are you saying *you* actually hate the Apaches?"

"I don't know about hate, but I don't plan to invite any to dinner."

He stopped a second time in front of her house. He offered a hand, helping her down.

"Come in for a cup of tea."

"Another time, perhaps. I should stop by the office, see if anybody's waiting. I'll see you in the morning . . . Marion."

"See you, Artemus."

She stood at the gate watching him off. The sun was lowering, the stifling heat abating. She did not want to go in just yet. She had finished unpacking and straightening up the place; she decided to go for a walk.

She headed back through town. She passed saloons already filled with noise, confusion, and laughter. The cafes and restaurants were already serving. Stores and shops had not yet closed for the day. She passed a rooming house; it sounded like a free-for-all going on upstairs. She was about to pass the open door of yet another saloon when a man came tumbling out, sprawling in the gutter. Hands on hips, the bartender glared down at him, seething. He caught himself and nodded deferentially as she passed. Blood glistened at the side of the bounced patron's mouth. She hurried on. Now and then she heard gunshots in other parts of town, but whoever was doing the shooting remained out of sight.

It took her less than ten minutes to reach the edge of town and the beginning of the north road, which curved away across the valley floor littered with cholla, tall saguaro, and organ pipe cactus. The cemetery was just outside town. Faded bouquets of flowers lay at the bases of a number of wooden and stone markers: mostly four-o'clocks, their lavender blossoms closed. At dusk they would unfold their delicate petals and, like the evening primrose, stand vigil through the night. Spiny hedgehog cacti abounded throughout the cemetery, their purplish-rose petals surrounding a ring of orange stamens with a cluster of tiny dark pods at their center.

She read marker after marker, curious to see what the local residents were dying from. There were more than a hundred. The inscriptions provided mute testimony to Tucson's way of life. She counted only four people who had died of natural causes. She recalled Artemus telling her that in the previous September alone, Tucson had had eight murders, three times that number of serious accidents, four hangings, two attempted suicides, and a fatal duel. Roughly half of his patients were victims of stabbings, shootings, and assorted misfortunes in the saloons and bawdy houses. For eight years he had made it his business to pack a stomach pump in his bag to disgorge the poisons swallowed by soiled doves who were continually trying to "end it all."

He told Marion not to expect to be paid in legal tender for her services with any frequency. His own bills were often paid in cord wood, canned goods, calves, cabbages, and chickens. And on many occasions he got nothing at all.

Marion had already seen garbage scattered about the streets attracting hordes of flies; they infested outside toilets and were a continuing menace. Spitting was condoned indoors and out. Dead animals lay unburied until coyotes or buzzards reduced them to bones. Water supplies came from seepage ditches, stagnant pools, uncovered cisterns, and the perpetually muddy river.

Illness struck with a vengeance. Only the hardiness of the people kept it from being worse.

Growing bored with her cemetery reading, she headed for home. In her brief absence, business appeared to have increased markedly in the saloons and bawdy houses she passed. She opened the gate and lingered in the garden inside the walls. A solitary century plant lorded over the flowers, its giant stalk rising well above the top of the wall; it looked to be on the verge of blooming. It would bloom, then die. Such a waste of effort in growth, all of it put into one brief, lovely display. Varieties of cacti predominated: pink-blossomed chin cactus, heurnia with its bell-shaped flowers, pale brownish outside and velvety black within; old lady cactus with its fat clusters of flat-topped, ball-shaped stems, the entire plant covered with silky white spines and crimson blossoms; the brilliant rose-magenta sour fig; golden-yellow prickly pear; red, yellow, orange, purple, and white portulaca, and hanging from the walls vermilion-flowered rat's tail.

Inez Alou, her landlady, came out smiling, fluffing her apron. Her hands and pudgy forearms were white with flour. She smiled graciously, revealing two shining gold teeth.

"It's so lovely," murmured Marion. "So peaceful here; the walls shut out the town."

"Not zee shooting. Eet goes on all day, all night."

"It doesn't seem to bother you."

"You get used to eet. After twenty years."

"You've been here twenty years?"

"*Si*. I come weeth my father and mother up from Pitiquito in Mehico. Een Sonora."

"I don't know Mexico, I know nothing about this part of the country."

"My father come to work building houses. He died last year; my mother died two years after we come here."

Someone emptied a pistol a couple blocks away. The walls muffled but did not erase the sound. Marion flinched; Inez yawned.

"You must like Tucson to stay so long."

"Eet ees home. I have my house, my boarders, my cooking, my garden. I have everything."

"You do indeed."

"I must get back to my oven. Ees your place satisfactory?"

"Lovely. I'm all settled."

"Eef you need anything, knock on my door."

She went back inside. Marion sat on a stone bench to relax, take the no longer insufferably hot sun on her cheeks, and drink in the beauty of her surroundings. A cactus wren arrived, settling on an old lady cactus, probing its spines for insects.

She sighed. Working with Artemus was going to be a

trial after Wills and Gabriel Cowan. She nevertheless decided that they would have to get to know each other better before she began to suggest changes. He would have to come to appreciate her in order to appreciate any innovations she might propose, any improvements. But he was satisfied with the old and suspicious of the new, making him about as tough as a steel nut to crack.

She should get a letter off to Gabriel, catalog the trip, leaving out the more harrowing aspects he had warned her about, play down Tucson's primitiveness, the heat, scarcity of fresh water, and the four hundred-odd other drawbacks and shortcomings. Tell him about Dr. Artemus Shaw, who confused consumption with lobar pneumonia. Tell him she was settled, busy, content, and eagerly looking forward to life in Ultima Thule, as he had called it.

Was she?

"You are."

At the sound of her voice the cactus wren looked up, and she swore it shook its head. Birds don't shake their heads; they bob, but not shake. The wren didn't give her the chance to confirm what she thought she saw. It flew off.

She thought about Captain Marcus Venable. He was in command now. It was he who had ordered his men down into the holes, and he would give the order to hang the prisoners. Looks were deceiving; he didn't seem at all vicious, but behind the handsome smile was evidently the mind and convictions of a sadist. A bastard with boots.

She would tangle with him sooner or later. She sensed it.

"Inflammatory adhesions to the parietal pleura,"
he muttered, eyeing the picture, an artist's
rendering of a consumption-ravaged lung. It depicted
various stages of the disease: enlarged lymph glands,
tubercles without tissue breakdown, and lastly cavity
formation.

"See how the lung tissue is denser in the afflicted
area?" said Marion.

Again Shaw squinted at the picture. And raised the
white flag slowly.

"You were right," he grumbled. "It is consumption."

His first admission that he was wrong! In anything!
Raise *all* the flags! She glowed.

They had worked side by side without any even mild
disagreements through the week, only because Marion
held her peace, difficult as it was at times. Dr. Shaw
continued to wade through his patients like a drunk wad-
ing through a wine cellar. Around two o'clock Saturday
afternoon, between patients—a rare phenomenon and
one Marion was quick to take advantage of—she got out
her microscope, placed a prepared slide in the clips, and
invited Dr. Shaw to have a look. While he peered through
the lens at Colonel Schreiber's sputum, she opened the
medical book to a page marked by a slip of paper.

He looked mildly stunned. "I was wrong, what do you know about that?"

"Shouldn't we make some changes in his treatment?" she asked.

"You're the doctor."

She could not believe it! Had he actually said that?

He smirked. "How about serum from a turtle? A drug with gold in it? Horseback riding? All acceptable medical procedures west of the Pecos."

"How about surgery?"

"I wouldn't dare. You either."

"I'd rather not, but it is coming to that." She restored the slide to the file box and closed the lid on Colonel Schreiber. "It is," she went on. "In Europe they're collapsing and putting out of commission the affected lung, when only one's affected, as in this case. They pump gas into the pleural cavity, collapsing the lung on that side. Open, repair the damage, close, reinflate the lung."

"Sounds like a last resort. Isn't there some other way?"

"Not surgically. Rest, fresh air, plenty of good food, encouragement. What he should do is step down, retire, go into a sanatorium where he can get attention around the clock."

Shaw's expression in reaction said that she was asking for the moon.

"He'd never. He's very image-conscious; to quit would be a sign of weakness."

"He may end up quitting whether he likes it or not. How old is he?"

"Around sixty."

"Time to retire."

"Old war-horses don't retire, Marion, they prefer to die heroically with their boots on. I don't see how we can manage that. He does seem to be improving the past three days, don't you think?"

The door flew wide. A skinny, freckled boy came bursting in out of breath.

"Doc, come quick . . . quick. Wall collapsed on a fella over to Pennington Street. He's passed out cold from the pain. Come on, come on!"

"Right there, Bernard. Watch the shop, Doctor, I'll probably be bringing him back on a plank."

"I can go."

"Watch the shop."

He snapped his bag shut, slammed on his hat, and followed the boy. She glanced about. The office examining room looked as if a tornado had passed through. She put away the book and microscope, and went downstairs and out back for a bucket of water. She added half a bottle of ammonia to it, and, after picking up the near misses and setting the slop pail outside the door to be emptied later, set about scrubbing the floor on hands and knees. She dusted, washed the windows, straightened, and was coming back from emptying the trash and washing out the slop pail when Captain Venable appeared in the doorway. His right hand was wrapped in a piece of deerskin.

"Dr. Shaw out?"

"Seeing to an accident victim. Let's have a look."

He was not at all reluctant to show her; he unwrapped his hand. It was badly swollen, black and blue. It had to be painful, but no discomfort showed in his eyes or face. This was a man, she thought, a sadist perhaps, but a soldier to the core.

"It's broken," he muttered self-consciously.

"I can see. How did it happen?"

"Accident."

"You were angry, you smashed your office wall."

"How'd you . . .? Can you set it? I'm in a bit of a hurry."

He seemed more embarrassed than rushed, Marion noted, as his cheeks reddened beneath his tan.

"Sit and set your hand on the table on the edge. Open it slowly." She felt it. "The first joints of the forefinger and second finger are fractured. It should be put in a plaster cast."

"For how long?"

He turned, looking at her apprehensively with one eye. He didn't want the answer she had to give him. He was as handsome in profile as full face, the sort who turns every woman's head walking down the street.

"Two to three weeks. Your hand should be immobilized completely."

"I won't be able to use it at all?"

"Not even to hold a pencil."

"Impossible." He was suddenly exasperated, even knowing, as he must, it would have to be that way. Bones, like broken hearts, took their time knitting. "I can't do anything with my left," he added lamely.

"You could have smashed the wall. I'm sorry, not funny. It's up to you: I can splint and bandage it or put it in a cast."

"What would you do if it were yours?"

"A cast. It'll force you to keep it still, especially when you're sleeping. You'll only be able to move your thumb. In two to three weeks we'll take it off and have a look. Probably replace it with a flexible wrapping."

"How long before it heals completely?"

"Four to six weeks. It looks lovely. When did this happen?"

He smiled for the first time. Marion was unprepared for the kindness that spread across his striking face, and her heart fluttered. "Couple days ago," he went on.

"Why didn't you come in right away?"

"Busy." Suddenly she wanted to bawl him out. "I thought the pain would ease up, it'd start to heal. I figured I could put up with it. I was wrong."

"Didn't it occur to you it should be set? Did you think it'd set itself perfectly?"

"How would I know? I've never broken anything before. I told you I was busy."

"That excuses it, of course. How's the colonel?"

"He seems better. He's sitting up most of the time. Even when he's in his room."

"He should be in bed when he's in his room. I'd better go back with you and check on him."

She bathed his hand in a weak solution of carbolic acid. He watched her prepare the plaster. They fell into friendly conversation; it got around to Tyson and the War Department's failure to return his remains. She still refused to believe that they were "irrecoverable." She was pleased to notice that Venable did not defend the government's laxity.

She asked about the fort and army life, the special requirements in such a hostile environment. This brought them around to the Apaches. She had heard that he had lost a number of men in a recent skirmish in the mountains, and assumed that his hatred for the enemy must be at its boiling point. It was, however, an assumption that begged confirmation.

"Did you hang your three Indians?"

It came at him like a blow from behind; it appeared to startle him, then his dark eyes narrowed. He looked, she thought, to be mentally girding his defenses. Why couldn't she mind her own business?

"Yes. But if you mean, did I personally, the answer is no."

"You did give the order."

"You rather we didn't hang them?"

"There's a war on, I know. It just bothers me, pricks my sense of justice or something. I mean if somebody had the patience and willingness to deal with them, as opposed to exterminating them, life would be so much easier for everybody around here."

"Believe me, Doctor, I wish we could work it that way."

"Do you really?"

"I do."

She believed him. She could believe everything he said. She recognized sincerity when she saw it.

"Has anybody tried to deal honorably with them?"

"Years ago. Now we're too busy fighting. Let me ask you something: you just finished saying the rebels killed your husband at Petersburg. Don't you hate them for it?"

"I don't even think about them. I didn't when I got the telegram, and not since."

It was his turn to believe her, she thought. His eyes said he did. Lord, but they were beautiful: somber, brooding pools. Did he have any idea how attractive he was? He had to. Did he care? Probably not.

Again he smiled, and nodded.

"Because it's a war and casualties, fatalities occur. No individual's at fault, no group; the war's to blame. It's the same here."

She had finished mixing the plaster. She began to apply it.

"I disagree. The South is fighting to keep slavery, against the tariff, against other policies. The whites out here want to get rid of the Apaches, drive them off their land, wipe them out."

"*Their* land?"

"Isn't it?"

"Whose land is really anybody's? They took it from the Papagos. Before the Papagos, the Anasazis; before the Anasazis, who knows? Maybe emigrants from Philadelphia. So who 'owns' the land, who has the God-given right to occupy it, is impossible to figure. It is with any land, right?"

"I simply don't understand why everybody who isn't an Apache wants them slaughtered. If you can live with the Papagos, why not the Apaches?"

"It's been tried, it has. Only any agreement depends on the two sides' willingness to observe it. They prefer not to."

"Because the whites cheat them, go back on their word, lie, break treaties."

It was foolish of her to draw him into a discussion of it; certainly neither had anything resembling a solution to the problem. He didn't agree with her in any respect; she didn't expect him to, but he did seem tolerant of her opinion.

She liked that; she liked him. He was logical, and sensitive for someone in his line. She would bet that his men admired and respected him. The colonel must think highly of him to invest him with temporary command. Under the armor of his manliness, inside the aura of the professional fighting man he seemed a trifle wistful, and lonely, and troubled. He was upset losing his men the other night, she was sure. Still, she sensed that something else was bothering him. Being stuck in the last outpost so far from the arena, the combat, the glory?

Footsteps set the stairs creaking. Shaw appeared in the doorway. His face was flushed, his shoulders drooped. He looked defeated and resentful of it.

"It crushed the life out of him. Heart burst from the weight. How'd you bust your hand, soldier boy, fist-fighting with your desk?"

Venable grinned.

"I'm going back to the fort with the captain to check on the colonel," she said. "All done, Captain, baby it now."

"Go ahead," said Shaw. "I'm going inside and get a little drunk. With your permission, Doctor."

"First lock the downstairs door."

"All right, all right, I'll hold off till five o'clock." He glanced Venable's way. "Women . . ."

Captain Venable and his cast sat at the desk out front. He leafed through reports. Marion got Colonel Schreiber back into bed.

"It's too hot out there, you'll be better off resting."

A well-used handkerchief stiff with sputum edged from under the corner of his pillow. She picked it up by one corner and, holding the opposite one, stretched the handkerchief. The dried spittle was yellow, but clear: no sign of blood.

"You're getting better, Colonel. Feel better?"

"Every day. How long do you think?"

"At least another week. Two would be better. You *are* going to have to ease back into your schedule."

Through the window she spied a lone soldier coming at full gallop toward the fort, yellow dust billowing from his horse's hooves. He pounded into the parade ground, circled without slowing, dropped a bundle in front of the office steps, and rode away. He came close enough for her to see that he wasn't a soldier, but an Indian in a blue uniform. His hair, his coloring, and unsaddled horse gave him away. And he wore moccasins in place of boots.

"What's that?" asked Schreiber.

She described the arrival. Through the open inner door she saw Venable rise, move to the outer door, and wrench it wide.

"Give it here, Olan."

He came into the sickroom carrying the small bundle: dried-out and ragged deerskin wrapped and tied with rawhide. By now the dust had settled in the wake of the vanished visitor.

"What the devil . . ." began Schreiber.

The captain had set the bundle at the foot of the bed. He opened it; somewhat tentatively, she thought, watching.

In it were a number of bloodied scalps. Nausea erupted. She turned from the sight. Venable exploded.

"The mangy bastards. Filthy animals! Just got to rub our noses in it."

The colonel scowled. "Wrap it back up, Marcus, get it out of here."

He did so, carrying it out front and throwing it away. Then he came back and stood in the doorway.

"I'm taking twenty men and going out to beat the bushes. They're up in the Tortolitas."

"Or the Catalinas, the Sierrietas, the Santa Ritas, or none of the above."

"The Tortolitas, bet on it. I'm going to get Namasa. I'll bring the spindly legged, cracked-brain son of a bitch back here, peg him down, cover him with honey, and leave him to the ants. Smack in the middle of the parade ground."

"Marcus . . ."

She watched him in awe. He was boiling. He looked like a man struck mad; his eyes were maniacal, his face rapidly reddening. The colonel talked to him, at first in placating tones, then irritably, angrily commanding him.

"Get a grip on yourself, man. Stop this nonsense! Calm down!"

Venable heard not a word. He whipped about and stormed out, slamming the door.

"Idiot! Imbecile!" Schreiber hurled his hands in the air.

He coughed sharply. She hurried to his side. He had risen from his pillow. She pushed him gently back down. She got him a clean handkerchief. He covered his mouth and coughed, his head jerking, color rising slightly. When he finally took down the handkerchief she saw the sputum was clear.

"Hotheaded numbskull," he muttered.

"I was afraid he'd snap."

"He's getting close. He needs out of this hellhole." He chuckled weakly. "Who doesn't. But they're getting to him. They're like typhoid, the way they get under a man's skin, into your blood."

She didn't quite know what to say. It was not her place to comment on the captain's outburst beyond what she had said already.

"You're doing fine. Get some sleep. Tomorrow's Sunday, I'll drop by in the afternoon."

"Appreciate it. Thank you for coming. I mean to Tucson."

She left, grateful for deciding to accompany the captain back to the fort. He had been charming, pleasant, smart, and witty when she had talked to him at the office. It had also been clear that he had problems, but she'd had no idea he was a smoldering volcano.

8

C aptain Venable's rage did not cool in the next ten minutes. If anything, it increased. He practically battered Lieutenant Sutherland's door down with his one good fist. It opened slowly to reveal him red-faced and in his long johns. His wife called softly from the bedroom, asking who was making all the noise.

They rode twenty-one strong, each man armed with a carbine, a hundred rounds, and close-quarter knives. Straight for the Tortolitas they sped, climbing all the way up to the caves at the top. The sight of the terrain brought back bitter memories to Venable. The ledge they had crouched under before dispersing and the knoll where the horses had been hobbled were particularly disturbing.

There was no sign of an Apache, but cook fires at the mouths of the two caves, although extinguished, contained warm embers. They followed a tricky, narrow trail down the north face, bringing the meandering Aravaipa Creek into view. The Indians had left tracks leading to the creek. Marcus and his men crossed the nearly dry bed and headed for the Catalinas, dominated by Mount Rice. The farther they ventured the sparser the tracks became. The ground was baked to granitelike hardness by the merciless sun. It was dark by the time they got to the foothills, where they decided to take a break. The sage-brush was unusually plentiful at the base of the mountains, girdling them to a width of a hundred yards. They spotted freshly broken branches.

"It's almost as if they rode through here intentionally, tearing up the vegetation, hoping we'd see it and follow," said Venable to Sutherland riding alongside. "Incidentally, I apologize for the interruption."

"Don't worry about it. Just don't apologize to Hannah when you see her. She'll turn six shades of red. You saying it's another trap?"

"When is it ever otherwise," said Venable wearily.

"Look over there. They headed back out away from the mountains—"

"North. Okay, boys, let's pick it up."

They circled the northern end of the range and headed northeast toward the San Pedro River. The moon flooded the landscape and vanished with predictable regularity. Presently they spotted fires burning through the darkness dead ahead. They drew to within about a mile before Venable signaled a halt.

"I count nine separate fires," said Sutherland. "You think it's them?"

"It's somebody. Just as long as they've got rags on their heads."

"You're out for blood tonight."

It dawned on Venable that neither Sutherland nor any of the others knew about the delivery of the scalps. He gathered them around and told them.

"I want Namasa. When the dance starts, shoot everything that moves. Everything. But leave him for me. For the benefit of those among you who've never had the pleasure of meeting the gentleman, listen closely. He's about five-foot-nothing, weighs about eighty-five, and looks like a puny skeleton with the ugliest face on God's green earth attached, and hair going from gray to white. It may even be all white since the last time I saw him. He's crazy as a bedbug, but like a lot of nuts, he's not stupid. As we speak he could be laying a trap for us. It's too early for them to be bedding down; they're probably finishing their meal. Maybe just sitting around the old campfire swapping tales. We'll find out soon enough."

Venable divided them into four groups, three with five men, the last with six, counting himself.

"Lieutenant, you and your boys will have the most ground to cover. Circle wide to the left, and I mean wide, and come up on their other side. Brennan, you and your men position to the left. Cabell, you and yours to the right. When you get into position, dismount and tether your horses. We'll approach them crawling, creeping, any way you think is safest, but nobody, I mean nobody, moves an inch toward them for twenty minutes. Set your watches. It's now twenty past ten . . . on . . . the nose. We'll start moving in at twenty of. Move out. Bob—"

Sutherland snapped to attention. "Sir?"

"Ride like blue hell."

They split up. Venable and his men waited. Marcus had kept Olan with him, because the boy had practically begged to go on his first dangerous mission. He was trying hard to look soldierly, cinching his belt as tightly as he could to help fill out his scrawny chest. His boots were not shining, but they were clean, and his hair was combed, with a cap perched straight on it.

"We gonna shoot squaws and little kids, too, sir?" he asked.

"What did I say, Olan?"

"Everything that moves 'cepting the old bastard."

"You think you'll recognize Namasa if you see him?"

"Ain't too many folks look like what you said, not even injuns."

"If you kill him, even accidentally, you'll get yourself thirty days behind bars. That goes for all of you."

They waited. One of the other men started to light a stogie butt. Venable grabbed his hand before he could thumbnail the match to life.

"Later."

And waited. Venable checked the time. Twenty-five of.

"Five more minutes."

They crowded around to study his watch.

"Remember, keep low, up and run in short bursts, no more than ten strides at a time, then down, freeze for thirty seconds, then move on. The closer you get the more careful. When I shoot, you shoot. And for chrissakes,

keep it low. Lieutenant Sutherland's on the far side.
When you start, pour it on; we'll throw everything we've
got in the first few minutes, stagger them, cut them to
shreds. All except him."

With thirty seconds to go, the second hand seemed to
reach bottom and stick a bit before beginning its ascent.
It crawled, passing a quarter to, climbing to the hour.

"Move out!" Venable ordered.

It took nearly an hour before they were close enough
to the camp to make out figures seated around the fires.
Faint strains of jabbering and laughter drifted toward
them. They were within twenty-five yards when Venable
signaled a halt. He had fanned his men out three on a
side with about ten yards separating them. Olan was
closest to him on his right. The clouds overhead were not
thick enough to hide the moon for any length of time. It
fairly flew through them; he could never recall seeing it
move so fast, as if evolutionary time had snapped its
leash to rush toward its destruction. Marcus looked over
at Olan. Terror gripped his homely profile. This was his
baptism.

Venable's first battle had been Bull Run—the battle of
the bumblers, with both sides seemingly doing their best
to lose. It had started on the eighteenth of July, a sweltering day on which his company commander had observed that a man could die as easily of thirst as by bullet
or shell. But the twenty-first, a Sunday, was the day
riveted to his memory. The rebels were on the far side of
Bull Run, flanking a tributary. The creek could be forded
at several points, but because of its steep banks and
heavily wooded approaches, cut up by many small tribu-
taries, it presented a formidable obstacle, particularly to
the east of Stone Bridge.

This was exactly where his brigade commander had
elected to cross. It was a most memorable Sabbath: time
for breakfast and prayers before the shooting began at
about five-thirty. It was barely light enough to see when
hell burst from the earth's core to spread over the rolling
green hills of northern Virginia. From the outset both
armies' tactics were clumsy, their attacks abysmally in-
ept, their blundering unparalleled in his experience since
that fatal day. The bucking, roaring cannon, billowing
smoke, the snapping of rifles from both sides so busy it

sounded like three times the number of men were engaged, the screams of the dying close by created a din that all but punctured his eardrums. Few recruits on either side knew anything about combat. He was as green as the grass he lay on. For hours they blazed away at three hundred yards until both sides were bloodied and exhausted, but long-distance sparring does not whip the enemy. Troops who grappled won, and the grappling was yet to come.

In the woods across the creek he had seen a tree toppled by a cannon ball fall on three men, crushing them. Another cannon ball had taken off a man's head not twenty yards away. A platoon of riflemen, foolishly bunched up fording the creek, was cut down to a man by a withering barrage. Bodies clogged the creek, damming it in half a dozen places. Wounded men lay helpless, run over by their own wagons. He himself had taken three bullets, and though none of them was life-threatening, the slug in his shoulder felt like a white-hot skewer plunged the length of his upper arm.

He had seen death that beautiful, bright Sunday in rampant profusion, taking souls like a gale plucks leaves from branches. Five thousand men on both sides. For many it had been their first and final battle.

Armed with an ancient Sharps box-lock breechloader that kicked like a mule, and by day's end had all but kicked loose his shoulder, bruising it black, he had poured lead into the woods. He'd killed at least five of them he could account for.

Marcus glanced at Olan again. Could he shoot straight? Could he shoot at all? It was a trifle late to ask.

Now all of his men were watching him, waiting for him to move. He nodded, waited for the moon to vanish, and crawled forward. Within seconds it came out and brightened the scene, then vanished again. Marcus snaked onward. Partially embedded, jagged stones hacked his ribs; he banged his knee on one, cursing eloquently and silently. He wriggled about ten yards before stopping, then raised on one knee, balanced his carbine on his cast atop it, set the butt hard against his shoulder, and fired. The slug plowed through the forehead of a giant sitting on the far side of the fire facing him.

Lead came singing in from all sides. The Apaches

reacted in total confusion. Their weapons were not at hand, and when they scrambled to their feet to collect them they were cut down before they could take three steps. The squaws shrilled, the children screamed and cried, the men died, leveled like cane under a machete.

The firing became sporadic, then died altogether. Smoke rose lazily, joining in a ragged ring over the scene. The breeze caught it, whipped it, dispersed it. Most of the women and children had scattered without drawing fire. Silence reigned. A solitary Apache sat by a fire surrounded by the dead, deserted by the living. He sat stiffly erect. He began to sing, swaying slightly in time, every bone in his torso and limbs sharply etched under his parchment-thin skin in the fire's glow. He looked two hundred years old to Venable, who had gotten to his feet with the others. He walked toward Namasa. Sutherland and his men came ambling in, looking about, appraising the dead. Eight warriors wore issue blue coats; others wore caps; still others showed boots in place of their knee highs; and the ground was littered with the weapons of the massacred and scalped soldiers. Venable stood before Namasa. The fire obligingly came to life, glowing brightly between them.

"*Oshuksu*," croaked the little man. "*Colo* Namasa."

He stressed his name, stretching the syllables proudly. Then he raised one scrawny arm and turned his claw hand down, pointing one finger at Venable. The other hand brought up a knife, which he plunged into his belly. He smiled broadly, triumphantly, and started to laugh before he keeled over.

"Son of a bitch loses and still wins," muttered Sutherland.

Sergeant Brennan, a burly, mustachioed New Yorker, a fearsome drinker and battlefield butcher, came up beside the two officers. Without a word he bent down, pulled the knife from Namasa's belly, and wiped the blade on the dead man's trousers. He held it up. Etched on the hilt were initials: J.F.T.

"John Francis Tumbelsky," said Venable, taking it from him. "Sergeant—"

"Sir."

"Take four men, retrieve our weapons and uniforms, and follow us back."

"Yes, sir."

Brennan saluted smartly. The fifteen other men, not one suffering so much as a scratch, were ordered to mount up, assemble nearby, and head back. Moments later Venable and Sutherland were on their way, the others following.

The lieutenant shook his head. "I still don't understand why he practically painted a trail for us to follow."

Venable shrugged. "Who knows what he was thinking. He probably never dreamed we'd be out looking. I didn't, until the package came."

A lone rider was coming up fast. Brennan came barreling up, reining sharply, smirking.

"Present for you, sir." He held up a dripping scalp. "His nibs'."

Venable scowled. "Put it back where you got it, Sergeant. The U.S. army doesn't take scalps, remember? We're supposed to be the civilized side in this to-do."

Brennan's massive face assumed a hurt look. He nodded. "Yes, sir."

Civilized, Venable reflected as Brennan sped off, that's rich. And more than a little presumptuous, considering this night's work.

9

Marion's apartment consisted of two large rooms with a small entry hall. It was on the ground floor where she could look out on the garden, which thrived in the heat and seemed to grow more beautiful with each passing day. The ceiling was low, but sunlight had no difficulty finding its way in. The two chairs were tolerably comfortable, and the bed was like a pile of down.

She lay in darkness thinking about the past, pushing it against the present. It was mostly at night when she was alone in bed that thoughts of Tyson drifted back. Not all were unpleasant, but most *were* frustrating. Brief though it had been, their marriage had been a good one. Apart from the love they shared, they had been best friends. It was not something they ever mentioned, but both of them knew it was there.

In spite of the war—almost in retaliation for its intruding into their happiness—they had made plans. The day he left for induction he swore he would be home for good within a year. How, he reasoned, could the South stand up against the industrial might of the North? There were nearly three million Northerners against a mere six hundred thousand rebels. And in the beginning, at least, only seven southern states had seceded. Subsequently only Virginia, Arkansas, Tennessee, and North Carolina had followed their lead. The Confederates didn't stand a chance. How could their leaders not see that? Were they so blinded by their hatred of the federal government they could not anticipate the disasterous consequences of their rashness?

But they turned out to be superb soldiers, excellent marksmen with gifted, intelligent leaders. And they were determined and prepared to fight to the death for independence. So the war dragged on, leaving its trail of butchered humanity, leaving Tyson Sturges. Had he survived Petersburg, they would have settled down. In a year or two she would have been pregnant. They would have a house, a garden. A child.

If he had survived.

She could not fall asleep. She got up, lit the lamp, and moved the night table to the garden window. She got out pen, ink, and stationery.

Dear Gabriel,

I hate to say you told me so, but the stage ride from Garden City, Kansas, was even more rigorous than I could have imagined, but I made it and have settled in. A Dr. Artemus Shaw has been the only physician in southeastern Arizona for the past eight years. We work together. He's a law unto himself and I tread on nettles, but we get along. He does know the area, the people, the politics, and problems like you know comparative anatomy.

The Apache is the gnat in the area ointment. The government's attempts to manage Indian affairs have so far been calamitous. They're cheated of the rations promised them in return for surrendering their hunting grounds. Western traders and Eastern political hacks get rich exploiting their misery. The bad blood is frightfully bad. Artemus says that the Indian Bureau under the Department of the Interior has been trying to placate the Apaches with weapons to increase their capacity to hunt. Only they use the guns to fight the Army and pester the settlers. In the long run, of course, they haven't a chance against the soldiers, because they have no base and can't hold what they win.

The Indians are a Stone Age people with neither the capacity nor desire to duplicate the white man's technology or social structure. They're more of a loose collection of tribes, each acting on its own. They see life controlled by magic, by spirits; they have no wish to improve their lot or to conquer the wilderness about them, which is their right. Only it does make for a tragic culture clash, with neither side interested in understanding the attitudes of the other.

Lillian and her husband had left for California by the time I got here. You probably wonder why I don't cut and git. Very simply because I like it here. I've found a home.

The town is different from Philadelphia in a thousand ways, and fascinating in many. At the local blacksmith shop they have an anvil made from a meteorite which came to earth somewhere in the Santa Rita Mountains. All Philadelphia has is a bell with a crack in it. I don't miss Philadelphia, I don't miss Wills. I miss you. Our long conversations, our lunches and dinners, our arguments, the operating room. How is Worth Hawkins working out? Better than you expected, I bet.

Write me, Gabriel, please? I'll write at least once a week. Also, if it's not a bother, send me your old journal copies, and the *Lancet* when you're done with it. If I don't keep abreast of what's going on in the outside world I'll sink into a rut like the one Artemus has dug for himself. Perish!

I'll close with a hug and a kiss and oops . . . that tear. Just one: moist testimony to my affection for my dearest friend in all the world.

Love, M.

Marion heard about the one-sided "battle" south of San Pedro Creek from her first patient the next morning, a little prospector with a barbed-wire beard carrying the smell of the stable about him and a bullet in his leg. Artemus was still asleep when the patient hobbled in. She could hear muffled snoring through the door and she hadn't the heart to wake him.

She dug out the slug, cleansed the wound, stitched it, and the little man paid her with what he claimed was two dollars in gold dust in a grimy drawstring sack. She took his word for it. Artemus could judge the value of a quantity of gold dust in five seconds with one eye; she had yet to master the skill. She sent the patient limping out the door.

She sat by the window watching for the next patient to show up. Saturday night in Tucson was one long, noisy, drunken revel. According to Artemus, he was busier with gunshot wounds Sunday morning than any other time. But the residents' aim must have been too befogged by alcohol to be effective because no second patient followed the prospector up the stairs for a full twenty minutes. She spent the time thinking about Captain Venable's bloody Saturday night and wondered when he would decide he had exacted enough revenge against the Apaches who had ambushed his men. She could not resist the temptation to judge him, and harshly. What, she wondered, made him think he was Almighty God's appointed wielder of the sword of vengeance? He was making it his personal war, a vendetta; in spite of all his arguments to the contrary, that was precisely what he was up to.

Tucson was slowly awakening. Across the way a Papago Indian turned the corner of Alameda Street and headed toward the stairs of the office. He was about thirty, a sad-looking man; he looked drained of pride and purpose, reduced to shuffling through life, carrying on his sloping shoulders the burden and disgrace of his tribe's conquest by the white man. He spoke English quite well. It surprised her coming out of the mouth of one attired in Indian garb, with not even a white man's belt to hold up his shabby trousers. His clothing was the last refuge of his pride, she thought. He rolled up his sleeve to disclose a bad cut on his right forearm. It looked like a knife wound; it was at least a week old and badly infected.

She made a solution of carbolic acid and set about cleansing it, debriding it of the infected tissue. It had to be painful for him, but he sat watching her work without a grimace or the flicker of an eyelid.

"I'll be done in a couple of minutes. I'll put some salve on it and bandage it. You must promise to keep the bandage on and keep it dry and as clean as you can. Understand?"

"Understand, Mrs. Doctor."

She was almost done cleansing the wound when a loud pounding came floating up the stairs from below. Two men came barging in. One wore a cloth wrapped around his head, covering his left eye. Both were sweating profusely, both dirty and disheveled and stinking of stale liquor, although neither was drunk. The injured man's visible eye was badly bloodshot. Both of his friend's were equally ravaged.

"Jess here got a bug in his eye, couldn't get it out nohow, and now it's all swole up."

"Hurts like hell!" boomed Jess.

"I'll be with you in a minute."

Both seemed mildly stunned.

"Wha'cha mean?" rasped Jess. "Hey, he can wait. He's a injun. I'm white like you. I told ya, my eye's killing me!"

She straightened and eyed him sternly. "Sit down and wait."

The man's companion grabbed her by the arm. "You see here, woman—"

She jerked free and scowled. "Keep your hands off me! Sit or get out!"

"Where's Shaw?"

"Asleep."

"Wake him up. I don't want no woman working on me anyways. Lucius, go bang his door."

"Don't you dare, and keep your voices down or get out."

"Don't you mouth-face me, woman!" burst Jess. He sent one hand to his injured eye, cupping it as if to catch the pain. "It's killing me, I tell ya!"

Lucius drew his gun, cocked it, and waved it. "Back off him, woman. Now!"

"And if I don't, you'll shoot me."

"I'll count to three—"

"Get out of here, both of you."

She had applied the salve, gotten out gauze, and was bandaging the Indian's wound. Before she could stop him, Lucius jammed his gun in its holster, seized the Papago, and jerked him to his feet. Artemus's door flew open. He stood in his nightshirt bleary-eyed, wretched-looking, stifling a yawn.

"What the hell's going on?"

"These two came barging in and refuse to wait until I'm done with this patient. You, sit down," she ordered the Indian.

He obeyed, ignoring the glares from the others. Swinging about on his stool, he offered them his back. Lucius whipped out his gun a second time, flipped it in his hand, and raised it to smash the Papago's head. Marion pushed him away.

"You cut that out!" bellowed Artemus.

"Fix my eye, Doc. Please . . . It's fair killing me with the pain. It's excruciating!"

"Get the hell out of here, I'll fix nothing on either of you."

"I'll take care of him, Artemus."

She finished bandaging the wound. The Indian got to his feet. He offered her a silver dollar. Feeling even sorrier for him than when he came in, she hesitated to accept it. She looked past the two seething intruders at Artemus. He shook his head.

"Put it back in your pocket," she said. "And remember what I told you about the bandage."

"Clean and no wet."

"Right."

He walked off between the two men.

"You, Jess, sit."

"Like hell, I ain't letting no female work on me. Not after you touched your hands to that redskin trash." He turned to appeal to Artemus.

"Dr. Sturges will tend to you or you'll tend to yourself. I'm going back to bed," he growled.

By noon her failure to stop ministering to the Papago and see to Jess was all over town. In Artemus's view it said more about her "rose-colored spectacle liberalism" than any speeches she could have made.

"I hope you're happy," he rasped when they got onto the subject between patients shortly before they closed the office for the day. "Everybody sure knows where you stand."

"Good, everybody should."

"Proud of yourself, aren't you?" He shook his head and sniffed.

"No, relieved that it's all out in the open now."

"That it is. Boy, nobody can accuse you of being subtle."

"You think I was wrong? I should have dropped what I was doing and examined that misfit's eye? Let the Papago sit and wait?"

"The Papago expected you to." Again he shook his head.

"I'm sorry if I disappointed him."

"Just don't be surprised if folks snub you on the street."

"I can't believe anybody would be that childish."

As she said it she couldn't believe he was being so petty about it; he seemed to be taking it personally.

"Marion," he said, "you're either with 'em or against 'em. Now you've told 'em which."

"Stupid me, I didn't realize there are two sides. Cumbersome arrangement."

"That's the way it is. Don't say I didn't warn you."

"You don't stop. I can handle it, Artemus. I'm going to get something to eat, then go out to the fort and see the colonel."

"Don't forget your other patient out there." He smirked and winked.

"He doesn't need attention. Besides, he's probably out slaughtering Apaches."

Nobody snubbed her in the street, although she did draw stares, and when people passed and she turned to look after them, most couples or pairs of women put their heads together to whisper. Monday morning, when she stopped by Solomon Warner's store to buy material for curtains on her way to the office, Artemus's prophecy came true. Two women were at the counter when she approached it. They received their change from Solomon behind the counter, turned, recognized her, sniffed in disdain, and raised their noses high. They looked like cartoons; it was all she could do to keep from laughing in their faces.

Solomon was not amused. Resplendent in a blue silk vest with black piping and a dazzlingly white boiled shirt, he affected a full white beard in contrast to his tar-black hair. His unkempt eyebrows gave him a grim look, but Marion had heard that he had a grand sense of humor. At the moment, however, he looked anything but funny.

"What'll it be, Doctor?"

Before she could answer, the taller of the two customers, a haughty, patrician-looking woman, addressed her companion. They had stopped at the door on their way out.

"Isn't it curious, Abigail?"

"What's that, Larcena?"

"Easterners. They can't do enough for the poor, poor savages."

"At the expense of their own kind, it seems," said Abigail. "Curious indeed."

"Good-for-nothing bullies may be your kind, ladies," said Marion sweetly, "not mine, thank you."

"You're not welcome, I'm sure!" burst Abigail lamely.

"Not in Tucson," added Larcena, glaring.

"Pardon my social blundering, ladies," purred Marion. "But then neither of you was around to advise me."

They sniffed and went out. Solomon Warner clucked and shook his head. "Where were we?" he murmured. "Oh yes, what'll it be?"

She explained that she needed material for curtains. He fetched four bolts of fabric and laid them on the counter.

"It's none of my business," he said. "You're entitled to your sentiments. Free country. But favoring a redskin over a white won't win you any popularity contest in this town."

"I don't plan to enter any popularity contest, Mr. Warner."

He shrugged. "Don't misunderstand. Some of us feel like you do. Poor, wretched heathens don't stand a chance between the settlers and the Army, never mind the Mexicans. And everybody's down on the Apaches. But me, I figure a man's a man whatever his color. We're all God's children."

Was this impromptu speech on race relations being delivered as a veiled warning like Artemus had already given her? Or was he simply expressing his true feelings? She gave him the benefit of doubt.

"Indeed we are, Mr. Warner."

"Solomon."

"Marion . . ."

"Any of these strike your fancy, Marion? I got more."

"I like this beige chenille. I'll need twelve yards."

"That'll be three-sixty. That's the best. You can have the lining for free. I always give new folks in town a break first time in here." He winked. "Makes for steady customers. How do you like Tucson?"

"Just fine, you?"

"Garden of Eden. Well, not quite, no stingtails and heat prostration in Eden, right? But I like it. You come from Philadelphia. I'm originally from upstate New York. Little town called Geneva."

"I went to medical school in Geneva."

"Is that a fact? I was operating a grist mill back there in '48. At the time I was courting an attractive widow with two little boys who loved to play around the mill. One morning I was startled by a terrible scream. Stand your hair on end. I rushed to the hopper. Got there just in time to see the four copper toes of the boots of those two darling little tads. Before I could stop the mill, the two of them passed between the top and bottom mill-stones and were ground into the day's grist. Of course, I couldn't face their mother. I'm ashamed to say it, but when she assumed the boys had been lost kidnapped, I just let her go on thinking that.

"But you know something? That day's grind of flour attracted considerable attention for its excellence. I wish there'd been a happy ending, but the widow's grief and my own remorse drove me to a wandering life, and I eventually ended up here."

"How fortunate for me," said Marion drily. "You did say the price was three-sixty—"

"My stars and body, you don't believe me."

"I do. I believe you said three-sixty."

She counted out three paper bills, five dimes and two nickels. He went to get his shears and yardstick. She followed him with her eyes, amusement playing at the corners of her mouth. The local storyteller's initiation rite for the green newcomer from the East. It was a ray of sunshine in the grayness of her ostracism. Was her fate as an outcast already determined in Tucson?

Time would tell.

10

Captain Marcus Venable sat at the colonel's desk writing his report on the Saturday night massacre. Thoughts of Dr. Marion Sturges kept creeping into his mind, which made the captain feel decidedly uncomfortable. He had work, a command to run, a career. What was he doing thinking about a woman?

Dr. Sturges stood at the supply cabinet straightening the contents and thinking of Captain Venable. He was certainly attractive, and her natural attraction to the opposite sex encouraged her to look. But that was as far as it went. He had already proven himself erratic with a vicious temper. The little she knew about his disposition she did not like; why think about him at all?

His face floated before her mind's eye and in annoyance she slammed a packet of gauze pads onto the shelf so sharply it bounced off and she had to bend to retrieve it. When she had applied his cast, she could feel his eyes drilling her. She remembered wondering, "What is he thinking? Why must he stare so?"

Before his blowup at the fort when the Indian dropped off those hideous scalps, he had been on his best behavior, as soft-spoken and polite as a choirboy. She'd gotten the feeling he was in awe of her. Why? It was as if he hadn't seen a woman in ages. What did she care? His social life was no business of hers.

Again his smiling face materialized on the screen of her imagination. Her heart sped up slightly. Why?

"Why, dammit!"

She would like to see him again, though, to see how his hand was faring. How would it be? Healing, of course. It was not yet time to remove the cast, so why see him? To look at it, stare at it, pretend she could see *through* it? Why was she thinking of him when she should be reminiscing about Tyson? What was she doing letting a perfect stranger usurp her thoughts, and block out the love she so desperately missed?

"You really must get a hold of yourself, Doctor," Marion murmured. "You're being ridiculous."

Venable's report would be forwarded to Prescott and Departmental Commander General George Crook. Describing the skirmish was a chore. He had to be careful, for the general demanded just cause for such an attack, so every such report required a bit of fudging of the facts. With the report would go the usual plea for reinforcements, another for weapons and ammunition, still another for additional food supplies and money to purchase food locally. It galled him: the area farmers clamored for protection from the hostiles and yet they charged exorbitant prices for their produce, figuring that the government's money supply was a bottomless well.

With every skirmish report sent to the Department of Arizona, subsequently sent on to Washington, went requests for essentials. He'd never dream of asking for a luxury like a bathtub or a new flag.

His right hand still in its cast, he wrote with his left. Rather he lettered, being unable to write legibly left-handed. It was tedious going. He could only take it an hour at a time, but he was nearly done and determined to get it over with. He had tried holding the pen between his thumb and the cast, but the writing looked like bird tracks. He paused to glance out the front window at the colonel sitting his chair, shawled with a blanket, taking the sun and fresh air. He was vastly improved. Within a week he'd be fit to reassume command. It couldn't happen soon enough for Venable. No more desk, no more paperwork, no reports, no more damnably niggling, pestiferous details to command his attention. He was happiest, most contented, away from the garrison, pursuing and engaging the enemy. The excitement of battle beat a desk and chair by six miles. When he got to be Schreiber's age he'd probably think differently, but for now . . .

Olan came in. He stood ramrod-straight before him, clicked his heels, and saluted.

"Barracks shipshape, sir."

"Good. Relax. I've been meaning to tell you, you did yourself proud the other night. Good soldiering."

"Easy as picking walnuts off the ground, Captain."

"It did turn out that way. Next time we may not be so lucky. It's the far side of different when they shoot back."

"I'm game for the roughest go-round, Captain."

"Good man. Olan, I want you to go into town to Solomon Warner's store." He tilted back from the edge of the desk and pulled open the belly drawer. He got twenty dollars out of the battered, flat, gun-metal gray strongbox and handed it to him.

"Buy blankets. As many as he'll give you for twenty dollars. As drab as you can find: gray, dark brown. When you bring them back, take them to Barracks C and replace the raggediest ones."

"Yes sir, Captain."

Again he saluted, pivoted less than smartly—too fast—and nearly toppled before righting himself and going out. Venable put back the strongbox. Beside it in the drawer lay Corporal John Francis Tumbelsky's gleaming knife. He examined it. Poor Tumble, he thought. What a cruel and needless way to go. What an ineffectual, misguided policy for dealing with the problem, with no end in sight. Confining the tribes to reservations wasn't working. The peaceful Indians, the Navahos, Hopis, and Papagos were cooperating, but they weren't the problem. If they weren't consigned to reservations, they would never cause the settlers any headaches.

It was the Apaches. For the most part they refused to be restricted to reservations. The result was that the bandage wasn't really being applied to the wound.

In the meantime every fatality at Fort Lowell went unreplaced in the ranks. And every survivor had to pick up the slack. The Olans found themselves attending to six different chores. The post commander's striker should, according to the book, be attending to the commander's needs and person exclusively, not straightening up barracks. It was a growing problem, one Marcus was in no position to solve; why brood over it? He turned the knife over again and examined the hilt, the corporal's initials.

He would have to write a letter to his wife waiting for him back in Springfield. He would have to write to all the widows and mothers. In the turmoil that followed the mountain massacre, he had completely overlooked that particular desk job. He supposed he could write pretty much the same words to every loved one. It seemed a trifle cold-hearted and mechanical, but the War Department did it that way. He couldn't letter them as he had the report; he would have to dictate to Olan or somebody. Could Olan spell? Could he even write? It wasn't a requirement for enlistment, not with the war on.

He put back the knife and went outside for a word with Colonel Schreiber. He could see the man was dozing and hesitated to wake him. He stood surveying the parade ground. At the far left corner four men were pitching horseshoes; the clink of metal against metal carried toward him on the breeze. They would be at it until supper, then resume until dark. In the barracks at least one marathon poker game was in progress. Noncoms only, keeping busy while the privates worked. The privates didn't have the money to gamble. Not on sixteen dollars a month. Corporals got a munificent nineteen; sergeants, twenty-two.

The garrison had an unmistakable atmosphere of decay about it. The aridity of the area, the broiling and brutal sun took their toll on wood; adobe brick stood up well under the combined assault, but it was more than the climate that afflicted the place: it was the feeling that here was a last outpost, too far from civilization for anyone back there to take steps to arrest the deterioration. One got the impression that Washington couldn't care less about Lowell. The shortage of supplies, the delays in delivery, the failure to replace fatalities—all of it was making it a downhill run. The war was a blanket excuse for official neglect.

Morale was perilously low, and after the armistice—

when it came—would sink even lower. But there was still the Apaches, the problem they were posted there to deal with. The trouble was that nobody east of the Mississippi was aware of the problem; those in high places failed to recognize the enormity of it.

Schreiber had awakened. Venable joined him.

"In answer to your question, I'm feeling much better," said the colonel, smiling.

"Good."

"Sick of riding a desk already?" It was Venable's turn to smile. "I've been thinking about your activities the other night. You ran out of here like you had a hornet in your drawers, like the Lord Himself going after Moab. I don't mind telling you I was annoyed."

"You were livid."

"I don't get livid, Captain. But I've thought about it since, calmly, objectively, and I have to say it did make sense. Too bad you couldn't take Namasa alive. You think they'll give the job back to Gold Eyes?"

"He's dead. Every man above the age of twelve is in that pack."

Schreiber sucked a tooth thoughtfully, rearranged his blanket, and fixed his eyes on the distant horseshoe match.

"About the only thing we've got working for us with the Apache is that they're divided into so many tribes."

"Divide and conquer."

"We can't take credit for that, it's their choice. But one of these days they'll see their mistake, they'll put aside their petty animosities and join forces. They've got the fellow who can get them together."

They talked about Geronimo. Venable knew little about the legendary chief; Schreiber knew a great deal. Gokhlayeh, "he who yawns," become Geronimo, had come to his eminence ethically and rightfully. Chieftainship was hereditary among the Apaches, and his grandfather had been a chief of the Nednis, a band that roved the wilds of northern Mexico.

"Geronimo got a bad break before he was even born. His father forfeited his own and his future son's inheritance when he left his people and married into the Mimbres. So when Geronimo was born, grew up, and attained manhood he had to go a different route to the top."

"War and pillage."

The colonel nodded. "The critical turning point came after a battle with the Mexican army, led by the military governor of Sonora, General Jose Carrasco. I say battle; it was a slaughter. Geronimo's wife, mother, and children were among the victims. Naturally, their murders had a profound effect on him. Up to that time he'd been an affectionate husband, an indulgent father, but then he turned bitter, quarrelsome, and unpredictably violent. In the meantime the Mimbres regrouped and gradually recovered their strength. Their chief decided that Geronimo was just the man to recruit warriors from other Apache bands for a massive attack on the Mexicans."

"So he's an experienced organizer."

"He is. He was sent first to Cochise, chief of the Chiricahuas. He did his job well. Another arrow in his quiver, he's a skilled politician. He brought the chiefs together and they chose Arizpe, a rich farming town in Sonora for their target. Wise choice: it was situated at the head of a narrow canyon, hard to reinforce, and the escape route back into the mountains lay through thinly populated farmland.

"I could go on for six hours about Geronimo, but to bring you up to date: Mangas Coloradas, chief of chiefs, was captured and killed; Cochise, of course, is still active down below, but here in the territory Geronimo's the one we should keep our eye on."

"If I knew where he was, I would."

"That, Marcus, is a favor he's bound to do us sooner or later; when he starts uniting the tribes he'll have to show himself here and there, up in the Gila Mountains, up in San Carlos, across the border in southwest New Mexico. Give him until next spring, word will come drifting in. He'll be spotted here and there, the proverbial will-o'-the-wisp." Schreiber's grin was one of admiration.

"We'll grab him before he can start his campaign of unification."

"If we can. Don't bet your horse on it; he's as wily as he is brazen. And he won't be riding around by his lonesome. But if he does wander into our bailiwick . . . Food for thought, eh, Marcus?"

"If we catch him it could go a long way toward breaking the back of their resistance. Wreck their morale. Or am I thinking like a white man? Still, it does make sense. Sooner or later they're bound to get together. It's ironic."

"What?" asked Schreiber.

"Wiping out the Mogollóns, I no doubt hastened the day."

"Don't flatter yourself, you didn't wipe out the Mogollóns. You massacred one arm of the one tribe. It's an octopus, they all are: Mogollóns, Mimbres, Chiricahuas, Jicarillas, Mescaleros, San Carlos, White Mountain. The Apache de Nabaju. A fragmented nation. I keep thinking, here we sit suffering all sorts of shortages, but we're not short Apaches." Schreiber scanned the horizon. "Sun's going down, I think I'll go back in." He brightened. "I think I'll sit at my desk a few minutes, just to get the feel of it."

"You're supposed to be in bed inside."

Schreiber leered. "My recovering does worry you after all."

Venable's cheeks flushed. The colonel laughed.

———————◆◀11▶◆———————

Steadfastly convinced that she was in the right in what she had done, Marion nevertheless held her breath every time she passed somebody on the street, fearing a confrontation. But as things turned out, her treating the Papago did not upset the community to the extent Artemus predicted. And the passage of time eased the episode's impact on the townspeople.

She discussed it with no one other than Artemus and Solomon Warner; the Tucsonians' resentment toward what Larcena Pennington termed her "scandalous behavior" did not extend to boycotting her services, although one man did show up at the office sporting a feather, telling her he hoped it would get him to the front of the waiting line.

Then calamity struck. Artemus got the news from Mark Aldrich. Marion was alone in the office when Artemus came bustling up the stairs panting and gesticulating.

"Did you hear? It's all over town. Larcena Pennington's been kidnapped by savages!"

"Good Lord!"

"Made off with her not two hours ago."

"What did they do, break into her house?"

He froze a scowl, blatantly if wordlessly questioning her intelligence.

114

"She took a buggy ride out on the Mesilla road. Filthy scum waylaid her, wrecked the buggy, killed the horse, snatched her."

"How do they know it was Indians?"

"Who else would do such a thing? Oh, it was the ragheads, all right; you should see the poor horse, they carved it into pie meat."

"What was she doing out on the Mesilla road?"

"Who knows?" He caught himself and eyed her critically. "What are you going to do, blame the poor soul for letting herself be abducted?"

"I'm not," snapped Marion.

"Sounds like it to me," he snapped back.

"It's just that anybody who hates and fears the Apaches like she does ought to have more sense than to go wandering off—"

"Tell that to her husband and children, I dare you, Miss Tolerance Personified!"

"Oh, shut up. Why must you twist everything I say?"

She waved off his response before he could get it out. She recalled telling him about her encounter with Larcena and Abigail Houghton at the store. She remembered Larcena as tall, dark-haired, a handsome if not beautiful woman who dressed with taste and seemed genteel—when she wasn't flinging spiteful remarks at Philadelphia liberals. Married to a prominent local feed store owner, she was reputedly very popular in town, something of a grand dame. She taught school and joined every crusade organized to improve the quality of life in Tucson.

The arrival of a patient interrupted discussion of the kidnapping. Marion tended to the man's fractured thumb, setting it in splints. As she worked she reflected on the abduction. The probable consequences were frightening. Imagination imposed no limits on what her captors might do to her. A shocking business, and Marion was shocked as well by the effect it had on her attitude toward the Indians. That they had seized Larcena in retaliation for Captain Venable's massacre seemed likely, but why take their revenge out on a helpless and innocent civilian?

The soldiers scoured the area, but failed to find her. Her husband and two grown daughters waited helplessly for word, dreading the worst. Mr. Pennington alternately badgered Captain Venable and Colonel Schreiber to do something and locked himself in his house, sitting at the front window, his eyes fastened on the Mesilla road. He kept his hopes up with a bottle.

Thirteen days after the kidnapping, when practically everyone had given up hope of ever seeing her alive again, Larcena staggered into town and collapsed by the whipping post in the square. A crowd quickly gathered. She was brought to the doctors' office covered with lacerations, badly bruised; the blankets covering her nakedness were torn and bloodstained. One look told Marion that she had been repeatedly violated. Her shoes had been taken from her; her feet were savagely cut and black and blue. Artemus administered luminol, and before she fell asleep, although she had been babbling incoherently up to then, she managed to tell them that she had walked barefoot nearly twenty miles to town.

"They—they a . . . bused me h—h—horribly. Vicious . . . ly. Stripped m—m—me. Had their w—w—way with m—m—me. Left—left me for dead . . ."

She fell asleep abruptly; it looked as if she'd died.

"You think she'll make it?" Artemus asked Marion worriedly.

"We'll know better in a day."

She smoothed Larcena's tangled, blood-matted hair from her forehead, revealing a bruise the size of a silver dollar.

Artemus sighed. "If she makes it through the night."

"What do you suppose she found to live on out in the desert?"

He shrugged. "Roots, berries, God knows what else. If she does come through it, it'll be at least six weeks before she recovers completely."

"She may never up here." Marion tapped her own temple. "It's the sort of thing that could haunt her the rest of her life."

The street below was filled with people. The curious crowded the stairs. Somehow the unfortunate woman's husband and daughters managed to wedge their way up the stairs. Pennington's mustache and his stone-gray hair parted in the middle lent him the look of a walrus despite his slender build and trim waist. He was red-eyed, white-faced, and his hands shook. His thirteen-day ordeal of waiting had brought him to the brink of a breakdown.

His daughters had borne up better under the strain. Although at least three years apart in age, they looked like twins and quite like their mother, though not the way Larcena looked at the moment.

"Larcena, Larcena," cried Pennington and threw himself across her unconscious form. The girls began to sob hysterically. It took both Artemus and Marion to pull Pennington loose and get him to a chair. He came apart completely.

"She's dead . . . dead!"

"She's not," rasped Artemus. "She'll be all right. She made it back, she's safe, she'll recover."

Marion's expression appeared doubtful and at the same time disapproving of his optimism. He avoided her eyes.

"Stop that infernal caterwauling!" he snapped at the girls.

Marion calmed them, talking soothingly to them. Pennington got control, dropped to his knees, and thanked his maker for his wife's safe return.

"Thirteen days, the poor darling. Dear God, what they must have put her through . . ."

Artemus finally got all three Penningtons out only after Mr. Pennington exacted Marion's promise that his wife would be returned home within a day or so. At supper that evening she and Artemus discussed the patient's prospects for recovery. They agreed it was too soon to tell. Marion figured that by dessert Artemus would get around to her opinion of the Apaches. They shared a table at Walton's Kansas City Restaurant, both ordering beefsteak dinners. Artemus didn't wait for dessert; he was halfway through his salad when out came his needle.

"This thing change your thinking any? Probably not."

"You actually think I can excuse such an outrage?" It was her turn to rivet him with a frown designed to make him squirm. "Rationalize it? There *is* no excuse, obviously, any more than there is for the Army's cruelty toward them."

"Rubbish, who's talking about the Army?"

"Isn't it two sides of the same coin?"

"You'll have a hard time finding anyone around here who thinks that. This has to be the absolute capper. Stealing horses and livestock, attacking stage coaches, burning and pillaging aside, when they attack a lone woman, helpless, defenseless, abuse her, leave her for dead—that tops it all. I can't wait for the war to end. Washington'll have no excuse for dragging their feet. They'll have to send troops, seasoned fighters, howitzers. The day'll come when they'll wipe them off the face of the earth. It can't happen too soon."

She stared aghast. "I don't believe you."

"I don't care what you believe."

"Is this going to make enemies of us? Is that what you want?"

"What I want, what I'd like, is for you to come down off your white charger and deal with the realities like the rest of us." He was suddenly angrier than she had ever seen him.

"I'm sorry, I can't honestly see what this case has to do with the overall problem." He jerked his head up and gaped; she ignored the reaction. "What happened to her is horrible, an outrage, worse than anything else they've done. But it's not the problem. Only a symptom of the problem. Genocide is no solution. I'm amazed somebody with your intelligence would think it is."

"It's the only damn solution, dammit!"

"Would you kindly keep your voice down? Let me pose you a hypothetical case, okay?"

"Here we go."

"Please, bear with me. Let's say the Apaches don't exist. Not a one. No Apaches, no Papagos, no Indians period. Do you think the Anglos and Mexicans would get along as well as they do now?"

"I do," he snapped.

"I don't."

"I do, and I know better than you. First-family Mexicans and Anglos meet, mingle, and intermarry on terms of perfect equality and mutual esteem. I can give you dozens of examples right here in Tucson."

"I'm sure you can. But if they weren't united in their hatred of the Apaches, there'd be friction. Oh, they wouldn't be at each other's throats, but there'd be prejudice, bigotry, resentment."

"Rubbish."

"There would. It's Catholic against Protestant, a difference of deeply emotional opinion that's been thriving since the Middle Ages. Since Martin Luther. And it thrives here. Under the circumstances, with the Apaches the pain in everybody's neck, it's passive, I grant you, but it's there. I've seen it. It's been less than ten years since the Mexican War. The bitterness between the two cultures that came out of that war is still with us."

"Rubbish." He waved it away disdainfully and took to his coffee.

"I'm not being hypothetical now, I'm talking fact."

"You're talking nonsense. You haven't been here six weeks yet and you've got it all figured out. And why do you keep straying from the subject? We were talking about the Apaches, remember?"

"Why is it so important to you to get me to change my way of thinking? So critical?"

"It's for your own good!" he burst.

"Rubbish."

"Talking to you is like talking to a rock."

He suddenly reminded her of Gabriel Cowan. There were similarities. Even with his dander up and active, his eyes held a kindly twinkle. Like Gabriel, he had a habit of burying his face in his coffee cup instead of bringing it up to his mouth. And both tended to lower instead of raise their voices when pushing home a point of view differing from hers, albeit not Artemus at the moment.

"Pay the check," he grumbled. "Let's get out of here."

"It's your turn."

He growled. "You are the pickiest female I've ever met, bar nothing."

"The expression is bar none."

Dear Marion,

Thank you for your letter. I promise not to throw stones at Tucson from here. You should be getting a stack of journals and other publications soon. If they travel by Jackass Mail, make that someday. I've underlined some things that merit particular attention. You might show them to Shaw; tell him one is never too old to learn.

Wills is a different place without your skills and smile. I miss you, but I won't go into that. Worth Hawkins is turning out better than adequate. He does drop things, and, sweet Jerusalem, but he sweats under pressure. Doesn't have much of a bedside manner, but does his job. Isn't lazy, but he doesn't go that extra mile like you used to. No sense of humor. I tell him *I'm* supposed to be the old fogy, not a twenty-seven-year-old like him. I don't mean to find fault."

Marion laughed aloud.

"Your description of Shaw is fascinating. Walter Ogren over at Pennsylvania Hospital knows him. They went through medical school together back in Milwaukee. It was probably Walter who told him you were coming and neglected to mention you were a woman.

The board of directors got the knot out of the purse strings and sprung for a new, fully equipped, modern operating room. On the third floor across from Ward B. It positively gleams. The black hole of Calcutta downstairs *was* getting a bit dingy. There's a move afoot to get surgeons to wear aprons while operating. Why not chef hats? Sweet Jerusalem!

If there's anything else you want, please holler. Samples, potions, or equipment. You must need everything. I fear for the jackass' back. In your letter you said nothing about specific cases. Do you and Shaw have *anything* to work with? I picture an army field surgery kit: trepans, knives, bone chisels, and saws; amputations for gunshot wounds, fractures, and dislocations. Please tell me it's not quite that primitive. I can't imagine what you do with eye and head wounds. Just remember, tobacco juice is no substitute for carbolic acid.

Hamilton, Hampton, Mrs. Childress, and a dozen others have recovered and been discharged. I'm sending you a Judson carbolic sprayer. I leave it to you to persuade Æsculapius Shaw of its inestimable value. Best of luck in dragging him into the nineteenth century.

I'll close now. I'm writing this in the office. I'm dining alone tonight as usual; Hawkins is married and I can't stand his simpering, bootlicking wife. After dinner I'll go home to my lonely rooms as I always do. If only I had a really close, true friend to hobnob with. But that's wishful thinking. When you get to my age, it's hard to make new friends.

Love,
Gabriel

Inasmuch as Fort Lowell's nemesis, Mogollón Apaches under Namasa, had been wiped out in the bloody encounter near the San Pedro River, the question arose in everyone's mind as to which other branch of the Mogollón tribe was responsible for Larcena Pennington's kidnapping. Could it have been another, wholly separate tribe? The questions arose in both Schreiber's and Venable's minds. Word was spread among the Papagos, and late one night the information came back that a roving band of Aravaipas was responsible.

By treaty the Aravaipas were supposed to be quartered on the San Carlos reservation near Globe, some seventy-five miles north of Tucson. Instead, these particular Aravaipas had wandered off to settle in their old home, the beautiful Aravaipa Canyon in the Pinatino Mountains. Their relocating placed them under the jurisdiction of Camp Grant, situated close by the canyon, and protocol dictated that dealing with them was the responsibility of the commander of Camp Grant. In removing themselves to their old grounds, the tribe came under the protection of the Army and were fed by the government, just as if they'd remained at San Carlos. In light of this beneficent treatment, it was little wonder that their alleged crime doubly infuriated the people of Tucson.

Tuesday at Fort Lowell commenced like every other day with reveille at five. The bugle call signaled morning roll call. Colonel Schreiber was no spit-and-polish commander. Distance lent itself to a relaxed attitude. The colonel's illness contributed as well. Even had he not been incapacitated he would not have required his men to turn out in full dress and equipment—no doubt because it would have proved an embarrassing sight. As the sleepy soldiers stood shivering in their places, the first sergeant of each unit called roll, after which the men were allowed to return briefly to their quarters to finish shaving and cleaning up or snatch a few minutes extra sleep while the sergeants prepared their morning reports. About thirty minutes after reveille came breakfast call, followed by sick call for the ailing and fatigue call for the fit. There being no doctor on the post, mildly ill patients were left to care for themselves or their friends looked after them; seriously ill patients were confined to quarters and Dr. Shaw sent for.

Fatigue duty for the well consisted of policing the grounds, digging drainage ditches and privy holes, cutting wood, repairing buildings and equipment, unloading and putting away supplies and similar chores. About eight o'clock the four-man fife-and-drum corps provided suitable music and the bugler sounded the call for guard mount. The sergeant major, the garrison's major-domo, formed the details into line, after which the adjutant supervised their inspection and then sent them to their respective posts. Each man stood actual guard only two hours out of every six.

Following this morning routine with about three hours to go before "roast beef," a derisive nickname for the noon meal, Captain Venable reported to the colonel, who had repossessed his desk and his duties without bothering to inform either of his doctors.

"I feel a hundred percent," he boomed to Venable without the captain's even asking how he felt.

He privately felt that Schreiber should have cleared this with Dr. Sturges, but prudently held his tongue. Schreiber waved him to a chair.

"Let's talk about the Aravaipas," said the colonel.

"I don't see what there is to talk about," responded Venable wistfully. "They're under Colonel Willoughby's jurisdiction up in the canyon. If anybody's going to call them to account, it should be him."

"Marcus, I know Thaddeus Willoughby. I like the man. He's witty, warm, and enjoyable company, but it generally takes two sticks of dynamite to get his nose out of a book and his rear end out of his chair. I can tell you right now, he's not going to bother."

"Somebody should."

"Not us, we have to play by the rules the same as everybody."

"I don't think the townspeople will accept that, Colonel."

It turned out to be a prophetic observation. Not three minutes later a delegation arrived from town headed by Larcena Pennington's husband, Solomon Warner, and schoolmaster-saloonkeeper Augustus Brichta. The colonel offered the three leaders chairs while their friends waited outside. Horace, Pennington was understandably ready and itching for war.

"Word is that the Aravaipas were the culprits," he said. "We want to know what action you intend to take."

Schreiber patiently explained Fort Lowell's position of responsibility regarding the tribe, emphasizing that the War Department decreed that the Aravaipas were under Camp Grant's supervision. Colonel Willoughby was the man they should approach. Schreiber's response was civil, manifestly clear, correct, and delivered in a sympathetic tone. But as Venable expected, watching Pennington take his words in, it wasn't good enough.

"What'd I tell you, boys? Didn't I say he'd try and wriggle out of it?"

Schreiber did not take this gracefully.

"See here, Pennington, all I can do is follow the orders of my superiors. The book is clear. Camp Grant has jurisdiction."

"Grant had jurisdiction when your men butchered the redskins back on that Saturday night, didn't it?" asked Solomon Warner.

"That's not the same thing," said the captain. "We can't chase a bunch of Indians out of our area and stop, hoping the next garrison will pick up the chase. But we simply can't ride into Camp Grant's backyard and raise hell. Not only would it be a breach of the rules and of etiquette, but a slap in Colonel Willoughby's face."

"My wife is kidnapped and nearly killed and he's talking about etiquette," growled Pennington.

"That's not good enough, Captain," snapped Brichta. "If you won't help us, Willoughby won't, either."

"Have you asked him?"

"No, and we don't intend to!" boomed Pennington. "Waste of time. We'll do our own dirty work, thank you. Come on, boys."

"See here," interposed Schreiber, rising from his chair. "You're being very foolish."

Solomon Warner shrugged. "It's either that or see nothing done. In which case the Aravaipas are bound to conclude nobody's interested in making them pay. And—"

"And," interrupted Brichta, "letting them get away with it will only encourage more trouble. Something worse."

"What could be worse than what they did to Larcena?" grumbled Pennington tightly.

"Playing vigilante is the worst thing you people can do," said Schreiber.

Warner was eyeing him critically. "If you won't do anything, you leave us little choice," said the storekeeper.

"Sorry we bothered you," muttered Pennington.

They filed out. Venable was about to call after them, but Schreiber gestured him not to bother.

"Let them go. All we can do is warn them."

"But they're no match for the Aravaipas. They'll be butchered. I bet Solomon Warner's never fired a rifle in his life. Or Brichta—"

"Relax, they're just spouting off. None of them will so much as set foot out of town. They'll go back and stir up the young bucks, just watch. Get me a man, Marcus, and tell him stand by. I'll write a note to Thaddeus Willoughby up at Grant to warn him what's on the way. It should be there well before any fracas can get started. Thaddeus can deal with things as he sees fit." He stopped and stared at the grim expression on Venable's face. "What's the matter?"

"Warner does have a point, Justin. We slaughtered the ones by the creek, the Aravaipas strike back, and we sit on our guns. It doesn't make much sense."

"I explained it to those three quite well, weren't you listening? Or is it your conscience buckling under the strain? I'm sorry, Marcus, alerting Willoughby is the best I can do."

Venable brightened. "How about if I mount a party and we follow them? The vigilantes—"

"And do what?"

"When they attack, pitch in and help. We could bend the rules a little. We could say we were out looking for renegades when we ran into the battle and did what any troop would, lent a hand. I can't imagine Willoughby would feel we deceived him. What does he care? He'll probably be grateful."

Schreiber pondered the suggestion; Marcus eyed him. Even though the colonel had stopped coughing, he did not look completely recovered. His color was not yet back to normal and although it wasn't even eleven in the morning, he appeared fatigued. Venable's eyes strayed to the cast on his own hand. It had been on the alloted three weeks; he wanted it off.

"Go ahead," said Schreiber quietly. He smiled. "Just don't tell me about it. We won't enter it in the book. No report to Prescott. Any casualties we'll chalk up to some planned, bona fide action. The way we're fighting this war, one brush fire after another, nobody back East will question it. Nor will General Crook in Prescott. You're on your own."

"Thank you, sir."

Horace Pennington, Solomon Warner, and Augustus Brichta lost no time in making good their threat. They had little difficulty lining up volunteers. Indignant Tucsonians could barely wait to get Larcena Pennington's abductors in their gun sights.

By late afternoon the planned retaliation began taking on the dimensions of a crusade by the Holy Mother Church. A committee of safety was organized, and the decision to wipe out the Apaches living in Aravaipa Canyon was unanimous.

It was a decision of necessity to those who made it. Living in an area surrounded by hostile savages was like living encircled by ticking bombs. At any time—the worst time—they could go off. The residents of Tucson, like the farmers and ranchers round about them, lived on the edge of the blade. As children they learned to sleep with one ear awake; as adults they kept their guns loaded and within reach. Whenever they ventured from the protection of their numbers, it was with fear.

To be sighted by wandering Apaches outside of town was certain death in the minds of the whites. There was no room in their minds for thought of the Indians' plight, the confiscation of their lands, their heritage of broken promises and treaties.

A wagon was drawn up to the military plaza and loaded with food, weapons, and ammunition. Local Mexicans and at least ninety Papagos swelled the ranks of the volunteers. By five o'clock, a hundred forty men had gathered in the plaza.

Marion and Artemus looked out the office window opened to admit the occasional breeze that drifted down from the mountains into the sweltering town. Tom Vidall, a suspected Confederate deserter twenty years younger than Pennington, Warner, or Brichta, took charge of the vigilante squad. The older men welcomed his leadership. He climbed onto the loaded wagon and whistled and waved for attention.

"This here's the plan, boys. We all wait till almost dark before we set out. Now keep in mind, this ain't vengeance we're going after. This here's a mission. It's the only way to protect ourselves and our loved ones. Somebody's got to, 'cause the army sure as hell ain't interested. They care more about them damned Indians. They issues 'em rations, help 'em farm, and pay 'em good money to gather hay for their horses. Pay 'em! Can you beat that? And the heathen sons of bitches pay it back by violating a defenseless wife and mother!"

"Butcher the red bastards!"

"Shoot 'em down like dogs!"

"Wipe 'em out!"

"Amen. That's just what we're gonna do. With the help of our Mexican friends and the Papagos. I have here in my hand a telegram from the headquarters of the Department of the Army of Arizona in Prescott, which was sent in answer to Augustus Brichta's telegram describing what happened and asking 'em to take appropriate action on our behalf. With your kind permission, I'll read their answer.

" 'Please be advised that the federal government cannot countenance any vigilante action on your part against the alleged abductors of Mrs. Pennington.' Alleged, boys, y'all hear?"

Catcalls and hoots greeted the question. Vidall went on.

" 'You are hereby instructed to use moral persuasion and diplomacy in dealing with the suspects.' "

"No hope in hell!" came a cry.

"Rip it up and send back the pieces!"

Upstairs in the window Marion glanced at Artemus.

"What are you looking at me for?"

"Don't be so touchy. Just wondering what you think. Are you for it?"

He was wiping blood off his hands from a blind boil he had just finished extracting from a farmer's back. The patient lay facedown and anesthetized on the table.

"Not for it, not against it. It's none of my business."

"It's everybodys! It's disgusting! When a mob takes the law into its hands—"

"Spare me the sermon, Doctor, I really don't care. Whatever the outcome, we'll have our hands full the rest of the week. We should have laid in more chloroform while we had the chance."

Below them a large crowd had encircled the vigilantes surrounding the loaded wagon with Vidall atop it. A lone rider came galloping into town. Marion had turned back to Artemus's patient when Artemus called her attention to the new arrival.

"Friend of yours coming to call."

She recognized Captain Venable. "Friend? I hardly know him. He's just another patient."

Artemus leered. "Nothing special, eh? Good-looking fellow. Of course, you haven't noticed."

She sniffed and assumed an expression meant to convey total indifference as she heard the captain come up the stairs.

"Afternoon, Dr. Shaw, Dr. Sturges. Dr. Sturges, the three weeks are up today. I'd like this thing taken off."

She set about removing his cast. Artemus had washed his hands, bandaged the unconscious farmer's back, and was putting on his hat and coat.

"Our friend owes us four and a half bucks when he wakes up. Three dollars for the chloroform. If he gets edgy about it, just remind him that he insisted on it. See you in the morning. Pleasure, Captain."

They were alone. She cut the cast off carefully and bathed his hand in clear water. Touching his hand made her feel strange. She realized her cheeks were warming. Why did he have this effect on her? It made her quietly furious. He's just another patient, she thought.

"Any pain?"

"A little."

"You're lucky. It's healed perfectly, though you shouldn't have put off coming in when you broke it. I'll wrap it so you can use it. We'll take another look a week from today. Try to favor it as much as you can for a time."

She felt him staring and looked up sharply. He lowered his eyes. His cheeks looked like hers felt, she thought.

Below in the square Vidall continued stirring up his listeners. She closed the window.

"Talk about your rabble-rousers," she said, hoping to start them talking about something to take her mind off him, if only temporarily. She had been thinking about him much too often lately, especially during the long, lonely nights. More than once she had berated herself for substituting him for Tyson. And Artemus teased her every time the captain's name came up, probably because she was so quick to deny any interest in him.

"You don't approve?" Venable asked.

"Do you?"

"Of course not. What do you take me for?" He bristled. "No, no," he added hastily, "I'm sorry, I shouldn't be so quick to take offense."

Silence fell between them. She released his hand. He took hold of her free hand. Instead of pulling loose, she sighed ever so softly, closed her eyes, and covered his hand with hers. But her heart suddenly caught in her throat as she realized how obvious she was being, and she jerked away.

"Please forgive me," he murmured. "I shouldn't. I have no right." He was blushing furiously, his expression sheepish. His glance strayed to his injured hand. "Is that about it?"

"For now. Till next week."

He got up from the chair. "Thank you, Doctor."

"Marion."

"Marion," he said. "And I'm Marcus. And . . ."

"Yes?"

"I just wanted to say we did try to stop the business down below before it could get any momentum. The colonel tried to talk them out of it, but they wouldn't listen."

He explained that Camp Grant had jurisdiction over Aravaipa Canyon and the Aravaipas' new *ranchería* there.

"It's out of our bailiwick."

"Tucson's not," Marion countered.

"We have no control over the residents, I'm afraid. A good many of them can't stand the sight of a bluecoat. And their frustration is coming to a boil. They've taken and taken it, now they're striking back. However it turns out, it's sure to be bloody on both sides. From now on. And if the locals win this round, the Apaches will only retaliate. It'll go on and on with no solution." He shook his head.

"You're giving up on it."

"On any possibility for peace. We'll just go right on fighting. Ours not to reason why—" He glanced at the still unconscious farmer. "I'll let you in on a secret. We plan to follow them to the canyon—at a discreet distance, of course. To help if they need us, which they will. But don't tell anybody, Marion, please."

"I won't, I promise. Only how can you be certain they're the Apaches who kidnapped Mrs. Pennington?"

"We have it from a very reliable source."

"Some Papago."

"More than one, actually."

"Couldn't they be deliberately misleading you?"

"Why would they?"

"They despise the Apaches. I'm sure they don't discriminate between the tribes."

"The Aravaipas in the canyon were the ones who kidnapped her." He stared at her. His eyes seemed to smolder. She was conscious of her heartbeat. "Can we make a pact?" he went on. "Agree not to talk about the Apaches ever again?"

"That's fine with me. We're not going to solve anything arguing."

"All we'll do is wear each other down. I'd much rather we be friends, because I've got enough enemies already."

"It's a deal, Marcus."

She shook his injured hand with exaggerated gentleness. He thanked her and started toward the door, but then turned back.

"Would you, I mean—"

"What?"

"Perhaps, I mean if you've nothing better to do, ahem, go for a buggy ride Sunday afternoon? If you're not busy, if—"

She brought her hands up defensively. "Please, I'd be delighted."

He glowed. "Great. I'll pick you up at your place at two. Is that okay?"

"Fine."

She went to the window and watched him ride away. He took it for granted she would be looking; he waved good-bye without turning back. Of all the gall! She laughed.

The patient groaned and awoke. She gave him a glass of water and helped him into his shirt. He paid her and left. By that time the vigilantes' wagon had rolled off and the plaza was deserted. The dying sun flung long shadows across the area.

She tidied up, locked up, and went home. She was secretly thrilled that she had accepted Captain Marcus Venable's invitation, but she knew she would have to set him straight on Sunday. As much as she liked him, she simply was not ready for another man in her life.

12

Tom Vidall and his friends had attacked an Indian camp earlier in the year, so he was the group's natural leader. He was an unusual man. Unlike most loudmouthed hotheads, he backed up his words with actions. Roughly half of the men who followed him had lost relatives or friends to the Apaches, and they saw this as their chance to even the score. Right, they knew, was on their side; every white man, every Mexican, every Papago in southern Arizona stood with them.

This time they didn't need the Army. Every man among them was confident that they would never again need "bluebelly help." They rendezvoused at Sam Hughes's house that night. Hughes was a slender, balding, black-eyed Welshman who had come to the area in 1858. He had gone to California with the forty-niners; he had been a professional cook, and his services at the diggings were much in demand. With his profits he bought a hotel and invested in mines and cattle. His lungs went bad, however, and he was heading for a warmer climate in Texas when he camped with a small party beside a Tucson irrigation ditch in May of 1858. It was said that he had been hemorrhaging so badly when he reached Gila Bend two days before that he could hardly go on.

Tucson became his home from the first day. In a matter of hours he was in business. He traded a good harness for some grain and sold the grain. He then went into butchering. He made money fast until the war broke out, buying and selling grain and meat to the Overland Stage Company and supplying stations between Maricopa Wells and Apache Pass. He married fourteen-year-old Atanacia Santa Cruz in the old church at San Xavier early that spring. Hughes welcomed the vigilantes hospitably. Vidall and a handful of others were put up in the house; the rest would sleep in the barn. At Hughes's suggestion Vidall posted a guard where the road crossed the Canada del Oro north of town to keep any messengers from carrying a warning to Camp Grant. No one suspected that Colonel Schreiber had already alerted Willoughby of their intentions, but neither Schreiber nor Venable could be sure Willoughby would act on the warning.

The vigilantes drank, planned, and slept. Shortly before dawn they reassembled and moved out. By the time the sun lifted free of the Tortolitas, they had surrounded the Aravaipas' *ranchería*, sealed off both ends of the canyon, and moved to the attack.

Venable and a dozen volunteers stayed a mile behind them. From the outset it was clear that their help would not be needed. The whites, Mexicans, and Papagos poured a fierce volley into the sleeping camp. In minutes more than a hundred Indians perished.

The sound of gunfire confined to the canyon was ear-splitting, even a mile away. Lieutenant Gaines stood with his binoculars fixed on the near end of the canyon.

"I can't see anything, Captain, only smoke. But from the sound of it they're not getting any return fire."

"They caught them asleep," replied Venable, but his sense of relief was overwhelmed by a deepening sadness.

"Shall we move up for a closer look?" Gaines asked.

"They don't need our help. Let's get out of here."

Sergeant Brennan protested. "Can't we at least ride up for a look, Captain?"

"What's the matter, Sarge, no bloodbath this week?" piped a man behind him. "Life getting boring?"

"Shut up, Ainsley, nobody asked you."

"Let's go," said the captain.

Vidall dismounted and with Sam Hughes watched the Papagos. The Indians set about raping the surviving squaws and methodically mutilating the bodies, slicing throats, scalping; one cut out an old man's heart, holding it up dripping, yelling triumphantly. Then he flung it away. Wickiups were set on fire. Children were clubbed to death. Death and destruction reigned.

"It's going to be a lovely day, Thomas," ventured Hughes.

Vidall said nothing. His brow was crinkled in thought. "Something's wrong here. Where's the men?"

"What you say?"

"There's no braves; only them two old men there, and the women and children."

"Bless my soul, I believe you're right."

They wandered among the bodies. A squaw screamed behind them. Both turned. A Papago had just finished raping her. He jumped to his feet; she caught his leg and tried to pull him down, but he bent over and punched her viciously. Vidall and Hughes turned their backs and resumed examining corpses.

"Where the hell *are* the men, do y'all think?" Vidall looked confused.

"Out hunting or powwowing with another tribe. I think we should collect ourselves and get out of here."

Vidall ordered the men to mount up. At least forty of the Papagos ignored him.

Sutherland and Venable stood at attention as Schreiber welcomed Willoughby into the office.

"At ease," growled the newcomer.

Willoughby was ten years younger than Schreiber, a strapping fellow, broad-shouldered, powerful-looking, not at all the physical personification of the classic bookworm Schreiber had touted him as being. He had a tireless vigor about him that tired the onlooker, so Schreiber claimed. At the moment, though, the impression he conveyed to both Venable and Sutherland was the last thing on Willoughby's mind.

"There's going to be red hell to pay for this hoedown,"

Willoughby rasped. "Those hotheads killed two grown
men. Only two, Justin. Goddamned Papagos carted off
twenty-five or thirty kids captive. Raped the women practically to death. All told, my men counted one hundred
and four dead, eight males—only two grown, as I said—
the rest women and children. Christ Jesus, wait'll Prescott gets wind of this. Crook'll hang me out to dry. And
the War Department, the newspapers back East . . .
there'll be holy hell to pay. You warned me it was coming, Justin. I should have set up picket lines at both ends
of the canyon. To tell the truth, I never dreamed the sons
of bitches would go through with it. Never have before.
Not on this scale. Of course, the Apaches never kidnapped and violated a white woman before, leave her for
dead and all . . ."

Willoughby dropped into a chair, clasping the back of
his bull neck with both hands, shaking his head.

"Hell to pay, yes sir . . ."

Schreiber had a strange look on his face, Venable
noted. It was part compassion for the man, part relief
that blame would not be laid at his doorstep. Willoughby
readily admitted he had no one to blame but himself. He
had chosen to ignore what could only be termed fair
warning. He babbled on about what a fool he had been,
and at length let slip the key reason for his failure to take
steps.

"I'd been reading as usual. I love nothing in this world
better than a good book. And I had a good one. Any of
you boys familiar with E.A. Poe's works? Fascinating
writer. I was reading a thing called 'The Descent into the
Maelstrom,' about a fisherman who escapes a whirlpool.
Most absorbing story I think I've ever read."

He looked upward in appeal to the colonel, then to
Venable and Sutherland.

"I couldn't put it down." His eyes continued to entreat
understanding. "I'm afraid I didn't read your message
until just before bedtime, Justin."

"I guess I didn't make it sound all that urgent," said
Schreiber, trying to ease the man's suffering conscience.

"But you did. I just didn't think they . . ." His voice
trailed off for a moment. " 'Descent into the Maelstrom,' "
he finally added. "Remember the title. You'll want to
read it yourselves."

* * *

Neither Marion nor Artemus talked about the vigilantes' triumph, though overblown descriptions of the action floated about town all week. Vidall and the other whites who had taken part were pedestaled as authentic heros and offered free drinks by the town's saloon keepers, including Augustus Brichta, who had helped to initiate the reprisal, but with Solomon Warner and Horace Pennington had stayed behind. The heroes of the hour earned the rapidly recovering Larcena Pennington's praise and gratitude, were interviewed by and quoted in the *Tucson Weekly Arizonan*, and serviced gratis by the admiring prostitutes from Mama Consuelo's crib and gambling house.

Marion worked evenings sewing her new curtains. Working by lamplight was tiring on the eyes. She got a letter off to Gabriel. She went to bed. Tyson no longer came to mind at night; he had been replaced by thoughts of Marcus Venable, and the guilt continued to mount inside her. By Wednesday morning she found herself wishing Sunday's buggy ride had already come and gone, and the understanding between them made clear. She was not ready.

Thursday night found her sleepless and thinking of Marcus—again. She lay back in bed and recalled their last meeting. She saw his eyes as she cut away his cast. Sad, wistful eyes mutely asking her attention. She saw him ride away from the office, and she remembered thinking how lonely his life must be. As lonely as her own?

A loud knocking broke into her fantasy. She jerked upright. The knocking became insistent pounding.

"*Doctora, Doctora* . . ."

"Just a minute. *Momento!*"

She threw on her peignoir, pulled open the door, and unbolted the outer door. A small boy with coffee-colored skin and enormous brown eyes stood clutching a wretchedly frayed sombrero.

"Come quick."

"What is it?"

"Come, come, *emergencia!*"

She ran back inside, slipped into her mules, snatched up her bag, and followed him into the night. I'm dressed like a visiting spirit, she thought. She had no idea what time it was. A gossamer haze shrouded the moon, and the few visible stars looked to be on the verge of burning out. The air was unaccountably still, not a whisper of a breeze, lending an aura of eeriness to the silent, sleeping town. The boy towed her along, babbling animatedly. She failed to catch a word. They half-ran down Pearl Street, across Main near the old Mexican barracks and up Alameda to a house set far back from the street and fronted by a neat garden that resembled Inez Alou's. Yellow light filled an upstairs window. They hurried up the walkway. The door opened to reveal Solomon Warner in a nightshirt and cap, holding a lamp. He looked grief-stricken.

"Hurry, hurry."

They rushed upstairs to a corner bedroom at the front of the house. An emaciated, deathly pale boy lay under the covers. His mother sat holding his slender hand. His eyes were closed; he looked dead, but he was breathing. Barely. Mrs. Warner stood up, letting go of his hand. It fell lifelessly.

"Doctor . . ."

Solomon had come into the room behind Marion. He nodded to the Mexican boy, who had been staring at the sleeping boy. He left.

"Jeremiah's been ill," said Solomon. "We both thought he was just running down, losing his appetite. Nothing serious. But in the last couple hours he's been getting worse and worse."

"He's dying," said Mrs. Warner bluntly.

"Emmaline, no!"

She was nearly as frail as her son, but she was pretty, her hazel eyes flecked with gold. She wore her blond hair knotted at the back of her head so tightly it seemed to stretch her face, one that confirmed the suffering raging inside her at the moment.

"He's dying," she repeated.

Solomon brought a chair for Marion. She pulled down the covers and listened with her stethoscope. His heartbeat was unnaturally rapid.

"Come along, Em."

"You can stay," said Marion.

She got out a tongue depressor and supported the back of the boy's head while she examined his mouth.

"Hold the lamp, please, so I can see."

Solomon did so. The boy was awake now. His eyes were glazed and floated uncertainly, and his breathing was labored. His skin had an unhealthy pallor, as did the mucous membranes in his mouth. She pulled the covers down all the way. His ankles were swollen.

"We were talking about an hour ago," said his mother. "He fell asleep in the middle of a sentence."

"I think he fainted," said Marion. "How old are you, Jeremiah?"

"Nine," said his mother.

"Have you had any headaches?"

"Today," said his mother. "For the first time. I gave him hot peppermint tea. Was that all right?"

"Yes," Marion assured her.

"His headache went away."

"But come back," said the boy, speaking for the first time and with difficulty.

"Came," his mother corrected.

She met Marion's eyes. They begged her to do something, to cure him. Marion stood up and closed her bag, then smoothed the covers, tucking them under the boy's chin.

"Does your head ache now, Jeremiah?"

"A little."

"I'll give him more peppermint tea," Emmaline replied immediately.

Marion opened her bag. She fumbled in the pocket and brought out a small bottle. "Give him one of these now and first thing in the morning. Just one with a full glass of water."

"Yes, yes . . ."

Emmaline hurried out. Marion felt Jeremiah's forehead as she brushed his hair back. He was running a slight fever. Fever was the least of his worries, she reflected. She walked down the hall with Solomon. They sat in a parlor dominated by a large parlor organ. A handsome oak regulator clock tirelessly ticked away the night. She could hear Mrs. Warner getting water in the kitchen.

"Will he . . . ?" began Solomon.

"Your son is very ill."

"What is it?"

"I'll need to take a little blood to examine under the microscope. I don't want to alarm you, but even without examining it the symptoms are clear. Anemia."

"Bad blood? Jeremiah? But he's just a boy. How—"

"Not bad in the sense you mean. It's weakened. You might say diluted. It's not carrying enough oxygen to the tissues."

"You're sure it's anemia."

"All the symptoms point to it."

"Can you help him?"

"Mr. Warner—"

"Oh my God. Oh no . . . Don't, please don't say anything to Emmaline. I beg you. There's nothing you can do? Not a blessed thing?"

"I'll do everything I can."

"But he's doomed. That's what you're saying. How could this be? How could it come on so suddenly?"

"Perhaps it didn't. Perhaps neither you nor his mother noticed his gradual loss of energy, his ankles swelling. He didn't complain."

"He wouldn't. He's a soldier, that boy. You're saying if we'd known in time something could have been done."

"No."

"He'll die, won't he? I mean, just like that it's all over for him."

"Please, Solomon, don't force me to make absolute statements."

"Speak! You call yourself a doctor!" He caught himself. "I'm sorry, forgive me."

Mrs. Warner came in with the glass of water. From her expression it was clear that she had overheard every word. She looked ready to faint. She did, dissolving in a heap, the pill dropping, the glass striking the floor, bouncing, spilling its contents. Warner picked her up and laid her on the couch.

"I'll get the water for his pill," he said.

"I will," said Marion. "Get a cold compress for her head."

She gave Jeremiah his pill.

"Go to sleep."

He tried a smile of appreciation and closed his eyes.

She turned the lamp down to a little crescent of light; it went out, plunging the room into darkness. She left quietly. Solomon was waiting for her at the bottom of the stairs.

"How long does he have?"

"I honestly can't say."

"Did you take the blood?"

"It can wait till tomorrow. I'm terribly sorry to have to say it, but it probably won't make any difference."

"You're absolutely sure? There's no chance?"

Her silence, her face said she was. Solomon sighed. He suddenly looked twenty years older.

"I'll have to tell her. It'll kill her," he said.

"It won't."

"She's not like you, she's not strong."

"Mothers can surprise you at how strong tragedy can make them. She'll bear up. Is he your only child?"

He nodded. "You'll be by in the morning?"

"First thing." Marion nodded reassuringly.

"We're very grateful. We'll pray. I'll go to church. I don't make a habit of it. God can help us; he will. God bless you, Doctor."

"Good night."

Before going to the office the next morning she stopped in at the Warners'. The moon-faced maid answered the door. Mrs. Warner was upstairs with Jeremiah. When Marion walked in she was struck by her appearance. She looked as if she hadn't slept in days.

"He's the same," she murmured. "He's having a terrible time getting his breath."

Marion explained the reason for this, adding, "He'll get enough. Did he wake up at all, at any time?"

"No. I've been sitting here for hours."

"You shouldn't. It's no good to him, and you'll do yourself harm. You need your rest. He'll be looking to you for strength."

"Yes."

Emmaline looked and sounded as if she had little to give, Marion reflected. How she hated discussing death or impending death with helpless loved ones, mother and father clinging to the worthless hope of recovery.

"I can give you something to help you sleep."

"I don't need anything, thank you."

"I have to take a blood sample."

She got out the syringe. She wiped the needle with alcohol and took a small quantity from a vein in his forearm. He slept through it.

"I apologize for caving in last night," said his mother.

"Believe me, I'd be taking it just as hard if he were mine."

"You wouldn't. You're a doctor."

Why do people seem to think that exempts me from feeling certain emotions, Marion wondered.

"How long does he have?" Emmaline asked shakily.

"I can't even guess until I examine his blood," Marion replied.

"When you know, I want to know. Solomon thinks I'm a weakling."

"He doesn't." Marion tried to sound as if this were nonsense, but she was hardly successful.

"But," Emmaline went on, "I can reach down and find strength when I need it. I have in the past. No more fainting, I promise. I'm glad Jeremiah didn't see it."

"He's such a handsome boy. And all boy."

"He's a jewel. Obedient, reliable, always cheerful. Never a whisper of complaint. I spoil him. Solomon says I do. But he's our only child, our world. How can I help it? He's exceptionally bright. Augustus Brichta says he's the most intelligent child he's ever taught. He reads books children twice his age read. He wants to be a teacher. Isn't that something? Nine years old and he's already planning his future."

She began to cry softly. Marion went around to the other side of the bed and put her arm around her. Jeremiah awoke.

"Mother . . ."

She straightened stiffly, sniffled, swiped at her eyes, and smiled. "Good morning, sleepyhead. How do you feel?"

"Okay, I guess."

"Headache?" Marion asked.

"Gone."

"Good. Jeremiah, your mother's going to give you some beef broth. That's a different breakfast, isn't it? You must promise you'll eat every drop."

"I like beef broth."

"Good boy. I'll be back this afternoon. I'll be coming every day."

She went out with his mother. "Beef broth and all the red meat you can get down him. We have to build up his blood."

"Is my boy going to die?" Emmaline struggled to keep her voice from breaking.

A moment of deafening silence was all the answer Mrs. Warner needed. Marion's heart tugged as the woman's expression slipped back into grief. She set a comforting hand on her shoulder.

"You and I are going to work; we'll build him up so he'll be able to bend iron bars. Give him lots of beef. All the red meat he can eat. I'll be back as soon as I've looked at this blood under the microscope."

Marcus stopped the buggy by a lush patch of soft, red sand dock. Tell him, Marion said to herself as he helped her down. Be fair to him. But the prospect of broaching the topic only threatened to ruin the afternoon.

And a glorious afternoon it was, the sun baking the world—too hot, as usual, but she was getting used to it. Prickly poppy grew close by, flaunting its lovely delicate white blossoms next to the prickly pear, its woolly areoles supporting large golden-yellow flowers.

"My private garden," said Marcus.

"Lovely."

"This time of summer it's at its best." He picked her a small bunch of sand dock, setting a prickly pear flower in the center. "I come here to be by myself and think."

"About what?" she asked.

"Mostly times gone by. Back when I was young and free of everything: responsibility, cares, woes, common sense. In those days I owned the world." He laughed. "At least the state of Ohio."

They had moved into the shade of a large mesquite tree. Its gnarled and twisted trunk was riddled with holes drilled by ladder-backed woodpeckers. Above them a host of yellow butterflies assaulted masses of pendant yellow flowers.

"Tell me about back then," she murmured.

"It's pretty dull."

"I'll be the judge, Captain."

He caught himself gazing at her again, entranced by her beauty.

Marion peered curiously at him. "What's on your mind? I know I've got Jeremiah Warner on mine. He's dying, poor child, and all I can do is stand by and watch him go. I feel like my hands have been cut off."

"What *can* you do? You're not God."

"People seem to think doctors can work miracles. I can't remember any case quite so discouraging." The feeling of helplessness prompted a small sigh.

"How is Larcena Pennington doing?" he asked.

"Surprisingly well. She's rugged. Not too many women could survive what she went through. She's Artemus's patient, which I'm sure she prefers. My attitude toward the Indians annoyed her before. She must despise me now."

"I doubt it. She's sarcastic and she can be childish, but she's not vicious. She wouldn't be as popular as she is." He glanced down at the bouquet in her hand. "You don't have to hold those flowers all afternoon," he said with a smile.

He took them from her, setting them on the buggy seat. When he came back she had reached up to pick a flower from a low branch. She twirled it and inhaled its fragrance.

She mesmerized him. He knew he wouldn't tell her, because he couldn't tell anyone but himself. Standing so close to her, it was all he could do to keep his hands by his sides. He wondered if her husband's death was still fresh in his mind. Perhaps she needed someone, man or woman, to whom she could reveal her innermost thoughts.

"Ohio," she repeated and smiled.

"Lorain, Ohio. Actually Charleston. Only everybody who lives there calls it Lorain."

"Were you born there?"

He nodded. "My father owns a drygoods store. I hated working there, being cooped up while all my friends were enjoying the great outdoors. Such as it is in Lorain."

"Did you have a girlfriend?"

"My very special girlfriend was Annie Ritchards. Her father was the neighborhood barber. Every time he cut my hair I was afraid he'd cut an ear off."

"He didn't like you?"

"I was going with his daughter. I'm sure he imagined the worst. But I was a perfect gentleman with Annie. After all, we were in love. We were only fifteen, but we thought we were in love. She wanted to get married."

"Every girl who falls in love at fifteen wants to. Fourteen, even twelve. I did with my cousin. He was only about thirty."

"But she was dying to settle down. The older we got, the worse it got. The way she constantly harped on it finally turned her against me. We stopped seeing each other. After I left for the Army I heard she married Walter Bystrom, the banker's son. He was sickly and deaf in one ear, ineligible for service. By now they probably have fifteen kids and argue and fight and make up and drag each other hand in hand through a great hulking bore of a marriage."

"How do you know that?"

She was looking upward again. A young quail, barely visible through the mass of flowers, was sitting on a branch near the top of the tree. Its sudden arrival sent a squadron of butterflies fleeing. Undaunted, the vermilion flycatcher remained.

"I don't. Sour grapes." He grinned.

She liked his smile. It was warm and genuine. "But you didn't want to marry her. Would you rather she became an old maid?"

"Oh no, I wouldn't have cared if she married Chester Carmicheal. He was our village idiot. He used to eat worms and beetles and sit on people's roofs all night. And he played the banjo."

"I think she's better off with Walter."

"She probably turned out to be a good wife and mother. She sure wanted to be both. She never stopped telling me. Annie Ritchards. Blond, pretty, cute—and persistent." He shuddered and grinned again. "Your turn. Tell me about Baltimore and your first flame."

"Oh no . . ."

"Why not, was he the village idiot?"

She threw back her head and laughed merrily. Her throat was beautiful, the skin flawless, a flush of pale pink on ivory. He wanted to kiss it. He couldn't resist it.

He kissed her throat, locking her to him with one arm around her back. She stiffened and spun free.

"I'm sorry, I'm sorry," he whispered.

Her reaction was impossible to read. It was neither anger nor pleasure, but her eyes blazed.

"I'm sorry," he repeated. It sounded pitiful. He felt like a total ass and knew that he looked like one. "I—"

"Forget it," she murmured. "Let's go back."

"But we just got here. It's not even three." He cleared his throat, and straightened himself. "I take it back, Marion."

She looked directly at him. "What?"

"I'm not sorry. I shouldn't have said it. I want to hold you, kiss you—"

"Marcus—"

"I can't help it. What's so terrible about it?"

She had sighed and turned away. The flycatcher fluttered its wings furiously, as if to test their strength, then flew off in a series of graceful dippings and risings. In seconds it was a speck vanishing into the sun.

"Take me back," she said. "It can't happen, Marcus."

"But it can if you want. And you do—"

"I don't."

It was pointless to talk further about it. He helped her onto the buggy seat. She picked up her flowers, and, for want of something to do with her hands, rearranged them. They drove back to town without either of them speaking. He let her off at the gate. She clutched her drooping bouquet and looked up at him.

"Good-bye, Marcus."

"Good-bye, Marion."

He sat on the edge of his bunk fully clothed except for his boots. They stood leaning slightly by his left leg. It was just past eleven-thirty. The darkness tightly pocketed the fort, crept through the open window, and seeped into his soul. It had taken him the rest of the day to dismiss the Sunday afternoon disaster. Even now her words came back with their painful finality.

It was as frustrating as it was discouraging. How was he to compete with Tyson Sturges? How does one deal with a memory, one so firmly entrenched and protected in the fortress of her heart? Tyson was dead, but her love and loyalty to him seemed to hold fast as time went on. Yet the suspicion lingered that, despite her rebuffing him, deep down she yearned for him as intensely as he did for her. Or was it only his ego encouraging self-delusion?

Outside on the near side of the parade ground he could hear the guard reporting to the officer of the day making the rounds: "All quiet and correct, sir." It snapped him from his daydream and back to the present. The looming problem was no longer Marion, but Willoughby. Would General Crook replace the hapless colonel? Would he make the rounds of the posts and lecture the commanders? Crook had his own reputation to protect. He had always dealt honorably with the Indians wherever he commanded, which was more than could be said of Sherman or Phil Sheridan. It wouldn't surprise him if Crook made an example of Willoughby for the rest of the CO's by throwing him to the wolves bone by bone.

No general in the Army better knew the importance of a combat reputation, and Crook kept his well burnished, even to bringing along news correspondents every time he made a tactical move. The biggest prize of all was yet to be garnered. Justin Schreiber was right: Geronimo would eventually develop into the most painful thorn in all their ambitions. Crook would go after him personally. Marcus was suddenly consumed with the desire to go with him.

Geronimo was in the future; the question of the moment was where and how would the Apaches retaliate for the attack on the Aravaipas' *ranchería*? The braves who had been out hunting at the time, probably for deer, would now substitute pale eyes for their quarry. If Schreiber were smart he'd billet twenty men in town from now on.

Venable marveled at the residents. It obviously did not occur to anyone that Vidall and his cronies had put them squarely on the spot. The Indians could ride in in force, spill blood from one end of town to the other, and be halfway to the Mexican border before the troops got there.

Damn Willoughby!

The fort slept save for the men on guard duty and the players in the all-night poker game in Barracks B. Someone called to Venable through the partially opened window. He went to it, crouching, squinting into the darkness. Olan brought his face up close.

"Visitor, Captain."

"This time of night?" Marcus looked up suspiciously.

"It's the doctor."

13

Marcus had no idea that Marion's spirits were even lower than his since they had said good-bye. She had watched him drive away, then gone in and put the sand dock and lone mesquite blossom in a vase. Going back outside, she sat in the garden and took in the vivid colors and arrival and departure of birds, butterflies, and dragonflies, and plunged into thought. She discovered that he had not really left with his buggy, but merely taken refuge in her conscience.

Why had she treated him so terribly? Though she had intended to set him straight, she never intended to do it so abruptly. It would hardly have been worse for him if she had screamed at him. Her eyes were drawn to the century plant rising above the top of the wall. It bloomed only once, then died. This seemed to be the ultimate termination for everything—even friendship.

Was this the way it was going to be from now on? Every time a man got close to her would she push him away? If so, the shell she formed around her heart would thicken as the years went by, never to be broken open. What sort of future was that to look forward to? Her glance drifted to the old lady cactus.

A breeze stirred the vermilion-flowered rattail in its

basket, hanging from the top of the wall across from where she sat. She stirred, turning to look toward the gate. She pictured him standing there smiling. She blinked and he was gone. The saddest part was he had not left; she had driven him away. The realization that she might only see him once more, to remove the flexible cast and pronounce his hand fit, dropped her into gloominess.

Now she sat on the buggy seat in the darkness, reins in hand, waiting. A three-quarter moon slid from behind a cloud, painting the parade ground a ghostly gray, the color of her mood. The flagpole stood stark, white, and bare. A passing breeze snapped its ropes against it lightly. A figure emerged from the darkness and came toward her. She wound the reins around the brake handle and got down.

"Marcus—"

He did not answer; he drew closer, raising his arms, embracing her, kissing her passionately. She submitted. His lips were soft, warm, capturing hers and in a fleeting moment she knew it was all over. Her defenses were swept away and her heart threatened to shatter as it pounded wildly.

He stood holding her, their lips parted. One last doubt sent up a final warning as it left: stop before it's too late. But it was already too late. She was surrendering, rushing, throwing herself into love. Or had she fallen earlier? He kissed her eyes and around her mouth and down her neck; she wilted and pushed against him, yielding.

He had driven her back to town.

"Come in," she said, "I'll make tea."

He held up his flexible bandage. "Can this come off? It's past midnight: seven days."

She laughed. Inside, she removed it and examined his hand. "It's knit perfectly. Any discomfort?"

He flexed it. "Not a bit. Thank you, Doctor, I owe you."

They didn't finish their tea. How they got to the bedroom neither knew nor cared. She lit the lamp, turning the flame as low as she could without extinguishing it.

"It's all going so fast my head's spinning," she said quietly.

"Because it's been delayed so long for us both," he said. "It's all pent up inside us."

"We're so lucky to have found each other."

He was looking toward the corner at the vase with the wildflowers in it. The water had revived them. He felt the same, as if he had been picked up, straightened, and set on a whole new path. And there she stood facing him, arms out to welcome him.

She began to unbutton his shirt. No more words passed between them, not a sound except their breathing. How could she not hear his heart drumming? he wondered. Presently they lay naked on top of the covers. He reached to turn off the lamp.

"Don't. I want to see your face. The rest of my life," she added.

His hand was warm; the fire in his fingers set the side of her neck aglow and a tremor passed from it down her breast, down her body. He brushed her neck with his lips, then kissed it lightly, teasingly. She marveled at his body. He was every inch sinewy grace, lithe, lean, and hard, pulsing with vigor, with the leashed power and energy of a panther. And yet he was so tender, knowing just where to touch her and how.

He began to caress her breast with delicate, feathery strokes, raising her nipple. She felt him stiffen against her. The spark ignited, the flames leaped and coursed through her, reaching every extremity, and massing about her thundering heart, leaving only the echo. She gasped and moaned as his gliding fingers found her and touched her everywhere. She whispered his name. But he did not answer; for him it had moved past words, even sounds into that realm of ecstasy ruled by the senses. He drew her into the golden circle of his passion. She raised her hips over his body, and he slowly entered her.

She sucked in her breath so sharply it sounded like a knife slicing leather. As she raised and lowered herself against his hips, she pressed her hands to his chest as she drove him deeper, swaying and rocking on top of him. They moved wildly as one, increasing the tempo and intensity of their love until their spines stiffened, arched, held, and they exploded together. She could think of just one thing as her mind still whirled and crashed around her: the fervent prayer that it would never end.

14

Marion straightened and stood aside. Artemus peered into the microscope.

"You say you give the boy a week? I say you're being too generous." He growled irritably deep in his throat. "That's not blood, it's water."

"I have to tell his parents."

"Go to the store and tell Solomon. He'll tell her."

"I promised her I'd be back." She paused. Even though she had known what would show under the microscope, the sight of it had shocked her. "I'll stop by the store on my way."

A pretty, perky young girl was behind the counter. She wore a starched apron over her puff-shouldered calico dress, and her long chestnut hair was braided and bound with strips of calico.

"Mr. Warner's not here. He said he was going to church."

Tucson had neither a Protestant church nor minister. She found Solomon sitting on the rear bench of San Augustan Church. Votive candles flickered in their racks before the altar. A large wooden cross painted gold stood at the rear. Dust hung in the sunlight slanting through the windows and whitened the aisle. The church had been built the year before by an energetic and dedicated priest, Father Donato Rogieri.

Born in Italy, he had spent five years in the Holy Land and could speak Arabic. No one knew what had brought him all the way to Arizona, but his heart must have dropped to his rib cage when he arrived in his new parish and found no house of worship, not even a favorite place under a tree for the faithful to gather. Within a week he was supervising the building of Tucson's first church. He went about it in ingenious fashion. He knew it would have to be built a little at a time and with next to no money. Within three weeks the concrete foundation was in place and it was time to raise the walls. The adobes were made on the property of Solano Leon near the edge of town. When services were over every morning, Father Donato would tell his congregation not to leave until he changed his robes. Then he would instruct them to follow him and they would go to Solano Leon's and each man, woman, and child would return carrying one brick. Father Donato would carry two. In this way the entire church was built.

Before it was completed, confident that it would be, Father Donato left. He was a restless soul and went looking for other fields to conquer. A few weeks later word came back that he had been killed by Apaches on the road from El Paso to Chihuahua.

Solomon heard Marion approaching and turned. He read her expression correctly.

"No hope?"

"I'm so sorry, Solomon."

"How long?"

"Perhaps a week; not much beyond that, I'm afraid."

He sat for a long moment taking her words in, examining them like berries, looking for edible ones, yearning more and more for the sweet taste with every discard. He found none.

His face began to redden; fire ignited his dark eyes. He shot to his feet trembling, his cheeks quivering. He growled and turned, shaking his fist at the altar.

"Goddamn you! I pray to you, this is the thanks I get! You miserable bastard! What kind of god murders innocent children? What heartless bastard!"

Marion watched wide-eyed, fearing that Solomon's impassioned ranting would suddenly turn violent. For a moment he stood with his arms outstretched, gazing blankly toward the ceiling. Then he fell to his knees, and his last bitter exclamation caught in his throat.

"You murdered my boy!"

"No, you'll only toss them out when my back is turned. [I]'ll keep them here. The sprayer goes to the office."

"It still looks like a coffeepot."

Captain Venable did not suggest to Colonel Schreiber [th]at twenty men be permanently billeted in town to pro[v]ide protection against the Apaches who might attack in [re]prisal for the Aravaipa Canyon massacre. His reason [fo]r not doing so was simple. The soldiers had a poor [re]putation among the people they'd been assigned to [p]rotect; whenever they visited Tucson they generally got [d]runk, got into trouble, took their frustrations and their [lo]neliness out on civilians. An even stronger argument [a]gainst posting men in town was the fact that the major[it]y of whites there were Confederate sympathizers and [c]ouldn't stand the sight of a blue uniform. Tucson's lead[in]g citizens—Solomon Warner, Augustus Brichta, and [H]orace Pennington among them—were from the North[e]ast, but a good seventy-five percent of the other whites [w]ere from states that had seceded, and the rebel flag and [r]ebel sympathies were much in evidence.

The Apaches bided their time. Colonel Willoughby suffered while he waited for the ax of authority to fall. Colonel Schreiber's cough came back, as both doctors knew it would, and he was sent back to bed. Captain Venable reassumed command at Fort Lowell. Tom Vidall went hunting.

Mark Aldrich opened his post office at seven-thirty the [s]econd morning after Jeremiah Warner's funeral. At one [t]ime Aldrich had been a successful businessman in Illi[n]ois before the gold fever infected him. He had been a [p]ersonal friend of Abraham Lincoln and Stephen Doug[l]as, husband of a lady of distinguished family and father [o]f several children, all of whom he abandoned when he [w]ent west to hunt gold.

Settling in Tucson after his mining days in 1860, he was [e]lected as the first American alcalde. He set up the [sh]ipping post in the military plaza and was making good [us]e of it in his efforts to control Tucson's criminal ele[me]nt when the turmoil raised by the murder of an un[nam]ed man convinced him that his fellow townsmen were [not] interested in cooperating with him. A number of [the]m witnessed the killing, but not one reported it or

---

●◀ 15 ▶●

Jeremiah Warner continued to fail, died peaceably and tragically, and was buried four days after Marion examined his blood sample. It was the most melancholy funeral she had ever attended. She stood over the grave opposite Emmaline, who seemed to be in a fog, paralyzed by her grief. Solomon stood beside her, furious; Marion half expected him to resume his ranting against God before Samuel Hughes could finish reading the verse from Ecclesiastes over the lowered coffin.

Marion had spent most of the previous four days at the Warners' house, keeping Emmaline company. It was, she thought, the least she could do; there was nothing medicine or surgery could do for the boy. Unlike her husband, Emmaline did not blame God for the tragedy. She blamed no one. Marion marveled at her willingness to accept the inevitable, once she recognized it as such. She was visibly suffering, but did not utter a syllable of complaint. Marion saw her fatalistic attitude as a shield against the pain of her loss, not preventing it, but perhaps numbing it. Throughout the four days, Emmaline concentrated all her efforts toward easing her son's discomfort, talking soothingly and lovingly to him hour after hour. She went without sleep, keeping her vigil through the nights. When Marion arrived at the house in the morning Solomon had already left for the store and Emmaline would be slumped over Jeremiah's bed asleep.

Marion knew in her heart that nothing in heaven or on earth could save the boy; the anemia was systematically destroying his blood and no amount of beef broth or red meat could reverse the pattern.

Her admiration for Emmaline's stoicism grew as the hours of dying dragged by. She lauded her to Artemus, who wisely commented, "Mothers have an astonishing reservoir of tolerance for tragedy, particularly that involving their flesh and blood. Fathers should only be so endowed." Such an observation coming from a staunch believer in the natural supremacy of the male surprised her.

Artemus also attended the funeral. It was mercifully brief; it occurred to Marion as it drew to a close that Jeremiah Warner, age nine, would be only the fifth deceased laid to rest in the cemetery to die of natural causes. She and Artemus paid their respects to the bereaved parents and started back to the office.

"I can handle things the rest of the afternoon," he said, "if you want to go over to their house and be with her. Solomon tells me you've been a cast steel buttress for her these past few days."

"She's been the buttress, Artemus. She's amazing. I don't think I should bother them now. I'll see her tomorrow."

"Did I tell you Colonel Schreiber has pronounced himself recovered and is back in command? Has been for nearly a week."

"He's being ridiculous. Damn!"

"What?"

"I haven't been out there in days. Too busy."

"You think you could have kept him in bed? In his chair? I told you at the start his masculinity would overrule his common sense."

"Not his masculinity, Artemus, his need to prove his manhood to himself. Men are such children," she concluded.

"That's a blanket indictment."

"Most men."

"I wouldn't worry about it; if he has a rel[...] have to get back in bed."

"He will. He's consumptive. His lungs are in [...] his life, not him."

They had come to within sight of the garden [...] on's house. Three large packages were stack[...] door.

"Mark Aldrich left them," said Artemus. "[...] from?"

"Gabriel Cowan."

Two were stacks of medical journals, includi[...] ple of dog-eared and well-worn copies of old [...] The third package was the promised carbolic acid[...]

"I told you he said he'd send it," she [...] him.

"What for?"

"Don't be dense."

"I know what it's for," he rasped. "I'm being [...] Absurd-looking contraption, looks like a coffeep[...] do we need with it? It'll only take up space, of w[...] have none."

"You've never read about Dr. Joseph Lister, have you? Have you even heard the name?"

"Only five hundred times from you."

"He noticed that his hands always came away [...] after an operation from the effect of the carboli[...] solution. But this device prevents it; it sprays a cl[...] yellowish mist. It covers every atom of the wou[...] distributes itself evenly, perfectly measured. All [...] to remember is to keep the windows closed. The [...] be absolutely still."

"You don't really think we'll use it."

"I will. And you, when you see how effective [...]"

"I'm sure."

"Artemus, why must you stubbornly resist [...] gestion, every idea I come up with for improvin[...]"

"I don't," he replied. "And if I do it's b[...] perfectly satisfied with the way things are."

"Ah, that's my point. Neither of us sho[...] satisfied, we should always be looking to im[...]"

"Ah, yourself. Spare me another of your [...] we have to lug these magazines to the offic[...]"

offered to testify. Aldrich resigned in disgust and took over the postmaster's job.

He lived with his Mexican mistress in rooms in the rear of the one-story building. When he opened the front door and stepped out for fresh air precisely at seven-thirty, he appeared to be the first Tucsonian to greet the new day. He glanced toward the military plaza. A shocking sight met his eyes.

Hanging from the whipping post was a man. Aldrich ran to him. When he got close enough to see his condition, it was all he could do to keep from wretching. Every inch of flesh had been peeled from his body. His eyes had been gouged from their sockets and replaced by dead scorpions. The blood had already dried in the early morning sun; he looked like he had been burnt at the stake, his body taken from the flames and painted red. His hair had been burned from his scalp. His face was a gory mass, his features all but indistinguishable.

But Aldrich recognized him. It was Tom Vidall. He had foolishly gone hunting alone the day before. But even if he had been with a dozen others, doubtless all would now be tied to the whipping post in the same grisly condition.

At eight o'clock the body was cut down and brought to Artemus Shaw's office. Why, neither Artemus or Marion had any idea, other than that the men who brought it in were simply at a loss as to what to do with it. Artemus took one look and offered a succinct observation:

"This boy died screaming."

They wrapped the body in a sheet, and later in the day Samuel Hughes officiated at his second funeral in a week.

The Apaches' revenge infuriated Vidall's cronies and most of the townspeople. A second vigilante group was speedily organized: another entry in the vicious circle. Mexicans and Papagos volunteered, swelling the ranks. More than a hundred men rushed off with fire in their eyes and no particular destination in mind.

Temporary CO Marcus Venable got wind of the escapade an hour after the vengeance seekers rode away. Which direction they had taken once they were out of sight was anybody's guess; annoyed and disgusted at the news, the captain refused to guess. It was Marion who told him about the return of Vidall's body and that the

vigilantes had gone back to work. She had driven
Artemus's buggy out to the fort to see the colonel. She
found him in bed coughing fitfully, spitting up flecks of
blood. He wore the sheepish expression of a small boy
whose hand had been caught in the cookie jar. She
resisted the temptation to castigate him roundly, settling
for a stern warning.

"The next time you decide you've recovered, send
somebody into town for me. Share the good news with
me."

"Yes, ma'am."

Venable, standing in the doorway to the colonel's room,
turned his head and slid a hand up to hide his grin. He
went back to his desk. Schreiber was eyeing Marion with
a gleam in his eye.

"Will I ever shake this damned thing? I know, not if I
keep getting up, but can it be cured? If it can't, tell me. I
can take it."

"It can be. You couldn't be in a better climate for a
cure."

"Am I too old to get rid of it completely, forever?"

"You're not exactly ancient. I can say this, I know of
few diseases involving lesions which manage to cure themselves the way consumptive lesions do. For some reason,
Nature tries her best in consumption. Of course, the
more acute, the longer it takes. You're back to spitting
up blood, we have to assume your condition is acute.
You've probably set yourself back to where you started
when I first saw you. But it did cure itself to some extent.
You stopped bleeding. If you'd stayed idle, eventually it
would have cleared up completely."

"How long?" He held his breath and squinched his
eyes.

"That's like asking how long you have to live. It's
impossible to answer. Your best medicine, and I'm repeating myself, is the outdoors: sunshine and fresh air.
Ideally, you should live like they do in the sanitariums in
Germany and Switzerland, in the open air twenty-four
hours a day, but of course sitting on the parade ground
all night every night—"

"I could."

"You might try it for a night. You'd have to bundle up
after sundown. You wouldn't have to stay awake."

"I do hate sitting out there, though. I feel so conspiciously frail; I present a sorry picture to the men. They see me as weak, helpless."

"Sit behind the building."

"I want to see what's going on."

"Sit wherever you want as long as it's in the sun. But don't start for a week. For the time being you're restricted to quarters."

"Yes, Doctor, whatever you say."

"No, Colonel, it's whatever you need."

She went out and closed the door. Marcus rose from behind the desk.

Marion sighed.

"If he doesn't do as he's told, he could be in and out of bed for the next two years. Keep an eye on him, Marcus."

"I will. Will I see you tonight?"

"If you don't come, I'll come here again. Which isn't easy, darling. I felt so embarrassed coming here last night."

"Why did you come?"

She cupped his cheek and kissed him fondly. "Seven o'clock. We'll have a candlelight dinner."

"It sounds delicious."

He came around the desk, embraced her, kissed her fervently. She broke free.

"Not here, Marcus, somebody'll see."

"Let them. I love you."

"You'd better. I'd hate to think I'm the only one who's lost his head."

"Seven, then."

He watched Olan help her onto the buggy seat. She threw him a kiss. Good, he thought, why *should* they keep it a secret? He suddenly wanted to climb up on the roof and announce it to the whole fort. The colonel's coughing broke into his musing. It kept up until he finally dozed off.

Moments later Olan burst in noisily. Marcus shot to his feet.

"What the hell—"

"Sorry, sir, important. Somebody here to see the col—"

It was as far as he got. In strode a cavalry sergeant, a saddler from the upright anchor symbol riding above the vee of the three stripes on his insignia. He oozed regular army: tough, proud, buttoned up, no nonsense. He stood aside holding the door, his chin high.

"InspectorGeneralMajorHamptonW.AllerdyceThird DepartmentalHeadquarters—DepartmentofArizona, GeneralGeorgeCrookcommanding."

Major Hampton W. Allerdyce III was in full cavalry dress, a luxuriant plume of dyed buffalo hair flowing from the brass pedestal atop his gold-eagle-emblazoned helmet, complete with sagging chain. His saber swung by the side of his double-breasted frock coat, the shoulders capped with gold epaulets, buttons gleaming, dress cord slung jauntily across his chest.

His boots shone as brightly as his buttons. He flung himself into a chair, the butt of his saber sheath banging the floor, pulled off his gloves, gestured with two fingers, and the sergeant withdrew. Captain Venable had gotten up at Olan's intrusion; he was still standing when the major sat down.

"Colonel Schreiber."

"The colonel's indisposed, sir. Down with consumption. I'm acting CO, Captain Marcus Venable."

"Venable, Venable; heard of you. Just come from town. Spoke with . . ." He paused and got out a notebook and pencil stub; he flipped pages. "Mr. Horace Pennington and Mr. Augustus Brichta. Investigating this sorry business with the Ara—Ara—"

"Aravaipas."

"The massacre. On my way up to Camp Grant. Answer me a few questions." He paused and looked toward the inner door. "Colonel's really sick, you say?"

"Very."

"Mmmm." The single utterance was heavily larded with doubt, but Allerdyce did not pursue it.

"You were present when Pennington and Brichta came here asking the colonel's help in apprehending the hostiles who had abducted Pennington's wife earlier. Somebody had determined that the ones up in the Ara—Ara —the canyon was responsible. Says here he turned down their request."

"The Aravaipa Canyon is out of our territory, sir."

"Mmmm. Camp Grant's."

"Yes, sir."

"Let me ask you—and this is important, so think before you answer."

Venable hated this, the Inspector General barging in, pinning him to the wall with questions. He had to protect the colonel, Willoughby, and everyone concerned. He didn't like Allerdyce; his head was swollen with his rank and the power of his job. He had the authority to push full generals into corners and browbeat them, and did it with pleasure.

"Did you or Colonel Schreiber warn Colonel Willoughby of the possibility that vigilantes would attack the hostiles' camp?"

"With all due respect, Major, shouldn't you be asking Colonel Willoughby?"

"I'm asking you. Answer me."

"Yes."

"Yes, sir," Allerdyce demanded.

"Yes, sir."

"So, correct me if I'm wrong: the attack went forward. Willoughby permitted it to; didn't lift a finger to stop it, *despite being forewarned.* Victims turned out to be almost exclusively squaws and children. Women raped, murdered; children carried off as slaves by the Papagos riding with the gang. Is that so?"

"That's what we heard, yes, sir."

"Any children been recovered?"

"Not that I know of, sir."

"You or anyone else, anyone you know make an effort to recover them?"

"No, sir."

"Not your responsibility."

"No, sir."

"Camp Grant's. Willoughby's. Question: when the dust settled, did you or Colonel Schreiber meet with him?"

"Yes, sir, he came here."

"He came here. You present?"

"Yes, sir."

"What was his state of mind? Was he contrite? Upset? Stunned, shocked, apologetic?"

"All of these things, sir."

"Did he admit he'd made a mistake?"

"Sir, I honestly think he's more qualified than I to answer that."

"Don't worry, I'll ask him when I see him. At the moment I'm asking you."

"You're asking me to characterize his inner feelings."

"Do it."

"He . . . well, he did confess that he'd made a mistake."

"Not heeding your warning."

"Yes, sir."

Allerdyce chuckled hollowly and snidely. "Mistake of his career. Towering boner. He's done for. Lucky if he gets off with a dishonorable discharge." He lunged to his feet. "Collins!"

The sergeant swung open the door. Out thumped the braid and gleaming brass of Hampton W. Allerdyce III. Olan came bustling in, eyes questioning.

"Close it, Olan."

He himself went to the colonel's door and opened it.

"You heard?"

"The whole fort heard. Poor Thaddeus. Poor, poor fellow."

Emmaline Warner was waiting for Marion at her door when she came back. She had on a short-sleeved pink-and-white frock with a lace collar.

"I guess you think I'm a hussy for not wearing mourning," she said, "but I can't. Our grief is in our hearts. We mourn in private."

Marion let her in, picking up a flat manila envelope leaning against the door. It was postmarked Philadelphia. "You don't have to explain to me," she said. "When I heard that my husband had been killed, I was stunned, of course, but I wouldn't wear black, either. Let's have a cup of tea, it won't take a second."

"I'd love some."

Marion put the pot on, readied the sugar and cups, and opened the envelope. There was no letter, only a few words scrawled inside the flap.

"Letter follows."

In the envelope were a number of newspaper headlines with the articles attached:

TUCSON INDIANS TAKE APACHE CHILDREN AS SLAVES

ARMY'S NEGLIGENCE RESULTS IN HORRIBLE MASSACRE OF INNOCENTS

WAR DEPARTMENT INVESTIGATING ARIZONA POST COM-
MANDER'S DERELICTION OF DUTY

INNOCENT SQUAWS AND WEE BABES MASSACRED BY
DRUNKEN VIGILANTES IN TUCSON, ARIZONA TERRITORY

TUCSON, ARIZONA. WHERE BARBARISM REIGNS!

There were more, mostly from Philadelphia and Baltimore papers. Marion crumpled them in a ball and dropped
it in the wastebasket. She was annoyed with Gabriel for
sending them, for digging her ribs with his elbow from
three thousand miles away.

"Who's Gabriel Cowan?"

"Doctor. We worked side by side at Wills Hospital
back in Philadelphia."

"A friend of yours?"

"An occasionally tactless friend. He didn't want me to
leave. He painted all sorts of grisly pictures of life on the
frontier."

"Most of which are turning out true."

They laughed. The water was boiling, so Marion prepared the tea.

"Marion, Solomon and I want you to come for dinner
tomorrow night. Can you?"

"I . . . of course, but are you sure—"

"I can play the smiling hostess? I'll try. It won't be any
fun if I'm a stump."

"That isn't what I meant—"

"Oh, it was, too!" Again she laughed. "You must come.
The last couple nights Solomon and I just sit and stare
at each other. We need to see people. I have a lovely
roast beef. Maybe later we can play whist. You do play?"

"It's been years. If you promise to bear with me . . ."

They chatted for another half hour. Emmaline finished
a second cup of tea. Marion marveled; she was determined to put the tragedy behind her without mourning,
brooding, or self-pity.

"I should be getting home," said Emmaline at length.
"Seven o'clock. Okay?"

"Fine. I'll wear my best dress. It's practically my only."

"Wait'll you see the roast beef."

*   *   *

Marion's "best dress" was a full skirt with slash pockets and her favorite Garibaldi blouse with epaulets and a single line of rickrack around the collar and cuffs. A double line escorted the buttons down the front. She also wore her mushroom hat with wide red ribbons trailing down the back, and satin pumps. She showed up promptly. Emmaline answered the door. Marion could hear the maid busy in the kitchen.

"Solomon's on his way. Inventory day. Let's sit and talk."

The delectable aroma of roast beef came wafting from the kitchen. They sat in the parlor. Marion eyed the upright organ.

"Do you play?" she asked.

"Solomon does. I don't know one note from another."

There was a pause. Sadness invaded the room and hung like early morning mist over a swamp. The struggle for emotional survival was beginning to wear on Emmaline.

"He was teaching Jeremiah," she added.

The silence continued. The clock ticked softly. The roast sizzled.

"Have you heard anything about the vigilantes?" Emmaline finally asked.

"I think they're still out looking," said Marion.

Emmaline clucked disapproval. "Riding around in circles a hundred miles from here. Begging to be attacked."

Like conversation about the organ, this promised to be neither cheerful or particularly interesting.

"How long have you and Solomon been here?" Marion asked.

"Since March of '58. Going on eight years." She rolled her eyes in a lighthearted plea for strength. "Sometimes it feels like eighty, but it's been more sweet than bitter. A lot more. Exciting, fascinating, satisfying, worth every drop of sweat."

"I'll bet you've seen some changes," she continued, happy to see Emmaline opening up.

"Oh, it's a whole different place from back then. When we got here it was still a sleepy Mexican village."

"No Americans?"

"A handful in town. A few ranchers and farmers around. When more came that's when the real changes began. It was Americans who built the first roads."

She was warming to the subject, eager to answer questions. And Marion was curious. Artemus saw Tucson through a narrow slit, in terms of the residents' injuries and illnesses for the most part. Emmaline knew the people who made things happen: the builders, improvers, the effectors of change. The first Americans had shrewdly recognized the great potential of the location, its destiny to provide Arizona's first stopover on the way to California. Emmaline's memory was an encyclopedia of facts and anecdotes. And she didn't depict her pioneering days in terms of a great struggle against discouraging odds, a battle for survival. Her story unfolded in funny, colorful, interesting facts and personal experiences: buying gold from an Indian at the back door; setting out every container they owned, from teacups to barrels, to catch a passing shower during the drought of the summer of sixty; their first Christmas without snow, carols sung around a stunted piñon pine serving as a Christmas tree.

"Marion, you should have seen us the first few weeks. We lived like hoboes with a hole in the ground for a necessary. I washed clothes in the river. The water turned everything we wore the color of coffee. Back then there was almost literally nothing here."

"Did the Indians cause much trouble?"

"Not a bit. The way we were living at the start, I'm surprised they didn't take pity and bring us food. They didn't start stirring things up until the whites began to pour in just before the war. *They* were the problem. Hardly a day passed without somebody getting shot and killed. In the streets, the military plaza. Tucsonians like to air their differences outdoors. Shootouts in the street are an institution around here. And whoever did the killing always got away with it. There was no law, no army, no authority of any kind apart from the alcalde. And he was helpless to stop the mayhem. As soon as we were able to move in here, we locked ourselves in nights. There was so much gunplay in the streets we slept with the windows closed on the hottest nights. It wasn't until Father Machebeuf, the vicar-general of the Catholic diocese of Santa Fe, came and brought religion that things began to quiet down. Somewhat. He had a knack for reaching people's consciences, for putting even the worst sort on their best behavior. I think it was the way he fulminated against the Devil. He sure put fear in the Mexicans' hearts, although they weren't the problem. He paved the way for Father Donato later on."

"How long have the Mexicans been here?"

"Ages, and some very good families. The Ochoas: Allagracia Ochoa is a sweetheart, she can't do enough for people. You'll meet her, you'll adore her. Then there are the Aguirres. He was a pioneer trader and rancher . . . the three Santa Cruz sisters."

"Did the Americans intermarry with the Mexicans?"

"Oh yes, Atanacia Santa Cruz married Sam Hughes when she was fourteen. I can think of a dozen intermarriages, but you really don't want to hear a slew of names of people you don't know."

Marion got her onto Solomon's store and business in general in Tucson.

"Business was piddling, we lived like mice in a poor box for the first few months. But gradually things picked up. Tucson was growing."

"How big was it before the war?"

"In 1860 we had six hundred permanent residents. Three stores, counting ours, two butcher shops, two blacksmith shops, livery stables. Just the one saloon." She laughed. "Our Mexican friends made enough pulque for everybody. Pulque is Mexican moonshine. And the stores sold tequila. Then Palantine Robinson began to advertise fine wines and liquors in his new place."

"But you had no police, no law?"

"Not until the Army came. Even back then we had hordes passing through. It was like a stranger opening your front door, walking through your house and out the back. Every day new faces in town."

"New guns."

"New blood. In the streets. As I said, Tucson's a natural way station. Freight was hauled from the West Coast through here from Guaymas on the Gulf of California. Men came through from the East heading for the gold fields. Settlers came through on their way to California. The transients caused most of the trouble."

"I've seen the cemetery."

"That's a small fraction of the people killed. Most of the bodies were dumped in the river."

"Did you and Solomon ever think of leaving?"

"We talked about it seriously, only by then we'd been here nearly five years. We'd worked like slaves to establish ourselves and the store. Solomon said it'd be sinful as well as cowardly to run off and leave it all. But for months and months life was absolute chaos. It was the wild West, Marion. Before Solomon set foot out the door to go to work, he strapped on a gun. We prayed it would change, life would get easier, less dangerous, civilization would find us. You should see your face, it says it must still be looking for us."

"It's not that bad."

"It's not Philadelphia."

"*I* like it."

"Why do you? Is it the challenge?"

"I like living in a new spot on the map that's young, growing, changing. I know I'm late getting here, but I still think of myself as a pioneer. Tucson's like a crude, clumsy child who doesn't know his own strength. It's exciting."

"It's never dull. I think of all the proper Bostonian ladies sitting back East sipping their tea, nibbling their scones, attending services in huge, beautiful granite and marble churches on Sunday, shopping, going to balls and formal parties, the theater, the opera. I think of them and feel sorry for them. Like Solomon says, people back there taste life; out here we swallow it whole."

The door opened. It was Solomon. With him in full dress uniform, a bouquet of desert poppies in one gloved hand, was Marcus. His jaw dropped, his eyes widened. The Warners had arranged a date for them! Emmaline fixed Marion with an odd but eloquent expression: *We tricked you. Don't be angry, we tricked him too.*

Marion's hand went to her mouth. It took every atom of willpower she could summon to hold back her laughter. Marcus stood smiling slyly, one tooth embedded in his lower lip to keep him from bursting out laughing.

Emmaline, meanwhile, had taken to looking as pleased with herself as a cat full of cream. Solomon was showing no reaction whatsoever. It was past seven-thirty; he'd put in a long day and he was famished.

16

Solomon's behemothian appetite seemed to be all the proof Emmaline needed that the roast beef was a success. The dinner as a whole was superb. Conversation was amusing, spontaneous, relaxed. Emmaline seemed surprised at how well and comfortably the couple she had "fixed up" hit it off.

The whist game turned out to be a minor catastrophe. Neither Marcus nor Marion were in a class with their hosts. After the second hand Solomon magnanimously suggested they switch partners.

"He's trying to tell us how bad we are," said Marcus to Marion.

"Nothing of the kind!" boomed Solomon.

He patiently tried to explain the basics of the game to Marion: "When you open a strong suit with a low card, lead with your fourth best. When opening a five-card suit with a low card, select your next-to-the-last card. With a six-card suit, instead of the next to the next-to-the-last card, play your fourth best."

Marcus looked so mystified she burst out laughing. Emmaline rescued them, suggesting they switch to penny-ante poker. It was loud, hilarious, and great fun. Marion won thirty-one cents. She and Marcus left at eleven.

Emmaline took her to one side as he and Solomon said their good nights.

"Do you like him?" she whispered conspiratorially and anxiously.

"He's okay."

"Just okay?"

"He's very nice."

"I'm glad." She looked relieved. "You're perfect for each other. You must get to know each other better."

"What if I'm not his type?"

"Oh but you are!"

"She's what?" Solomon asked, joining them along with Marcus.

"Lovely in that outfit," said Emmaline. "Don't you think so, Marcus?"

"Yes, yes."

Outside Marion pulled the woolen stole Emmaline had thoughtfully lent her tightly about her shoulders against the night chill.

"Is this crazy?" Marcus grinned and winced his eyes shut. "When he asked me to come to dinner I thought I'd be the only guest."

"Me, too, when she did. You didn't tell him we—"

"Already know each other? Of course not. Why spoil Emmaline's fun?"

They walked hand in hand to the corner. Artemus's upstairs windows were in darkness. She pictured him asleep in his back room.

"How are you two getting on?" asked Marcus.

"We're too busy to step on each other's toes, if that's what you mean."

"He can be crotchety."

"So can I."

"No you can't, you have to have a talent for it. You have none. I have a funny feeling about him."

"You suspect him of a double life?"

She tittered.

"In a way."

She stopped. The breeze set the loose ends of her stole flapping lightly. Somewhere a dog yapped. Marcus looked extraordinarily handsome in the moonlight, she thought, an Anglo-Saxon Adonis. His expression suddenly turned serious.

"If I tell you, promise you'll never breathe a word to him."

"I promise, I promise."

"Shortly after I got here last year, one of the men, Sergeant Brennan, came down with mumps. His glands were badly swollen. Fever, terrific sore throat. Artemus came out to examine him. Ordered him quarantined for three weeks. Gave him a hot water bottle and put him on fluids until the swelling went down. When he was done he was getting ready to leave when another man came up complaining of a toothache. Before you knew it there was a line of men with toothaches and Artemus standing at the head pulling one tooth after another. I was watching with Bob Sutherland and his wife. Some of the men had set up a small table in front of the colonel's office with a basin and towels and a couple bottles of whiskey. Artemus would examine the tooth, give the man a swig of whiskey, jerk out the tooth, make him bite down on a wad of towel, give him another swig, and move onto the next. He went through two full bottles and when he was done the basin was almost half full of rotted teeth. Lovely sight. He must have pulled teeth from half the men at the post, officers included. He was good; skillful, dexterous; clamp and twist, clamp and twist. Out it came first try every time.

"The thing of it is every time since that day when I've had occasion to see him doctoring, especially cutting, I've never gotten the same feeling. He never looks as sure-handed. It makes you wonder what kind of school he went to, medical or dental?"

"Medical. In Milwaukee, Wisconsin."

"Then how come he doesn't hang his diploma on the wall? All doctors I've ever seen put up their diplomas, certificates, licenses. How better to impress your patients? His office walls are bare."

They were, she thought.

"That's true. It was one of the first things I noticed when I got here. I was planning on putting up my diplomas. I have three, all framed, but when I didn't see any of his I thought he either wouldn't approve of mine or it'd hurt his feelings. I didn't want to start out offending him. I still treat him with kid gloves; he has a fragile ego."

"You think I'm right? He's really a dentist passing himself off as a doctor? There's a lot more money in doctoring."

"If he was in it for the money, he wouldn't be here. He'd be back in Milwaukee."

"I just remember the impression I got watching him, and what Bob Sutherland said: 'Like picking grapes. He missed his calling. He should have been a dentist.' "

"There's more to dentistry than pulling teeth. Anybody can do that."

"Not like he did that day."

"He's a doctor, sweetheart, believe me."

"If you say so." He smirked.

"What's funny?"

"I wonder what would happen if people found out he's been shamming it all these years . . ."

She invited him in.

They sat at the little kitchen table, waiting for the teakettle to heat up. She examined his healed hand.

"Read my palm," he said.

She turned his hand over. "I see a new friend."

"Look closer. That's a new love," he said.

"You're right."

"Let me read yours." He grabbed her hand. She eluded him.

"Let me finish," she said. "See the way the crevice deepens under your baby finger? That means it's serious." He poked a finger into the crevice. "What are you doing?" she asked.

"Measuring the depth. Amazing."

He took her hand and kissed her fingers one by one. Then he rose, leaned across the table and kissed her face lightly all over; by the time he got to her lips she was trembling.

A knock rattled the outer door. A voice called through the window.

"Oh my God," moaned Marcus.

His face fell, dropping into a pained frown. It was Mark Aldrich.

"Artemus says come fast as you can. He's got his hands full with walking wounded."

"The vigilantes," said Marcus. "I'll come help."

They hurried toward the office. The vigilantes had

blundered into an ambush in the Chiricahua Mountains about eighty miles east of Tucson.

"Tsoka-ne-nde stronghold is in the Chiricahuas," said Marcus.

"The Apaches killed nearly half in the first few minutes," said Aldrich. "Hit 'em from all sides."

"My God," whispered Marion.

"A bunch got away, came straggling in about ten minutes ago. Talk about Napoleon's retreat from Moscow."

"Good!" burst Marcus coldly. They both stared at him. "Great! Maybe this'll teach them. Maybe now they'll stay home, stay alive!"

They found the stairway crowded with wounded; a chorus of groaning punctuated with cursing rose upward to the office. Aldrich left them at the street door. They pushed their way up the stairs. Artemus was barefoot and in his nightshirt, busily extracting pieces of arrows. At the moment he was snipping the feathers from the end of a shaft so that he could pull it through the wound out of a burly patient's thigh. The man sat trembling, sweating, his teeth clamped to his wrist against the pain. Artemus did not look up when she spoke to him.

"About time, Doctor. Set yourself up on the other end of the table there or on the floor, wherever. What do *you* want, Captain?"

He looked up for the first time.

"To help."

"Good. Don't just stand there, get started bandaging. Soon as a wound's stitched, pad and court-plaster it. If you get too far behind, just tie 'em up with gauze."

"Right."

"No place for a dentist here," Marion whispered to Marcus.

Most of the wounds she could see appeared painfully serious. All had been inflicted by arrows. All required stitches and dressing. They worked for two hours without letup. She was cleaning a Mexican's shoulder wound, preparatory to stitching it, when the man Artemus was working on nearby spoke to the next man waiting in line.

"I did too see Klee."

"You seen a ghost."

"I seen him! Live. Big as life. No mistaking that red beard and hair down below his shoulders."

"Klee's dead," said the other. "Killed last year."

Marcus worked swiftly and sure-handedly beside her.

"Who's Clay?" she asked.

"K—l—e—e Swiss-American. Resident bad penny. Bootlegger, profiteer, general all-around nuisance. Turns up every now and then. He's been killed ten times and keeps coming back to life. Indestructability makes for legends. If people really lived the tales others tell of them, what an extraordinary world it would be."

Artemus snickered. "Larger than life, that's Erasmus Z. John Klee. When big trouble with the tribes is brewing, he's usually holding the stirrer."

"I seen him," said his patient.

"*I* didn't," said his friend. "And nobody else."

"I did, Senor Hartley," said Marion's Mexican. "Not shooting at us, standing near a big boulder with a bunch of them. His beard like a red flag, *si.*"

"Told ya!"

The wounded continued to file in. Out of comments, bits of conversations, even arguments, Marion managed to piece together a tapestry of the ordeal. As she had earlier presumed, the vigilantes had ridden away simply looking for trouble. They had found no Indians and by the end of the first day had ranged far to the east. Their leaders had decided to continue even farther in that direction, to the San Simon Plain with the New Mexico border just beyond it. When they reached the plain they planned to start north, describing an enormous circle around Tucson, spiraling it tighter and tighter in search of Apaches.

But the Chiricahua Mountains blocked their way to the San Simon Plain. Halfway through the mountains they had blundered upon the Tsoka-ne-nde stronghold. They had not actually reached the camp, being set upon a hundred yards from it by lookouts whose numbers were speedily reinforced by the men they were guarding.

"I saw Raymond Coulter take eight arrows, hitting him all the same time. Looked like a porcupine, he did. One clean through his skull. Damnedest sight. Make your blood run cold."

"You couldn't see the bastards till late on, nary a one."

"Not till they had us on the run for fair."

"I smelled 'em coming."

"Did like hell!"

"Did too! Everything was quiet, but I could feel something running through my horse, like electricity coming up out of the ground. Next thing there was shrieking and whooping all around us."

"Then the first arrows. Like steel rods. God, it was awful! Terrible!"

"Some throwed burning brands down from up top. They'd land on bodies and burn away. One hit Clement Woodward in the shoulder; scared the hell out of both of us."

One man had dismounted and started running, carrying a shaft that had passed through his chest with just the feathers showing at his breastbone. He covered six strides and dropped. Another watched his brother shot through the neck, tried to reach him, and was driven back. When he started away he had his horse shot from under him. He fell, broke his shoulder, and finally managed to scramble to safety.

It was from all accounts the reverse of the Aravaipa Canyon massacre. The final count was thirty-four dead, every single corpse left behind.

It was nearly two-thirty by the time the last wound was treated, bandaged, and its bearer sent on his way. Artemus, Marion, and Marcus sat over coffee. Pieces of shafts littered the floor. Marion examined a whole arrow.

"I never realized they're so long."

"Up to two and a half feet," said Marcus. "That one's cane; the foreshaft there is mountain mahogany. Work of art."

"Don't they use arrowheads?"

"Not the Apaches. They whittle the point sharp and harden it with fire. Some tribes rub the tip with snake or spider venom. The Apaches never use snake venom; they shun snakes. The Chiricahuas use a substance made from rotted animal blood mixed with prickly pear spines."

"Even with poison on the tip it can't be any match for a rifle."

Artemus scoffed. "Don't fool yourself. They can hit a man's chest at a hundred yards as easy as you can toss that thing into the slop pail. They can reach up to a hundred and fifty yards."

Marcus nodded. "With tremendous force. When they shoot a deer at close range the arrow goes clean through. They pull it the rest of the way to retrieve it."

"Fascinating," she murmured.

"Effective."

"What sort of wood do they use for their bows?"

"Different kinds," said Artemus.

"Mulberry's supposed to be the best. Locust, oak, even maple. What's interesting is the bowstring. The best are made from the sinew of a deer's leg or back. They soak it in water, peel it into strands, and splice them end to end to form one long string. They chew the bumps out to get an even thickness, then fold and twist it." Marcus shook his head grimly and admiringly.

"Fascinating," Marion repeated.

"Not enough to sit and chew over this late. If you two'll excuse me, I'm going to bed." Artemus glanced about. "We can leave this mess till morning."

"I'll clean up," she said.

He leered at Marcus. "Miss Tidy. She's got a phobia against germs."

He went into his room. Marcus helped clean up.

"I wonder if the Apaches are satisfied?" she said. "If this makes them even."

"Not a chance. What a slaughter. What a pack of idiots. And what does it all prove, the bloodshed, the martyrdom on both sides?" He was suddenly incensed, the banners of his indignation unfurled and flying. "Why can't people share the world without killing each other?"

She looked at him with mock seriousness. "And why don't rocks give milk?"

The sheets twisted around their limbs. He closed his hand over hers and slid it down over his thigh. The heat of his stiffness sent a chill through her body, and she ran her hand slowly over him. The tremor radiated down from her breasts, suffusing and consuming her body. His taut stomach muscles rippled as he reveled in the fire of her touch. He turned his head and began moving his lips across her eyes and face, then back down her neck, across one milky white shoulder and around each rising breast. Her hand drew away from his body as she luxuriated in the warm moistness of his mouth capturing her flesh.

He lay beside her, his member hard against her thigh. She ached to have him inside her, to never let him free.

"Take me," she whispered.

He did not answer. The only sounds were the anguished moan building in her throat and the hammering of her heart. He lifted himself and rolled over her, poised. Her hands traveled up his inner thighs and grasped his manhood. It pulsed powerfully in the coil of her fingers, the head massive, magnificent. He guided himself into her, his body lowering and easing forward, forward . . .

17

Dear Marion,

I apologize. I shouldn't have sent you those grisly headlines. It was petty of me, and nobody exaggerates like reporters. That said, let's move on to something more agreeable. I presume you got the sprayer; I hope you'll be able to talk his nibs into using it.

Guess what? Worth Hawkins is deserting the ship, taking his passably fair skills and eagle-winged ambition to Boston. He leaves at the end of the month. Just when I was beginning to get attached to him; now I'll have to start all over with somebody new. Why can't I hang onto assistants? Could it be my charming personality? He does act like I intimidate him. Do I? Am I an ogre? I can't believe it.

We're adding a new wing to the mausoleum. It was announced at the monthly board meeting. No one asked my opinion, but of course I gave it anyway. I told them they'd be better off tearing down the place and building a new hospital from scratch. That prompted some icy stares.

Expect more *journals* and *Lancets*, whenever I get my hands on the latter. Say, I almost forgot. Some juicy gossip is flying around Philadelphia's medical circles. It concerns Walter Ogren, your friend Dr. Shaw's fellow student back in Milwaukee, was it? Somebody at Pennsylvania Hospital uncovered a skeleton in the poor fellow's closet. Would you believe *he never attended medical school!* He studied dentistry and apparently changed his mind about practicing when he graduated. For which I can't blame him. Set about filling his head with books on medicine and surgery and successfully passed himself off as a physician all these years. And, from all reports, a good one. He's been fired, of course, and has left town in disgrace. I wish I knew where he's gone so that I could write him a letter of condolence, perhaps help ease his pain. Only what would I say? Poor man. A dentist. How bizarre.

Miss you, my dear. I wish you'd never left, but we won't go into that. Wish me luck in finding a halfway decent replacement for Hawkins. If I do find one, I'll swear him to a blood pact not to leave for twenty years.

Much love,
Gabriel

Walter Ogren a dentist, Walter Ogren a fellow student of Artemus Shaw. She reread the portion about Ogren, then put the letter in the drawer with Gabriel's other letters and set about making supper.

She couldn't possibly confront him, couldn't even tell Marcus. Nor would she tell Artemus what had happened to his friend Ogren. What would be the point? All she could really do, in the interest of ethics, would be keep an eye on Artemus as he worked. But even then she saw little need to watch him closely. He obviously knew what he was doing. He had saved a great many more patients than he lost, so what would be gained by exposing him to disgrace?

Yet there was another side to it. She was a legitimate professional; he was not. Could she silently allow him to continue to practice, to dupe people who put their faith in him, their lives in his hands?

She thought about it all through supper and until bedtime. She fell asleep shortly after deciding that she had a large problem. At the moment she could neither dismiss nor solve it.

She would write to Gabriel. He would tell her to let well enough alone. She would do so. But she would still write. Maybe he would advise her differently.

18

F rom July through September, thundershow-
ers dashed and darkened the arid land and
muddied the indolent waters of the Santa Cruz River.
These storms brought most of the year's rainfall to southeastern Arizona. With the onset of autumn the sun began
to lose its ferocity, a seasonal reprieve most welcome in
Tucson.

Winter arrived. The gila woodpecker no longer swooped
and darted among the saguaros; the black silky flycatcher
absented itself from its favorite perch atop the mesquite;
no longer was the sweet song of the cactus wren heard
greeting the dawn; white-winged doves ceased their gath-
ering at the springs. The million locusts that had filled
the cottonwood groves vanished, taking with them their
tireless, undulating anthem. The hognose skunk no longer
rooted in the desert soil for larvae. Among the graythorn
the piglike collared peccary no longer snorted and ran,
and the jackrabbit could not be seen taking its ease,
sitting beneath a cactus with its ears backlighted by the
lowering sun.

The creosote bush dropped its leaves to conserve its
water, as did the yellow paloverde and other plants.
Where earlier waters flowed in roiling fury, cascading

over the edges of cliffs and down sheer canyon walls, silence reigned and trickling remnants of the late summer storms laced the land.

Winter reigned and ruled that nature quit its labors and rest. It slept to reinvigorate itself for the great eruption of growth and green, the explosion of color in spring.

In no way did the seasonal change affect Marion and Marcus's relationship. It flourished and bound them closer. They saw each other every day if only long enough to refill the well of happiness they shared.

Marion also spent much of her little free time with Emmaline, who tirelessly heralded the romantic possibilities involving the captain and the doctor, convinced as ever that it was she who had brought them together.

Since the catastrophe of the Chiricahua Mountains, the more militant residents rested their arms and animosities if not their fears. Colonel Willoughby was stripped of his command, reduced in rank to second lieutenant, and sent to Fort Randall in southeastern Montana. Why he didn't resign Marcus could not understand.

Colonel Schreiber and his men continued to protect the town and the surrounding area; their efforts produced mixed results. Battling the Indians wasn't the problem. It was finding them. And all the while the threat of their joining forces under Cochise, Geronimo, or some other chief shadowed everyone's lives.

Time at the fort hung increasingly heavy for officers and enlisted men alike. Men of every rank were bored, restless, and homesick. They took to fighting among themselves, more out of frustration than dislike for each other. The heat, scarcity of fresh water and decent food, the shortages and ever present danger posed by the Apaches, made life increasingly miserable for everyone. Matters reached a point where an average of two men a month were deserting. Some were found and brought back to face punishment; most were never seen again in the area.

The tension finally snapped. On a chilly Sunday night in March, a gang of drunken hotheads, reluctant to go out after Apaches on the heels of the Chiricahua Mountains debacle, let off steam by marching to the fort under cover of darkness and setting fire to it. Four soldiers died in the flames and scores were injured. The immediate result was to reduce the number of able-bodied men fit for duty to fewer than seventy. It had been nearly three years now since the last replacement had come in. Feelings between the military and the townspeople were perilously strained. Marcus confided to Marion that they had never been worse. Colonel Schreiber tried to calm the troubled waters. Riding into town with an escort, he made a speech in the military plaza. He talked of the ongoing and urgent need for cooperation between the two sides. He announced that his door was always open to civilians, and insisted that he and his men held no prejudice against the town's Southern sympathizers, that all of them were good Americans, and none should lose sight of the fact that unity was their staunchest ally against the common enemy. Well intentioned though his message was, it was greeted with stony silence. He thanked the crowd for listening, mounted his horse, and led his escort back to the partially reconstructed fort.

His first act upon returning was to cancel all the enlisted men's leaves into town. Until further notice Tucson would be off-limits. Overnight his popularity with his men was running neck and neck with that of the townspeople.

Over the months Dr. Artemus Shaw carried on his practice nobly, at times downright brilliantly, his lack of a medical degree notwithstanding. On one occasion he performed a Caesarian section in under sixty seconds; in Marion's opinion his speed saved the mother's life. He shrugged off her compliments with "all in a day's work."

One evening in early April, Marcus was visiting the apartment for a candlelight supper. He was helping Marion with the dishes when a stranger came to the door. It was after nine o'clock. The man was a squat little peon, barefoot and hatless, wearing a seedy lambskin jacket and two Navy Colts straddling his stomach. He introduced himself as Emilio Quintero. As he did he glanced past Marion and reacted with an expression of concern at discovering Marcus. The captain joined them at the door.

"Emilio Quintero," he said. "One of Erasmus Klee's cronies, aren't you?"

She recognized the name. Both Marcus and Artemus had told her about the legendary renegade Swiss who was more Apache than white man, who lived with the tribes and enjoyed their respect and trust. Klee dealt in all sorts of contraband and the Army had been trying to capture him for years.

"Senor Klee is my employer, *si*," said the little man.

"What do you want?" Marcus asked.

"To speak with the lady doctor, *Capitaine*."

"Come in," said Marion.

"Wait, let's not be hasty," protested Marcus.

"I mean no harm, I swear by the Virgin. I come to you on a mission of mercy, Doctor."

"Come in."

"I am sorry to interrupt you. I know it is an imposition. He said it would be."

"Klee."

"*Si*. He is very sick; dying. He asks you to come to doctor him, please? I escort you to him in perfect safety, and back here, *si*."

"Forget it!" burst Marcus.

"Would you mind letting me speak for myself?" Marion flared. She turned back to the young man. "What's the matter with him?"

"Down low. Sweating like a horse, throwing up. He doubles up." He demonstrated, contorting his own body, writhing absurdly.

"His kidney."

"He suffers." Quintero seemed to be suffering in telling of it.

"How long has he been ill?" she asked.

"Maybe three days."

She turned to Marcus. "Stone."

"You must come quickly. Please, I beg you," Quintero pleaded.

"Don't go, Marion. You'll be taking your life in your hands," Marcus warned.

"No, no, she will be safe, I swear!"

"He needs a doctor," Marion said evenly.

"He needs a rope. He's vermin, a white Apache."

"I have to go." She could feel the back of her stubbornness rising, stiffening.

"I have a horse waiting for you, a fine mare. Please hurry!"

"Don't go," repeated Marcus. Advice had become a command.

"I must."

"I'll come with you."

"No. One look at that uniform and they'll kill you. Besides, this has nothing to do with you, you shouldn't get involved."

"*You* shouldn't. Damn . . ."

He sighed heavily, drew his pistol, flipped it in his hand, and offered it.

"At least take this."

"No, no guns."

"This is insane. You're not thinking. You can't trust this man, you don't even know him!"

"I am telling the truth, I swear."

"Shut up!"

"Stop it, Marcus."

She got her coat and gloves on as Marcus continued protesting. She checked the contents of her bag and went out, feeling his eyes stabbing her back.

"I'll wait here," he said, flinging a final glare at Quintero.

"I may be all night," she flung back.

"I'll wait."

"This way," said Emilio Quintero. "Hurry!"

She had anticipated a long, arduous, pell-mell ride east to the Chiricahua Mountains to a place in the vicinity of the ambush; instead Quintero led her south. They followed the Santa Cruz River toward Nogales and the Mexican border. Some twenty miles down they veered away from the river to the southeast. Presently tiny orange lights punctured the darkness ahead. He was riding beside her. He pointed and grinned.

"Soon we get there, *si*."

Even before the lights of Tucson had vanished behind them, misgivings began to pile up in mind. She did not see the situation as dangerous, despite Marcus's warnings. Klee needed her desperately; Quintero would protect her. What worried her was the stricken man's condition. From Quintero's catalog of symptoms and the area of discomfort, it sounded like a stone obstructing the flow of urine from the kidney, blocking it in or above the bladder. It could also be stone in the ureter or pressure on the ureter from elsewhere in the abdomen. It could be clots of blood blocking the ureter, or even a tumor blocking the outlet of the ureter into the bladder.

Whatever the cause, to relieve the pressure the stone had to be removed. This decided, her heart sank in her breast. In hastily checking the contents of her bag she had neglected to look for chloroform. Cutting without some type of anesthesia was unthinkable, but it was useless to stop and check now, within sight of the *ranchería*.

She had only cut for stone four times. It was not the most difficult surgical procedure. An eight-to-ten inch incision was made, starting in the loin on the afflicted side and extending around the side toward the front of the body. The level of the incision should be just below the last rib and above the hip bone. She would cut through the fat tissues under the skin and through the muscles of the loin. The kidney exposed, the stone could be removed in one of two ways: through a cut made directly through the substance of the organ or by opening it over the stone. Remove the stone, insert two drains and close. Leave the drains in for at least a week.

It's so simple, she thought, running it through her mind step by step.

They rode into the *ranchería*. The stench of human sweat and waste mingled with that of rotten meat. Other, undefinable odors rose in her nostrils like decay from a stagnant swamp. They dismounted. The Apaches stopped what they were doing, cooking, eating, conversing, freezing. Quintero indicated a wickiup ahead of them and walked her to it through a gauntlet of stares. When they ducked inside she could hear the activity resume behind them. The air within was intolerably close, almost unbreathable. The smoke hole open at the top was useless. She turned and pushed the blanket flap outward, draping it over the yucca-thatched frame to admit at least a breath of air. At once two curious squaws came up to the entrance to gawk. Quintero shooed them away.

Erasmus Z. John Klee lay in agony on a straw mat with a saddle for his pillow. He was covered by a thin, ragged blanket. His condition, his suffering notwithstanding, he was an impressive sight. His thick, long straight hair was fiery red, as was his full beard. His eyes were pale blue; he was handsome, bull-chested, powerful-looking. He smelled utterly foul, he sweat so copiously.

At first she thought he had been dashed in the face with
a bucket of water. The glow of a makeshift candle, a strip
of rag hanging from the lip of a sardine can filled with
oil, lent him a fearsome appearance.

"Help me. Agony . . ."

She knelt and opened her bag. Immediately she found
a half-filled can of choloroform. Quintero, meanwhile,
got out a torch and lit it, holding it aloft, brightening the
interior.

"It's too smoky, put it out. I'll manage. Bring that
sardine can around to this side. Find something to set it
on to raise it. At least a foot or two."

"A basket. A big one."

"A drum," rasped Klee.

Quintero went out. She pulled the blanket down.

"Where exactly is the pain?"

"If I move—"

"Don't. I'll touch you; tell me when I hit it."

It was where she expected it to be.

"It's like a knife. God in heaven—" His agony twisted
his face.

Quintero returned carrying a large drum. He set the
burning wick in the can upon it. Raising the light helped,
but it was still feeble. She unbuckled Klee's belt and
pulled his trousers down gently, and his shirt upward,
exposing the area. She began to explain the procedure.
He interrupted.

"Just get on with it."

She folded gauze into a pad, placing it over his nostrils,
and handed the choloroform to Quintero squatting on
the opposite side.

"A drop at a time till I say enough."

"Count backward from one hundred," she ordered.

Klee began. The improvised candle flickered and went
out, plunging the interior into blackness. She could not
even make out Quintero inches from her. She could hear
him getting out matches. He relit the wick. Klee continued mumbling the count, then stopped. Quintero resumed administering the chloroform.

"Enough," she cautioned.

She swabbed the area of incision with alcohol. He
should be shaved, but there was no time for procedural
refinements; under these circumstances Gabriel would

approve. Artemus would approve under any circumstances. She got out her instruments and a towel and laid them in a neat row along with two gutta percha catheters.

Two minutes into the operation, Quintero paled, lurched to his feet, and staggered out, his hand cupping his mouth.

It went well; she finished, held the bloodied, jagged stone up to the light, set it to one side, carefully inserted the two catheters and stitched the incision. Klee slept on. He had stopped perspiring and was breathing normally. He was very strong, vigorous, he would have no trouble recovering.

Quintero stuck his head in; his color had returned. He looked sheepish.

"All done," said Marion. "He'll sleep awhile. Whatever you do, don't move him, don't let him move himself for at least two days."

"Two days, *si*." He cleared his throat. He looked apologetic. "Doctor, there is a boy here with a bad arm. Crushed by a big rock. Can you . . . ?"

"Of course."

He was about nine, a beautiful child with perfect features, perfect teeth, and bright, snapping, mischievous eyes. His right forearm was under siege by infection. The Indians crowded around as she tended to him. They stared and pointed and mumbled to each other. Their suspicion upon her arrival fled. They could not have been more in awe if she were bringing triplets into the world. Some of the women wore expressions of envy as well as admiration. They struck her as being like children seeing Santa Claus in the flesh for the first time.

She cleansed the site, applied a mild carbolic solution, and set about gently debriding the wound. The boy did not wince, setting his small jaw, fixing his eyes on his wound and not looking up. The crowd continued to watch in wonderment. Two women started a fire to give her more light to work by. She thanked them. They beamed as they drew respecting glances from the others.

Through a break in the circle of onlookers as she worked she saw two other women roasting small furry animals, hides intact.

"Wood rats," explained Quintero.

"Squirrels."

"Rats. Apaches eat almost anything, except prairie dogs, *si*."

"Why not prairie dogs?"

"Because they eat snakes."

He explained that the wood rats would be roasted until half-done, then skinned and gutted and the cooking finished.

"They won't eat the peccary or javaleena, either. They call them white mans' hogs, snake-eaters, disgusting."

"But they eat rats."

"And mountain lions, too; deer, elk, mountain sheep, goats. The unborn young is a great delicacy with them."

She asked no further questions about food.

A few of the men were drunk, drinking *tiswin* brewed, according to Quintero, from mescal plants, cooked into a gluey state, which was squeezed to extract the liquid, which was set aside to ferment.

The women seemed to be doing all the work—carrying wood, hollowing gourds, crafting spoons and dippers from them and from tree burls and the leaves of the broad-leafed yucca.

The clothing of both sexes differed markedly from the pictures she had seen of Plains Indians' attire. The braves' breechcloths were voluminous compared to those worn by the northern tribes. The Apache wrapped his about his waist and it fell to his knees in front and to ankle length behind. They wore buckskin shirts, fringed on the shoulders and lower sleeves, with round neck holes. Their moccasins had rawhide soles and buckskin uppers for protection against the cactus. Some uppers reached to the wearer's thighs. A peculiar round tab extended vertically from the ends of the toes.

The virgins or unmarried women wore their hair vertically bundled at the nape of the neck and wrapped in a hair bow, a piece of leather shaped like an hourglass, worn vertically with the upper and lower loops studded with beads. The strands that fastened the bow to the hair were of brightly colored cloth and hung well down the back. When a woman married, according to Quintero, she destroyed the hair bow and let her hair tumble down her back, squaring it off at the bottom. He told her it was a serious insult to her husband if a woman failed to destroy her hair bow when she married. It signified that she might take lovers behind his back.

Nearly every woman she could see wore layers of necklaces. Some displayed tattoos: small circles or line patterns on their cheeks and foreheads. The men also wore jewelry, some conspicuously decorative, but mainly to signify their power.

She spread ointment over the boy's wound and began to dress it. Squaws and some warriors crowded around to watch, moving in very close. Marion had to use her elbows to give herself room to work. One woman brazenly poked a finger into the gauze pad Marion had set on the wound.

"Don't!"

The woman started as if stabbed. Two men upbraided her loudly. Away she slunk in disgrace. Marion was tempted to call after her, bring her back, save her from humiliation, but she vanished inside a wickiup. Marion finished dressing the wound.

"Tell him," she said to Quintero, "he must keep the bandage dry and wear it for five days. And when his mother takes it off he must keep it clean."

"He has no mother; the vigilantes killed her and his father. He has only an older sister and little brother. His name is Coo-wanta, Little-Hawk Hunter."

"Clean," murmured the boy, speaking for the first time.

She patted his cheek. "Good boy, Coo-wanta."

"Clean!" boomed a warrior, grinning broadly, approvingly.

"Clean!" echoed the others.

"Clean," repeated Marion, nodding. She restored the tube of salve and what remained of the gauze in her bag and was closing it when a loud rumbling shook the ground under her. It seemed to be coming from the north, the direction she and Quintero had arrived from. In seconds a cavalry troop came thundering through, bellowing, cursing, swinging their sabers, hacking everything in reach. Caught by surprise, the Indians panicked, the women shrieked, the children exploded with screams. Everyone ran. The attacking blue wave passed through, leaving carnage and desolation in its path. Throughout the havoc she sat stunned and rigid, holding the boy's wrist, not daring to breathe, telling herself it wasn't happening.

The Apaches reacted swiftly, snatching up weapons as they fled, running southward, reassembling about two hundred yards away, spreading out, and moving to counterattack.

"Inside!" boomed Quintero.

He grabbed her arm. She was still hanging onto the boy. They rushed into Klee's wickiup. He was still unconscious. The three of them crowded the opening, looking out. From where she crouched she could see five corpses, three squaws, and two older men.

"There are only fifteen or so. The people will drive them away." Quintero nodded, convinced he was correct.

He had not touched either of the guns in his belt, content, it seemed, to distance himself from the fray, to observe, she noted.

"They came in so fast. No warning. Doesn't the tribe have sentries?"

"Not tonight. Not down this far. Look there."

He pointed across the open area that spread between two large wickiups, both sending huge tongues of flame skyward, framing a panorama of bloody conflict: braves and bluecoats fighting hand to hand. As she watched, a trooper lopped off a brave's head with a single swipe of his saber, then took a lance full in the back, killing him instantly. Another plunged his blade cleanly through his adversary; a third had dropped his saber and was going for his pistol. A knife plunged into his gut and froze him before he fell.

The battle raged evenly for the next few minutes, but the Apaches outnumbered their attackers by at least three to one. The *ranchería* itself was by now deserted, the escaping squaws, children, and older men swallowed up by the darkness, the regrouped braves carrying the fight to the intruders. A few yards from where the three of them crouched watching, one of the fallen women stirred. Before Quintero could stop her Marion rushed out.

"Come back, come back! She is finished!"

The woman's left shoulder had been all but completely severed. It hung by a thread of flesh. Blood poured copiously from the wound. It was impossible to stanch. Marion backed away horrified, turned, and lunged for

the opening. Inside, she scrambled to her feet. Klee
groaned. He was awake. Coo-wanta, meanwhile, squat-
ted unmoving on his haunches and was gaping at her. His
eyes said that she was a ministering angel from heaven
who had taken away his hurt and for this he worshiped
her.

She bent over Klee. Quintero adjusted the strip wick
in the can of oil. The flame flickered and diminished,
then flared brightly.

"How is he?" Quintero asked.

"He'll be all right," she replied.

Outside the din of battle was gradually lessening, as if
it were moving away from the campsite. The gunfire that
had erupted following the initial saber attack was becoming more and more scattered.

"It is over," said Quintero. "The troopers have had
enough. They will withdraw."

Klee was now fully conscious.

"How do you feel?" Marion asked.

"Remarkable." He appeared awed by his recovery.
"New man. Sore down there, but no pain."

She held up the still bloodied kidney stone. He smiled
and was about to comment on it when a trooper burst in.
He waved his Colt. He eyed her malevolently, not at all
surprised by the sight of her.

"Get out!" she snapped. "Out! Leave us alone . . . "

Ignoring her, he swung his weapon toward Quintero,
setting the muzzle against his cheek. He then jerked one
gun, then the other from the Mexican's belt, tossing them
behind him. Quintero swallowed and slowly raised his
hands. The trooper spat at him, then turned back to
Marion, and grabbed her by the shoulder. He was nearly
as big as Klee; flowing mustaches spread across his pink
face. Three stripes yellowed his sleeve.

"Out, woman!"

She shook loose. "Don't touch me! *You* get out!"

Quintero took speedy advantage of their dispute; he
threw himself at the opening and scuttled through it. The
sergeant took after him, got him in his sights, and was
about to fire when she shouldered his arm aside. The gun
exploding in the restrictive confines of the wickiup sounded
like a cannon fired into a barrel. Coo-wanta jumped and

yelled, then resumed his rigid stance, round-eyeing the trooper fearfully.

He had pushed her down. Her interference had incensed him; he was suddenly livid.

"Meddling bitch! Now see what you've did!"

Klee was trying to rise on one elbow. She saw and moved quickly to him.

"That there's Klee!" burst the trooper.

"Leave us alone. He's helpless, can't you see? Get out of here!"

"You get, woman, if you know what's good. Take the boy with ya. Leave that thieving, bush-faced renegade scum to me!"

"Keep away from him!"

He pushed her aside. Leering sadistically, he raised his pistol slowly. Coo-wanta jammed his fingers in his ears, his face flooding with fear. Again she tried to push the sergeant's gun hand aside, but he was too strong; she could not budge it. He fired. The boy shrilled. She screamed. The bullet slammed through Klee's skull; blood flowered. Astonishment wreathed his face and he tried to speak, his lips moved soundless. His eyes widened, then shuttered.

"Bastard!" she roared. "Murderer!"

She exploded, attacking him, flailing with her small fists. He shoved her from him as easily as he would a small child and went out. She stood stunned, staring down at the dead man. The blood glistened in the glow of the candle. She could not believe it; it hadn't happened. She began to shake. She fought to get control. She shook so it felt as if her bones would crack. The boy stood gawking at Klee. She heard a horse gallop off, the last horse to leave.

Silence was broken only by the soft moaning and whimpering of the wounded. Marion looked outside. The Apaches were coming slowly back into camp singly and in pairs, walking like dead men animated by some supernatural force moving them through the nightmare of the onslaught. She looked back at Klee.

"Madre de Dios."

Quintero was back. He gaped at Klee. Coo-wanta fled.

"No."

He crossed himself, then shook it off, and addressed her.

"Come, we will find horses. I must take you back."

He retrieved his guns. Moments later they started out. They had not covered twenty strides when she reined up.

"Coo-wanta."

"He will be all right."

She glanced back. He was standing watching her. An older girl had come up on one side of him, a younger boy on the other. They clasped hands. He did not wave, did not move.

19

Marcus woke and glanced at his watch. It was almost four-thirty in the morning. He rose from the chair wearily, stretched, and went to the front window. The garden wall completely blocked the view of the street. He buttoned his tunic and went out, leaving the door ajar. He stood at the gate looking up and down the street. All was quiet; Tucson slept.

He returned and was about to close the door behind him when the sound of horses came drifting up the walk-way. Seconds later he heard both horses stop, and moments later resume, moving off. He stood at the open door. She came slowly toward him, her head down. When she raised it her face was masked with fury.

"You bastard!"

"What the—"

"You sent them after us, they followed us to the camp. Did their usual thorough job. I hope you're satisfied, hope you're proud of yourself, you deceitful pig!"

"What the devil are you talking about?"

"Go ahead, deny it. I dare you—"

"Marion—"

"Get out of my sight. I never want to see you again!"

He bristled. Without a word he walked away.

194

She locked and bolted both doors after him. She was still seething. He had left his hat. She flung it into a corner. She sat on the edge of the bed, turning over the night's grisly events. She hated Marcus, despised him for his treachery. She hated the nameless sergeant even more. She would see the ruthless savagery twisting his face till her dying day. Marcus had certainly sent the right man for the job.

She went to bed, but, as she expected, could not turn off her mind. It was filled with the horror of the bloody hour, the carnage, visions of the dying and dead, the stunned and terrified boy; Klee, Quintero, the loathsome sergeant: vicious, sadistic animal! And she vowed she would never forgive Marcus for using her to lead the soldiers to the camp.

She lay for what seemed hours until, summoned by her exhaustion, sleep came, blacking out the turmoil roiling her thoughts.

A loud pounding woke her. The sun was high. Through the window the garden glowed in myriad colors under its brilliant assault. She glanced at her watch. It was after twelve. Emmaline was at the door, visibly agitated.

"Marion, what have you done?"

"What are you talking about?"

She yawned, covering her mouth; she felt wretched.

"Larcena Pennington stopped by the house. A soldier from the fort told her maid. It's all over town that you went into the mountains last night to doctor some Apache chief. Marion, Marion, whatever possessed you—"

"It's a damned lie!"

"You didn't go to them?"

"I—"

"You did? Oh, Marion, how could you?"

"I didn't know that's where I was going! Didn't know there'd be Indians there—" She began to explain, only to stop abruptly in mid-sentence. "Stop shaking your head like a ninny!" she burst. "What is this? Why are you browbeating me? I thought you were my friend."

"I am. Why else would I be here? Oh my dear, you've no idea what you've done. You really don't, do you?"

"I'm trying to tell you. Klee was suffering horribly. If I hadn't shown up he would have died. I cut a stone out of him. I did what any doctor would do. God, am I to be pilloried for that? Look at you, you'd think I'd committed some hideous crime."

"*They* think so."

"To hell with them!"

"You'll have to explain. Tell them everything. What you did, why—" She brightened. "You could say you didn't know it was Klee you were going to help, you'd never even heard the name before, didn't know his man was taking you to a *ranchería*. Only when you got there, you didn't turn around and come back—"

"How could I? Aren't you listening? He was in agony, I had to operate. I don't care who he is or what he's done. He could have been the devil himself."

"That's just what he is."

"Was."

"Marion, Marion—"

"Will you please stop it? Go away! Leave me alone!"

"I'm only trying to help."

"I don't need—" She stopped and sucked in a breath, steeling herself, letting it out slowly. She took hold of Emmaline's hands.

"I know, I understand."

"What are you going to do?"

Emmaline took a step inside. Marion indicated a chair.

"I don't see as I have to do anything. If *they* don't like it, they disapprove, that's their problem. Let's not talk anymore about it."

"They think you've betrayed them. Everybody . . ." Emmaline shook her head sadly.

"You, Solomon, Artemus?"

"Not us, of course. You know Solomon and I'll stick by you."

"Marcus sent men to follow us. They raided the camp; it was horrible. I'll never forgive him. I trusted him."

"He *admitted* he sent soldiers after you?" Emmaline looked astonished.

"He didn't have to. When I accused him he looked guilty as a thief."

"Why would he do such a terrible thing? It doesn't make sense."

"Oh, but it does. Duty above all, above any feeling he might have for me, any value he places on our friendship, the conniving bastard. He used me!" Marion swung about and pounded the wall with her fist.

"How can you be sure? It seems so blatant to deliberately and so obviously incriminate himself."

"You think he cares about that? He's doing his job, don't you see? That comes before all else."

"I still can't believe it of him; it's not like him, he's so honorable, so straight."

"He's a fraud, Emmaline! For the first time he's shown his true colors. Forget it, forget him. I have. I'm late for work. Artemus will wonder. I have to go."

"I'll walk you there."

"You don't have to. Nobody will attack me in the street."

"Be careful."

Almost the moment she walked in she could see that Artemus had not yet heard. She found him between patients, passing the time while he waited fiddling aimlessly with the carbolic acid sprayer.

"Well, sleepyhead, about time you showed. Although you haven't missed much. Only Mrs. Ferguson. I changed the dressing on her incision. My, my, we do look like the wrath of God today. Bad night?"

Heavy footsteps below interrupted before she could answer. A horde of men came surging up the stairs, led by Mayor William Oury. They all wore hateful glares.

"We figured we'd find you here, *Doctor* Sturges," rasped Oury.

"What is this?" asked Artemus. "What's going on?"

"Ask her. Ask her what all she was doing last night down below, rubbing elbows with her Apache friends, tending to Klee himself. Y'all deny it, doctor? Speak up, we're listenin'."

"Who do you think you're talking to, Oury? How dare you barge in here and accuse me. What I do with my time is nobody else's business!"

He smirked. "So y'all don't deny it, you were out there. Y'all treated him!"

"Where I was and what I did is no concern of yours. Any of you!"

"Your Honor, I'll thank you to get the hell out of my office!" boomed Artemus. "Out! Everybody!"

"You go to hell, Artemus. This is serious. I'll make it short, Dr. Sturges: we want y'all out of Tucson. Eastbound stage is due in nine tomorrow morning. See that you're on it. Go back where y'all belong, back with your bleeding-heart liberal friends in Philadelphia. We don't need you here, don't want y'all. And think yourself lucky: if y'all were a man we'd tar and feather you, and run you out on a rail."

"Go to hell, Your Honor." Marion stood, fists on hips, eyeing him hard.

He smirked and sneered. "Fair warning. Get out of Tucson and stay out. Y'all show your face around these parts again, y'all wish you'd never seen the light of day out of your mama!"

He turned and pushed through the crowd to the top of the stairs. To a man they glared viciously at her.

"Damn bleeding heart!"

"Apache lover!"

"Traitor!"

"Get out!" burst Artemus. "All of you."

They left muttering insults. Marion stood red-faced, eyeing the floor.

"Congratulations, Doctor," Artemus said softly.

"Please, don't start."

"Relax. They're just blowing off. Oury's a master at it. You won't have to leave town." He set a reassuring arm across her shoulders. "I won't let you."

"I want to. I wish there was a stage in ten minutes."

"Marion, don't talk rubbish." Artemus frowned.

"I'm fed up with Tucson," she murmured.

"Sit, please. Tell me about it."

"I can't be bothered; it had to come to this sooner or later. I've been expecting it for weeks."

"So just like that you're ready to toss it all away. What happened?"

She told him.

"Erasmus Klee? His friend told you up front he was taking you to Klee? Didn't the name sound familiar? Didn't you remember the talk here when the vigilantes came back after the ambush? Klee's another Simon Girty, Judas Iscariot, a traitor to every white in the territory."

"He needed a doctor, Artemus. If it was you, would you have refused him?"

"Well, I—"

"You know you wouldn't. They've got it all twisted to fit their stinking prejudices. I took a kidney stone out of him. I treated a little boy's injured forearm. I was about to leave when the troopers came thundering in. Marcus alerted them after I'd left, sent someone to the fort or went himself. They set out, picked up our trail—"

"Marcus Venable? That's nonsense." He waved both hands in rejection.

"He used me—"

"Rubbish! He'd no more betray you than I."

"Maybe I was a bit hasty . . ." She bit her lower lip.

"If you know what's good for you, you'll get out there and apologize to him." He thrust his face up into hers. "I mean it, Marion."

"No."

"Marion—"

"Why bother? We'll never see each other again anyway. You heard our esteemed mayor. He means business."

"Rubbish. Oury's all wind, putting on a show for his cronies. You are not leaving!"

"I am. I want to. Nobody in town, outside of the Warners, will come within a block of me now. What good am I? What good is any doctor without patients?"

"That didn't occur to you when you set out last night?"

"Please, I don't need to hear it from you, too."

"I'm sorry."

"So am I. For letting you down. Don't stick up for me, Artemus, they'll only come down on you the same way."

"They wouldn't dare. I'll speak to Oury privately. I can handle him."

"I wish you wouldn't bother."

Someone was coming up the stairs. Three, perhaps even more people.

"Patients," said Artemus, "let's go to work."

But the four arrivals had nothing that needed either bandaging or dosing. The medicine cabinet had no nostrum for indignation. Larcena Pennington, completely recovered from her ordeal in the desert, her friend Abigail Houghton, and two other ladies came sweeping in under full sail, red-faced, angry, and spoiling for a clash.

"Dr. Sturges!" boomed Larcena, immediately appropriating center stage.

"Good morning, Larcena," said Marion pleasantly.

"*Mrs.* Pennington if you don't mind, or even if you do. We represent the F.D.A.T.—"

"Founding Daughters of Tucson," explained Artemus out of the corner of his mouth. "What they've found is tea, sugar cookies, gossip, and do-good."

"This doesn't concern you, Dr. Shaw," sang Abigail.

The four women stood in a semicircle, stabbing Marion with their glares.

"She's already gotten the good word from Oury," said Artemus, ignoring Abigail. "Save your breath."

Larcena drew herself up like a rooster inflating his lungs, preparing to herald the dawn.

"Save your own," she snapped. "Please—it smells to high heaven. Our business is with Dr. Sturges. We'll be brief."

"Let me help," said Marion. "You want me to leave town, I'm gone."

"Like hell you are!" boomed Artemus, so loudly all four visitors recoiled. "Who do you dragons think you are? Do you have any idea what went on out there last night? What she did because it had to be done?"

"We don't care," purred Larcena.

Her tone sounded like she was patiently indulging an irritable four-year-old. Marion watched and listened, hovering between disgust and grudging regard for the woman. Larcena was nasty, sarcastic, and overbearing, but she was also tough, practically willing herself into full recovery from her ordeal, taking charge of her companions like a schoolteacher. Larcena caught Marion staring and eyed her resentfully. Marion suddenly felt like an insignificant handmaiden who, having sinned in service, was about to be banished by her queen.

"Don't bother, Artemus," said Marion. "They wouldn't understand."

Larcena produced a ticket. "Here you are. Compliments of the Founding Daughters of Tucson. It'll get you to Garden City, Kansas. Our farewell gift. Have a safe journey now, and a long one."

Her audience tittered.

"Keep it, I'll buy my own."

Larcena fairly oozed false sincerity. "I hear Philadelphia is charming this time of year. You know what they say: be it ever so humble, there's no place—"

"Out!" snapped Artemus. "Everybody! Go home and catch up on your backbiting."

Larcena ignored him, her gaze fastened on the object of her scorn. "One last thing," she purred. "We can't let you leave with any doubt in mind, can we? Failure on your part to recognize the enormity of your—"

"What, crime?" Marion stiffened. "is this going to be a speech?"

"Not at all. It's a bit late to help you overcome your prejudice against us."

"I have no prejudices against you," said Marion sweetly. "I feel sorry for you. You're playing right into the Apaches' hands. It takes two to quarrel, and you and your kind are certainly holding up your end."

Even before she finished speaking, Larcena had turned to her friends. She smiled sweetly. "Brace yourselves, my dears, *she's* going to make a speech. Pay close attention. She's an expert on the Apaches. Everybody knows Philadelphia's overrun with them."

Laughter.

"No," responded Marion quietly, "but we certainly have our share of narrowminded, holier-than-thou, professional hate mongers."

Larcena waggled a finger. "Sticks and stones. Shall we, ladies?"

They swept out before Artemus could get a word in. More footsteps sounded on the stairs, and a woman appeared with a small boy in tow. His face was red, his eyes puffy. Clutching her son's hand, the woman rustled past Marion as if she did not exist. She looked worried and upset. The boy blinked rapidly; he shaded his eyes with his hand and started to cough.

"Howard's got the miseries, Doctor. Bad cold. Stand up straight, Howard."

Marion watched as Artemus stood Howard by the window and checked his throat with a tongue depressor. The boy covered his eyes with the heels of his hands against the bright sunlight.

"It's from running around barefoot," said his mother. "I tell him and tell him, but it's like talking to the bedpost."

Artemus grunted. He was checking behind the boy's ears.

"Feeling pretty miserable, Howard?"

"Shitty."

"Howard!" burst his mother.

"Awful," he muttered.

Marion moved to assist in examining him; the woman frowned.

"He can do it. Don't need you, thank you all the same."

"I'll be going, Artemus," said Marion.

He looked up. "Where? What are you going to do?"

"Start packing."

She headed for the apartment, changed her mind, and turned toward the Warner's house. Every person she passed displayed some reaction of disapproval, ranging from a simple turning of the head to avoid her eyes to a mumbled, unintelligible remark. There was no need to hear what they said, for the tone certified their resentment.

It infuriated her. She could hardly wait to leave.

Marcus Venable slouched in a chair in Colonel Schreiber's office, glaring into space as Schreiber read the written report Sergeant Brennan had handed him. Brennan stood smartly at attention, head high, cap tucked under his arm. Schreiber read to himself, his lips moving slightly. He paused and looked up.

"Four casualties?"

"Two killed: Cabot and O'Leary. Two wounded: Incavelli, thigh wound, not serious, and Corporal Tremont, a busted finger, sir."

"Mmmm. Eleven braves killed. And Klee."

"Yes, sir. Mr. White Apache himself."

"You saw him die?"

Brennan inflated his chest an additional notch and gilded his tone proudly. "I killed him, sir. It's all right there. I come onto him in his wickiup. He fired and missed, I returned fire. Got him clean through the head."

"You're certain it was Klee."

"No mistaking that hair."

"Just making sure, Sergeant. He's been killed before, you know. Man has more lives than six cats."

"He used up his last one last night, sir."

"That'll be all for now. Good job."

Brennan saluted, wheeled smartly, and marched out. Schreiber's eyes remained fixed on the closed door for a moment before he returned his attention to the report.

"He says here he came upon your friend Dr. Sturges in Klee's wickiup. Evidently she'd been treating him. Weren't you at her place in town last night? Were you there when Klee's man came to get her?"

"Yes."

"I don't follow. Couldn't you talk her out of going?"

"She told me pointedly it was none of my business."

"Marcus—"

"When Brennan and the others chanced upon that *ranchería*, they did their jobs. She was only doing hers."

"It's not the same," said Schreiber.

"She seems to think so." Marcus pounded his fist on the desk. "Goddamn Brennan!"

Schreiber jerked his head up sharply, his eyes questioning.

"Why that particular camp? Why last night?" Marcus continued "And his timing was perfect. She thinks I sent them after her. She came back breathing fire. I swear, if she'd had a gun—"

Schreiber tittered. Marcus scowled. The colonel sobered.

"Excuse me, Captain. I know you've been seeing a lot of each other . . ."

"What?"

"Sorry, I'm prying. As for Brennan, as you said, he was only doing his job."

"What happened to Bob Sutherland last night? Didn't he have patrol?"

"His wife's been laid up. He asked to be relieved. Gaines was officer of the day. He let him off, didn't replace him. Sent the patrol out with Brennan in charge. It wasn't any deep, dark conspiracy—"

"I didn't say it was."

"He'd been in charge before. He could handle things, he did." He whistled softly. "Klee dead, my, my. That's one chronic headache cured. Quite a coup for the sergeant. He's probably expecting a rocker for his stripes."

The door squealed open. It was Olan holding a brown envelope.

"From Departmental Headquarters, sir."

Schreiber unwound the string binding the flap and got out a single sheet of paper. His eyes brightened; a beatific smile stretched his face. He whooped and pounded the desk, then handed the paper to Marcus.

"At last! At long last!"

It was from General Crook. General Lee had surrendered to Lieutenant General Grant at Appomattox Court House. Eight hundred men were to be immediately reassigned to duty in Arizona Territory.

"To be apportioned among the eleven posts," read Marcus.

"We'll get at least seventy!" Schreiber cried ecstatically. "New blood, Marcus, the first in three years!"

"And the war over at last. Just like that."

"Everybody could see it coming. Wait'll Tucson hears. We should send a man in to tell the mayor. He'll put on black, hang the town with crepe, and declare a week of mourning."

He was up and pacing, swinging his arms, clapping, beaming, exulting.

"When does it say the troops'll get here?" asked Marcus.

"It doesn't, just that they're coming. They'll probably report to Prescott en masse and be apportioned. Great Scott, isn't this exciting? We'll need mounts, gear, weapons. The works. Our manpower doubled, just like that! Hey, I have an idea. Why don't you go up to Prescott?"

"What for?"

"Find out all the specifics. Represent us. Make sure we get a fair shake."

"Lobby General Crook. He'd love that—"

"You know him, he likes you. With you there to protect our interests—"

"In his face, you mean." Marcus shook his head.

"Come on, I don't mean badger him, just . . ."

"Stroke him."

"Take a couple men with you. It's only a couple hundred miles— "

"Only."

"You can be there in two days. The other posts'll be sending representatives. If we don't have somebody up there, we'll wind up with the leavings."

"We could send a telegram."

"Be serious, we haven't gotten through by telegraph

since before the war. Every time the wires are repaired the Apaches cut 'em again in a different place. I want you to go. Bring back something with his signature on it. A guarantee we get *x* number of bodies. I'm not ordering you, Marcus, I'm asking."

"I suppose, but I can't say I like the idea of standing in line with my hand out."

"Oh, it won't be like that. Besides, it'll be good for you. You need a break."

There was no way he could see it would be good for him—or his horse. But there was no denying it was double-barrelled good news: the war was over, and reinforcements were on the way—and none too soon. Their arrival would bolster manpower, elevate morale, and bring closer the day of reckoning with the Apaches.

"I do wish you'd reconsider." Emmaline stared soberly at Marion.

They were having coffee in the parlor. Sunlight spilled across the carpet. Emmaline offered her a cookie. Marion had stated her case for leaving twice how, but neither Emmaline nor Artemus were convinced.

"Where will you go? Not back East."

"I haven't decided: I guess to Wilmot or Vail. Stop off, unwind, get my second wind, then decide. Maybe I'll catch up with my cousin Lillian and her husband Joe in California."

"This is dreadful! It's all wrong—"

"It's not. I don't belong here, Em. I don't fit. I never should have chosen Tucson in the first place."

"That's ridiculous. You never thought so before."

"Maybe I just never said so."

"You'll be deserting us."

"The mayor doesn't seem to think so."

"He's an ass! They all are. What about Marcus? He loves you. I've thought about what you said he did. I don't believe he'd do such a thing, and neither do you. And don't try to tell me you don't feel something for him. You've become inseparable. Marion, you can't get on that stage tomorrow. Tucson's your home."

"I won't deny I've gotten used to it. It's far from paradise, but that's its appeal. Like a mongrel dog: scruffy around the edges, boisterous, nothing to look at, no breeding, but somehow it worms its way into your heart."

"You love it, scorpions and all. Look me in the eye and tell me you want to leave."

"What I want doesn't matter. It's right. It's best for all concerned."

"I dare you to say that to Artemus. You go and he'll be swamped with patients. He's the one you'll really be deserting. He'll work himself to death."

"Never. He was on top of things when I got here—"

"But Tucson's practically doubled its population. And when the war's over, more emigrants will come. We'll need half a dozen doctors."

"They'll come." She laughed. "Like swindlers and gamblers, they always go where they're needed most. Doctors'll come, and if Tucson's lucky, none of them will share my misplaced sympathies for the underdog."

"I won't let you go. Neither will Artemus." Emmaline searched Marion's eyes and lowered her voice. "You *are* going to see Marcus, aren't you? He won't let you go. He'll tie you up to keep you here."

By the time Marion drew up to the fort in Artemus's buggy she was a bundle of nerves. She worried Marcus would take it badly, and they would end up quarreling. But she could see no way out of telling him. Olan showed in the doorway.

"I'm looking for Captain Venable."

"He's over at the stables. Behind Barracks B." He pointed. "Leaving for Prescott on business for the colonel. Maybe already gone. Didn't you hear? the war's over. General Lee gave up. Word come from Departmental Headquarters."

Marion gasped. "When did he surrender?"

"Yesterday. Isn't that something?"

As welcome as it was, it seemed strange and almost inapplicable in Tucson. They had been so far from the action it might as well have been taking place on another planet. Only the undercurrent of bitterness between the Southerners and the Northerners in town reminded people it was even going on. The only thing anyone cared about was the problem with the Apaches. That was Tucson's war.

Peace had arrived a bit late for Lieutenant Tyson Sturges, Marion thought as she drove to the stables. There was no sign of Marcus. Her heart sank. Two bare-chested and perspiring enlisted men were curry-combing horses.

"Captain Venable?"

They exchanged looks.

"Him and his escort left for Prescott about twenty minutes ago, ma'am."

"Did they take the Rillito road?" she asked, alarm creeping into her voice.

"Yes'm."

"Twenty minutes ago," repeated the other man. "Riding hard on their saddles. You'll never catch up in a buggy."

Marion drove slowly back to town. She would have to write a letter. Perhaps that would be best; at least there would be no way to argue.

Marcus and his two companions did not even slow passing through tiny Rillito. Red Rock and Picacho Peak loomed beyond. Since his conversation with Schreiber after Brennan left the office, Marcus had discarded his foul mood and shrugged off his resentment over Marion's accusation. It did appear as if he had alerted Brennan and the others. The pieces fit too neatly together, particularly the timing.

But none of it was true. She could have at least given him a chance to deny it, to swear he had never left the apartment and had no idea the patrol was working the south-center sector that night.

Because he had not been able to defend himself, she undoubtedly still thought him the culprit. If she had cooled down and changed her mind, she would have gone to the fort in the morning and apologized. But her apology was not the issue; her helping Klee was. The townspeople would never forgive her when they found out. They would probably run her out of town, and by the time he returned, she could be halfway to Kansas City.

"Damn!"

He could forget her bitter outburst. It had been a

simple misunderstanding. Marcus's heart lurched as he thought of never seeing Marion again. He was hopelessly in love, but suddenly he felt only hopeless.

Picacho Peak drew closer.

◄20►

I've a good mind to get on board and go with you," Artemus grumbled. "Leave these bone-headed ingrates to dig out their own bullets and dose their own miseries."

Emmaline had given Marion a parting gift of pen, ink, and stationery. She stood teary-eyed, shaking her head as Marion got into the coach. Solomon handed her a small package through the window.

"My going-away present," he said. "Nothing much. Book on whist."

Marion managed a grin.

"Solomon Warner," snapped Emmaline. "Couldn't you think of something more useful?"

"What in the world could be more useful than a book on whist?" he asked.

"I appreciate it," said Marion. "I'll read it cover to cover. Thank you all for coming."

Two-thirds of the town had come to see her off, but there were flames in their eyes rather than tears. The people crowding closest made no effort to keep from airing their sentiments. She appreciated her three friends' willingness to show up and lend moral support, though they seemed like three slender reeds standing against the inrushing, storm-roiled tide.

One other passenger was already seated when she boarded. He introduced himself as the Reverend Joseph Chatterton from Yuma on his way to Nutt, New Mexico, to assume the pulpit of a new church. He looked somewhat awed, dismayed, and slightly fearful when, after she took her seat, the crowd assembled around the stage, filling every window with scowls of disapproval. It must have appeared as if she had murdered some beloved pillar of Tucson society and that the townspeople deeply resented her escaping the hangman by leaving.

The driver cracked his whip.

"Write, please write," called Emmaline.

"I will, I promise."

"This stinks!" boomed Artemus. "You hear? Stinks!"

The coach rumbled off. Looking back, she could see the crowd breaking up. The show was over. A few of the more militant among them shook their fists after her. Her heart tugged; she got out a hanky and touched her nose. Artemus and Solomon were waving. Emmaline was crying.

"Good-bye, my friends," she whispered. She felt Reverend Chatterton's eyes boring into her.

He smiled sympathetically. "Anything I can do?"

"No, thank you."

"Shakespeare said parting is such sweet sorrow."

"Actually, my feelings are somewhat mixed."

"Care to talk about it?"

"No, thank you."

They had traveled only a hundred yards when the driver called to the horses and reined up. Mark Aldrich came running up waving a letter.

"Marion!"

He passed it through the open window. "I'm damned sorry to see you leave. It's wrong and stupid. That came for you early this morning. I completely forgot about it. Lucky I caught you before you left."

He glanced up at the driver, let go of the sill, and nodded. The stage rolled on. The letter was from the War Department. It was addressed to her apartment in Philadelphia and subsequently rerouted. She tore it open.

Dear Mrs. Sturges,

Through a most regrettable error the War Department previously informed you that your husband, First Lieutenant Tyson Matthew Charles Sturges, was killed in action at Petersburg, Virginia. The President is pleased and happy to inform you that such is not the case. Lieutenant Sturges was badly wounded in the aforementioned action, but was removed to Sheppard and Enoch Pratt Hospital in Baltimore where, after nearly a year he has completely recovered. He received his honorable discharge on March 27 last.

The President apologizes for this most regrettable error, recognizing that it could not help but cause you pain and anguish. He most humbly and earnestly asks your forgiveness.

Yours most sincerely,

E. M. Browder
War Department
Washington, D. C.

Marcus and his men got well beyond Phoenix before reining up for the night. They
did not quit until almost midnight. He reasoned that if
they rose at sunup and maintained the same pace, they
could reach Prescott shortly after sundown the following
day. On the far side of Phoenix, skirting Alhambra,
Glendale, and Peoria, they would pick up the Agua Fria
River and follow it through the wide valley west of the
Black Hills.

Ordinarily this was not renegade Apache country. It
was too well patrolled by troops from nearby Fort Whipple. Rising with the sun, the captain and his men ate
hurriedly and got back on the trail. By noon they were
well north of Peoria. The bulk of conversation continued
to focus on the expected reinforcements. Private Ephraim
Moody, a native Arizonian, and Private Elmer Colfax,
his buddy, who hailed from Hibbing, Minnesota, agreed
that Fort Lowell would get at least double the number of
men Colonel Schreiber was expecting.

"It figures, Captain. Posts up north and west don't
need manpower. All their boys do is sit and scratch their
hindends. And pot jackrabbits and snakes. They don't

get any ruckusing from the Apaches. Us and Grant and Fort Huachuca is the ones got our hands full.''

"He's right, sir." Colfax nodded.

"Only if you assume the Apache stays put. And don't we know better? They're constantly on the move, which means all eleven posts will need their share of the replacements."

"Talk around the barracks is the injuns are gonna join up together under Cochise or Geronimo. What do you think, sir?"

"I think, boys, we've got company."

Marcus pointed ahead and to the left. A puff of smoke rose steadily on a thermal draft against the high white sky. Another followed it upward.

"Damn Sam!" burst Moody. "Wouldn't you know we couldn't make it up to there without the ragheads coming calling!"

"That signal's about two miles from here and he's at least a thousand feet up," said Marcus. He glanced back the way they had come.

"There's another across from it," piped Colfax. "What'll we do, sir?"

"We'll run between 'em."

They stared, wide-eyed. Moody gasped. His Adam's apple looked as if it was trying to break out of his throat.

"They know we can see them signaling," explained Marcus.

"They're likely readying to bushwhack us up ahead," said Moody worriedly.

"Maybe they don't care about us," said Marcus. "Maybe they have other things on their minds."

He wanted to sound convincing, but his command was feeble.

"Let's go."

They broke into a full gallop. The horses were rested and eager to run, though how far and how fast remained to be seen. A scattering of boulders beckoned about three miles directly ahead, an ideal site for an ambush. Riding straight into them could be suicide, but their only other alternative was to turn around and flee, which would add another full day or more to their journey, circling the mountains to the east or west.

He figured they had a fifty percent chance that hostiles lurked behind the boulders ahead. If they did they wouldn't open up before he and his men reached them. They would bide their time until the three men started through, then hit them like a spiked vise.

Marcus slowed and pulled up. The others stopped ahead of him and looked back questioningly.

"You two stay here. I'm going ahead and have a look."

"But, Captain," protested Moody.

"Do as I say."

He took off, galloping straight into the canyon's mouth. He imagined dozens of armed savages concealed behind the boulders, hundreds more posted in nooks and out of sight on ledges in the mountains on both sides. The sun glared like a sheet of red-hot brass. He tasted dust, his horse's sweat, the dust collecting and caking; his teeth were enameled with grit. He spat repeatedly.

He rode cautiously, glancing left and right at the mountaintops, looking for more smoke signals. He saw none. It raised his hopes that it had only been two braves signaling each other, and that neither was concerned with the three intruding bluecoats. He would know for certain very shortly. He was sweating in earnest, the back of his shirt soaking, the sun boring into his neck. Two hundred yards from the boulders he drew and cocked his Colt.

A hundred yards. He swallowed so hard it felt as if he had pulled a muscle in his throat. The pain persisted. He tried to gently swallow it away. His eyes teared and collected dust granules. When he blinked he could almost hear the grinding. He heeled his horse.

Fifty yards.

Twenty-five.

He burst between the first two boulders. Not a soul crouched behind any of them. He pulled up sharply; his heart was pounding like Tubal-cain's hammer, threatening to shatter his rib cage. The horse was blowing hard, its sides heaving. He got down, holstered his weapon, and scanned the area. Not a single sign, not so much as a cast-off deer bone to suggest recent occupancy of the area.

He stiffened and listened, but the only sound was the wind. He climbed onto a boulder and signaled Moody and Colfax to join him. Moments later they came dusting up. He'd never seen two men look more relieved.

Ahead of them the all but completely dried-up Agua Fria turned eastward. Beyond lay tiny Bumble Bee, and roughly fifty miles beyond it, Prescott.

"Chrissakes, sir," blurted Moody. "I plumb had my heart in my mouth for you."

"We're not out of the woods yet."

"But ain't this Fort Whipple country?" asked Colfax.

Marcus smiled. "Tucson is Fort Lowell country; we still run into hostiles now and then."

"Every time we turn around, seems like," added Moody. "Chrissake, what a lousy, dried-up, no-good stretch this is."

Colfax leered. "Your home territory, Private."

"Not through choice, Private. You just watch my butt when I get that little old piece of paper in my hand."

"Let's go," said Marcus.

He stopped sweating from fear as they pressed on, although his glands continued to drain copiously from the heat. A surge of relief inched through his heart, quieting its thudding. The burl at the nape of his neck softened and dissolved as he relaxed.

He was premature. Ten miles farther on, well past Bumble Bee, thirty braves came whooping into view ahead. They spotted them, they gave chase. The way had widened considerably, and now nearly twenty miles separated the mountain ranges. The three riders had stayed close to the Black Hills on their right, almost within their shadow. Marcus took immediate advantage of this, veering right, leading them even closer to the slopes until they were within a few hundred yards of the oncoming savages. Then he cut sharply left, heading across the valley in an obvious all-out effort to circle the attackers.

The three of them had one invaluable advantage: their horses were grain-fed and therefore stronger, speedier, blessed with more endurance than the Apaches' grass-fed ponies. In a long chase they could not help but outdistance them, and the Apaches, unlike the Comanches, the Cheyenne, and other Plains tribes, were not superior horsemen. Although among the first North American Indians to acquire horses from the Spanish, they had never put them to such extensive use, or relied on them as much as the Plains Indians, and in reservation times never mastered the art of breeding horses.

But all these swift rays of optimism were collectively offset by one undeniable black fact: many Apaches were fond of racing horses, and from what he could see at a distance, their pursuers were among the fondest.

The Apaches also turned to ride laterally, bent on cutting the troopers off before they could turn the corner and slip behind them, which in effect, would turn the chase completely around. Moody and Colfax looked to be holding their own, but both, Marcus noted, were pale with fear when they might better be red from exertion.

The floor of the valley was cluttered with growth: mesquite, stunted pine, cacti. Ahead the mountains rose, looking closer than they actually were, uncomfortably close. Marcus spurred his horse, easing up between his men.

"Listen. When I say 'now,' cut as sharp right as you can. Pull all your weight right, scissor your horse with your legs tight as you can, and hang on."

"We're kicking dust up real good," said Colfax. "Maybe they won't see and catch on right off."

"Maybe," said Marcus.

He slipped two lengths behind, then yelled "Now!" and reined so sharply right his mount stumbled and nearly fell, but made it, finished the turn, and headed back toward the Black Hills. The maneuver caught the Apaches completely by surprise and it was long, precious seconds before they turned back. By the time they did, the three men had added a good twenty yards to the distance between chased and chasers. Back in the lead, Marcus swung left, Colfax and Moody following. They were now heading straight up the valley, and it crossed Marcus's mind that the Apaches were so eager to catch them they weren't thinking; had he been in their position he would have spread his men in a line, creating a barrier that his quarry would either have to break through or retreat from. If they tried to break through, they could be shot at, and at a distance of less than twenty yards any Apache worth his head cloth could put an arrow through a man-sized moving target at twenty yards.

He felt his horse beginning to tire. Arrows came singing at them like a swarm of angry hornets. He yelled; they spread out and began weaving, flattening in their saddles. They fired blindly back. But still the arrows came, winging, singing death. Moody cast a quick look behind.

"Can't see 'em, too much dust!"

Out of the cloud came a flurry of shafts.

"How far to Prescott, sir?" yelled Colfax.

"Too far," shouted Marcus. "But Cordes is just ahead. Only about forty souls last time I was through here, but sight of the buildings should be enough to discourage them."

"My horse is getting winded," complained Moody. "I feel it through my knees."

"So are their ponies. When we see Cordes, they'll quit."

Death came from behind. Blind death, Sutherland called it. The worst of it was not knowing when the arrow would hit, feeling it a dozen times before it happened. If it did find its mark, when the point shattered vertebrae and plowed through, pain would strike like a red-hot poker and radiate in every direction, shooting to the tips of the fingers, down the legs, up the spine to the brain and exploding. Eyeballs would roll upward for one final glimpse of blue sky, then blackness and nothing.

Moody was sneaking a second look behind, unconsciously raising his trunk slightly. He had emptied his gun, wasting cartridges on the dust cloud. Colfax's gun, too, clicked harmlessly. Marcus did not bother to shoot.

"Keep down!" he bellowed at Moody.

He could not guess how much of a lead they held, but he knew that it was not enough.

His rolled-up blanket was draped over his horse's back and snugged under his cantle. Had they had time to prepare for the chase, he would have gotten it out, folded it four-square, and stuffed it up under the back of his shirt, or tied it to himself with a rawhide thong.

An arrow whirred over his right shoulder so close he could almost feel the shaft pass his neck. Praise God, the Apaches had only bows, though in their hands they were as good as rifles.

A speck on the horizon became a squat cluster of

low-lying ramshackle buildings: little gray wooden boxes bunched like chicks around a mother hen. Cordes! The instant Marcus sighted it, the arrows stopped.

They barreled into town, slowing, reining up, the horses so exhausted it amazed Marcus that they could still stand upright.

Moody dismounted, patted his horse affectionately, and led it to a nearby trough.

"I wish it was beer, little lady. You deserve it."

Marion was still in shock. She read the letter three times before it sank in. She sat quietly holding the single sheet. Tears streamed down her face.

Reverend Chatterton stared at her in alarm.

"Oh, my dear, is it bad news? I'm so sorry, how dreadful for you."

"It's good news."

She explained.

"How marvelous! I'm so happy for you. Oh my. Oh gracious! The Lord moves in mysterious ways His wonders to perform."

"How could they do such a terrible, such a heartless thing?"

"I beg your pardon?"

"Why didn't they make absolutely sure before they sent that awful wire?"

"Oh yes, well, mistakes are made in the heat of battle and the confusion that follows. It's unfortunate—"

"They're a pack of idiots! Putting people through needless agony, misery . . ."

"But now you have him back. To err is human, to forgive—"

"Please!" She softened her tone. "I'm sorry. You're right, of course. I should be celebrating."

"Rejoicing. Let all bitterness, and wrath, and anger, and clamor, and evil speaking be put away from you, with all malice."

"Yes, yes."

Would he continue to fling quotes from the scriptures at her all the way to Nutt? They were coming into tiny Wilmot, situated about seven miles to the southeast of Tucson. She decided to get off as she had originally planned. Everything had happened so fast, the rush of events confused her so she wanted time to sit down and think things through. Her first inclination had been to keep going to Garden City, Kansas, then catch the first train back to Philadelphia, or even directly to Baltimore.

But that made no sense. Tyson had long since been discharged from the hospital in Baltimore. The letter said he had been discharged from the army two weeks ago. He had probably gone straight to Philadelphia looking for her. By now he would have found Gabriel and been told that she was in Tucson.

By now he was probably riding a stage coach through New Mexico along the route she herself had taken last year. It would be stupid to distance herself farther from Tucson, making him chase her all the way back.

Wilmot boasted only one hotel, though it looked like more of an apology than a boast. But it would have to do until Tyson got there. One of them would have to stand still; he would find her. She would send a message back to Artemus. When Tyson arrived he would direct him back here. She could also keep an eye on the stage coaches passing through. There couldn't be more than one or two a week coming through from the East. Tyson would be on one.

She registered and was given a corner room at the front overlooking the main street—the only street. She ordered up a plunge bath and immersed herself in the steaming water with her last bar of Pears soap, determined to wash Tucson off her body and out of her memory.

Erasing Marcus from memory would be more difficult. She wished she could have said good-bye to him properly. It would have been nice to part company with good feelings, no matter how sad they were.

She would write. He would be happy for her. And she would miss him.

She lounged in the tub for more than an hour, until the water became tepid and the bubbles vanished. Getting dressed, she felt better; the prospect of being reunited with Tyson dominated her thoughts. Anticipation consumed her.

Before going out for lunch she gave a message to the

desk clerk with a dollar. He promised to have it delivered to Artemus. It contained her good news, which he would tell Emmaline and Solomon. Before nightfall all of Tucson would know, though few would care.

Marcus would hear. It was a shame that he would have to learn of it in such a manner, but he would understand. And when the shock passed, he would be happy for her.

—•◄22►•—

Three days passed. On the morning of the fourth day Marion had an unexpected visitor. Emmaline drove over from Tucson. They sat in the hotel room. Next door a child was crying and down the street a blacksmith's hammer rang. Marion told her the good news.

"Fantastic!" burst Emmaline. "Marvelous!"

"And infuriating. I'd like to mass hang the entire War Department."

"They did botch things awfully, didn't they? But it's all worked out. You'll be together again. I'm so happy for you!" Her smile glowed, then slowly gave way to a worried look. "Only poor Marcus . . ."

"Yes."

"You'll tell him."

"Of course. I started a letter. About thirty of them, actually. I can't seem to get past the first few lines."

"You love him, don't you, Marion?"

"I did. But it's over."

"Oh yes, it has to be. Poor Marcus. I haven't seen him around town. Is he away?"

"Gone to Prescott.'

Emmaline's eyes suddenly widened, and she smacked

221

her forehead with her palm. "I'm forgetting why I came. To bring you back."

"No, thank you."

"Artemus sent me. He said if I don't bring you back I'm not to come back myself. He needs you desperately. Remember little Howard Barker?"

"I remember. He had measles."

"He was just the first; since you left there've been seven more cases. Artemus says it's an epidemic. He's so busy he hasn't slept more than two hours in the past three days. He said to tell you if he dies from overwork, he'll come back and haunt you. Marion, you must come back and help."

"I'd really rather not. The thought of seeing all those faces again—"

"You're not afraid of them. Besides, Artemus has fixed everything. Last night he stood on the whipping post platform in the plaza and made a speech. Practically the whole town was there. Artemus bawled them out till his face was blue and theirs were red for the way they treated you. Shamed the britches off them. Painted lurid pictures of what a measles epidemic can do. He said instead of hounding you out they should have pleaded with you to stay, and the only way to make amends is to welcome you home like the ministering angel from heaven you are."

Marion was flattered, but all she could do was laugh.

"He was something. He heaped fire and brimstone on their heads like the Lord sent down the day Lot left Sodom. After he was done Mayor Oury came up to him looking like a whipped hound and practically begged him to get in touch with you and talk you into coming back."

"Did Artemus really call it an epidemic?"

"Seven cases. And probably six more since I left. Solomon says he's never seen Artemus so worked up. We talked to him after your stage pulled out. He was in a daze, honestly, Marion. And when Oury and some of the others came up to him he wouldn't speak to them. But that was some speech. He hit them smack in their consciences."

"That's assuming they have any."

Emmaline studied her archly. "You're not bitter . . ."

"Not really. Mostly let down. I suppose I was bitter when I left, but staying that way is childish."

"You *will* come back. Tyson will come for you, won't he?" Emmaline paled. "Oh dear—"

"What?"

"When he comes, when you get back together, you won't leave again, will you?"

"I don't know, Em. I don't know if he'll want to settle in Tucson. He may have too many unpleasant memories of Petersburg and Southerners to want to live among so many Southern sympathizers."

"But the war's over. There isn't any North or South anymore, just one country."

It was a pleasant prospect, but Marion knew it was much too idealistic. Yet from the look on Emmaline's face, it was obvious she believed what she'd said and that could be turned on and off like a faucet. Would that such was possible, Marion thought, that scars might disappear at the blink of an eye.

Riding back with Emmaline in the buggy, her emotions were churning. Part of her wanted to return, and not just because Tyson would be showing up. It was the part that had developed a fondness for the town, pride in being a resident, in seeing it grow and prosper. The other part of her remained apprehensive over her reception. It was hard to believe Oury and his cronies had undergone a complete change of heart. It was more likely, as Emmaline had hinted, the fear of measles Artemus had burned into their minds with his scary oratory. She wasn't so naive as to expect to be welcomed back. She expected to face a few snide remarks and insults, but hopefully only a scattering of scowls. Klee was dead; what she had done for him was choked on or swallowed. There was nothing she could do about that. And she couldn't win back the favor of the more resentful residents by performing some heroic act, running around saving lives. She would have her hands full helping Artemus keep the measles from spreading.

It was highly contagious. Almost everyone exposed who had never had it previously, caught it then. It was a universal childhood experience and adults were not exempt from its ravages. Its clinical course was characteristic. The time that elapsed between exposure and the onset of the symptoms varied between a week and twenty days. Fever signaled the onset. Eye symptoms like Howard Barker's followed in about twelve hours. It continued with coughing, a runny nose, fire in the throat, and conjunctivitis. Lastly, the eruption: the final fireworks display, as Gabriel Cowan used to call it, a splotchy, reddish-purplish set of crescentic masses that showed on every part of the body. But when they emerge, the patient begins to feel better and his temperature drops.

It was very important to isolate the afflicted from the rest of the family, because cross-infections were common and complications resulted in middle-ear disease and possibly pneumonia. Death, although far from common, could result. Gabriel Cowan had a theory that one was most vulnerable during the catarrhal stage which preceded the rash. To prevent an epidemic, any head cold accompanied by an irritating dry cough was treated as measles.

Marcus was so sore and exhausted he nearly collapsed. The Old Gray Fox had smilingly promised him ninety seasoned troopers for Fort Lowell, a figure that more than doubled its existing strength—more than he had expected, but fewer than Colonel Schreiber had hoped for. Schreiber greeted him.

"Jesus, Mary, and Joseph, you look as if you'd ridden nonstop from New England!"

"I feel like it."

Marcus gave him the results. Schreiber accepted the figure with tolerance if not grace.

"Oh well, if that's the best the old stable boy can do."

"What's been happening around here? Anything? Any fracases?"

"It's been unbelievably quiet. There doesn't seem to be a single Apache for miles around. Of course, the men on patrol don't turn over rocks. But that surprise raid last Sunday night seems to have chilled their ardor for the fray. I dug deep into the kitty and purchased a dozen fine mustang mares from a farm on the Mesilla road. And we got a shipment of about half a ton of canned corn beef. The War Department's getting positively lavish now that the shooting's stopped. Oh, there's a bit of personal news that might interest you, concerning Dr. Sturges. She's left town."

Marcus sank his teeth into his lower lip to keep from exploding. "She didn't 'leave,' did she, Justin? They drove her out."

Justin nodded. "They're stupid. The population's more than doubled since she came. Shaw can't possibly handle all the sick and injured. Those people are morons. I swear!"

"Oh, I'm sure other doctors will be settling here," Justin reassured him. "Tucson got its first minister a couple weeks ago, and two days after that its second. I hear the Presbyterians are collecting money to build a church."

"Hounded her out, narrow-minded ingrates!"

"She may have left you a message. If you're going into town, stop by Shaw's office. If there is one, she'd leave it with him."

Marcus stopped abruptly. "I almost forgot the biggest news of all from Prescott. George Crook is leaving."

Schreiber's jaw dropped in astonishment.

"I got it in confidence from his adjutant. It's not official yet, so we can't spread it around, but he's decided. He's leaving for the Department of the Platte."

The colonel's initial surprise gave way to an understanding smile. He nodded knowingly.

"Phil Sheridan."

"What?"

"Nelson Miles. A blind man could see it coming. I keep an eye on military politics, especially those that affect us. Fascinating chess game. General Miles has had his eye on this hot end of nowhere for some time. He recently married Sheridan's favorite niece. Intensely ambitious fellow. Every general is ambitious, has to be to get his star and hang onto it, get another. But Nelson Miles makes Caesar seem retiring by comparison. And he's wanted the Department of Arizona for years."

And, Schreiber went on, Sheridan wanted just as badly for him to have it. Sheridan had a strong personal dislike for George Crook, and even though Crook had made his reputation as an Indian fighter, Sheridan considered him soft on Indians. For his part Crook regarded Sheridan as unnecessarily cruel and vindictive, and couldn't stand the sight of him. Nelson Miles, one of the few non-West Pointers to make a name for himself on the western plains, had started out buying his commission.

"A slap in the face to the regular West Pointers," Schreiber scowled.

But Miles had risen to the rank of brevet major general on merit and was a field officer to Sheridan's particular taste: courageous and ruthless. He attacked Indian encampments ferociously and showed no concern for the humanity of his enemies.

"Remember Thaddeus Willoughby? General Crook reduced him to lieutenant and shipped him practically to Canada for that Aravaipa Canyon mess. Had Miles been in charge he'd have bumped him up a grade and given him a medal."

"How can you be sure Miles will be the one to replace Crook?"

Schreiber tapped his temple.

"Very sure. I'll bet you my month's pay against yours. And when he takes over he'll turn this territory upside down, shake out every dirty little brown savage and cut their hearts out. Personally, if he can. He'll see that every post has troopers in the field twenty-four hours. Just you wait, you're going to see some changes. Did Crook's adjutant suggest any time frame?"

"He doesn't know, but soon."

"Very soon. Maybe even next week. You don't know Nelson Miles, do you?"

"Nothing about him."

"He'll toss out every policy Crook's instituted and replace them with his own. No more persuasion, no more helping the Apaches learn farming and sheep herding. No more land set aside for them. No more digging irrigation ditches. It's going to be guns and blood from the New Mexico border to the Colorado River. No, thank you, that does it for this old war-horse."

"What are you talking about?"

"What does it sound like? I'm resigning."

"You can't!"

"Who says? The war's over. I promised myself when it ended I'd call it quits. It may have escaped your attention, but I haven't climbed on a horse, except to ride into town a couple times, in months. Not a lick, not two minutes of action. And that's what you'll see day and night when Miles takes over. Orders'll come thundering down to wipe them out. If I were thirty years younger, I'd be jumping up and down on this desk. But I'm taking myself out of the game.

"I never told you, but I have a house in Monterey. Not Mexico, Monterey in western Massachusetts. It's empty, just waiting for me. Has since my wife Kate, may the saints bless her, passed on to her reward. There's a rocking chair on the front stoop and room over the fireplace to hang my saber. I'll get my pension. It won't make me rich, but I'll get by. I'll sit and rock and listen to the birds and sip iced tea and think back on the past thirty-five years. Thirty-six come next week."

"A week. That's how long it'll take to get to you. Send you climbing up the walls."

"No. I won't let it. Other men retire, so can I. Gracefully, Marcus, comfortably, enjoyably. Wouldn't you say I deserve a rest? And you, my boy, deserve your chance. I intend to recommend you to take my place, take permanent command. Beat the drum, get you your gold leaf. You've earned it. I'll see that you get it. Now get out of here before you collapse on me. And thanks again, *Major* Venable."

Marcus left the office more than slightly stunned by Schreiber's disclosure. He had never mentioned owning a house back in Massachusetts, never told him he was a widower. He really knew very little about the man, mainly because he kept his private life private. He did know that he had not started out intending to become a career officer. A devout Catholic, Schreiber's ambition had been to enter the priesthood. He would have, but evidently fell in love and changed his plans accordingly.

And the military was a priesthood itself, demanding devotion, unflagging loyalty, a rigidly regulated existence that deprived one of the freedoms and luxuries and opportunities of civilian life.

Marcus yawned. It was all too much to assimilate at the moment. His brain was closed for the day. He started across the parade ground toward his quarters and his waiting bed.

Marion had left. So be it. He could hardly expect her

to wait around for him with the way Tucson felt about her.

"Narrow-minded idiots. They don't deserve a decent doctor!" he muttered to himself.

She was gone, probably on her way back to Philadelphia. She had tried on Tucson, buttoned it up only to find it did not fit. And that was that. It was over. They would never see each other again. In a few days or a week he would get a long letter: apology, kind words, warm sentiments sincerely felt, blame heaped upon herself for running out on him.

He saw nothing he could do about it, so he refused to rake his soul over it. He decided instead to crawl into bed with a pint of whatever he could find in his locker, soften the aching with a few stiff belts, and fall asleep.

And wake up in the morning still in love. Now, tomorrow, forever; shaking her out of his heart would be impossible.

There had been no good-bye.

So deeply did he plunge into the morass of discouragement, he failed to hear the buggy approach behind him.

"Marcus . . ."

He turned. She was shading her eyes from the sun, smiling down at him. For a second he imagined his eyes were playing tricks. It was the sun. Then she spoke again.

"How was your trip?" she asked.

"You're back!"

He ran to her, helped her down, and hugged her so tightly she squealed in protest. He covered her face with kisses, holding her, reveling in her dizzying warmth.

"Marion, Marion . . ."

She broke from him gently and glanced about. No one was watching them. The wind whipped the brim of her straw hat. She took it off. In the bright sunlight she looked radiant.

"When I heard," he went on, "I thought you were gone for good. But you couldn't leave, you had to come back!"

"We have to talk, Marcus."

"Great news, sweetheart. Justin Schreiber's retiring. I'm to take over permanent command. And I've been promoted to major!"

"Wonderful!"

"You mean it? Because if you want, I'll refuse it. I'll quit the Army. I've saved quite a bit of money, enough to buy a place of our own. A small farm, a ranch, even a store in town if you'd rather. Will you marry me?"

It struck her like a blow coming at her unseen. She gasped. He was too excited to notice. He kissed her tenderly, but as their lips parted a troubling thought shadowed his joy: something was wrong. She was not responding.

"What is it?" he asked.

"Marcus, there's something I have to tell you."

"Good news, I hope, but what could be better than this? I love you!"

"Please."

"I missed you so, to not even see each other for almost a week."

She had to tell him. The longer she delayed the harder it would be for her, the harder for him to accept. But she simply could not do it; he was ecstatic. To shatter his mood would be devastating and heartless. It would be better to wait for a more opportune time, like later that night. It would give him time to come back down to earth.

She eased from his arms and picked up the reins, preparing to climb up onto the buggy seat.

"What are you doing?" he asked. "Where are you going?"

"I have to get back to the office. Come by tonight. Seven o'clock all right?"

"Fine. But what was it you wanted to tell me?"

"It can wait till tonight. Get some sleep, you look exhausted."

"Till seven," he murmured. "It'll be years till then . . ."

He kissed her hand and waved her away.

Artemus was out of the office, but came back shortly after Marion showed up. He looked even more harried and fatigued than usual, but a broad, beaming smile warmed his face at sight of her.

"The prodigal returns!"

"As if you didn't expect me. I heard about your speech."

"Some speech. I lost my temper. Even we saints do

once in a while, you know. Actually, I think what turned our numbskull clientele around was that they finally came to their limited senses."

"How bad is the measles, really?"

"You think I exaggerated to your friend Mrs. Warner? That Howard Barker and I are in cahoots? We already have nine cases, and more on the way. Have you ever had it?"

"Yes."

"Lucky you. I haven't."

"Oh, Artemus—"

"Relax, I'm too old to catch anything communicable. I'll die in bed at a hundred and fifteen."

"If you didn't have it as a child you're as susceptible as a child."

He grunted. "Is this going to be your measles lecture, Dr. Know-it-all?"

"Just don't catch cold and don't get your feet wet."

"In what, blood? This is Arizona, lady, the waterless wonderland of the Western Hemisphere. I'm keeping the little nippers and Judge Meyer completely isolated. The judge is in a pretty bad way; you may want to look in on him. And don't worry, he's not down on you for treating Klee. He doesn't care."

"A pity the others don't share his indifference."

Artemus leered. "Relax. That's where we got 'em, missy. They won't dare beat up on your sensitivities now. Not with little Johnny lying in his darkened bedroom looking like a polka-dot calico."

He was taking fistfuls of tongue depressors from the cabinet and putting them in his bag. One would have thought the measles was spreading like bad news all over the West.

"I hear the captain's back," he said.

"I saw him."

"Mrs. Warner told me your good news, the resurrection. Did you tell him?"

"No."

Artemus continued working without looking at her. "In case you haven't noticed, he's in love with his doctor. Worship may not be a strong enough word." He turned and put on his most serious face. "You should play straight with him, Marion. Tell him. Get it over with before Lazarus shows up."

"I know, I know."

"Do you want me to tell him for you? I'm good at breaking bad news."

"You enjoy it, you mean." She shook her head and smiled.

"So when do *you* plan on telling him?"

"That's none of your business, Artemus."

"I'm only trying to help."

"I'll tell him tonight. He's coming over." Marion stepped toward the door.

"Make sure he's sitting down. What are you doing? Where are you going?"

"To look in on Judge Meyer."

"Oh, he's not as bad as I made out. His rash is starting, he's in the home stretch. Damned fool never even told anybody he'd come down with it. I'm sure he's been lying in bed dosing himself with every homeopathic nostrum he carries in his store. You coming back?"

"After lunch."

"Good. We've got at lot of catching up to do, Marion."

"I've only been gone three days."

"I took the liberty of speaking to your landlady. Told her you'd be back and not to rent your apartment."

"You're incorrigible!"

He leered. She held back a grin. It was good to be home.

Marcus came early. He looked rested, and his ebullience had not diminished in the least. He looked ecstatic. He looked like a man so in love he couldn't contain himself. Her heart sank at the sight. He carried a bunch of desert poppies.

He kissed her hello. "I'm a little early."

"That's okay. Marcus, we have to talk."

"Me first. Before I burst. Sit down, please."

He fumbled in his pocket and brought out at small, square, velvet-covered box tied with a ribbon. Oh, how I hate this, she thought, trying to hide her disappointment.

"I was so happy this morning when you showed up, I guess I didn't make much sense. But I got a few hours' sleep and woke up with a clear mind. I rode into town to

Cleary's." He undid the ribbon and proffered the box.
"Open it."

She did.

"It's called pear shape. I walked into the store, up to
the case and it hit me in the eye. I said to Mrs. Cleary,
'that's it, that's the one!' "

"It's beautiful."

"I love you, Marion. When I thought I'd lost you for
good—"

"Please, I have to tell you something."

She rose from the divan, looked through her handbag,
and got out the letter. She unfolded and handed it to
him. He lowered his questioning eyes to it and began to
read. His smile slowly faded, his face darkened. Pain was
clearly visible in his eyes when he back to her.

"The stage was leaving," Marion said. "Mark Aldrich
caught up with it and handed me that."

"You said he was killed at Petersburg."

"The War Department made a mistake. He was
wounded, but survived. He ended up in a hospital in
Baltimore. He was there almost a year. I have no idea
what was wrong, why he didn't contact me through Gabriel Cowan in Philadelphia. Maybe he was in a coma,
maybe delirious, amnesia, who knows?"

"Have you heard from him since he got out?"

"Not yet, but I expect to any day. He has to be on his
way here."

"But if you haven't heard—"

"He must be. When they released him from the hospital and he was discharged from the Army, I'm sure he
went to Philadelphia and spoke with Gabriel."

"Do you still love him?"

"He's my husband."

"You love me. You know you do." There was more
hope than certainty in his tone, she noticed.

"I . . ."

"You don't?"

"I can't, Marcus."

"No. Of course not. I'm sorry."

He stood, looking devastated, so crushed that for a
moment he could not go on. He groped for something to
say. She eyed him pityingly.

"Oh, Marcus . . ."

He had returned the ring to its box. He snapped it shut. It sounded like a pistol cracking.

"Well, doesn't this beat the devil? Talk about being in the wrong place at the wrong time." He laughed thinly. "Wrong man. Congratulations are in order, Doctor. I mean it; it's wonderful, a miracle. You deserve it after what they put you through. I wish you only the best."

"I hate this, hurting you."

"Don't be silly. I'm a soldier—battle-hardened and all that. I can take it." He grinned. "I admit I'm stunned. I certainly have made a gigantic fool of myself, haven't I?"

"Don't talk nonsense."

"I do love you."

Marion looked at him for a long moment. "And I love you," she said softly.

"It's good to hear you say it."

"I mean it." She took his hand. "We'll always be friends. Oh God, that sounds so pathetic."

"I'd better go."

"Please don't. Dinner's on. It'll be ready in a few minutes. Chicken—"

A knock interrupted her. She went through the inner door to the front door and opened it.

She gasped.

"Tyson!"

23

Tyson looked fit, as handsome as ever; the only change she could see was the small, slender lines that darted from his eyes. He kissed her passionately. Her heart thundered as she yielded, she could feel her eyes beginning to fill with tears, then she suddenly remembered Marcus. He stood awkwardly behind her. She freed her mouth from Tyson's and turned.

"I'll be going," he said and managed a smile.

She introduced them. They shook hands.

"It's marvelous," Marcus said. "I'm very happy for you both."

"Thank you," said Tyson.

Marcus left. Tyson closed the door and came back inside, going to the window to watch Marcus pass through the gate.

"Who's the handsome soldier boy? Your lover?"

"A friend," she snapped.

"I'm sorry, my love. That was uncalled for. Jealous husband, that's me. Can you blame me? My wife is so beautiful."

Again he kissed her, a thousand kisses held in abeyance, combined in one. It came from their souls. He trembled slightly.

"Are you all right?" she asked.

"Physically, so they tell me. Mentally—oh, not loony, just still a little worked up. Upset. Chip on my shoulder, thanks to those blundering idiots. Did you get my letters? I wrote you from Philadelphia right after I saw Cowan. And the next day."

"The mail is insidiously slow. All I've gotten so far is this."

She showed him Browder's letter.

"Isn't this something? Isn't it incredible? A stinking note of apology. You'd think they'd stepped on your foot. We killed him; oh no, we didn't, sorry. Do you know I didn't find out they'd sent you that first wire until la couple weeks ago? They had everything in a mess. Had me listed in the hospital records as Lieutenant Edgar Thompson, whoever he is. Six feet under, probably."

He was up and pacing. He appeared extremely nervous.

"How were you wounded? Where?"

"You name it. In the shoulder, the thigh; in the head mainly. I was in a haze for months and months. They could have called me by number and I wouldn't have known the difference."

"Shell shock."

"I don't know what they called it and I don't care. Anyway, I lay there day after day all last year, the first three months of this one, Lieutenant Nobody. They couldn't do a thing for me. I finally snapped out of it. Woke up one morning clearheaded, completely recovered and they say congratulations, Lieutenant Thompson. I got it all straightened out by noontime. Got out of the hospital, went straight to Philadelphia to Wills. You should have seen me, I was worked up to a frenzy. When Cowan told me you'd moved to Arizona it stunned me so I nearly passed out. I settled some business and caught the first train. I changed to a stage coach from Garden City, Kansas, to Santa Fe. Got off there, bought myself a horse and gear, and here I am. Oh, my darling!"

He threw his arms around her. Her heart surged and sang.

"It's been a thousand years," she said.

"Not to me. The way my head was, it's like last week."

"You look tired."

"Long ride. Over four hundred miles to Lordsburg,

New Mexico, alone. I stayed over two nights there, got my second wind. Gave the horse a chance to get hers."

"Wouldn't you like to lie down?"

"In a while maybe. Right now I just want to sit here and look at you and thank God for miracles."

"Oh, Tyson, we are lucky, aren't we? What a crazy thing."

"Ah, that's number one on the agenda. It *was* crazy, but it never should have been. Before I got on the train I met with a lawyer, two lawyers, matter of fact. They say we have an ironclad case. We, my darling, you and I are suing the federal government for . . . one million dollars?"

Marion was shocked. "*Can* you sue the government?"

"We can, we are, and we'll win. We don't even have to show up in court. I signed a deposition, just my signature's required. Thirty-one pages detailing the whole horror story. It's all the lawyers need, according to Mr. Staley. Staley and Barton, one of Philadelphia's most prestigious law firms. They'll fight for us, get us our money, and they don't charge a nickel until the settlement. A million dollars, darling! They've already released it to the papers. It'll be all over the country. Staley promised to send me copies of the stories in the Philadelphia papers. The War Department will rue the day they killed me with their stinking telegram."

"I don't care about the money. Having you back is all that matters, Tyson."

"But don't you think we deserve it? I'm suing for you, for all they put you through. You wouldn't have come all the way out here if it weren't for their blundering." He chuckled. "You couldn't have gotten much farther away from the scene of the crime. *Their* crime."

"When I heard, I wanted to get away from everything familiar and start over. Only Gabriel was right, my heartache was the last thing I packed and the first I unpacked when I got here."

He held her hands and kissed them. "Well, it's over now. We can both start fresh. When I got here I asked one of the locals where I could find you, Aldrich the postmaster. He said you're the best thing that's happened to Tucson in years, these people are lucky you're here. I could have told him that. And you should hear Cowan rave about you. Darling?"

"Yes?"

"Why am I sitting here babbling on and on?"

His arms flew around her. She drew her breath in sharply as she yielded to the touch of his hard body. In his embrace she felt pliant as a reed. She groaned as a rush of eager anticipation swept down to her sex. His hands moved slowly down her back. He lifted her to her feet. They stood, arms clasped tightly around one another. She pressed herself against him and felt his enormous hardness. She fought to catch her breath, weakening in his embrace.

He was back, his arms around her, his heart against hers, his kisses warm and loving. All the loneliness, the despair and regret, all the gray days and nights were swept away by the glow of his smile, the passion in his eyes. The painful memories vanished and their love was restored.

"At last," he murmured.

She clung to him, burying her face in the crevice of his shoulder. The fire of his kisses trailed down her cheek and moved to the hollow of her throat.

His hands cupped her breasts, gently caressing, teasing her nipples with his fingertips, driving her slowly mad with anticipation. He slid his mouth down to one white mound, and her heart leaped. She moaned as his hand slid below her stomach, stroking her and releasing her desire.

They lowered themselves on the bed. Returning his mouth to hers, he moved his firm, strong, beautiful body upward, hovering over her. She arched her back, mutely imploring him to begin.

Slowly he descended. She wrapped her legs around him, drawing him deeper and deeper. He thrust, and his features were transfigured by the mask of passion.

They began pounding faster, their bodies meeting and separating in the quickening tempo of lust. He seized her waist and pulled her high against him, driving, rushing to climax, exploding.

She let out a cry of ecstasy as she came with him. He twisted and thrust madly inside her, still hard and pumping after he was spent. All her nerve endings came alive as his pelvis continued to rock against her.

"I love you," she rasped.

"I adore you," he whispered.

His voice seemed to reach her from a great distance. It touched her ear, a feather of a sound.

"Adore you," he repeated.

She moaned and a dim vision of him appeared behind her closed eyes. His features were indistinct in the haze.

"Worship you," he whispered.

"My love," she murmured. "My dearest Marcus."

24

H istory has no strict pace. Events moved quickly at Fort Lowell following the cessation of hostilities between North and South. The Old Gray Fox, General George Crook, had indeed decided that his work in Arizona was at an end. The handwriting was clearly inscribed on the official wall of resistance to his humane policies formulated in what he considered to be the best interests of the Apaches and their pale-eyed, would-be conquerers. He favored neither side; he favored and sincerely believed in the possibility of a lasting peace.

His successor, General Nelson Miles, wanted no part of Crook's policy of pacification. Miles had been a drygoods clerk in his hometown of Westminster, Massachusetts, when the Civil War erupted. He entered the army in September 1861 as a lieutenant in the 22nd Massachusetts volunteer infantry and served with distinction in the Peninsular campaign and at Antietam, Fredericksburg, and Chancellorsville, where he was wounded and incapacitated up until the opening of Grant's Virginia campaign of 1864. He commanded a brigade at the Wilderness and Spottsylvania, and in May 1864 was rewarded for his gallant leadership, being named brigadier general of volunteers.

General Philip Sheridan had personally selected Miles to replace the departing Crook, just as Colonel Schreiber prophesied he would. Sheridan and Miles were of like mind in their disapproval of Crook's policy of appeasement. For some time Crook had been under fire from Americans in the Southwest who felt the Apaches should be eliminated to the last squaw and child. Crook was also under fire from his superior, Sheridan, a traditionalist who heartily disapproved of the use of Apache scouts. The whip stroke that killed the mule came as a result of the Old Gray Fox's abortive secret meeting with Geronimo. In response to his report came a curt telegram:

YOUR DISPATCH OF YESTERDAY RECEIVED STOP IT HAS OCCASIONED GREAT DISAPPOINTMENT STOP IT SEEMS STRANGE THAT GERONIMO AND HIS PARTY COULD HAVE ESCAPED WITHOUT THE KNOWLEDGE OF THE SCOUTS

Crook was furious at this insult. He resigned and went off to Omaha to assume command of the Department of the Platte. General Nelson Miles arrived in Prescott. His first decision was to arrange for all Mimbres and Chiricahua Apaches on the reservations—including scouts who had fought with Crook—to be exiled to Florida.

His second order was to formally acknowledge retiring Lieutenant Colonel Justin Schreiber's request to name Captain Marcus Venable to succeed him as post commander at Fort Lowell. Assuming command and being promoted to major should have set Marcus aglow with pride and satisfaction. But other things occupied his mind.

On the morning Colonel Schreiber bid formal farewell to his command and his private good-byes to Marcus, the colonel took note of the major's dismal mood. They sat in the major's office. The colonel's bag was packed. He wore a broadcloth suit recently purchased in town and, he confessed, the first mufti he had put on in thirty-six years. The two joined in a glass of port and Marcus broke out a box of Cuban panatellas.

"Shake it off, my friend," said the colonel. "Forget about her."

"I wish I could."

"You're not even trying. She didn't really throw you

over, you know. It's not that he's the better man. They're husband and wife."

Marcus puffed his cigar and eyed the wall beyond the colonel.

"It's not that she loves you any less," Schreiber went on.

"She loves me period, Justin. She doesn't love him. Not anymore. She can't."

"Did she say that?"

"I *know*."

"But face it. There's nothing you can do short of sending him home. Cheer up, you'll get over it."

"How? Every time I go into town I bump into them. It's a wound that'll never heal."

"It will if you let it alone. All you need is time."

"What I need is to leave here."

"You just took over!"

"I'm not saying quit. Miles has only been here a few days and he's already talking about mounting a big campaign to go after Geronimo. Crook let him off the hook, Miles wants him back. He's right to focus on him, because Geronimo's the linchpin. Pull him out, the wheel falls off, the whole wall of resistance will collapse. I've made a decision. I'm going to volunteer to join the campaign. It shouldn't take more than a year or two to run him to ground."

"You could grow a beard below your knees before you even spot him."

"Whatever it takes. Bob Sutherland can run things here. He's perfectly capable. The reinforcements'll be here shortly, maybe even this afternoon. I can take one troop with me, leave him the other four. He'll still be stronger than we are now. He'll never miss the one."

"You really think you'll be able to get along with Miles?" asked Schreiber, his eyes filled with skepticism.

"I can take orders."

"I don't mean take orders. Marcus, he's as different from George Crook as you are from Napoleon Bonaparte." He chuckled. "Come to think of it, Miles has a lot of Bonaparte in him. They could trade egos and neither one would be the loser. But he'll *use* you. Capable field commanders are rungs on the ladder of his ambition. Do you really want your head hanging on his office wall?"

"He can't be that bad."

Marcus searched his eyes for agreement, but it was not to be found.

"You best be on your guard if you serve him directly," Schreiber warned.

"I don't think it'll be directly. At first sign of a threat, Geronimo will run down over the border into Mexico, into the mountains. He'll be safe there. He'll think so."

Schreiber laughed. "Me too. It'll be like looking for a collar stud in a silo full of corn."

"The longer it takes, the better for me. I don't think Miles will want to bury himself in the wilds of northern Mexico far from the photographers and newspaper reporters. He'll much rather play puppeteer, glued to his desk up in Prescott. Feeding reports to the newspapers and his wife's dear Uncle Phil."

"Well, it's up to you. If you think going hunting will get her out of your head, go to it."

"Do you agree that Bob Sutherland is competent to take temporary command?"

"He is."

"Then it's settled. I'll send a messenger up to headquarters. Miles should recognize my name. He just promoted me."

"Whatever you do, be careful. I just hope you've thought the thing through. It'll be a lot different than what you're used to. You won't be able to come back here between skirmishes. You'll have to live out of your backpack and off the land, and not a very hospitable land at that. You don't know those mountains. No American does, but Geronimo does. He's tough as wire, clever, gutsy, and desperate. You'll be fighting to capture him, he'll be fighting to survive."

Marcus nodded. He was digging in his breast pocket. He got out a handkerchief. One corner was tightly knotted. He undid it. he held up the engagement ring. It caught a ray of sunlight and sparkled beautifully.

"What are you doing with that thing?" asked Schreiber. "I would have thought you'd turned it in and gotten your money back by now."

"I'm hanging onto it. Someday I'm going to put it on her finger."

"Jesus, Mary, and Joseph, will you make up your mind? You just finished saying you want to get away so you won't have to see her."

"I didn't say 'her,' I said 'them.' "

Schreiber's response to this was to merely shake his head, eloquent if silent expression of his feelings. Marcus restored the ring to its knot.

Measles, quipped Artemus, works in mysterious ways its mischief to perform. Tuc-
son's epidemic was to peak at twenty-seven cases before
leaving town. Twenty-three of the victims were children.
Only four adults were infected. Two came for office
visits, the other two were treated at home. Marion called
on one. Her knock was answered by Mr. Pennington.
She was pleased to note he did not look behind her for
Artemus and did not ask what she wanted. He was cor-
dial and mannerly. He practically dragged her inside
bodily. The couple's daughters were not at home. Larcena
was sitting up in bed supported by six pillows; the erup-
tions had already appeared. She looked as if she had
stood behind a screen and had reddish-purple paint flung
at her. Her nose ran steadily; tightly balled and damp
hankies littered the covers. She hacked. The mucous
membrane lining the inner surface of the eyelids was
fiercely inflamed.

She did not react at the sight of Marion. She appeared
too weak to react to anything.

"I'm very very very ill," she murmured by way of
greeting. "I'm almost never, I'm blessed with excellent
health, we all are."

"Don't talk, it'll only irritate your throat." A stern look underscored the command. Larcena nodded obediently.

"It's very sore."

"I'm sorry," said Marion. "You can talk." She smiled. "Just no speeches."

She took her temperature. It was 102 degrees. She reacted involuntarily as she shook the mercury back down.

"Scary high, isn't it?" said Larcena.

"It could be worse. I'm glad to see you're keeping out of the sunlight."

"Horace insists." She looked away. "You must hate me."

"I don't hate anybody. I don't want to disappoint you, but I don't even dislike you."

"I tried hard to make you."

"Pull down your nightie, let's have a look at your chest."

Larcena resumed coughing, more a dry barking than a cough. Her chest was liberally splotched, as were her forearms, legs, and behind her ears.

"How about your eyes?" Marion asked.

"They're sore."

"Have your husband or one of the girls make up an eyewash: one teaspoon of salt to one pint of tepid water."

"Will this get worse?"

"It seems to be peaking now. It's not the measles that are particularly dangerous, it's the possible complications. But you do look to be on the mend. In two or three days your rash will begin to fade and the skin will start peeling."

"And I thought this was as bad as I could look—"

"Be glad when you start to peel. It'll mean you're definitely getting well. But watch for complications: cough becoming worse, breathing faster, earache or discharge, infection deep inside your ear."

"I do appreciate it."

"You mean my coming? I'm a doctor."

"I mean telling me what to look for, and what to expect. You're a good doctor, everybody says. Tucson's lucky to have you."

"Thank you, Mrs. Pennington."

"Larcena, please." She began playing aimlessly with

the hem of the sheet, her eyes downcast. "I should apologize for all the nasty things I said to you."

"Go ahead."

She grinned through her spatterings. "You're a card, you know that? I do apologize. Everyone's entitled to his opinion."

"Even Philadelphians?"

"Especially."

Marion didn't altogether understand this, but it did sound sincere sentiment. She snapped her bag shut, reminded Larcena about the eyewash, and said good-bye. Before she left, Larcena invited her to tea "when she got back on her feet."

Justin Schreiber boarded the Jackass Mail for Yuma and the West Coast, to eventually take passage on a schooner out of San Diego, heading south to Cape Horn then around and up the Atlantic to Boston. His doctor advised a long sea voyage would have a salutary effect upon his consumption-weakened lungs.

The reinforcements arrived at Fort Lowell, ninety men, a mixed shipment of grizzled oldsters, fresh-faced youngsters, and everything between, all battle-hardened veterans who had signed up for additional three-year hitches in preference to going home.

Spring rains battered the territory. The Santa Cruz refilled; muddy and swollen, it coursed it is way northward out of Mexico. Belligerent, bullying peals of thunder shook the heavens; lightning flashed like the swords of angry god-warriors flailing at each other in combat. The rain fell in torrents out of massive thunderheads into summer, and when each storm had spent itself, the sun parted the clouds, the darkened sky fragmented, and each little piece became a white cloud which was seized by the wind and pushed along to other sectors. The shiny green saguaro cactus thrust upward from the earth like a giant hand with malformed fingers. From its tips burst clusters of lovely white blossoms, and below the brilliant claret cup cactus bloomed, the pineapple cactus flaunted its delicate lavender blossoms, and the prickly pear cactus its butter-yellow loveliness.

Marion and Tyson Sturges were finding their marriage somewhat difficult to resume. Tyson had moved into the apartment, but proximity to his wife was his only concession to the relationship. He refused to speak, limiting his contribution to conversation to monosyllabic grunts. Marion tried to break the wall of ice that her slip of the tongue had formed between them, but she met no success for nearly a week. She came home from the office at six o'clock one evening to find him immersed in one of the two books on mining that he had brought with him from Philadelphia. She had reached the limit of her patience; she was fed up with the barrier separating them and pointedly said so. To her surprise he spoke.

"I asked jokingly if he was your lover."

"You weren't joking, Tyson."

"You said he was a friend. Why lie?"

"He is my friend and yes, he made love to me. I made love to him."

Triumph set his eyes glistening. "You're actually proud of it!"

"I was a widow, remember? So lonely at times I could scream. You were officially dead. When I first heard I refused to believe it, but after a time I obviously had no choice. I went into mourning. For a time I was so sick at heart, so depressed, I thought I'd never shake it off. My husband, the man I loved, the only man in the world for me, was dead. I carried the burden for a long time, Tyson, long after I got here."

"Right up until you met your handsome captain."

"Tyson, the last thing I wanted was to fall in love, but it happened, and it pulled me up out of my doldrums. It was the fresh start that had eluded me up to that time."

"How touching, you poor creature."

She stiffened and said tightly, "It happened because we were both lonely. We needed each other's support. We fell in love. As soon as I read Browder's letter I knew it was all over between Marcus and me. When I came back from Wilmot I went straight to the fort to tell him. But when we came face-to-face I just didn't have the heart to. It was cowardly of me, but I simply couldn't. He was so up I couldn't knock him down."

"Up meaning crazy about you and ready to shout it from the nearest belfry."

"That's right. He'd been away. He had no way of knowing you'd come back from the dead."

"How inconvenient for you both. How inconsiderate of me."

"Can I finish? He invited himself here that evening."

"And you let him, you wanted him to come."

"To give me a second chance to tell him, which I did. He proposed to me, he showed me the ring he'd bought. I couldn't let it go on, of course. I told him about you. He had just finished reading Browder's letter when you knocked on the door. When I opened it and we saw each other, we were so absorbed you didn't notice his expression. But when I remembered he was standing behind me, I turned around. Darling, he was stunned.

"Put yourself in my position. I didn't just worry that you'd been killed at Petersburg, *they told me you were dead*. The telegram made it official. You were dead, it was all over. Dead when I left town, dead when I got here, and all these months. Now you've come back from the dead, and it's the most beautiful, the most marvelous thing that could ever happen. This is our chance—not to start over, better than that—to pick up where we left off, wipe away all these months. Can't we, Tyson? I want to so much."

He said nothing. His eyes said it all. He took her hands and pulled her gently to him.

"My wife."

"My husband."

"Forgive me. The damned thing is still hanging on me like rags. I need time to shake them off."

"I'll help."

He kissed her affectionately; her heart rose.

"Good news," he said. "I got a letter today from Benjamin Staley, the lawyer. It's here somewhere."

He went on talking as she read it to herself. Getting even with the government was becoming an obsession with him. He wanted the blood of the bureaucratic beast that had made them suffer so. She had been thinking about it all week: a million dollars in compensation for the needless suffering inflicted on her by their error.

It was the worst possible thing one could do to a wife beside herself with worry. If by some quirk of fate she knew the name of the guilty party, she would never forgive him. There could be no apology for such cruelty.

But she didn't know the person responsible; the nameless, faceless federal government was to blame. Far too late they had discovered their error and they'd informed her that they were sorry it happened.

Now he was demanding a million dollars in reparations. But what good would money do? Would it eradicate that black period from their memories? Would it rearrange their lives so that it had never actually happened?

Staley's letter glowed with enthusiasm and optimism. He even extolled his client's courage in tackling the giant and was sure that others made to suffer in the same manner would follow his lead. How many combat soldiers had been killed by telegram Marion could not guess, but it couldn't be too many. Still, at a million dollars a mistake, even a dozen amounted to a large sum. This brought another point to her mind: who were they suing? The government. What was the government? The people, the people who had fought the damned war. So in a sense all the others involved at Petersburg, at least on the Union side, were being asked to pay for somebody's carelessness in Washington.

She sensed that she could go on reasoning, rationalizing, hypothesizing, but she would rather not. She changed the subject. She picked up the book he had been reading when she walked in.

"*A Manual of Mining* by Professor Conrad Kolb Steiger."

"Did you know gold was discovered around here three years ago? A woman by the name of Pauline Weaver found it on the Colorado River north of a place called Ehrenberg," he said.

"Ehrenberg's on the California border, not exactly 'around here,' darling. They've found gold and silver all over the territory."

"Practically in your backyard. In the Patagonia Mountains down below. It's destiny, darling. Tucson is destined to become the mining capital of the region."

His enthusiasm, if not infectious, was at least encouraging. Getting involved in something, anything, was the best thing for him. She could only applaud.

"Why this sudden interest in gold mining?" she asked.

"I read up on Arizona before I left Philadelphia. I have to do something to make a living. Can you think of a better line? I'll admit I don't know beans about it, but

I'm learning, and I'm sure darned few others knew any-thing when they started out. That's no hindrance. Ac-cording to what I've read so far, many more strikes are made by amateurs than professionals."

"You want to stay here?" she asked.

"Don't you?"

"What *you* want is just as important."

"I like the little I've seen so far: the town, the land, the weather, the opportunities, possibilities."

"You may not find the people up to your expectations. Not all of them, of course . . ."

She told him about the dominance of Southern sympa-thizers among the populace.

"They're still bitter over losing the war, and they won't get over it by next week."

"The losers are always bitter, but you're not answering my question. Do you want to stay here?"

"I do. Our practice is growing, I'm saving money. Wouldn't it be nice if we could build a house? Some lovely tracts of land are still available."

"We wouldn't have to wait till the suit is settled or for me to strike gold."

They made supper and talked about the future well into the night. They made love very late. She ws careful not to slip a second time, but afterward, lying beside him, listening to him sleep, she thought about Marcus. It saddened her.

General Nelson Miles made a tour of inspection of the eleven posts in the territory under his command. He was due to arrive at Fort Lowell on Thursday morning. The day before Major Venable held a squeaky-tight dry-run inspection of all grades, after which the troopers paraded in close formation, then lined up in cavalry-manual per-fect order and he addressed them.

The general had yet to respond to his request to join the planned Geronimo campaign, but Marcus was not worried; he expected his answer when Miles arrived and could not conceive of the possibility of being turned down. So certain was he that he took time to brief Lieutenant-become-First Lieutenant Sutherland on his re-sponsibilities as temporary CO.

General Miles came riding in with his fifty-man escort

promptly at ten the next morning. A strikingly handsome man, he affected, in emulation of Napoleon III, an imperial, a tuft-of-hair beard and matching mustache as pointed as he could twist the ends without using wax. He wore his jet-black hair short, parted on the left and weaving across his upper forehead. His eyes too were dark, and as penetrating as those of a mesmerist. The overall effect provided him with a distinctly magisterial air. One look would convince any observer that the man considered himself superior to all others. Popes, princes, and presidents were his peers; common soldiers were useful as tools, officers as puppets, women as playthings, Apaches as annoying mosquitoes to be swatted and squashed before they could bite. As one would pour oil in a swamp to rid it of mosquitoes, he had resolved to pour power throughout the territory to exterminate the Apache.

The bugler had sounded assembly when the lookout spotted the column a half mile away. By the time the visitors rode in, the troopers were firmly implanted in position and the CO and his staff stood stiffly at attention, white-gloved hands to foreheads prepared to offer a salute of welcome to the commander.

The general acknowledged it in kind, dismounted, came forward, and was greeted by the major. Miles removed his glove and offered his hand.

"Major Venable." He swung about in cursory appraisal of the formation. "Splendid, splendid. Fine body of men. Numbering . . ."

"One hundred fifty-nine able-bodied, sir."

"Splendid, splendid. Dismiss them. Where can we talk?"

Marcus put forth a conscious effort to keep his face from falling. The men had been preparing all week for inspection. Every loose thread was snipped, every button polished, every boot gleaming like a mirror, every horse brushed for hours, every weapon cleaned. The breeze flapped Old Glory at the top of her freshly painted pole, its base surrounded by newly whitewashed stones. The formation looked picture perfect. A photographer should have snapped it, developed, and preserved it for all time as the shining example of what every cavalry regiment should look like prior to inspection.

"Dismiss the men," said Marcus to Sutherland, and

stood aside, permitting Miles to precede him into the office.

The general did not just sit his chair; he transformed it into a throne. He made his listener feel like a peasant supplicant. He proceeded to put Marcus through the wringer, firing question after question: battle experience, current activities against the little men. He did not call them Apaches; that he even called them men mildly surprised Marcus. The general wanted to know tactics in the field; results over recent months, over the past year; knowledge of enemy movements; names of enemy principals encountered, engaged, slain, wounded, escaped. The inquisition completed, the general turned to the projected campaign.

"Our predecessor, General Crook, as able, fearless, and successful an Indian fighter as any man in uniform, pursued a policy of appeasement. Far be it for us to criticize George's judgment, but we view the situation as calling for a markedly different approach. In brief, it is our opinion that the territory will never be safe for the settlers, their lot will never improve, new immigrants will never be attracted to Arizona in large numbers, it will never be entitled to statehood until the little men are driven out. Permanently.

"Geronimo is the key. Eliminate him and you break the back of their resistance, destroy their morale. He's more than a chief. He's a god in their eyes. He got away from George. He's gone to ground. Where, do you think?"

"Down over the border."

"And how do you assess his strength?"

"That's hard to say, sir. My guess is no more than a few hundred."

"Few . . . ?"

"Three hundred."

"Three hundred. Well, you'll be pleased to know that we are mounting a force of two thousand troopers to capture him. Two thousand men whose sole and single duty will be to find him and bring him in dead or alive. We are also building a dozen heliograph stations to flash Morse code messages from mountain to mountain across southeastern Arizona and into northern Sonora. Our forces will be spread to guard every spring, every source of water, every pass to prevent them from moving about.

We will lasso them, then slowly tighten the noose. It will be the most massive manhunt in American history, and we will get our man."

"Two thousand men? Washington is sending additional reinforcements?"

"No, we already have sufficient manpower. You volunteered to join us. Splendid, splendid. Other post commanders would do well to emulate your initiative. We're pleased to say your request is granted; happy to have you along. We'll need three of your four troops as well."

"That'll leave only one troop."

"Three from four does leave one, Major. So?"

"We protect the town and the surrounding area settlers up to the Galluro Range, east to the Chiricahua Mountains, west to the Santa Rosa Valley—"

"Yes, yes, yes, and you do a splendid job. Splendid."

"One troop will spread us pretty thin."

"Whoever's left in charge can make do. We shouldn't have to underscore the importance of the campaign. Our success will solve our problem with the little men. It's really that simple. When we're done we won't even need a post here."

"Yes, sir."

"Splendid, then it's settled. Any questions?"

"No, sir."

"Excellent."

Splendid, thought Marcus wearily. He could see the expression on Sutherland's face when he told him.

"With your permission, sir, I'd be pleased to escort you on a tour of the post."

"No need. When you've seen one, you know. We *will* join you for noonday mess, after which we'll be heading on up to Camp Grant. Which reminds us, what did you think of that business at the Aravaipa Canyon a few months back. Refreshing, didn't you think?"

"Refreshing?"

"We mean the way the settlers took matters into their own hands. Gutsy chaps. Didn't turn out too good for Colonel . . . what was his name?"

"Thaddeus Willoughby."

"Black eye for him. But whipping the little men was good for everybody, don't you think?"

"As I recall, they only killed a couple braves. The rest were women and children."

"Nothing wrong with that. Women breed more braves; little boys grow up to become braves."

Miles talked until noon, mainly about himself and his experiences fighting Plains Indians. It was on these experiences that he planned to draw in the effort to subdue the Apaches. Marcus let him expand on the subject without interrupting. He fancied himself a good listener; a good listener was obviously all the general wanted. Twelve o'clock arrived and they went to lunch.

The first territorial officials were carpetbaggers. Under the circumstance of the war, the people of Arizona tolerated them. But when the war ended they campaigned bitterly against their rule; the root of all evil touched off the explosion. The carpetbaggers were involved in contracts and government business. In time they became sarcastically known as the "Government Ring," and it was believed that they worked with a group of Tucson's most successful merchants known as the "Tucson Ring," men who supplied the military posts and Indian reservations.

It was hard to prove that the two groups were in collusion, but suspicion flourished. With the onset of peace, citizens began calling for a government of Arizonans, by Arizonans and for Arizonans. The *Tucson Weekly Arizonan*, the town's first newspaper, put everybody's feelings into words: "It is time the people of Arizona choose for officers men from among themselves. There is no just reason why we must be represented by starved-out politicians . . . who do not remain a single hour in Arizona if divested of official patronage. It remains for the Democrats to explode the carpetbag system of representation."

Tyson, meanwhile, paid no attention to the political furor, nor did he launch his proposed new career. He continued to research gold mining, and talked about it to his newly acquired friends in Brichta's saloon. But he did not turn his hand to mining. To Marion he seemed to be playing a waiting game: watching the mails, holding his breath, waiting for word from Philadelphia that his lawyers had either triumphed in court or the government had settled out of court for a sizable sum.

Marion and Artemus got around to discussing the situation late one morning between patients.

"Why should he work when he has a wife who's willing and able to support him?" Artemus asked.

"Oh, he's not like that, you don't know him."

"Give him a chance, it's only been a few weeks. Let him unwind."

"I just wish he wasn't so all wrapped up in that stupid lawsuit."

"What's stupid about a million dollars?"

"It's blood money, Artemus."

"It's green. It spends like the other coin of the realm. You don't approve?" He couldn't understand her and she could see he wasn't pretending.

"I don't know. I keep telling him to go ahead if that's what he wants. I just don't see that it solves anything."

"It's not supposed to, it's compensation. It's like an insurance policy paying off. You see something immoral in that?"

"I suppose not. Only I don't like what it's doing to him. It's all he talks about; it gnaws at him. He wants his pound of flesh and he practically foams at the mouth trying to justify suing. If he believes it's right, why does he feel he has to justify it?" She shook her head discouragedly.

"He evidently feels you don't think it's right."

"Do you?"

"Absolutely. It won't wipe out the past, but it'll sure make the future a lot more comfortable. A million shinplasters; my, my, it boggles the mind."

Emmaline came sailing in smiling and bubbling. She greeted Artemus.

"Ready?" she asked Marion.

Marion nodded. "We're going to Mama Elena's for chili."

Artemus grinned and grimaced. "Better take along the stomach pump."

Marion could not accept Artemus's out-of-hand assessment of the lawsuit. His thinking was lockstep in stride with Tyson's; neither seemed interested in considering the ethical or moral aspects. Emmaline did.

"Solomon mentioned it at the supper table last night," she said. "Not judging whether it was right or wrong, only . . ."

"What did he say? I want to know what other people think."

"He just wonders if the federal government *can* be sued. It's so big and complex. I said it must be possible or Tyson's lawyers wouldn't bother to pursue it. Then he said if that's the case, if a man volunteers to serve in the army and is killed in battle, why can't his loved ones sue? I said that's different, when somebody signs up he knows what the possibilities are and is willing to take his chances for God and country and all that. That's when he said a curious thing. He said Tyson's suing because he *wasn't* killed. He was serious."

"He's right."

"I don't follow . . ."

"This lawsuit is strictly retaliation. Tyson's angry, he wants a million dollars worth of revenge. I think it borders on extortion."

"I wouldn't go that far."

Emmaline was eyeing her strangely. Was she sounding terribly disloyal? wondered Marion.

"I just don't feel comfortable about it," she explained. "It bothers me. Am I being ridiculous?"

"I . . ."

"If you think I'm wrong, say so."

"I don't."

"Then I'm right."

"I don't know."

Marion dropped it there, vowing to dismiss it from her mind altogether. She would not discuss it with Tyson. It could only cut a breach between them, and in a few months, perhaps sooner, it would be resolved one way or the other. That would end it.

The chili arrived steaming and smelling delicious. Emmaline got onto the subject of Marcus. "Solomon heard that he's leaving for Mexico tomorrow with a hundred men to go looking for Geronimo."

"Oh my God!"

Marion caught herself; why the reaction? It was his job, what he wanted in life: carry a sword and gun and protect the flag. Except now the war was over, why didn't he get out? Get a real job? Buy a ranch or a farm? She suddenly felt Emmaline's eyes boring into her.

"What is it, Marion?"

"What's what?"

"All I did was say his name and you plunged into thought."

"Plunged?"

"The fire's still burning, isn't it?"

"No."

"I bet his is. I bet he's carrying his torch high and burning brighter than ever. You don't want to talk about him."

Strange, thought Marion, all her friends—Artemus, both Warners, Mark Aldrich, the Penningtons, the Brichtas—had an opinion about Tyson. They were all pleased for her that he had come back, but not all of them liked him like they did Marcus. No one came right out and criticized Tyson, but she could tell from their expressions when his name came up how they felt about him. Artemus, for instance, seemed to feel a pressing need to defend him as he had just before Emmaline walked in earlier. But that crack, "Why should he work when he has a wife to support him?" gave away his honest opinion. he really did not spark to him probably, she decided, because he so admired Marcus, and felt sorry for him. He had done his best to throw them together, and when they finally did he was as pleased as if he had been one of their doting fathers. And Emmaline liked Marcus too much to like Tyson; she was very fair-minded, but that didn't keep her from looking upon him as an interloper. Solomon, on the other hand, although fond of Marcus, carried on as if Tyson were a long-lost son. He seemed dedicated to making a close friend of him.

It wasn't possible for Marion to compare them. Marcus was the past; Tyson was the present and the future.

Then why every time Tyson made love to her did she think of Marcus?

That afternoon she and Artemus were unusually busy; the line seemed endless. That night she was exhausted. She and Tyson went to bed early. She woke up around eleven with a sharp pain in the pit of her stomach. Tyson woke.

"Something wrong?"

"I don't know. It feels . . ."

"What?"

"Pain here and it feels like it's moving upward."

He lit the lamp. "You're really pale and sweaty. Don't you have something you can take for it?" He started to get out of bed.

"No, there's no medicine for this."

He started. "You know what it is?"

"I wish I didn't. Let's give it a couple minutes. I want to be sure."

He got up, lit a cigar, and got her a glass of water. She waved it away.

"The verdict's in," she said. "Appendicitis."

"It could be just a stomachache. You said you had chili for lunch."

"I wish to God it was a stomachache. But it's definitely moving upward to my navel. Then it'll move down to my appendix. I'll feel nauseous, probably throw up, fever—"

"You better be sure."

"I'm a doctor, remember?"

"Can I do anything?"

"Not unless you want to take it out."

"We'll get you over to the office. I'll wake up Shaw." She stiffened. Concern darkened his face. "What's the matter?"

"*I'll* have to do it."

"Operate on yourself?" He looked stunned. "Are you crazy? He can do it, it's not that complicated. Is it?"

"Not at this stage, but it has to come out. Before it gets acute."

"So what are we waiting for? I'll help you get dressed. He'll get it out, you'll be fine. He's a good doctor." He was studying her. "Isn't he?"

She began to laugh, wincing with the pain along with it.

"Are you all right?" He looked as if he thought she had snapped.

"There's something I think you should know, Tyson. Artemus is actually a dentist." He laughed and waved this away. "I'm serious, darling. He's never been inside a medical school. Never worked in a hospital. He went to dental school."

"My God."

She sobered. "I'm thinking the same thing."

"What'll you do? You can't cut yourself open. I won't let you. I don't get it. Artemus has been practicing here for years."

"Going on nine. Hundreds of patients, thousands."

"You said he was a good doctor."

"In some ways he's great. Listen to me, Tyson. Don't you breathe a word of this. Not a hint, even jokingly. If people knew, they'd tar and feather him—or worse. If word gets out, I'll never forgive myself."

"How the hell do you know all this?"

"Long story." She sucked a breath in sharply and grimaced. "But true. He really is a dentist. And he's going to remove my appendix. He'll want to and if I refuse to let him, I'd be the worst sort of hypocrite. Oh, this is priceless. Talk about the horns of a dilemma. Get my robe and slippers, would you?"

"I'll get a buggy next door. Better yet, I'll carry you over. It's only a couple blocks and faster and easier on you."

"You'll get a hernia."

"You're as light as a bouquet of roses."

He was staggering by the time he reached the stairs leading up to the office, but he managed them. By now the pain had shifted to the appendix region and she was feeling nauseous. She was about to take a true test of faith.

"Ooooooooo . . ."

Tyson got her inside and laid her gently on the table; he found a blanket and covered her, then went to wake

Artemus. Shaw came out in his nightshirt and battered slippers, yawning, scratching.

"Appendicitis, Doctor?"

"Would you kindly remove it?"

"I don't think you'll want to watch this, Tyson," he said, smiling. "Go wait in my room. It won't take long."

He washed his hands, brought up the carbolic acid sprayer, and exposed the afflicted area. He tested it with his fingertips. She winced.

"Tender, rigid. Diagnosis correct. Relax, Doctor, this'll be easy as pulling a tooth."

He got out a bottle of chloroform and a gauze pad, doubling it.

"Only take a jiffy and a half. I said relax, this is your doctor speaking. You look like you're holding your breath. Is it that painful?"

"Would you please get on with it?"

"What time did the first attack come?"

"Around eleven."

"It's now twenty-five past. You're well under a day. There can't be any danger this early."

She watched him lay out his intruments. Her heart felt as if it were trying to beat its way out. He double-checked the sprayer. She held her breath as he picked up the gauze pad and set it over her nose and mouth. Drops of chloroform spilled down. She closed her eyes in capitulation, then changed her mind, and tried to stay awake. Another drop, yet another and the gray curtain dropped.

Tyson was smiling down at her. He looked relieved; she felt as if she had come back from the dead. Her mouth felt stuffed with cotton. There was a numbing pain at the site of the incision. Artemus stood leering like Lucifer, as if he'd successfully stolen a prize soul.

"It practically jumped out. Lie still. I've stitched you, but I still have to bandage it."

"Can I see?"

He rustled through a drawer and got out a large hand mirror. The incision was about three inches long. The stitches were neatly aligned. He had a particular knack for stitching, and for appendectomies, too, it appeared.

"Well?"

"It looks beautiful."

"It is. I do beautiful work. Want to see your appendix? Close your eyes, Tyson."

"I'll pass," she murmured.

"You'll be happy to know you were days away from peritonitis."

"What time is it?"

"Almost one-thirty. You'll spend the night here. You go home, son. Get some sleep. You, Doctor, can go home in the morning if you promise to stay in bed all day."

Tyson kissed her good-bye and went out.

"Boy's a horse, carrying you up those stairs like he did. I'd hate to tangle with him." He stared down at her. "You look very relaxed. You were tight as a spring when I anesthetized you. So tight I was afraid you'd explode on me. Not your appendix, you. Worried sick, weren't you?"

"Why should I worry?"

"I would, knowing I was being cut open by a dentist."

"What are you talking about?"

"Come off it, Marion, you know I'm no doctor. You've known for months. You know I went to school with Walter Ogren. They discovered his guilty secret back in Philadelphia. He wrote and told me, though I never told you he did. I figure your friend Cowan must have told you what happened to him. It had to be the talk of the town. It doesn't take a genius to put the pieces together. You knew."

"Yes."

"But you never said a word. Not to a soul. Not even to me."

"You're a good doctor, Artemus."

"Terrific dentist. You do know I'm not the only fake practicing medicine out here in the boondocks."

"You're no fake."

"I'm no doctor. Not licensed. I suppose I should tell my patients. That'd be the honorable thing. Don't think I haven't thought about it. Then I think about all the others dosing and cutting, all the tinkers who call themselves doctor. It doesn't seem to trouble their consciences. Witch doctors. Bleeders and hackers. Some with diplomas are even worse. Listen to me rationalize."

"No need to. The people in this town are grateful."

"For you, not me." She sucked in a breath sharply. "What's the matter?"

"Artemus, there's something you should know."

"*You're* a dentist?"

"Seriously. I'm afraid I did tell Tyson just before we left the house. But I swore him to secrecy, and I won't tell anyone else, cross my heart."

"An exceptional heart, Doctor, filled with charity. I appreciate it. Still, maybe you should give it a little more thought. You'll be making yourself an accomplice to my campaign of deception."

"Rubbish. How can you be deceiving anybody when you have the skills? And you do. Pieces of paper in frames don't make doctors. They're self-made and you did a good job." She squeezed his forearm affectionately.

"Trial and error, plenty of error." He laughed. "You know, practicing under false pretenses does have one benefit. However badly I mess up, nobody can take away my license. Why don't you get some sleep? We can talk about it in the morning before the herd comes thundering up the stairs."

"We're done talking about it. Neither of us will ever mention it again. And thank you for coming to my rescue. Now go back to bed, doctor's orders."

He kissed her on the forehead.

"Sleep well, Doctor."

Marcus presumed correctly. General Nelson Miles returned to Prescott following his tour of inspection and began orchestrating the great search from behind his desk. He would not run the show from a distance forever. When Geronimo was found and the noose began to tighten, Miles would come galloping down to be in on the kill. But for now he would sit at his desk, secure in the knowledge that no one would think him a coward with his enviable record in Indian fighting.

As head of the two thousand-man search force, Miles selected Colonel Thompson Bragg Betteridge, a veteran of Grant's campaign in the Wilderness and Cold Harbor. Grant's object had been to secure the road to Richmond, but the difficulties of the terrain—the almost impenetrable growth of the wilderness south of the Rapidan River—prevented a decision. Subsequently at Cold Harbor the two sides engaged in one of the most desperate battles of the war. In attempting to dislodge the Confederates from their entrenched positions, Grant suffered a severe defeat. Colonel, then Major Betteridge, had nevertheless managed to drape himself with glory and forge his reputation for leading men intelligently and effectively in difficult circumstances over terrain ill-suited to normal travel, much less battle.

The mountains of Sonora promised similar problems. Movement would be restricted to narrow, rugged, steep trails which in most instances were little more than paths. Hiding places from which the troopers could be ambushed abounded. When the colonel echoed Miles's opinion that the troopers would locate Geronimo and his followers in weeks, thanks to sheer force of numbers (two thousand men were four thousand eyes) Marcus put his tongue into his cheek.

Knowing Geronimo from Justin Schreiber's accounts of him, he would flit about like a will-o'-the-wisp. Twenty thousand men could search for years and not find him. He could follow them and they would never realize it. He traveled light, he traveled fast, and he and his people knew the area far batter than any white man.

What neither Miles nor Betteridge seemed to take into account was that the Apache was no ordinary Indian. In no way could a Plains Indian be compared to him. The Cheyenne, Pawnee, Comanche, Kiowa, and all the others were tough, resourceful, wily foes with or without rifles, but the little men were in a class by themselves as fighters.

The Apache survived in a domain far more rugged and treacherous than that occupied by any other tribe. Every Apache male was drilled from boyhood in the cardinal virtues of cunning and toughness. He was taught that trickery ranked above pure courage. He was forced to stay awake for long periods to learn how to deal with exhaustion. He trained as a long-distance runner; he was required to race up the side of a mountain carrying water in his mouth and was made to spit it out on his return to show that he had breathed properly through his nose.

As a grown man he was expected to cover seventy miles a day on foot over the most difficult terrain and in the worst weather. From the age of ten he fought mock battles against his peers with arrows and rocks flung from slings, relying only on hide shields and agility to emerge unscathed. By the time he was fourteen he hunted with the men.

Above all, the Apache learned better than any other

Indian on the North American continent to obliterate his tracks, conceal his camp, and keep his horses at a distance.

Major Venable and his men rendezvoused with Betteridge and the main force at Fairbank, about thirty crow miles north of the Sonoran border. Betteridge impressed Marcus. He guessed he was about forty and weighed close to two hundred-thirty pounds which, save for a respectably small potbelly, was all muscle. He carried himself like an athlete and it was apparent that he was a man of action. He was clean-shaven; he was almost completely bald and the top of his head displayed an old saber scar.

They sat in the colonel's Sibley tent in privacy. He had greeted Marcus and invited him in effusively, but as they talked and the major formed his initial impression of the colonel, tiny seeds of suspicion sprouted in Marcus's mind. Betteridge was being overly friendly, carrying on garrulously, smiling and looking over his shoulder. Marcus looked people in the eye when he spoke to them; he liked others to afford him the same courtesy. Betteridge seemed to have either a hard time doing so or had no desire to.

And the more he prattled on, the more patronizing he became. Marcus began to feel like a raw recruit being lectured by a battle-hardened superior. The colonel paused to swipe his helmet lining with an already soggy handkerchief. The tent was like an oven. Why they didn't find a tree and take advantage of its shade Marcus couldn't understand. The colonel had turned to inspecting his helmet in a manner that suggested it had just been issued to him.

"How long have you been in Arizona?" he asked without looking at Marcus.

"Three years."

It came as a surprise. The colonel looked straight at him and immediately jettisoned his condescending air. But as far as Marcus was concerned, the damage was done. He could not say he immediately disliked the man; he would have to scrutinize him closely. He didn't think they could become as close and trusting as he had been with Justin Schreiber. Ordinarily he gave everybody the benefit of his doubts starting out, but this one would have to prove he could be trusted.

"You know these savages. How long do you think it'll take us to catch up with him? Two weeks? A month? The reason I ask, I'm getting married first of September."

"Congratulations."

"Thank you." He showed him her picture. She was blond and attractive if a little heavy. "In Santa Fe. Myrtle's from there. You a married man?"

"No, sir."

"Hey hey, let's have none of that. When we're talking man to man, call me Tom."

Otherwise call me sir, reflected Marcus, and tingled slightly with amusement.

"Just haven't found the right girl, eh? I didn't till last year and I've got a few years on you. Cheer up. You'll find her." He leaned over and patted him consolingly on the knee. "So what do you think, two weeks? A month?"

He couldn't possibly give an answer of any value to such a question. But from the expectant look on Betteridge's face he wanted him to give it a try.

"If we get lucky, maybe two or three months."

The expectant look dropped a good two inches. "That's pretty pessimistic."

"If I might make a suggestion . . ."

The colonel gestured. "Feel free."

"I think some experienced scouts would be very helpful."

Betteridge winced as if he'd been pinched and sucked through his teeth. Then shook his head.

"The general's dead against Apaches scouting Apaches. Besides, he's shipped most of them out. At least the Mimbres and Chiricahuas."

"There are others, tribes that are fairly peaceful."

"Fairly." Betteridge had taken to rubbing his chin, scratching the side of his head, then rubbing his chin again. "I don't know. An Apache's an Apache, all brothers under the skin. General Miles would have my arse for cat food. Oh, he didn't specifically order no scouts, but he leaves no doubt as to how he feels about them. Let's pass on that one. Anything else on your mind? If not, let me show you around the camp. We leave in three days. By then we'll have every piece of equipment we'll be taking. Which reminds me, I've got something to show you that'll tickle you."

It was the strangest-looking field piece Marcus had

ever seen. It sat its carriage like a howitzer—a short cannon, though it looked more like a mortar, ranging in caliber from 8.27 to 23.5 inches. Marcus saw immediately that this was neither cannon or mortar. It had ten barrels clustered around a cylinder that could be turned by a hand crank. According to Betteridge, a five-year-old could crank out a thousand rounds a minute. There were six such weapons lined up and gleaming new, the Cosmoline still shining in their muzzles.

"It's called a Gatling gun, put out by Colt. Latest thing. If we'd had a couple at Cold Harbor we would have slaughtered the rebs in twenty minutes. Impressive, eh? What's the matter?"

"How much does it weigh?"

"Around two hundred pounds. Why?"

"That's twelve hundred plus ammunition. Won't they be terribly awkward in the mountains? From Pitiquito east to the Santiagos, that's all Sonora is: steep rock, trails that go straight up."

"We'll have mules."

"These things could rake flat terrain like a scythe leveling wheat, but we're not going to find a flat spot bigger than a fair-sized backyard, not unless they head south down out of the mountains into Chihuahua."

The colonel was looking miffed. Marcus decided he had better quit finding fault with the man's new toy.

"A thousand rounds a minute," he murmured.

"We corner them and let loose with all six at the same time, and they'll throw down their arms and give up on the spot. And look over there, two howitzers. Two twelve-pound balls a minute. If they try to hole up on us, we'll blow them into their Great Spirit's lap!"

He introduced him to the senior staff officers, two lieutenant colonels and three majors. One of the latter, Major Andrew Colclough, looked very familiar, but Marcus could not seem to place his face. His curiosity aroused, he took him aside.

"Major Colclough—"

"Andy, and you're Marcus." They shook hands. "I know you by reputation. My younger brother Henry was stationed at Lowell. He was a big admirer of yours."

The past came rushing back: the Tortolita Mountains, the pursuit of the renegade band of Mogollón Apaches,

Corporal Tumbelsky, Orpheus Tchakarides, Private Henry Colclough, the lot surrounded, killed, scalped. Marcus sighed deeply.

"Henry Colclough," he murmured. "Good soldier."

The major was studying him with earnest eyes, exuding friendliness, and looking so much like Henry they could have been the same man.

"The folks got the usual letter from the War Department: regret to inform. How exactly did he die?"

Marcus's conscience twinged; he felt compelled to unburden it, purge it, tell all about the chase turned ambush, the dog's breakfast that had taken the lives of eight good men. He took pains to skip over the more grisly aspects of the tragedy. Colclough listened without altering his expression.

"If we'd gotten back ten minutes earlier . . ." Marcus shook his head and sighed again.

"You couldn't have. It was fated to happen. I really believe that. We mortals don't control a blessed thing in this world, least of all our lives."

"I liked Henry. Everybody did. He was special."

"And green. Oh my God, was he ever. I ranted and raved trying to talk him out of enlisting, but he wouldn't listen. He was seventeen and looked twelve. That squeaky voice, face as smooth as an apple."

"He worked like a Trojan to make himself a man. You had to admire him. We all did."

"Green as grass."

"You know the colonel—"

"Oh yes, I was with him at the Wilderness, Cold Harbor. Other scrapes before. He was a major back then, I was a first lieutenant. He's good. He doesn't sit behind the lines out of range poring over maps like some I've seen. Got good instincts; he'll look over the scouts' reports and visualize the whole picture. He can pick out soft spots in the enemy's defenses like a boxer picks out his opponent's."

"That's strictly instinct, Andy. I know, I sure don't have it."

"They say it's because he's so good at chess. He plays a battle like a game. He's got a genius for countering: the right number of men, type, placement attack strategy. He doesn't squander his firepower."

Marcus shook his head. "I've seen field commanders try to kill a fly with a sledge hammer. Like when Sumner wiped out the Second Corps at Fredericksburg."

"Not Thompson."

"He sounds like a gem. How come he hasn't made general?"

"He will. He really outdid himself at Cold Harbor, even though the rebels whipped us."

Colclough's eyes said his thoughts were winging back to that bloody time and place. He gnawed his lower lip as he reflected. Cannons roared and wrought their destruction, the dying screamed, and the bloodied woods sent up a cloud of smoke visible ten miles away in Richmond.

Marcus broke through Colclough's reverie. "What sort of man is he?"

Again Colclough chewed his lip; he studied the ground. "Okay."

"Is that the best you can say for him?"

"He has his faults. He's complex, and he tends to take you only so far into his confidence and no further. He's a backslapper. He'll call you by your first name, he'll smile you to death, but he's sincere. Still, he likes you to stay on the right side of him."

"He likes people to suck up."

"That's a little strong."

"Does he suck up to Miles?"

"He looks up to him, even though Miles is ten years younger. Be careful of one thing: Thompson doesn't take kindly to people who disagree with him."

"He's always right."

"It's more he'd rather not be told he's wrong."

"What's the difference?"

"Let me put it this way; if he likes something you don't, it's better to say nothing than knock it. Some pretty fine people are like that, you know. You question their judgment and it rubs their fur the wrong way."

"I'm in trouble. I as good as told him his precious Gatling guns are worthless."

"Oh boy. I'm afraid that's exactly what I mean."

"I'll try not to make an enemy of him," said Marcus dryly.

"He won't let you. Can't. He'll be depending on you in

the days to come if we're to stand any chance of catching Geronimo. And he's got to."

"By September first. He old me."

Colclough grinned, then his face darkened. "Are you saying it's not possible?"

"I think next spring is more like it. If at all."

"Oh boy. General Miles isn't going to like that. Everybody in Washington thinks he has a magic wand that turns rocks into gold. We're supposed to work his miracles for him. Of course, he takes the credit. But you'll be okay, you've got an insurance policy."

"You've lost me."

"You've been fighting the Apaches for three years. Nobody else around here comes close. Thompson knows your reputation."

"Such as it is. I sure haven't turned any rocks into gold. Let me get this straight. I'm supposed to work a miracle so the colonel can take credit and Miles can take it from him?"

"Well . . ."

"Hey, I'm not surprised. That's the way the Army works. Only against the Apaches, I'm only running about fifty-fifty."

"That's better than George Crook. He fell on his beard."

"Only because he took on the War Department, Sheridan, Sherman, just about everybody along with the hostiles. Do me a favor, Andy."

"If I can."

"If you get a chance, point out to the colonel that Indian fighting is Indian fighting, but the Apache is as different as pigs from peacocks. He never quits and almost never gives up, only when he's cornered with his women and children. Braves by themselves fight to the death. Usually the other fellow's. He's devised a whole new system for waging war. If Betteridge can concede that, we'll stand a chance. A good one. If he refuses to—"

"That's just what I'm saying. He's in no position to, he has to show results. To Miles, to Myrtle." He laughed and threw a friendly arm around Marcus's shoulders. "And you put it very well. Why don't you tell him yourself? Come on, let's eat."

* * *

Two hours before the two thousand-man search party was scheduled to depart, Betteridge came into Marcus's tent. Marcus was talking to Sergeant Brennan, whom he had never completely forgiven for lying about the killing of Erasmus Klee, covering his brutal act. But Brennan was a seasoned trooper; he would know how to conduct himself and direct the men under him in the days and weeks ahead, and Marcus saw little sense in alienating him by calling him to account for his deceit. And it was history, along with much else: Klee was dead, every white settler from Yuma to Santa Fe applauded, breathed easier, and was indifferent to the details surrounding his passing; Justin Schreiber was gone; Tyson Sturges had arrived; Marion was lost to him forever and time crept on.

Brennan shot to his feet, snapping a salute at the colonel. Betteridge was all smiles.

"Got something to show you, Marcus, if you'll step outside."

"Yes, sir."

"I know you think I put the damper on your suggestion that we consider taking along a few scouts, but I *have* been thinking about it. You know better than any of us what we'll be going up against. It'd be shortsighted of me not to take what you say into account."

Three Indians stood waiting outside. One wore a tattersall vest, a disreputable pair of blue serge trousers, and a government-issue dress-plumed helmet missing its gold rope sash. He also wore a supercilious smile. Another had on a badly stained cowboy hat with the brim turned up both sides and an outfit of fur-trimmed deerskins that lent him the look of Buffalo Bill Cody in caricature. His face was as blank as a pie tin. The third affected a plainsman's hat and infantry uniform. Oddly enough, it fit him perfectly. He also wore a rusty sword and a somewhat haughty air.

"These men are scouts," said Betteridge in a tone clearly calculated to impress. "George Wide Hand, Konosa, and Little Owl. I've had a long talk with them. They've agreed to join us. They'll receive daily rations equal to the enlisted men's. They're responsible for their own ponies and feed and whatever weapons they see fit to bring with them. I've notified Departmental Headquarters and expect authorization from General Miles shortly." He noticed Marcus's uncomfortable look. "Is something wrong?"

Marcus nodded to the three and moved out of their hearing. The colonel walked with him.

"They're Papagos, sir."

"I know, but they know the Sierra Madres—every rock, every tree, every arroyo—"

"Is that what they told you?"

"Why would they lie? They volunteered. Why would a man take a job he can't handle? They still have to prove their worth. I made that very clear. See here, surely you know they hate and despise the Apaches."

"They do, but—"

"But what, Major? You wanted Indian scouts."

"Apache scouts," said Marcus mildly. "I believe in them. On a jaunt like this they'd be invaluable. They'd find Geronimo for us."

"No Apaches." The colonel was suddenly breathing through his nose, sounding a partial whistle. "I thought I made that very clear."

"You did, sir, but these men would be useless. Only an Apache can catch an Apache. A hundred and fifty years ago the Papagos were fighters. They could give as good as they got from the Apaches. No more. They're a beaten people, farmers when they work at all. They don't know how to fight. Oh, they're as good as the Apaches at living in the desert, but in the mountains they'll be worthless. And if they claim to know the mountains down below, they're lying. They've probably never seen the border, let alone crossed it."

"You don't want them."

Marcus's eyes asked pointedly: *do you?*

"Suit yourself, take 'em or leave 'em."

Betteridge leaned close. His pleasant and friendly manner had fled. He looked to Marcus like one whose hand had been painfully bitten by a creature he was feeding. His eyebrows crept closer to each other. His nostrils flared. His voice lowered an octave and a half.

"They're all you'll get!"

With this he spun around and marched off.

The following day at ten, the two thousand officers and

men assigned to find and capture the elusive Geronimo broke camp and set forth, heading southwest for Nogales and the border beyond. The three scouts did not accompany them.

━━━━━━━●⟨*28*⟩●━━━━━━━

He removed it with his left hand, Gabriel, as
easily as yawning. This has to be the first time in
medical history that a dentist has removed a doctor's
appendix. I can't wait for *him* to come down with a
toothache!

Most of the letter was devoted to Tyson. He had gone
to work. His head crammed with technical information,
he took to the field to explore, to search out what,
according to Professor Conrad Kolb Steiger, would be
ideal ground in which to find auriferous deposits. He
spouted mining terms with the ease of an experienced
professional. He knew a giraffe from the cable that let it
down or pulled it up the shaft. He learned that a horse
was not a four-legged creature but the barren rock that
interrupted a vein of ore. He discovered that silicon and
oxygen under certain circumstances could combine to
form a mineral that was often mistaken for gold, but was
the gold of fools called pyrite. He read up on claims, on
claim jumping, on coyoting, crevicing, and crosscutting.
He went to school inside his two books, absorbed the
information down to the last punctuation mark, and
graduated.

It took him only two weeks to find gold. It was not a strike to rival the fabled Comstock Lode, discovered in the Washoe Mountains of Nevada in 1859; it was not to be confused with James Marshall's historic find in Sutter's millrace in California, but it wasn't pyrite.

It was gold. He first found all Professor Steiger's signs indicating its possible presence. He staked out the area, filed his claim, doubly protected himself by purchasing the land outright, and announced his discovery. He invested in equipment, he tried to hire men. He finally talked two Mexicans and four Papagos into working for him by promising them shares as well as wages.

He had made his discovery on land northeast of town in the shadow of the Catalina Range approximately ten miles south of Mount Rice. The lode was tracable on the surface by scattered quartz outcroppings; he persuaded himself and his men that the bulk of the ore was hidden, although in places it was so shallowly buried that he could almost scuff it up with his boot. The heavy spring rains had washed away the last remaining surface soil, bringing the quartz to light. It was, as is the case with nearly all discoveries of precious metals, an instance of being in the right place at the right time. Luck played a significant role, but he *was* out searching. He knew the type of rock he should be looking for; he knew roughly the area to concentrate on. So it was a combination of factors that led to the discovery.

Nevertheless his success amazed almost everyone else in Tucson—including himself.

It also pleased Marion. For the first time since his arrival, Tyson was out of his books and into a job. She was proud. She only hoped the telltale indications on and near the surface would develop into a bonanza. It was highly possible. A nugget weighing only a quarter of an ounce discovered by James Marshall in Sutter's millrace had triggered a stampede of nearly ninety thousand forty-niners to California. Thousands had become rich unearthing gold from Truckee in the north down to the Colorado River and across it into Arizona. Prospectors had begun digging up Arizona as early as 1863, encouraged by the Weaver find just north of Ehrenberg the year before.

Marion sincerely wanted the Eleanor, named after Tyson's mother, to turn out a bonanza, but she took a realistic view of the situation. Husband and wife discussed it over dinner one night. Tyson's enthusiasm had reached a height that put the mountains to shame. Hope yielded to conviction.

"They've found gold near Prescott, Wickenberg, on the Hassayampa River, in the Harquahala Mountains. Camps have sprung up on Big Bug Creek. Lynx Creek, Weaver. All over the territory!"

"But with mixed results, darling. Don't misunderstand, I hope and pray the Eleanor turns out to be the biggest gold mine in the country. All I'm saying—"

"I know what you're saying. You keep saying. You throw cold water on everything, you know that? Miss Pessimism, that's you."

"That's ridiculous."

"Is it? Don't get your hopes up, don't get your hopes up. Is that the only string on your violin? It sounds like it. A man's wife is supposed to encourage him."

"I do."

"You don't. Not in anything." He shook his finger reproachfully. "Don't think I don't know what it is. You're jealous."

"Tyson—"

"You are. I'm finally getting my teeth into something big, something that can make me. I could become one of the richest men in the whole Southwest, but you don't like the idea. You hate it. You like being our sole support. It makes you feel superior, doesn't it? Admit it."

She hurled down her napkin and started up from the table. "I don't have to listen to this."

"But I want you to, 'darling.' It's time we opened up. I'm willing, why aren't you? What's the matter, does playing queen bee with me the drone make you uncomfortable? That's what I've been until now, thanks to those fumbling bastards."

"How convenient, to be able to blame everything on what happened."

He did. Every setback, every disappointment seemed to be tied to the tragic telegram with the string in his hands. He was deeply embittered and growing worse every day. His lawyers did not write often enough. He got a letter every week, but he wanted one every day. What they could say of substance to fill a page every

day without repeating themselves was beside the point.
He wanted his pound of bloody flesh. But Marion was
getting the feeling that even if he got it, it would not
satisfy him.

War changes men. It had changed him. He had never
been the sort to feel sorry for himself, never sought hers
or anybody else's sympathy for anything. Now he demanded it for everything. He had always been cheerful.
Now all he did was gripe and harp on the lawsuit, the
focus of his existence.

He had changed almost magically. Horribly. She
wouldn't compare him to Marcus, for she knew that
would be terribly unfair. She compared him to the old
Tyson, and recalled a Sunday afternoon walk in the Druid
Hill Park in Baltimore. He was to leave for the Army in
three days; she was understandably down. He tried to
pick her up, clowning, carrying on, telling bad jokes.
Late in the afternoon they turned a corner and came
upon a vicious dog fight. Tyson pulled his jacket off and
pitched in, saving a little terrier whose heart was bigger
than he was from a bullying German shepherd. The little
dog was badly mauled; his owner, a boy about ten, was
upset and crying. They consoled him and Tyson insisted
they take the dog to the nearest vet. It was dark by the
time they found one willing to remove his nose from his
Sunday paper and see to the patient. The dog was patched
up and the vet announced that he would be completely
recovered within a week. Tyson paid him and sent the
boy home smiling gratefully with his dog in his arms.

Tyson had dropped everything to help. They had reservations for dinner and tickets for a concert that night. All
was forgotten in the emergency. How could she complain? It was the sort of gesture on his part that endeared
him to her. It added new and extraordinary dimensions
to his heart. His first concern was the dog's pain, his
second, the boy's. He worried about everyone in trouble
and always tried to help if he could. He was people-
centered. He could have sent boy and dog home to the
boy's family to take care of matters. But it had never
occurred to him to do so, not when he was there on the
spot and could lend a hand.

He couldn't pass a beggar on the street without giving
him something. Nor could he pass the frowsiest alley cat

without calling to it, petting it, often even buying it food and feeding it. It was impossible for him to give enough of himself to others, to her. And he was the sweetest soul she had ever known.

The old Tyson.

She wished to God the suit would go to trial and be decided, no matter what the outcome. If he won he would go back to being himself.

She tried not to think about what might happen if he lost. At the moment she was edging perilously close to the end of her rope. He was pushing her. Worst of all, this appeared to be his plan.

"I'm going to make a strike that'll set this burg on its ear. You watch. Things'll be different around here. You might even come to respect me. I know that seems farfetched—"

"Will you stop it!"

"Are you ordering me?" He stiffened and saluted. "Whatever you say, my queen. You can't say I don't know my place." Marion strode toward the door. "Where are you going?"

"Out."

"Where?"

"Nowhere. For a walk."

"I'll come with you."

"I'd rather be alone."

"I'm sorry, sweetheart, honest. It's this waiting, holding my breath for word to come. It's got my nerves jumping in my skin like whips. You understand—"

"I don't understand. I should think you'd put it out of your mind rather than mentally pacing the floor, waiting for the baby to be born."

"I should, only I can't. It's not just the suit. It's the root cause, what they did to us. I don't mind telling you, I'm bitter."

"No kidding!"

"*You* should be." He glared.

"Maybe. If sharing your resentment is a test of wifely loyalty, then I am guilty of lack of interest. I just don't think it is."

"I'm suing for you, sweetheart!"

"So you keep saying."

She got a stole down and threw it about her shoulders.

"Let me get my jacket."

"Please, Tyson, I'd rather go by myself. I want to be alone. I won't be long, I promise. It'll give us both a chance to wring out our tempers and put them away."

"Whatever you say. And I'm sorry."

He kissed her cheek and held both doors for her.

He was always sorry after they had it out; he always said he was. She chided herself for being spiteful. Sincerity, even if dredged up for the occasion, is still sincerity. She did wish they got along better—like before. Even more she wished she could love him like before. It was becoming increasingly difficult.

And in the effort, she mused, closing the gate behind her, in the fact that she consciously had to make an effort, was she deceiving herself?

There is no Geronimo." Colclough grumbled, spitting tobacco juice viciously between his feet. "He's a figment of the imagination. Miles's. This is like searching for a ghost."

Marcus laughed. "He's not going to come walking into camp ready to shake hands."

They had scoured the mountains for nearly nine weeks without a sign of an Apache—not a single deserted camp, not even the dead coals of a cook fire. From all appearances Geronimo and his followers were down in Honduras drinking *tiswin*, celebrating their success in eluding the bluecoats, laughing till their scrawny ribs ached.

The soldiers had made camp the night before on a small plateau. Morale was low, discouragement flourished. Something good had to happen soon. To the south of the campsite, a trail wound down through the rocks, across a *cañón* floor, and up the opposite side to a family of four peaks of varying height. The vegetation was thick, boulders and outcroppings roughening the slopes down to the *cañón* floor and up to the peaks.

Colclough spat again, got up, stretched, grunted goodbye, and went off to talk to his men.

"Be back," he called.

Marcus surveyed the peaks, watching a lone buzzard wedge the sky above the peak farthest to the left. He thought about Marion. Not a day went by without his thinking of her. Not a night passed without her face lighting the screen of his mind.

He got out the diamond and was studying it, turning it over, catching sunlight in its facets, when he heard steps.

"Why, you rascal!"

It was the colonel.

"That's an engagement ring. You've been holding out on me. Who's the lucky lady?"

"Back in Phoenix," he lied.

"Do tell. Don't be bashful, you sly dog you, let's have a look at her picture. Blonde, brunette, redhead?"

"I don't have a photo."

Betteridge looked mildly shocked. "No picture of your fiancée?"

"Just the one big one." He gestured measurements. "In a frame on my desk back at the post."

"When's the big day?"

"Sometime next spring."

"Lucky you. In ten more days I'm supposed to be waltzing up the aisle with Myrtle. Poor little girl's going to be crushed. Goddamn, I know I am. Here we are into the ninth week and we haven't even seen a footprint."

Major Colclough joined them. The colonel was carrying a rolled-up map under one arm. He knelt and opened it, setting stones at the corners. It was riddled with pencil markings, his own hieroglyphics, which were impossible for Marcus to decipher.

"We're here," he said indicating. "There's the canyon, these are the peaks over there. The canyon peters out about a mile down the way. Here. We haven't seen hide or hair of the son of a bitch up to now, but he's seen us. He's probably been watching us every step of the way since we crossed the border."

Probably, Marcus thought grimly.

"Here's my idea." The colonel set the point of his pencil on the plateau on the map and started it slowly down the trail. "What if we send a good-sized party down the trail, across the canyon, up the other side. On foot, of course. Up top over there they'll spread ten, fifteen yards apart. At the same time the rest of us'll move left and right."

"Circle the canyon," said Colclough.

"Exactly."

"You think you'll catch them in the middle?" Marcus asked.

"I think it's worth a try. We've got to do something. God help us, we could go for six months without success. My father used to say: if you corner a wolf, you don't wait him out. Go in after him and force him to make a move."

"This bowl's not exactly a corner," observed Colclough.

"I believe it'll work, Major Colclough. Marcus, I want you and your men to go down the trail then up to the peaks. The rest of us'll move into position in an enormous circle. Do you want to do it in daylight or wait for dark?"

Marcus did not want to say what was running through his mind, that anybody who went down the trail had no chance of making it up the other side. Once separated from the main body of troops, they would be painfully vulnerable to attack. They could be wiped out in minutes before the rest of the force got within three hundred yards of them. It would be easy and safe for the Apaches to sit at the top and rain arrows on the hapless line threading down the trail in full view.

"So what'll it be, Marcus, now or after dark?"

"With all due respect, Colonel," interposed Colclough, "either way they'll be begging to be massacred."

"Nonsense. We'll be keeping an eye on you every step of the way. You'll be covered from every point of the compass. The first sign of attack and we'll rake the area."

"We'd have to see them to shoot at them," said Colclough.

"Andrew, be a good fellow, and let us talk in private, okay?"

"Yes, sir," Colclough replied. He walked off dusting the seat of his pants.

"How do you feel about it, Marcus?"

"He said it all, sir."

"I think he's wrong. He's underestimating our superior position, immensely superior firepower and overestimating the hostiles."

284 • A.R. Riefe

As the colonel continued talking, it became clear he was aching to start something, hoping to bring their quarry into the open if even just to see them and confirm that they really were in the area. He would set his trap; Marcus and his men would serve as live bait. He was careful not to use the word "trap," but he had the horse of initiative under him and was off and running. All he wanted was agreement and obedience. He might not get the first, but could not be denied the second.

"After dark, sir," Marcus finally said.

"Excellent. I knew you wouldn't let me down."

The colonel clapped him on the back. Marcus nearly pulled his shoulder out of range to avoid it, but checked himself just in time.

Marcus finished explaining the assignment to the men, and a chorus of protest immediately swept forth.

"We'll be dead meat and stinking by sunup!"

"They'll pick us off like cans off a fence!"

"Jesus, sir, he's calling for a goddamn suicide mission."

"It's an order, men," Marcus called out. "And if you calm down and think about it, it's not all that dangerous."

"The hell it ain't!" boomed Brennan.

"Cover the cannon, Sergeant. Listen up, everybody. Last night you couldn't see a single star or the moon. It'll probably be the same tonight. I'll lead the way. We'll keep ten paces between us. You won't have to stick to the trail. If you come to a boulder, a tree, whatever, use it for temporary cover—two or three seconds. Move from one to the next, keeping the line spread out. Just don't stray too far from the trail, got it? We're pulling out at twenty-two hundred hours. It'll be tactical, pistols cocked and ready."

"Sitting ducks!"

"Dead ducks!"

"I said quiet. That's all. Dismissed. Go clean and check out your weapons."

They dispersed grumbling and glaring. Marcus shook his head. They had every right to protest. He studied the surrounding heights. It was not a perfect bowl. To the east it ws wide open, creating a horseshoe—one more advantage for the Apaches. One of the men had termed it a suicide mission. Marcus hoped with all his heart it was an exaggeration. If they made it to the *cañón* floor without incident . . .

But the watching braves would probably *let* them get to the bottom, because they'd present ideal targets climbing up the opposite side.

Colclough came back looking extremely concerned. Marcus's expression was even darker.

"Cheer up, Marcus. It could end up being nothing more than a midnight hike."

Marcus reacted as if he had not heard Colclough's remark. "I want you to do me a favor," he said. "I'm going to write a letter to a friend and leave it with you. If . . ." He paused and tilted his head. "See that it gets back to her. Stick it in Betteridge's dispatch case, okay?"

He found a pencil stub in one of his pockets and began sharpening the point on a rock.

"I'm worried about Thompson," said Colclough. "He's getting desperate. These past two months have been rough on him. Every three days the dispatch case goes back to General Miles with the same report, a page of meaningless drivel. He's got nothing *to* report. He sits in his tent scribbling, imagining Miles reading the report and throwing it in his wastebasket, cussing him out and blaming him for the Apaches eluding us. Miles wants results. Thompson would love nothing better, but all he's been able to do so far is wander around like Hagar in the wilderness."

"Have you got paper and an envelope?" Marcus cut in.

"In my tent. I'll get them for you." Colclough stopped and tossed one final comment back. "He's ready to try anything to get something started."

"If you've got pen and ink, I'll borrow them, too."

It was the middle of a broiling August afternoon. Fetid, stifling air filled the office in a single huge chunk. The windows were wide open, but not so much as a wisp of breeze found its way inside to penetrate the unmovable air. Below in the military plaza the flag drooped; an ancient hound, its rib cage clearly visible, lay panting in the shade of the whipping post, the pink ribbon of its tongue spilling from its mouth. The streets were deserted, not a soul intrepid or foolish enough to venture from the shadows.

Artemus leaned against the wall between the windows, arms folded, watching Marion cut away the crushed big toenail of a prospector. The man sat rigidly on a stool, his little head pushed down between his shoulders, eyes clamped tightly shut, face bunched in a grimace.

"All done," she said. "That wasn't so bad, was it?"

"Mmmmm."

"We'll tidy it up, bandage it, and you'll be done."

"How's Tyson's mine doing?" Artemus asked.

"He's working it. Starts at six every morning. He likes to get in at least five hours before the sun gets high. He stops between eleven and three, then goes back until six."

"I take it it's no Ophir."

"Not yet. It takes time, he expected that."

Artemus eyed her skeptically.

"Oh, they've found gold," she went on.

"Whereabouts?" asked the prospector.

"The Eleanor. This side of the Catalinas. They've finished the adit, set the timbers, installed the tracks."

"I know the place," piped the man. "They's wasting their time. Like fishing in a rain barrel. Me and my partner went over that whole patch six years ago. There's gold, but not enough to fill your tooth. Want to know where it's really at? Down below in the Patagonias. That's where me and Buck been digging. We had us a small strike over to Nugents Pass back in '62, worked it cleaner than Buck's glass eye. Got out every speck. Didn't make neither of us rich, but enough to keep us from starving. The Patagonia Mountains is the hot spot these days. Boys is flocking down there ever since Cap Mowry hit pay dirt. That's the spot, alright, not the Catalinas."

Marion said nothing and resolved not to mention it to Tyson. Any slightly pessimistic remark was taken to heart. He fueled his labors with faith, and she let him. He believed that if he kept at it long enough, he would eventually find a vein half the width of a barn door that reached clear back to Mount Rice.

She finished with the prospector. He paid in gold dust and left. She watched from the window as he crossed the plaza, pausing to pet the dog. A man came out of the post office. She could not see his face, and though his bearing was recognizable, he was walking like a man who had just been dazed by tragic news. She stiffened. He crossed the plaza and came into the building. She heard him start up the stairs.

"It's Tyson," she murmured to Artemus.

He came in slowly, plodding as if every step was to be his last. She went to the head of the stairs to greet him. His face was black with rage.

"Darling—" she began.

"Is he up there?" He had stopped halfway up.

She nodded. "What's the matter?"

"Come down, we have to talk in private."

She had not heard Artemus come up behind her. Tyson looked past her, where Artemus stood with his hat in hand. He put it on.

"Come on up, Tyson. I'm going out." Marion turned to Artemus. "To Meyer's Drug Store. We need a few things."

She sat on the patients' stool. Tyson paced, a letter from the lawyers in his hand.

"They can't sue. The government won't let them. The attorney general, Speed, he's blocking us. Stymieing us."

"How can he?"

"Read it."

He practically flung the letter at her. Attorney General James Speed, a holdover from Lincoln's administration, had seized on Tyson's case. He had petitioned Congress to enact legislation barring such suits. In his opinion, just cause was absent. Litigant must prove that the government "willfully, maliciously, and deliberately" misinformed litigant's spouse. Simple error, regardless of the tragic consequences of such error, was insufficient grounds for legal action. If such an action were permitted to be brought in a court of law, it would set a precedent that could lay the government open to hundreds of similar suits.

" 'Willfully, maliciously, deliberately.' The sons of bitches are guilty of all three," he rasped. "Only they won't admit it. That's the roadblock."

"Solomon Warner said he thought this might happen."

"What the hell does he know? Stupid ribbon clerk—"

"Didn't *you* think it might come to something like this?"

"Of course. Do you think I'm stupid? I knew they'd try, but Staley didn't think they could. Oh, you should have heard him toot his horn. 'You've got an ironclad case, Mr. Sturges. They haven't a leg to stand on, Mr. Sturges. They bungled, they lied, misinformed, that telegram is all the proof you'll need. They can be made to pay and pay and pay, Mr. Sturges. And if they try to wriggle out of it, we'll go after them in the newspapers. There'll be a public outcry that'll shake the walls of the White House. Every heart will be touched by your poor wife's suffering.' Fourth-rate shyster. That's our mistake, don't you see? We need a real lawyer, somebody with the guts to tackle the War Department, the Honorable Mr. Speed, the Congress. Stand up in court and tear them to shreds for their incompetence, their stupid bungling!"

He paused; he was suddenly glowering at her. "What's the matter with you? You're taking it all very calmly, I must say. Aren't you upset? Furious? Say something!"

She held out the letter. "Tyson, drop it. It's over."

"That's the spirit. That's my loyal, supportive, loving wife."

"It's over," she repeated.

"Not yet, my love. I'm going back to Philadelphia and hire a real lawyer, a whole battery of lawyers. We'll fight this thing to the Supreme Court. I refuse to give up!"

He shredded the letter, hurling the pieces violently. He was livid, touched with momentary madness. He shook all over.

"Tyson, calm down."

"Shut up!"

"Grow up! Take it like a man. It's a lost cause, so forget it and concentrate on the mine."

He went rigid, stabbing her with his glare.

"I have to go back to the mine."

She stood at the window and watched him cross the plaza, mount his horse at the hitching post in front of the drug store, and ride away. Artemus emerged from the store with a bagful of purchases. He looked after Tyson, shook his head, and started across the plaza.

He had no idea what had happened, but he clearly disapproved of Tyson. She only wished her feelings were that mild.

◆❙30❙◆

It took Marcus most of the afternoon to compose his message to Marion. It was not exactly a love letter, but his feelings did find their way in. He said simply that he loved her and always would, and if anything, their separation the past few months had strengthened his devotion. He told her he thought of her constantly, missed her dreadfully, but now at last he was able to accept the fact that there was no hope for him. They could never be together and would have to go on with their lives and put it all behind them. He promised to try.

He admitted his reason for writing was selfish: he couldn't go on letting his feelings gnaw at him and hoped that by putting them down on paper it would bring him some relief. He did not ask her to love or remember him. He did not even ask that she understand this final effort to gain her attention. He did not use the word "sympathy." He did not mention the mission.

When he was done he read the letter. Then tore it up and started over. It was nearing six in the evening when he finished his second attempt. He made so many changes the draft was scarcely legible. He copied it on a fresh sheet, but it pained him when he read it, and it struck him that it would have the same effect on her. The letter was weighted by self-pity, despite his conscious efforts to avoid it.

He tore it up. He decided against writing. She didn't expect to hear from him, and it was better not to run the risk of her husband intercepting the letter. Marcus would forget her as she had forgotten him.

If she had.

Sergeant Brennan came into the tent after Colclough left. Brennan looked gray with worry, his beady eyes questioning, his salute halfhearted.

"I'll be leading the way, Sergeant. You stand to one side and send the men down one at a time, three paces between."

"Yes, sir."

He saluted again and left. Minutes later the men formed up and started down the path, Marcus in the lead, feeling Apache eyes from every quarter. There would be no owl call signals like that night against the Mogollóns in the Tortolita Mountains the year before. There was no need, for every blue-clad man was clearly in view, popping from behind the temporary concealment of rocks and trees. They made their way down to the *cañón* floor, a dried-up streambed lined with small stones, the banks nearly hidden by weeds.

Marcus clattered across and started up the trail on the opposite side. Above, about thirty yards ahead, an out-cropping jutted forth. He scrambled up to it and rested a moment in its shadow. The man behind him came up out of breath, pale with fear. Neither of them spoke. Marcus grasped the edge of the outcropping, swung, and kicked himself over to the top, then resumed climbing. He had not taken ten steps when the mountain erupted with rifle fire. Bullets slammed the ground from every angle. Arrows sang. He could hear screaming and scrambling behind him. The man directly behind him was hit and dropped from the ledge. Panic seized the troopers up and down the line. High along the rim, the others had opened fire, shooting at unseen targets.

An arrow came winging in from the right, catching him in the bicep, tunneling deep, detonating pain. He fell, the screams of the dying hammering his ears, the side of his head striking the ground.

* * *

The stench of human excrement lanced up his nostrils and triggered nausea. His head pounded. He could barely move. He looked to his right. His sleeve had been ripped off, baring his arm to the shoulder. Where the arrow had struck, a poultice was tied on with a strip of rawhide. Using his other arm, he pushed upward to a sitting position. The effort set his head ringing, dizzying him so he had to brace himself to keep from falling on his face.

A chorus of laughter greeted this awkward action. The glaring sun struck his eyes, sending twin needles through them into his still swirling, aching brain. He blinked and lowered his face, then raised it to look at the laughers. They sat in a semicircle, grinning idiotically, pointing.

He blinked again and recognized the one sitting directly opposite: Juh the giant. There was no mistaking him. Even sitting, he was a head taller than the others, as tall as the legendary six-foot-eight-inch Mimbres chieftain Mangas Coloradus. He was Juh, the stutterer, Geronimo's war brother. The ends of his heavy, braided hair fell to the ground. He giggled and pointed.

Deliberately ignoring them, Marcus got his bearings and looked about. The camp was small. He could not estimate the number of braves and could not know if there were other camps, but the Indians had to have a fairly large force to have poured such heavy fire down at the soldiers the night before. Marcus saw no other prisoners. Am I the only survivor of the carnage, he thought.

"My God . . ."

His wound throbbed. Juh rose and stood blocking the sun, pointing at the poultice.

"W—w—w—wound."

So powerful was the stench around him it was all Marcus could do to keep from gagging. His nose ached, his eyes stung. He felt like a piece of fruit mashed to a pulp under a heel. But he was alive. Barely.

Why?

What use did they have for a prisoner? They didn't take male prisoners. Had they kept him alive to entertain them? A torture show? No, they were on the run; they had no time for amusements.

"Oh Jesus . . ."

"Je—Je—Je . . ." Juh was looking at him with a stupid

expression. He lifted a finger the size of a sausage and pointed again. "W—wound. P—p—pain?"

"It's fine."

A group was approaching. One of them stood no more than five-foot-eight. He was the leader; his haughty manner confirmed it, for he acted a foot taller than he was. He had a big chest which seemed inflated in permanent display. A nose like a hawk's beak shadowed a short, thin mouth. His brows protruded, overhanging his eyes. His cheekbones thrust outward and looked as if they had been planed.

It was Geronimo.

He was smoking a frazzled cigar. The Apaches did not smoke the peace pipe, Marcus knew. Peace and its symbols was as alien to them as the ocean or the railroad. But they enjoyed tobacco. They smoked it wrapped in a single oak leaf. The acid in the leaf lent an acrid taste, but they seemed to like it.

Geronimo wore his hair, black as a grackle, parted in the middle and falling straight down to his shoulders. He had on knee-high moccasins and the traditional long, full breechcloth. He also wore a vest, which Marcus had heard about from Justin Schreiber: it was fashioned of braided human hair taken from the scalps of white men he had slain. It was a badge of honor which no other Apache chief wore.

He approached Marcus and looked down at him, his nut-brown brow furrowed in thought, cigar smoke wafting over his face, partially obscuring it. Only his unblinking stare pierced the cloud. Juh had obligingly backed off. Upon Geronimo's arrival his manner became almost servile.

"Officer," growled Geronimo. He tapped his own shoulder. "Major. What name?"

Marcus told him.

"You have many men with you."

It was not a question. His face said he knew how many. All he actually wanted to know was if Marcus was capable of telling the truth.

"How many did you kill last night?" Marcus asked, and held his breath.

"Foolish. Stupid. Why you take men down trail in

moonlight?" He whirled a finger at his temple in the crazy sign.

"I was ordered."

"Stupid. Not Crook's order."

"Crook is gone. General Miles has taken his place."

"Miles?"

Geronimo made a face that said the change was inconsequential. It was the same foe with a different name.

"How many were killed last night?" repeated Marcus, sensing the answer would be honest.

Geronimo held up both hands, fanning his fingers. Every one, even his thumbs, looked broken in a number of places. Marcus's heart sank as the hands were pushed forward repeatedly. Seventy.

Geronimo repeated the crazy sign. Then knelt and offered a cigar. Marcus declined, but with a friendly smile. He was in no position to play the indignant superior. Geronimo returned his smile. He began to question him at length. He wanted to know where Crook had gone, where Miles had come from. Marcus told him the war was over and great numbers of soldiers were coming to the territory. He was not so presumptuous as to demand or even advise that Geronimo surrender.

The chief's knowledge was astonishing. He remembered Venable's name, repeated it, and correctly linked it to the deaths of Namasa and Gold Eyes. He knew everything about the Aravaipa Canyon massacre. He was able to recall the ambush in the Tortolitas. As he prattled on, showing off his knowledge, Marcus reflected on the chief's chilling response. Seventy killed? Could he be lying, exaggerating? Could one of his men had told him that was the number and he had accepted it?

Geronimo grilled him for hours. The sun climbed to its zenith and started down. They gave Marcus water and fed him some kind of meat he did not recognize. It tasted good, if somewhat salty, and he devoured it, not wanting to know what it was.

When Geronimo was done questioning, Marcus was helped to his feet and escorted to a spot behind a wickiup and ordered to sit. There they left him. The stench was mercifully much less powerful removed from their midst. The meat had restored his energy. His wound was sore, but the pain bearable, and moving his arm did not increase his discomfort.

He had been face-to-face with Geronimo, carrying on like two old friends. Marcus had answered his questions honestly, suspecting that he already knew the answers and was mainly seeking confirmation, and testing his veracity. From the way they had treated him so far, he felt he had won Geronimo's respect. Geronimo had impressed him. He was sharp, did not miss a word, evidently understanding English much better than he spoke it, understood and analyzed each response immediately. He could understand now why Crook, Geronimo's only enemy contact, had been so impressed with him. Crook had never trusted him, but he could hardly be expected to trust the bane of his career.

One could almost assume that Crook had quit as much out of frustration with Geronimo, with his failure to dent the chief's resolve and get the better of him in any meaningful way, as out of resentment against Sheridan.

Marcus had to admit that he had always felt uneasy in conversation with anyone whose intelligence was superior to his own. Superior intellects knew when they had the upper hand, and used that edge. Geronimo had made him feel that way, and the same might have held true for Crook.

It didn't seem to occur to the chief that in time, against such vastly superior numbers, he and his people would go down. They were doomed. If it did occur to him, he didn't let it show in resentment, in anger or frustration. In the more than three hours they had talked, not once had he raised his voice or changed his expression. He remained cool, self-possessed, quietly intimidating. He was everything Justin Schreiber had claimed.

They had not tied Marcus, and they were not guarding him. No one even peered around the corner of the wickiup to check on him. He had been sitting unattended for nearly ten minutes. Clearly they wanted him to walk away. If he tried, would he catch an arrow between the shoulder blades? He weighed the pros and cons of an attempt. He decided that Geronimo wanted him to return to the colonel and tell him about his captivity in detail, tell him how strong the Apaches were. He looked around. In the distance he spotted the four peaks. Measuring the distance to the right of them, he fixed the position where the troopers had camped the previous night. Were they still there? He would never know if he didn't look. He got to his feet and stretched, favoring his wound. The poultice, whatever it was, was still damp. It appeared to be working a miracle cure. It had been a relatively short time since he had been hit deeply by the arrow, and it was almost completely free of pain.

He could hear activity on the far side of the wickiup and see them sitting around cook fires talking, women scraping hides, cleaning bowls, upbraiding children. Emaciated dogs wandered about. He saw braves, but not Geronimo or Juh.

He started away. He found a path and picked up speed as he entered it. He felt the muscles in his neck and across his back tighten, expecting an arrow. It was much too easy, so easy his suspicions could not help but arise. He had covered about twenty paces down the path when an arrow flew by his right ear, so close that a feather in the fletching brushed it. He cringed, froze, and stopped. The arrow had lodged deep in the trunk of a tree ahead where the path curved to the left. It vibrated with a soft, twanging sound. Someone laughed behind him. With his heart pushing up to his throat, he slowly turned.

It was Juh. He smiled broadly and waved.

"Son of a bitch," muttered Marcus.

31

Marcus stumbled and nearly fell as he came
into camp. Men rushed to him from all
sides. He was brought to the colonel. Colclough and the
other officers crowded around them.

"This is marvelous!" crowed Betteridge. "We thought
we'd never see you again."

Marcus did not want to lift his head to look him in the
eye. Everyone peppered him with questions. The colonel
rescued him.

"Give him a chance, boys. Can't you see he's practically out on his feet?" Marcus looked into his face for the
first time. It hung darkly with guilt, shame, and uneasiness.

"Did they torture you?" Betteridge asked solemnly.
Marcus shook his head. "How in the world did you get
away?"

"Walked. They let me."

"I don't understand."

A ripple of surprise passed through the others. No one
appeared to understand.

"They *wanted* me to come back. To tell you where
they are."

"We'll go back!" burst the colonel. "You'll show us
the way."

"No, Jesus. That's exactly what they want!"

Betteridge's face clouded.

"They won't be there," rasped Marcus, stunned by the man's incomprehension. "They'll be hiding close by. We'll find the camp empty. We'll start poking around, and by then they'll have us surrounded. They'll massacre us."

"See here—"

"I know what I'm saying!" he snapped. "Sir."

Betteridge started.

"They let you go," he murmured, then looked about worriedly. "And followed you back."

"They didn't have to. They know where we are. They've known every step of the way."

He was becoming exasperated with them, all of them, even Andy Colclough. Had they learned nothing about Apaches over the past two months? He had talked and talked to them, answering the same questions over and over.

"They know our strength to a man. How many did we lose last night? Seventy, right?"

"Sixty-eight," said Colclough. The colonel flushed slightly and looked at the ground.

"It was my fault," he said quietly. "Tactical error. Of course if the damned moon hadn't come out at the last minute . . . Rotten luck, plain rotten luck."

Marcus felt the urge to jump him and grab him by the throat.

"Sixty-eight," he whispered.

"A few wounded," added Colclough, "none seriously."

"You look awful," said the colonel, patently wanting to drop the slaughter as the subject. "Aren't you hungry? You look like you could sleep for a week. Anything you want?"

"We got a few of 'em," said Colclough. "A handful. Bastards just melted away."

Marcus looked at him. "Out the open end?" He indicated the mouth of the horseshoe. "No. They'd be cleverer than that."

"They were. A couple of the men found a cave that turned out to be a tunnel on this side."

"They had their getaway all planned," said the colonel. Marcus said nothing. Betteridge persisted. "Are you sure there's nothing we can get you? Just name it. Can we talk privately? Come into my tent."

The others began to drift off. In the tent a chessboard on an upended barrel showed a game in progress. Marcus sat facing the colonel.

"I can't tell you how sorry I am about this," said the colonel. "It's been eating at me. It was the moon. If it hadn't come out, we'd have made it over to the other side and up the face."

"Not a chance, Colonel. Even in pitch darkness they would have clobbered us. I told you they would."

"I know, I know, I should have listened." He sighed heavily. "But what's done is done."

Five words dismissed the needless deaths. Betteridge didn't see it as sixty-eight killed; he saw it as his force reduced by slightly more than two and a half percent. That was the way he would report it, the way Miles expected him to. Battle casualties were considered a percentage of overall strength. The War Department had little choice but to issue numbers; the public demanded it. But many field commanders considered losses in terms of a percentage of the force involved. It sat more lightly on the conscience, for one thing. Nevertheless, Marcus reflected, it would take some masterful fiction writing to explain it in a report. He *had* to report it; there was no covering up such a loss. But he could couch it in terms that Miles would find more acceptable than the painful truth.

Marcus's anger was gradually giving way to disgust. How many men would be sacrificed so rashly before the Apaches were either defeated or exterminated?

"You need a break from all this," Betteridge went on. "You've earned it. I'm sending you back with the dispatch case. You can take a couple of your men with you."

"I'd rather not, sir. The men—those who survived— might take it funny."

"I don't see how they can."

"They might feel as if I were deserting them."

"Nonsense. They know you better than that. You'll be doing me a service and yourself a favor by delivering the case to General Miles. And you don't have to go all the way to Prescott. We've gotten word that he's set up temporary headquarters at Huachuca. I told you those heliograph stations would come in handy."

He got out a map and indicated.

"We're here. I make it approximately thirty miles to the border. And Huachuca is only about ten miles above it. You get yourself some rest and leave first thing tomorrow." He picked up the dispatch case. "There's the usual progress report, a personal letter from me to the general, and the officers' and men's mail. You'll be pleased to know I've already started on the letters to the loved ones of the men who were killed last night. Sixty-eight letters. Quite a pile. I'll be all week."

He seemed not to tire of talking. Marcus was too tired to care, to even listen. Let him ramble, he thought. Maybe it will cotton his conscience.

"After you've reported in and delivered the case, don't turn around and come back. That, Major, is an order." He tapped the case. "I've advised the general that I want you to take a week off, longer if you want. Go back to Tucson, see your fiancée. Rest, relax, go on a seven-day drunk if you like. Forget about us, the Army, everything."

Again he indicated on the map. "When you do come back we'll be right around here. Double-check with Huachuca before you head on down. If there's any change over the next few days, they'll know by way of the heliograph network."

He looked at Marcus with the most earnest expression he could muster. "You've been through hell, Marcus. You deserve a rest, and I have a selfish motive for giving it to you. I need you fit and clearheaded because you're the expert on the Apaches. We're all agreed on that."

So when are you going to start listening to me? Marcus thought.

"While you're gone we'll keep after Geronimo. We could get lucky, you never know. It's like chess. You never can tell when your opponent will make a mistake that will open the door for you. It looks like it'll be too late for my wedding, unfortunately, but Myrtle understands. Lucky she's an army brat. Let's hope we wrap things up by next spring so as not to interfere with your own wedding plans, eh?

"I guess that does it. Go get yourself something to eat,

get some sleep. And oh yes, it's good to have you back. We all thought for sure you'd—really great."

I have to get out of here, thought Marcus. In ten more seconds he'll start apologizing for last night again.

Tyson had second thoughts about returning to Philadelphia to press his case. A second letter from his attorneys explained the course of action the government could be expected to take in defense of its mistake and the obstacles the Justice Department could legally raise appeared formidable. Mr. Staley also advised that pursuing the matter further would be prohibitively expensive. Tyson sought the opinion of a local lawyer, the astute and highly regarded former governor of Wisconsin, Coles Bashford. Upon reading the letter Bashford said, "You stand about as much chance of suing a tree that falls on you. Even if you get into court, which I see scant possibility of, any judge worth his gavel would probably dismiss."

Tyson was furious. Marion was relieved. She did not tell him this, but he recognized the signs and continued to make it an issue between them. Unhappily, while he was still smarting from the summary dashing of his hopes, he suffered a second blow.

The Eleanor petered out.

For eight straight days he and his men enlarged the mine in search of the vein he *knew* was there. Up to that point they had uncovered a little under two thousand dollars worth of gold, all of it at or close to the surface. Artemus, whose knowledge of gold mining had been gleaned from prospector patients over the years, pointed out that gold found on top of the ground does not necessarily mean that it came from underneath. It could as easily have been carried to the area by surface water. Marion agreed. Tyson's reaction was that Artemus was talking the rot of total ignorance.

He hired Iris Alderson, a mining engineer from Phoenix, to look over the mine and give his expert opinion of its potential. Alderson charged a hundred dollars for his services. He spent six hours underground examining every inch of the Eleanor. He took soil and rock samples and examined and tested them exhaustively with the most modern equipment. He examined two samples of the first gold Tyson had unearthed.

Alderson informed him that of the minerals containing gold, the most important were sylvanite or graphic tellurium, calaverite, and nagyagite or foliate tellurium.

None of the three natural settings for gold was found in the mine.

Alderson was knowledgeable, thorough, articulate, sympathetic, and dismally, blatantly pessimistic in assessing the mine's potential.

"It has none."

Tyson paid his fee and Alderson went back to Phoenix.

When Tyson told Marion about the report, adding that in Alderson's experience, nine out of ten strikes petered out, she tried to console him. It was a mistake. He made it clear that he didn't need her pity. When she curtailed her efforts to build him up, he accused her of cold indifference.

His dive into the doldrums did not worry her; she saw it in combination with the bad news from Philadelphia as a passing dark cloud over their lives. What concerned her was the drastic change he had undergone. He was a completely different person than she had married, a stranger whose emerging personality she was growing to despise.

He continually lamented his rotten luck. He was unhappy, he was neurotic, he was frustrated, and he lashed out at his most convenient target. Marion resented it and told him so.

Artemus had a theory. "Men come back from war changed. It ends, they leave, but they still can't put it behind them. It anchors itself in their systems like a virus and lingers and lingers. They're bitter. Even if they didn't suffer in combat, even if they sailed through their enlistment, they still had to sacrifice precious years. That could be a part of his problem, Marion. Not only what they put him through, but bitterness at being separated from you."

"Others come home and pick up where they left off."

"Some, I suppose, but I think the experience changes every man in one way or another. Who can blame him for feeling he's been cheated out of a part of his life?"

She accepted this and could sympathize with him for it,

but could not accept his unwillingness to at least try to shake it off. In the old days he would have broken his neck trying. And she was getting fed up with his moodiness, his readiness to blame her, his perpetual scowl, and his ceaseless carping against the government. Having failed to find gold on his first try, he gave up completely. He began sleeping until noon, then loafing about town for the rest of the day. His evenings got later and drunker, although he was not staggering home bouncing off walls and fences every night.

Their marriage came apart. He systematically destroyed it. She tried to mend it, but without his cooperation it appeared hopeless. It infuriated her. She too began to sink. Artemus brought it to her attention.

"You're getting as miserable as he is. He's making you miserable. That's very wrong, Marion. No one has the right to pull another person down into their personal black pit. It's getting worse, isn't it? It's never going to get any better. I think you should divorce him."

"No. I'm not giving up on our marriage without a fight."

"What have you been doing ever since he got here but fighting? What good has it done you? Not a bit so far. Besides, you're overlooking the most important thing of all. You don't love him. You did once, but no more. You love Marcus."

"You talk rubbish."

"Do I? Then so does your heart. Just listen. I'll tell you what you do. Go home tonight and have it out with him. Give him an ultimatum—either he straightens out or you'll leave him. If he won't listen, dump him. If you're not happily married, you shouldn't *be* married. Get a divorce. Marry Marcus."

"Rubbish," she snapped.

Artemus focused his patented leer.

"I'm sure by now he's forgotten all about me," Marion added.

"Just like you've forgotten him."

32

Geneneral Nelson Appleton Miles's temporary headquarters at Fort Huachuca was an office-cum-shrine. Had a stranger wandered in when the general was absent, one look around would have speedily confirmed whose office it was. In one corner on an oak burl pedestal stood a bronze bust of Miles. A smaller one of pewter occupied his desk. Adorning the walls were no fewer than seventeen photographs and three paintings of the general. They depicted him in various types of uniforms, everything from full dress to fur hat and coat. Not a single picture that showed his chest failed to show his decorations. Full face and left profile or right—he preferred the right—the general's eyes stared challengingly at whoever looked upon him. Not one photograph or painting included anyone else.

Various souvenirs of his military exploits adorned his desk: mounted favorite pistols, a calendar supported by a piece of shrapnel resembling a diminutive meteorite on a small slab of marble, an array of spent bullets of varying calibers on a wooden pedestal. Crossed sabers were brightly polished and hung with golden tassels. A miniature carving of his favorite horse shared shelf space with books on warfare, military law, and history.

His desk also contained a large, gilded mirror.

When Marcus arrived he turned the dispatch case over to the officer of the day and was ushered into the outer office to wait. He waited for an entire hour. Then the general's orderly came up to him, clicked his heels smartly, saluted, and cleared his throat.

"The general will see you now, sir."

Miles had the contents of the case spread all over his desk and was engrossed in Betteridge's letter.

"Come in, come in, Major. Sorry to keep you waiting. Have a chair. We've just been going over Colonel Betteridge's report. Frankly, we can't help getting the feeling you boys are running around in circles down there. Worse, that Geronimo has you jumping through a hoop. This campaign, if we could call it that, could go on till hell freezes and cracks. We're not blaming anybody, but the situation is exasperating. Tell us confidentially, Major. You've been out here fighting them how long?"

"More than three years, sir."

Miles lowered his voice and leaned closer to Marcus.

"If you were calling the shots, how would you go about catching him? Tell us what you think, we want to know. What would you do?"

"I wouldn't try, General."

An eyebrow crawled up Miles's forehead. He lowered his handsome face slightly and fish-eyed Marcus.

"It's Mexican territory," Marcus went on. "I think, at least while he's down there, he should be their problem. They should be chasing him. We should post men along the border to make sure he doesn't come back into Arizona."

Miles did not say a word; he appeared to be chewing on the suggestion now that his initial surprise had vanished.

"The Mexicans have as much to gain by capturing him as we do. They're not lifting a finger," Marcus continued.

"True. Nevertheless, the settlers expect us to catch him. As does the War Department. We might disappoint one, but not the other. Ours is not to reason why, Major."

He had turned to sifting through the papers. He found the two he wanted.

"This is a personal letter to us from the colonel. In part it concerns you. We'd like you to read it if you will. Start at the top of the second page."

Marcus read: " 'After two fruitless months we finally managed to engage the hostiles. We lost sixty-eight men.' "

He went on to describe the suicide mission.

"Skip over that. Go down to the next paragraph. Read it aloud."

" 'It was, in short, a suicide mission. When Major Venable proposed it to me—' what the devil, I didn't propose it, he did. It was his idea!"

"Just continue reading."

"Sir!"

"Read!"

" '. . . proposed it to me I didn't like the idea. It struck me as too rash, too risky, but he pointed out that if we didn't draw them out into the open we might never get a crack at them. He saw the risk he and his men would be assuming, as did I, but inasmuch as I did not reject the idea, I don't think it fair for me to ascribe blame. I, after all, am in command.' General—"

"Keep reading."

" '. . . command. I agreed and gave him the go-ahead. I felt that the major's experience against the hostiles, being far more extensive than my own or that of the other officers, entitled him to his chance. I was wrong, I freely admit it. Those sixty-eight men went to their deaths like lemmings over a cliff while the hostiles managed to get away with only a few minor casualties. So it turned out a slaughter, a terribly costly exercise in futility, but again, let me make this very clear, I blame myself for agreeing to employ a strategy which, under normal circumstances in a shorter and less complicated operation, I would have rejected out of hand as far too reckless and with no possible assurance of success.' "

"What do you say to that, Major?"

"I did not propose the mission. He did, and when he did I spoke against it. Strongly."

"He says it was your idea."

"Every one of my men knew where the idea came from, and the other officers, Major Andrew Colclough in particular. He used the phrase, 'lambs to the slaughter.' "

"We're not interested in what the enlisted men or the other officers say. They weren't directly involved. Let's keep it simple: it's the colonel's word against yours."

"I'm telling the truth, goddamnit!"

"No need to raise your voice. No need for profanity. Too bad he isn't here to tell his side of it. Still, the letter does that for him. He'd hardly write one thing, then turn around and disavow it verbally. That doesn't make sense, does it?"

"He's a liar. That's all there is to it."

"You want us to believe you—"

"I don't care what you do," Marcus cut in. "I don't have to take this. From him, you, anybody."

"Watch yourself, Major. You're upset, just calm down. We're not making any rash judgments. We're trying to be impartial. We're not for him and against you. We don't even know you. Be patient. It'll all come out in the inquiry. You realize, of course, there has to be an inquiry."

Miles paused to light a cigar. He offered the box to Marcus, who shook his head. He was boiling, gripping the arms of his chair so tightly his knuckles were drained of blood. Miles lofted a perfect smoke ring.

"Thompson goes on to say that he's given you a week off. Use it, unwind, grow a beard, go fishing. Take it easy. When you go back—"

"Back? There? How can I? I can't place myself within a hundred yards of that two-faced, back-stabbing son of a bitch. Lying bastard! I'll break him in half!"

"Now, just a minute. We've asked you to get control of yourself. Now we're ordering. You'll go back. You'll rejoin your unit. You'll not mention this to him or anyone. You'll take orders, you'll give them, you'll conduct yourself as an officer and a gentleman. When the operation's over and you return, the three of us'll thrash this out. What the hell is it, anyway, but a difference of opinion."

"The hell it is, he's dumping manure on me and getting away with it. Pulling rank so he can. I've taken my share of shit over the years and shrugged it off, but not this. I don't need it, the operation, him, you!"

"Enough!"

Miles pounded his desk so hard his heaviest souvenirs bounced and the mirror toppled. He set it back up.

"You shut up and listen. Nobody on God's earth talks to Major General Nelson Miles like that." He narrowed his eyes. "What are you, some kind of troublemaker? Or do you have a problem? Oh, we've seen it before. You've been at it too long, too many fracases with the little brown men, too much heat, loneliness, frustration. You're burned out. Lost your ability to make decisions, your energy for the fight, your pride, your toughness. Your stomach.

"It happens. The war ends, something clicks in a man's brain. Suddenly none of it's serious anymore. Appomattax ended all that. Since then you've just been going through the motions. The little brown men aren't a threat, just an annoyance."

"You've got it all figured out," Marcus sneered.

"Silence! One more interruption and we'll break you and toss you in the guardhouse. You can nurse your grudges, and hopefully figure out where you went off the track."

"Go to hell, Miles, with your track and your goddamn guardhouse. I quit!" Marcus ripped off one epaulet, then the other and tossed them on the desk. "I've got a life to live. I've done my share for glory and the flag. From now on I'm looking out for myself."

Miles released another perfectly proportioned smoke ring.

"Excellent. Wise decision. You've abandoned your sense of commitment, and your patriotism. By all means get out. The Army doesn't need your sort. The taxpayers deserve better. We'll look for your resignation in writing on our desk within the hour. Dismissed!"

On the way out Marcus slammed the door, hoping that Miles's mirror would fall again.

33

How's your wound?"
Marcus chuckled.

"What's funny?" Sutherland asked innocently.

"Miles never noticed it. I guess the talent for overlooking minor details is part of what makes a great general. It's doing fine, thank you."

"I'm impressed. You actually talked face-to-face with Geronimo."

"He did all the talking. That's another thing Miles and I never got around to."

Sutherland sat at his desk, toying with a pencil and studying him. Outside, an officer was marching the men about the parade ground. A bellowed command turned Marcus's attention to the window, then he looked back at Sutherland.

"Do I see a smidgen of regret in your expression? Having second thoughts about resigning?"

"Yes and no."

"Is that both or neither?"

"Not about getting out, just how it worked out. I can't help feeling I'm being driven out by Betteridge and Miles. I boiled over in his office, but when I got out of there I calmed down in a couple minutes. I told myself I'd done the right thing. I sure couldn't go back to the operation, and he as good as told me he wouldn't let me off the griddle. But what about you? How are you doing in the big chair? Anything happening?"

"Nothing. I could have slept the past two months and not missed a thing. The tribes are quiet up and down the territory. It gives you a queer feeling, Marcus, like when you know a gun's going off, but you don't know when. They're waiting for Geronimo to come back and rally them. Do you think he can?"

Marcus grinned. "He didn't mention it when we talked."

"What *did* you talk about? How did he look? Impressive? Is he as sharp as everybody says? How did they treat you?"

"Whoa, whoa. He's everything Justin said he was, starting with brilliant. Shrewd, wily. Homely as fungus on a stump. Not big like Juh or Mangas Coloradas, but there's something about him, the sort of aura that a king or president has. He's . . . commanding without raising his voice, without getting all worked up. Sitting listening to him you feel like a schoolboy in the principal's office. Oh, he's a liar. I wouldn't trust him from here to the end of my arm, and he'd slit your throat in a second if you crossed him. I walked on slippery stones, but he *is* impressive. His men treat him like a god."

"Is he coming back?"

"After he wipes out Betteridge. All the tribes expect it of him and he wants to deliver. And once he's united them, he'll be in a position to bargain with Miles. The son of a bitch thinks like a statesman, Bob. He'd be a match for Tallyrand or Ben Franklin."

They talked on, Marcus questioning him about the post, learning that Lieutenant Gaines had resigned, more reinforcements had arrived, and Sutherland was expecting to be replaced soon by a higher-ranking officer, which didn't appear to bother him. He asked Marcus to tell him about the suicide mission in more detail, but when he started, the names of the dead men upset him.

"What are your plans?" he asked Marcus, abruptly changing the subject.

"I haven't really made any. I submitted my resignation, he accepted it. It takes effect end of the month, but that's only two days. For all practical purposes I'm already out."

"How do you like civilian life? Seriously, will you be sticking around?"

"Tucson? For now. Take it easy for a while, then get a job. Maybe get into ranching, start a business, I don't know. I'll have to look around. First thing in the morning I'll go into town and buy a suit, maybe two. It should be an experience. I haven't worn civvies in almost six years. I'll turn in my army issue, my gear, weapons the day after tomorrow."

"No hurry. Some of the boys hang onto some things. Supply looks the other way."

"I'd rather not. No souvenirs. One of my wool shirts is missing a sleeve. The Indians ripped it off when they treated my wound."

Sutherland grinned. "Let me write that down. One wool shirt missing a sleeve. Two major epaulets missing."

Marcus eyed him. "Have you been getting into town much?"

"Now and then. Hannah goes in every day with some of the other officers' wives." He paused and smirked. "Aren't you going to ask me if we've seen her? I did yesterday. Not to talk to. She doesn't know me from your maiden aunt, but she looks good, pretty as ever."

"Mmmmm."

"Yes, mmmm. By the way, I've a letter for you."

Marcus's heart quickened. He brightened as Sutherland fumbled in the drawer.

"It came a couple days ago. I stuck it . . . Here it is."

It was from Justin Schreiber.

"I was going to forward it to Huachuca with the rest of the mail. I didn't think you'd be back this soon."

"Neither did I."

"You'll have to forgive me, Marcus. I'm still a little stunned over your quit—resigning."

"Quitting."

Sutherland got up, drew on his gloves, buckled on his saber, and put on his hat.

"I've got to review. Give you a little privacy."

"Where's Olan?"

"Probably napping out back of the stables."

He went out. Marcus looked about the office. It ap-

peared unchanged since he had last seen it. He looked
into the inner room occupied by Justin Schreiber, now
vacant. Bob and Hannah Sutherland occupied quarters
on the opposite side of the parade ground. Looking at
the bed, he pictured the colonel lying in it, Marion attending him, Artemus Shaw standing by. It seemed a
century ago. Coming back was unsettling. He would miss
the office, the desk, the post; Olan, Bob Sutherland, the
other officers, the men, although most were newcomers.
Colfax, Moody, and Brennan had survived the massacre.
How long they would survive the campaign was something else. His conscience took a thorn that almost made
him flinch. In a way he was deserting them, though they
would not think of it that way. They would be pleased
for him; Colfax and Moody would, though he could not
be sure about Brennan. He and the sergeant had never
been barracks blood buddies.

He sympathized with all the survivors, with every man
in the campaign. Their opposition was formidable. Namasa,
Gold Eyes, none of the other Apache chiefs, with the
exception of Cochise, ranked with Geronimo.

He examined the envelope. It bore a Monterey, Massachusetts, postmark. He read the letter.

Dear Marcus,

How are you, my friend? Excellent, I trust. Healthy,
happy, and giving the Apaches fits. I finally made it.
Arrived in Boston and home to Monterey to this old
house. It took me a week to clean out the cobwebs,
the dust, and ghosts. I've started painting the outside.
I work till noon every day and sit in my rocker and
read and nap and reminisce through the afternoons.

I'm writing this sitting on my front porch with a glass
of iced tea at my elbow. There's an enormous maple in
the frontyard, a majestic tree. It belongs to a robin.
He sings his heart out all day long. I've been planting
rose bushes to replace the old ones. They were all long
dead, a tangle and run riot. I got home a little late to
plant vegetables around back so the plot will just lie
fallow until next spring. I have petunias, begonias,
marigolds, and nasturtiums along the sides of the house,
but all along the front facing the street are roses, red,
white, pink. I had to replace the trellises, too. They'd

rotted away to nothing. Thirty-six years. I was surprised to find the old place still standing.

Thirty-six years. It flew by. No distinction, no glory, a job, a career. I don't regret it. Still, I can't help but wonder what life would have been like if I'd gotten into some other line. I did miss out on some things. I never had a chance to plant roses and watch them thrive. Never sat in a rocker drinking tea and listening to the birds. Never slept till noon.

As you might gather, I like retirement, Marcus, no more reports, no more niggling details, reviews, inspections, the nuts and bolts of commanding a post. I miss you and the others, though, and hope you miss the old war-horse a little.

I'll close now, finish my tea, smell my roses, and maybe spruce up and go into town for a bowl of clam chowder. I've been devouring seafood since I got home. Take good care of yourself, my friend. Keep your head down and don't shoot until they show theirs.

Your friend,
Justin

Marcus folded the letter and restored it to its envelope. He pictured Schreiber smelling his roses. He looked out the window. Sutherland and the other officers were astride their horses, the men at attention on foot. He could see their faces, but they weren't their own. They were Corporal Tumbel's, Orph's, Henry Colclough's, and the others who had passed on. The men were saluting. The familiar notes of "Retreat" floated over the parade ground. Across the way the officers' wives stood watching. The flag was being lowered.

He felt a sudden wrenching sadness. It was all coming to an end. *His* flag was coming down.

Solomon Warner welcomed Marcus at the counter.

"You're a surprise. How did it go down there?"

"It's still going."

He told him he had resigned his commission, not explaining why; Solomon didn't pry into his reasons. He did ask if he planned to stay in Tucson.

"If I can find a job."

"You won't have any trouble. There's plenty of work for those willing to."

Marcus got a strange feeling that Solomon wanted to talk about Marion, but hesitated to rummage through that closet without being asked.

"How's Mrs. Warner?"

"Fine. What can I do for you?"

"I want to buy some clothes."

"Do you know your sizes?"

"Regular, I guess. My uniforms are all regular."

"I'll get my measuring tape. Go on down to the men's clothing department. Around the corner just past shoes. I'll be right there."

There was a wide choice of summer-weight suits, jackets, and trousers—crash linen suits, linen dusters, summer cotton, pinchecks, light blue- and white-striped jackets, brown lined summer coats, black alpaca. Solomon came back.

"Put on a vest, any one. I have to measure with a vest on."

Marcus did so, raising his right arm with difficulty.

"What's the matter?" Solomon asked.

"I took an arrow in the shoulder muscle."

"Hurt?"

"Not now. Just stiff. I had a very good doctor, whoever he was."

Solomon ran his tape across his shoulders, down his back and arms, around his chest.

"Some chest you've got there. See anything you fancy? This alpaca goes for sixty-five cents, but you're entitled to the serviceman's discount."

"Is there one?" Marcus eyed him skeptically.

"In this store. I'm one of the one's who's grateful for Fort Lowell." He finished noting down the measurements. "I should get back out front."

He indicated a table. "These'll fit you, and the coats on the corner rack. If you see anything you like, try it on. I'll be back in a bit."

He pulled the full-length oval mirror out into the light and went back out front. When he returned ten minutes later, Marcus had selected two suits, two vests, and a jacket.

Marcus came away from the shopping spree feeling

down. He was out of touch with the new styles and the shoes felt especially strange. They were not uncomfortable, but not roomy like boots. He had ended up deferring to Solomon's judgment in practically everything he bought. Solomon didn't pressure him; he was considerate, helpful, and patient when Marcus had trouble making up his mind. Still, Marcus couldn't help but feel like a small boy being outfitted without his mother present to guide him.

What he really felt was miscast in his new role. But he had to start getting used to civilian life. His days in blue were all over tomorrow.

He wandered about town the rest of the afternoon. He talked to Mark Aldrich, Augustus Brichta, and others. Everyone seemed pleased that he was thinking of settling in the area, though he was not absolutely certain he would.

He had volunteered to join Betteridge in the chase to get away from Marion. At the time he didn't think he could stand to see her walking down the street arm in arm with her husband. But running away hadn't solved a thing or changed his feelings in the slightest. He still ached for her. Perhaps confronting the problem was his only recourse.

He went into a saloon for a drink at about four o'clock. Approaching the bar, he saw Tyson sitting with four other men at a corner table. They were arguing politics. They were the only other customers. Tyson's back was to him when he came in. Marcus had a rye at the bar, listened to their conflicting opinions regarding the relative merits of Lincoln and Andrew Johnson as presidents, and heard Johnson, a Tennesseean, vigorously defended by the three Southerners. None of them brought up the fact that he was a former slave owner. Tyson and another man thought that because he had been an energetic prosecutor, he would bend every effort to punish the die-hard Southerners further. The other three maintained that Johnson was a Southerner first and prosecutor second, despite his working for the Union and being elected Vice-President in 1864. It was a friendly dispute without any possibility of agreement.

Marcus paid for his drink and was leaving when one of

the men called Tyson's attention to him. Tyson turned in his chair toward the door.

"Major Venable? Join us for a drink."

Marcus sighed and went over to the table. Everyone greeted him amiably.

"I'd like to, Mr. Sturges—"

"Tyson, please."

"I have to get back. Perhaps another time."

"Look forward to it."

He left. As he stepped outside a gale of laughter erupted at the table.

Artemus was out on house calls. Marion was busy with patients. She was examining a woman's sore throat when Tyson came in.

"Got a minute?" he asked.

"I—"

"This won't take a second."

She lowered the tongue depressor and walked him out of range of her patient and the four others seated by the door waiting.

"How much this time?" she asked.

"Fifty."

"Fifty dollars!"

"Shhhh, it's nobody's business."

"They have eyes."

"Let's go into Shaw's room."

She fumbled through her bag, folded the money tightly, and thrust it into his hand.

"That's my girl. Good news, I'm starting out Monday morning bright and early."

"A job?"

"Better. I'm going out after silver." He stopped. "What's the matter? Why the face? Are you giving up on me before I even start?"

"I'm not giving up on you."

"I don't hear any encouragement. It's not going to cost anything. I still have all the tools and equipment from before and I know I can get men. They're finding silver down south near Tubac in the foothills of the Sierrieta Mountains. And near Tombstone."

"That's quite a ways."

"We're not going down there. I plan to start looking

north of Wilmot. Don't worry, I'll be home every night. Isn't it exciting?"

"You're not gambling, are you?"

"Of course not, what do you take me for? This isn't a loan, it's an investment." He kissed her cheek. "Thanks, sweetheart. I love you." He started off.

"Remember, we've been invited to the Warners for dinner tonight."

"Damn, that's right. Tell them I may be a little late. On second thought, you go ahead; make some sort of excuse for me. Tell them I'm into a new venture, really big. There's a lot of preparatory work. See you."

He left. It was almost four-thirty. There was a poker game starting in George Hand's Saloon, after which everybody would be going to the bullfight at Smith's corral.

Emmaline answered the door. Solomon called from upstairs.

"Where's my new silver stud?"

"In the box in the second drawer where it always is," Emmaline called up to him.

She ushered Marion into the parlor, closing the pocket doors. Marion made Tyson's excuse for his absence.

"Guess who's back in town," said Emmaline. "Marcus!" Marion stared, wide-eyed. "He came into the store today. Bought a whole new wardrobe. He told Solomon he's resigned his commission. Isn't that something?"

"How did he look?"

"Okay. He was wounded—"

Marion gasped.

"Oh, not badly, just his shoulder. He's all right."

The doors slid open. Solomon's collar gaped. At the sight of Marion he brightened, then his face fell.

"Marion—" He looked at Emmaline. Concern mingled with appeal in his eyes.

"I told you the Sturges were coming for dinner," she said. "You don't remember a thing lately."

"I still can't find my stud."

"Did you look in the bottom drawer?"

"You said second drawer."

"Well, if you can't find it there, look in the bottom one."

He tilted his head, indicating he wanted her to step outside. She did so.

"Excuse us, Marion." He closed the doors. "What are you doing?"

"Ssssh."

"What's the matter with you?"

Solomon looked sheepish. "I have a confession. I . . . invited Marcus over tonight."

"You didn't!"

"Sssh."

A knock rattled the front door.

"Oh, my Lord, this is priceless. Tyson didn't come. Even if he did—"

"Ssssh. Calm down, it's not the end of the world. They may even be happy to see each other. They *are* friends. It *has* been awhile. You let him in, I'll go find my stud."

"*You* let him in. I'll try to explain to her. You are a prize, Solomon Warner!"

She reopened the pocket doors. Solomon welcomed Marcus. Marion heard his voice and jumped from her chair. She savaged Emmaline, then Solomon with her eyes. She was suddenly livid.

"Emmaline—"

"I'm sorry, Marion."

"How could you? Solomon, how could *you*!"

He swallowed. "It's not her fault, it's all mine. A simple misunderstanding. Cross my heart, Marion. Honestly, Marcus."

Emmaline was nodding vigorously. "He forgot I'd invited you and Tyson," she explained. "Neither of us planned it. Please believe me, dear."

"It's the God's truth," said Solomon.

"I'll go," said Marion.

"I will," said Marcus.

"Neither of you will," said Emmaline. "There's no reason. We have a wonderful dinner waiting. We're all grown-ups, so why can't we just sit down and enjoy ourselves? Like old ti—we can, can't we, Marion? Please? Please stay, both of you."

Marion sighed and nodded. Marcus nodded. There really was no reason to leave, she thought, and she did want to see him. It seemed like years.

She looked lovely, he thought. Oxen and chains couldn't drag him away.

"If you two'll excuse me a moment," said Solomon, "I'm missing a stud."

"I'll help you find it," said Emmaline.

They practically sprinted away, closing the doors after them. Marion gestured futilely to stop her. Marcus took a chair. A long moment passed before they looked at each other.

"You—" both began.

And stopped. He studied the carpet.

"I—" both said.

She laughed. He grinned.

"Em says you were wounded."

"Nothing serious. That isn't why I came back."

"Was it awful down there?"

"Awfully boring. Riding around looking for Geronimo. And when we couldn't ride, walking. How have you been? You look great."

"I'm okay. Fine."

"How's Tyson?"

"Fine."

A long, excruciatingly awkward pause followed. The clock ticked, the floor above creaked.

"I wonder where Solomon's stud got to," he murmured.

It drew a smile. "He says you're leaving the Army."

"As of midnight tonight I'm out."

"You'll be staying in Tucson . . . ?"

"I guess. For a while. I missed you terribly," he blurted.

"Oh, Marcus, please don't."

"I'm sorry."

"No, no. I don't think either of them planned this, do you?"

"No. But I'm glad it worked out. I wanted to see you. Just to look at you."

"It's nice seeing you again. I did worry about you."

"This is all fits and starts, isn't it? Would it be better if I open the doors?"

"If you want."

He opened them. It triggered a pounding at the front door. Solomon was coming down the stairs, Emmaline following. He had put on his collar stud and tie. From their expressions neither had any idea who it could be at the door. The maid rushed in from the kitchen to open it.

Tyson stormed in.

"I knew it!"

He glared at Marion and shoved Marcus to one side. He started toward her.

"Tyson . . ."

He scowled at Marcus. "Friend of mine said he'd seen you coming here—"

"This isn't what you think, Tyson," said Solomon behind him.

He whirled. "And what is it I think, Warner? That you and your doting wife set up this little rendezvous for the star-crossed lovers? Oh, I don't think that. How could I possibly?"

"You'd better go," said Solomon quietly.

"You bet. Get up, you slut!"

Marcus bristled and stiffened.

Tyson eyed him. "She'll have to meet you another time, *Major*." She had not stirred. "I said get up, bitch!"

He strode to her and slapped her cruelly. Solomon started. Emmaline gasped. Marcus grabbed Tyson by the shoulder, spun him around, and smashed his jaw. He fell into a chair. Solomon ran to Marcus and held him back. Marion cried out and dropped to her knees beside Tyson. He pushed her from him.

"Don't touch me!"

He started up from the chair at Marcus. Solomon pushed between them.

"I said you'd better leave, Tyson."

He got up rubbing his jaw. Marion followed him out. She was speechless, crimson with embarrassment. She could only shake her head and fling her hands helplessly. Her face was reddening where he had struck her.

Tyson wrenched the door wide and went out, half dragging her by one arm. Solomon closed the door and leaned against it.

"I'm sorry," murmured Marcus. "I shouldn't have. I'll go after him . . ."

Solomon shook his head.

"He'll hurt her," Marcus protested.

"He won't. You mustn't interfere, they're husband and wife."

"He will too hurt her!" burst Emmaline. "He's an animal, Marcus!"

"No!" bellowed Solomon. "We must stay out of it. There's been enough damage done—"

A knock sounded. Marcus exchanged glances with Solomon. Before either could do so, Tyson opened the door.

"Soldier boy, you've come between me and my wife for the last time. We'll see who's the better man." He eyed him malevolently. Marcus had never seen hatred so burning, so compelling in any eyes. "I challenge you to a duel. Dawn, day after tomorrow. You choose the weapons. Your privilege."

"You're crazy."

Tyson leered. He started to turn. "Oh, one last formality. Must observe the proper etiquette, right?"

He slapped Marcus viciously. Marcus did not flinch, did not send his hand to his cheek. Marion had come up to the door behind Tyson. She cried out.

"No gloves," said Tyson, "that'll have to do."

"Tyson, don't do this!" burst Marion.

"Shut up, you whore. This is between him and me."

"Tyson—"

"Shut up or I'll kill you!" He turned back to the three of them. "Good night, all."

34

Marion awoke to a stinging sensation where Tyson had slapped her face. Even more painful, was the throbbing at her right temple like a hammer inside her head pounding at the bone. He had cursed her all the way home and at the front door, as she fumbled the key into the lock, he exploded. He began to slap and cuff her viciously, cursing like a madman. Nothing she could say or do could calm him. A blow to the head had knocked her cold.

She lay stretched on the bed fully clothed, spread-eagled, wrists tied to the headboard. He stood at the foot of the bed leering at her.

"Back with us? My, aren't we the fragile one, though. Like a rose."

She struggled against her bonds. It was useless. "Tyson . . ."

"The Iron Rose, that's what I'll call you. It's perfect. So delicate, and yet so hard. The Iron Rose. I hold you and you make me bleed: all beauty, all thorns. If your lover only knew. He's bedded you, but he doesn't know you. Doesn't know what a calloused, iron bitch you are inside."

He leaned over her. His breath stunk of liquor, but he

wasn't drunk. His eyes were clear and wild. Madness danced in their blue depths.

"We're going to settle this once and for all, my sweet, my Iron Rose. Which of us is the best man."

"Untie me."

"When I'm done."

Before she could say another word he jammed a balled-up handkerchief in her mouth, and, ripping off a strip of the sheet, gagged her securely. She screamed; the sound rushed from her throat into her brain, splitting and dying in her middle ears. She tugged against her bindings. He laughed and ripped off her blouse.

"Oh, clumsy me, I've torn your lovely blouse. And your skirt."

She continued to struggle and kick as he tore away her underclothing. She lay naked, staring up at him fearfully.

"That's the least you can do, my sweet, give your husband a chance to prove he's a better man than your lover. You've always been a stickler for fairness. That's fair."

He had undressed. His member rose in erection. He climbed onto the bed and mounted her, roaring and driving with full force against her, ripping inside her, sending a shock wave of pure agony through her. Again she screamed. Again the sound did not make it out of her head. He began pumping furiously.

"How . . . is it . . . my . . . love? Does . . . it . . . please . . . you? Love . . . love . . . love . . . love . . ."

Sweat dripped from his brow, landing on her face. She shuttered her eyes in a vain effort to block out the nightmare. Terror daggered her heart. He wanted to kill her, fill her with pain, with agony.

"Love . . . love . . . love . . . love . . ."

She was bleeding. Above the upper line of his pubic hair his stomach was spattered with blood. And still he pounded relentlessly. She tried to slip the traces of consciousness to escape into insensibility, but it was impossible. Again and again he drove full length into her. No lust, no arousal, only the fixed purpose of violating her with all possible pain.

She was dying little by little. He was surely mad, over the brink into the dark pit where all reason is lost. All feeling, all sensibility were destroyed. And the horror moved forward.

It was moments after Tyson had taken Marion away. Marcus was on his feet and pacing; Solomon and Emmaline both tried to calm him with no success.

"I've got to go," he snapped.

"No!" boomed Solomon. "No," he added quietly. "Don't you understand, man? You go chasing after them, you'll only make it worse for her. You can't tie yourself to them to protect her. They're man and wife. He won't hurt her. He just lost his temper—"

"Oh Solomon, you're so stupid!" exclaimed Emmaline. She ran from the room, pounding up the stairs.

"Sit down, Marcus, please. Let me get you a whiskey."

"No."

"Yes. You need it. Look at you, you look like a wildman."

"He's the wildman. Didn't you see? He's snapped. I'm going—"

Solomon was on his feet, backing against the entrance, closing the pocket doors behind him.

"You interfere, you'll wreck things for her. You want to make things worse? That's what you'll do. She can handle him. What you have to be now is patient. She's divorcing him."

"How do you know that?"

"Artemus. There's nothing left for her with Tyson. Whatever they had before is gone. No love, no friendship, nothing. He came back a changed man—not surprising after what he went through. Anyway, she's leaving him for good."

"If she lives to."

Solomon had poured him a whiskey, gesturing, urging him to drink it. Marcus hurled it down. Solomon refilled his glass.

"What are you trying to do, get me drunk?"

"Good idea," said Solomon. "You pass out here and you won't be able to interfere." He smiled and shook his head. "I still don't believe he challenged you to a duel. Where does he think he is, back on the old plantation? I thought he fought on our side. He won't go through with it, of course, it's just a bluff. She'll talk him out of it."

"In the frame of mind he's in, she won't dare open her mouth."

"Drink."

"No more."

Marcus had slumped into a chair, elbows on his knees, head between his hands, eyes on the rug.

"If he hurts her, Solomon, so help me God I'll kill him."

Tyson stood fully clothed at the foot of the bed gazing down at her. A large red welt crept horizontally under her right eye; her left eye was blackened; bruises discolored her face, shoulders and upper arms. Her wrists were raw where the ropes had burned the flesh, and her pelvis was splattered with blood. She was semiconcious.

"My, the Iron Rose seems to be softening a bit around the edges of her petals."

She groaned.

"Oh come now, my sweet, you can do better than that. You're not hurt. You can't be, you're indestructible." He came around the bed and leaned over her, speaking directly into her ear. "Well, what do you say? What's the verdict? Who's the better man? Tell me, don't be afraid. Here—"

He removed her gag. She came fully awake.

"My arms," she murmured. "Shoulders. Broken."

"Oh my, that'll never do."

He went into the kitchen and brought back a knife. He cut her wrists loose, then got his pistol out of the night table drawer and strapped it on.

"Where—?"

"Am I going? Out hunting. I'm going out to bag me a major. Kill him, stuff him, hang his head on the wall there. Trophy."

"No—"

"Oh yes. Oh my, yes. Don't tell me you're surprised. What do you think I am, gutless?"

"Tyson, don't—"

"Not Tyson, my sweet, Mar . . . cus. Say it."

"Don't go—"

"Say it, bitch!" He raised his fist threateningly. She cowered.

"Marcus."

"You'll call me that from now on. Make it easy on yourself. It's always on the tip of your tongue. Marcus—"

"Don't go, Tyson, please don't."

He laughed hollowly and went out. She heard the inner door slam and the muffled echo as he closed the outer door behind him.

"I have to go, Solomon."

"So soon? You haven't even eaten. Come to think of it, none of us have."

"I'm not hungry, thanks."

Marcus got up and looked for his hat.

"Don't do it, son. You'll only make it harder for her."

"I'm not going to knock on their door. I just want to go over there . . ."

"And do what?"

"Listen."

It sounded absurd, he thought, like a Peeping Tom describing his technique.

"And what do you think you'll hear?" persisted Solomon. "You think he's got her tied up and he's horse-whipping her? If you must go, go home, go to bed."

"I guess." Marcus extended his hand. "Thanks for everything, Solomon: the advice, the whiskey, you're a true friend. She's lucky to have you and Emmaline."

"She's lucky to have you."

"Mmmmm."

He put his hat on and left thinking what a nightmare the night had become. He should have never come back to Tucson. It would have been better if he had stopped off at the fort, cleaned things up, and left the area. Still, how could anyone have known it would turn out like this? The extent of Tyson's insane jealousy could never have been predicted.

Marcus hoped Tyson had not hurt her. Maybe that slap would be enough to drain his aggression; hopefully his conscience would take over. Then again, it was after he slapped her that he had slapped Marcus and challenged him to the duel. What it came down to was that she wasn't safe under the same roof with him, no matter what Solomon thought. Emmaline knew; she had refused to stay and listen to his rationalizing.

He set out for Inez Alou's. If they were still up and arguing, he would be able to see them through the lighted front window. He quickened his step, worrying that Tyson might be getting violent again.

Down Alameda, across Main near the old, abandoned Mexican barracks and up Pearl Street he ran. He came within sight of the house. It was in darkness, as were the houses around it. It was not yet ten, but Tucson's respectable element retired early and rose with the sun. This was not true of the carousers. They could be heard in almost every block in every cantina and saloon. He crossed the street, stood at the gate, squinted at the window, and listened. There was no light, not a sound.

Until someone spoke behind him.

"My my, this is a pleasant surprise. Here I thought I was going to have to go looking for you."

Marcus turned. Tyson stood smirking about six feet from him, holding his pistol pointed at Marcus's stomach. Moonlight silvered the barrel. Someone was shouting over by the barracks. Loud laughter followed. Tyson waved the weapon, his eyes glinting, sparkling. He looked to be aching to fire it.

"Put it away, Sturges," said Marcus, with much less command in his tone than he wanted.

"Is that an order, Major?" Again he waved it, telling Marcus to move to his right. "Walk to the corner of the wall and turn down the alley. We're going to need privacy."

"You're crazy."

"Everybody seems to think so. Though not so crazy I don't know what I'm doing. Do *you* know what I'm doing? I'm going to kill you. What do you think of that?"

"Why?"

"That's a stupid question," Tyson sneered. "As if you didn't know. You raped my wife, you degenerate son of a bitch. Took advantage of her, used her. You're going to pay. Get going."

His eyes were absorbed by the gun. The sudden, unexpected imminence of death made him stagger slightly. He had come so close so many times, but in every case death was the chance by-product of dangerous circumstances. Here in a quiet street while everyone slept close by, it had picked him out and was directly approaching. He walked to the corner and down the alley ahead of Tyson.

"Far enough. Turn around."

"Put it away, Sturges. Use your head, man, you can't get away with it. Somebody'll hear the shot."

As he said it a gun went off a couple blocks away toward Alameda Street. Tyson laughed.

"Like that one, you mean."

"Everybody, even your friends will know who did it. She will."

The triumphant smirk gave way to a glower. Tyson's head shook slightly. He thrust out his jaw.

"You mean your whore, the Iron Rose? I fixed her. Good."

"If you hurt her—"

Marcus took a step forward. The gun jerked up. Marcus froze.

"Hurt her? I'm her husband, you jackass. I protect her. From lechers like you. Besides, nobody can hurt her, she's indestructible. She destroys others like every queen bee. The Iron Rose."

He smiled, then scowled. Marcus could see the battle raging behind his eyes, but he held the gun steady, his finger grasping the trigger. Marcus swallowed and imagined it going off, the world exploding.

"I don't want to talk about her," Tyson went on. "She's a whore. Bitch whore. She give it to you good? Tell me! No, don't. Let's talk about you. I'm going to kill you. Put your hands on top of your head and turn around."

"You'd shoot me in the back."

"What's the difference, front or back you're just as dead. And nobody'll see. Turn around, damn you!"

Marcus turned. The cords in his neck began to twist and bind, pulling his shoulders toward the nape. A shudder flew down his spine and he tautened his upper back. The night air chilled the sweat under his tunic. He heard the gun cocked. The sound was curiously sharp and hollow, as if it was being done inside a metal barrel. His heart repositioned in his chest and the beating became thrashing. He tried to take a deep breath; his throat was beginning to constrict. Pictures flashed through his mind: the mountains of Sonora, men's smiling faces, Andy Colclough's, Betteridge's, Nelson Miles's, Bob Sutherland's, Justin's. Marion's. Each gave way to the next until hers materialized. It stayed and came floating toward him.

"No!" she shrilled.

Tyson fired. In the closeness of the alley the sound was like a howitzer. The bullet sped past Marcus's shoulder. He instinctively ducked and dropped to one knee. The slug struck her, driving back her left side. She cried out, grabbed her hip, and went down. Her yell had surprised Tyson, tilting his hand, spoiling his aim. Smoking gun in hand, he bulled past Marcus, nearly knocking him over. He dropped beside Marion.

"Marion, darling . . ."

Two passersby across the street had heard the shot. They called out and started toward the alley, moving cautiously. Up on his feet and approaching husband and wife, Marcus could see that Marion was not badly hurt. She held her hip tightly, but he saw no blood seeping through her fingers. Tyson must have also seen she was in no danger; he sprang up from her side, whirling, bringing his gun around. Marcus sledged his wrist with both fists before he could fire, sending it flying from his grip. The two men came running up. Both yelled. Tyson ignored them and dove for the gun. Marcus's knee caught him in the chest, knocking him backward. His head struck the wall with a sickening, cracking thud. He hung suspended in midair, then seemed to flow down the wall. He sat, gaped, and fell slowly forward.

"Tyson!"

Marcus brought his hand back from the side of Tyson's head where it had struck the wall. His fingers and palm were gloved with glistening blood. He pressed his jugular vein and looked up at her.

"Oh my God," she whispered.

"I've killed him," murmured Marcus.

"In self-defense, and accidentally. He was going to kill you." She set a comforting hand on his shoulder.

"He was," said one of the two strangers. "We saw, didn't we, Roy?"

"She's right."

Marcus heard nothing. He could not take his eyes off the body.

"I didn't mean to," he said softly.

He rose tiredly to his feet. She came to him and held

his arms. He was trembling. Up close he saw her bruises, the marks of Tyson's abuse. He gasped.

"What did he do to you?"

"Never mind." She looked down at the body. "It's over. All over."

Epilogue

Colonel Thompson Bragg Betteridge failed to locate the elusive Geronimo and his followers, prompting General Miles to add three thousand more soldiers, bringing the total in the operation to nearly five thousand. But pursuing the savages and at the same time detailing men to guard every water hole, spring, and pass in the Sierra Madre proved impossible. Despite his personal reservations, Miles changed his mind and agreed to use Apache scouts. At the same time he increased the number of heliograph stations to thirty. The scouts were to prove invaluable, but the heliograph stations only made the search more difficult, for when Geronimo saw the mirror flashes, he thought they were magic and began avoiding the mountaintops.

Assuming personal command, Miles spread his men throughout Sonora, but Geronimo remained more mobile and more elusive than ever. In their travels the Apaches recrossed the border into Arizona, killed a cattleman's wife, her thirteen-year-old child, and a ranch hand. A few weeks later they killed two men outside of Nogales, Arizona, then ambushed the pursuing soldiers in a narrow canyon, killed two of them, and seized horses and supplies. In none of these or any subsequent engagements did they suffer any casualties.

Hysteria spread throughout the region as Geronimo continued to elude the massive manhunt, raiding at will. The newspapers exaggerated the horror stories, invented others, and inflated the number of American and Mexican casualties. It was variously claimed that Geronimo was leading a hundred fifty to five hundred men. When he tired of raiding and withdrew deep into the Sierra Madre to rest, he had not suffered a single casualty. But some of his followers wearied of the chase and deserted.

In contrast to the sporadic violence and bloodshed that led up to it, the end was undramatic. In desperation General Miles decided to try to negotiate with the enemy. He sent as his emissary, Lieutenant Charles Gatewood, a seasoned veteran of the Indian wars who understood the ways of the Apache, having been stationed on a reservation for years. To make contact with the band, Gatewood crossed the border and began to patrol the flanks of the Sierra Madre with two scouts and an escort force of twenty-five troopers. In time his scouts brought him word of Geronimo's whereabouts. When he learned the chief was sending women into the small Mexican town of Fronteras to trade for mescal, he rushed to the scene. In Fronteras he discovered the Mexicans were hoping to lure the Apaches into town to massacre them.

Gatewood decided on a different tactic. Paring his force down to his two scouts and a half dozen soldiers so as not to alarm the enemy, he trailed an Apache woman out of Fronteras and deep into the front range of the Sierra Madre.

Alerted by his sentries, Geronimo watched the scouts come up a canyon ahead of Gatewood. A warrior was sent to escort them into camp. Geronimo kept one scout as a hostage and sent the other back to the lieutenant to say he was ready to talk. The next day Gatewood and his six men moved up the canyon. They were met by a warrior who said that Gatewood would have to come on alone. A compromise was reached. Leaving the soldiers behind, Gatewood continued on with his remaining scout.

Geronimo met him. At a distance he lay his rifle on the ground and came forward to shake hands. But when they sat down to talk, Geronimo deliberately sat so close that Gatewood could feel the concealed revolver on his hip. Geronimo asked what the U.S. government would offer if he gave himself up. When the lieutenant replied that he could only accept unconditional surrender, adding that Geronimo would be sent to exile in Florida, the chief exploded.

"Take us to the reservation or fight!" he demanded.

Gatewood played his ace. He informed Geronimo that his family was already in Florida with the other Chiricahuas. At this news, coming from a man whose word he believed, the fighting spirit, the iron-willed defiance, the fierce and unflagging hunger for independence, drained from the old warrior.

He agreed to speak to General Miles.

Miles kept him waiting for nine days. When he finally arrived, he offered Geronimo nothing apart from the assurance that if the fugitives surrendered, they would be reunited with their families in Florida.

With thirty-seven followers, among them fourteen women and children, Geronimo surrendered, only to find himself the victim of one final treachery. Arriving in Florida, he was imprisoned for two years, denied even a glimpse of his family. In time, upon being removed to Fort Sill, Indian Territory, most of his followers and their families died of disease and despair.

Geronimo himself was turned into a human showpiece. He marched in President Theodore Roosevelt's inaugural procession in 1901 and was exhibited at the St. Louis World's Fair in 1904. Proudly spurning a belated offer of financial assistance from the federal government, he eked out a meager living of his own, making and selling bows and arrows, and his autographed photographs.

His resistance in the Sierra Madre was to be the last stand of the Apache. By the time he died in 1908 at the age of eighty-five the Apache nation was reduced to a shadow of its original power. But on his deathbed he could claim a niche in history, a moral triumph no other Indian chief could equal: in the end it had taken five thousand whites to subdue his thirty-eight Apaches.

On the day General Miles assigned Lieutenant Gatewood as his personal emissary to Geronimo, Marcus Venable and Marion Sturges were married. Their wedding took

334 • A.R. Riefe

place one week after Marcus's acceptance of Solomon Warner's offer to join him as his business partner.

Tucson continued to grow and thrive. Throughout the Indian wars it held the distinction of never having been abandoned. In the late 1860s and 1870s it became a general pack train center. It was the territorial capital from 1867 to 1877. The Southern Pacific Railroad arrived in 1880. In 1883 Tucson was chartered as a city.

> We have a strong city; salvation will *God* appoint *for* walls and bulwarks.
>
> —Isaiah. 26, 1

Ⓢ SIGNET BOOKS

BLAZING NEW TRAILS
(0451)

☐ **THE BLOODY SANDS by E.Z. Woods.** Jess McClaren's dad owed his life to Joe Whitley, and now Whitley was at the end of his rope. Jess's dad was dead, and the father's debt was now the son's. So Jess arrived on a range where he could trust no one that wasn't dead to pay a dead man's debt with flaming guns.... (152921—$2.95)

☐ **GUNFIGHTER JORY by Milton Bass.** Jory draws fast and shoots straight when a crooked lawman stirs up a twister of terror. When Jory took on the job of cleaning up the town of Leesville, he didn't know it was split between a maverick marshal and a bribing banker. Jory was right in the middle—and he only way to lay down the law was to spell it out in bullets ... (150538—$2.75)

☐ **SHERRF JORY by Milton Bass.** With the town full of kill-crazy outlaws, Jory had not time to uncock his guns. Could Jory single-handedly stop this gang of bloodthirsty killers? Nobody figured Jory had a chance against them ... until his bullets started flying and their bodies started falling. (148177—$2.75)

☐ **MISTR JORY by Milton Bass.** Jory's guns could spit fire ... but even then he had his work cut out for him when he took on a big herd of cattle and a gunman faster on the draw than he could ever hope to be. (149653—$2.75)

☐ **DREAM WEST by David Nevin.** A fiery young officer and a sixteen-year-old politician's daughter—together they set out to defy every danger of nature and man to lead America across the Rockies to the Pacific ... to carve out a kingdom of gold ... and to create an epic saga of courage and love as great and enthralling as has ever been told. (145386—$4.50)

☐ **ALL THE RIVERS RUN by Nancy Cato.** Here is the spellbinding story of a beautiful and vital woman—the men she loved, the children she bore, the dreams she followed, and the destiny she found in the lush, wild countryside and winding rivers of Victorian Australia. (125355—$3.95)

Prices slightly higher in Canada